FIREWATCHING

FIREWATCHING

Russ Thomas

G. P. PUTNAM'S SONS

New York

PUTNAM
—EST. 1838—

G. P. PUTNAM'S SONS
Publishers Since 1838
An imprint of Penguin Random House LLC
penguinrandomhouse.com

LIBRARY OF CONGRESS CATALOGING-IN-PUBLICATION DATA

Names: Thomas, Russ, author.
Title: Firewatching / Russ Thomas.
Description: New York: G. P. Putnam's Sons, 2020. |
Summary: "A taut and ambitious police procedural debut introducing
Detective Sergeant Adam Tyler, a cold case reviewer who lands
a high-profile murder investigation, only to find the main suspect is
a recent one-night stand." —Provided by publisher.
Identifiers: LCCN 2019042363 (print) | LCCN 2019042364 (ebook) |
ISBN 9780525542025 (hardcover) | ISBN 9780525542049 (ebook)
Subjects: LCSH: Detective and mystery stories.
Classification: LCC PR6120.H658 F57 2020 (print) |
LCC PR6120.H658 (ebook) | DDC 823/.92—dc23
LC record available at https://lccn.loc.gov/2019042363
LC ebook record available at https://lccn.loc.gov/2019042364

Printed in the United States of America
1 3 5 7 9 10 8 6 4 2

BOOK DESIGN BY KATY RIEGEL

For Mum,

who never once told me to get a proper job,

and for Dad,

I miss you and I hope this does you proud

FIREWATCHING

sparks

the firewatcher

It starts with the striking of a match: the thin, dry snap of red powder scratched on white. It is the sound of chemistry—of sulfur, phosphorus, and glass. It is a warm and gentle caress, a pair of thick, strong arms that take hold of you, envelop you, and tell you everything is going to be all right.

But you shouldn't have come back. You know that now.

You should never have returned to this crumbling Victorian mansion, like something from a horror film, with its grand architecture and Gothic features. The rusted iron gates that lie discarded in the rhododendron bushes. The long, winding, weed-infested driveway. The house itself, squatting in faded glory, brick-blackened and scarred, windowpanes cracked and stained with milky cataracts.

The workmen unload their long pipes of scaffolding from the van, laughing and joking, questioning each other's parentage and boasting of their sexual prowess. They lift their tools and cans of paint, and slip back into the gaping maw of the house, back to their great work of restoration.

These hired hands dig at your past, knocking down walls that were placed there for a reason; unearthing all the buried secrets. You can hear him now, just as before, and only now do you realize that he never

3

really went away. He was there all that time, lying dormant, waiting to be found. Waiting for you to drop your guard. His voice grows louder as he surfaces, clawing his way up through your mind, echoing and barreling around inside your head. He looks out through your eyes . . . and then he screams.

You reach for another match, feel the warmth and the beauty and the comfort offered . . . but it's over far too soon, the wood consumed from top to bottom in mere seconds, the flame drawn down into your empty hand, where it gutters and snuffs until there is only the cold and the damp and the dark.

The scream is louder now, and this time the match will not be enough.

This time the whole world will burn.

POSTED BY **thefirewatcher** AT 5:45 PM

0 COMMENTS

The man with the scar on his cheek looks down from the window of the apartment building and wonders if someone has thrown a blanket over Sheffield. Summer has swaddled the city in a haze reminiscent of the smogs of its industrial heritage. Sunlight is funneled through rows of terraced houses just as molten iron once sludged and pooled in the blast furnaces and steel mills of the Don Valley. It spills down from the hills and through the parks, weaving its way between the trunks of trees and out onto the ring road.

From several stories below, the man hears the deep bass rumble of music. The latest addition to a chain of real-ale pubs. This city, with its proud tradition of industry and purpose, now courts only leisure. Productivity turned to idleness, he thinks. And the devil makes work for idle hands.

He turns to look back at the estate agent standing nervously behind him. He looks over the open-plan living room the agent just referred to as "a blank canvas." Whitewashed walls, not so much as a hint of magnolia; the cheapest kind of laminate flooring, all spongy underfoot where the surface hasn't been prepared properly.

The man wonders if they even bothered to clean away the blood before they laid it.

The flat is unbearably hot, the air so thick he can taste it. He feels the sun pushing in through the south-facing glass, the heat rising up from the apartments beneath. He wonders what it would be like to live here. Like being buried alive, he imagines. Still, at least it would be cheap to run.

The estate agent struggles to hide his nerves. He smiles too much. And his eyes flick constantly toward the bedroom, betraying the fact he knows full well the history of his "one-bed pied-à-terre."

The agent finally meets the man's eye, doing his best to avoid the scar. "Of course," he says artfully, "the rooms are much larger than you usually get in this type of property." He crosses to the window and looks out for himself. "And the views . . ." He seems content to leave it at that, unwilling perhaps to push his luck.

The man ignores him and heads straight to the door that opens into the bedroom. He has to push hard against the spring-loaded mechanism, and he imagines the room wants to keep him out. His pulse quickens. He half-expects to see the tableau as he remembers it—walls coated in arterial blood, the girl lying splayed across the futon, her head bent unnaturally backward, her dark, lifeless eyes staring up, pleading with him for help. The organs. Laid out in neat little piles around the room, liver, kidneys, spleen; like choice cuts in a butcher's window.

But there are only the same whitewashed plaster walls, the same uneven faux-wood flooring. It has been a little over three years since the butcher came for the girl in this flat, and now she lies in the Abbey Lane Cemetery, her innards restored.

The man feels a fat bead of sweat launch itself from his armpit and streak down his right-hand side. He resists the urge to scratch it away. The fire door pushes back against his outstretched arm.

Behind him, the estate agent clears his throat. "En suite?" he says faintly.

But the man doesn't bother to look. He's seen enough. He's disappointed, though he never really expected to find anything after all this time. He tarries now, only out of some perverse pleasure he takes in discomforting the agent. He steps back into the living room, allowing the bedroom door to shut them out. "Eighty-five thousand," he says, as though giving it some serious consideration. And then he realizes he actually *is* considering it. He needs a new place, and it really is a good buy.

The estate agent nods encouragingly and echoes his thoughts: "I doubt you'll find better at this price."

The agent's opportunism irritates him. "So what's the catch?" he asks.

The obsequious salesman wrings his hands, and the man with the scar remembers the warm, clammy palm he was forced to shake when he arrived.

"The owner wants a quick sale. It's been on the market for some time now." The agent glances once, quickly, at the bedroom door. "I understand the vendor *is* open to offers . . ."

"I'll give it some thought," he says. A good deal is a good deal, after all. If he could get past the fact a woman was once gutted in his bedroom. Could he get past that? Perhaps, for the right price.

Back downstairs the agent leaves him at the entrance to the building with another sweaty handshake. "I'll call you toward the weekend then," he says. "Give you a chance to give it some serious consideration."

"You do that."

The agent begins to turn and then, almost as an afterthought, says, "Sorry, remind me what the name was again?"

"Tyler," says the man with the scar. "*Detective Sergeant* Adam Tyler."

The ever-present grin on the estate agent's face finally slips. His hand falls away to his side, and he wipes his damp fingers down the right leg of his trousers. He turns and hurries away to his car.

Now Tyler is the one smiling, the scar tugging at the corner of his mouth.

The pedestrianized city center is beginning to empty, security gates inching their way protectively across shop windows. Tyler stops outside an estate agent's window. This evening's visit has reminded him he really does need to find a place and start putting some of his meager salary toward a mortgage instead of into the equally slippery palm of his landlord. He scans down past the country mansions of the Peak District through the detached leafy suburbs, to the bottom row and his own more modest price range. It leaves him a choice of three: a bungalow in a highly sought-after part of town (*in need of extensive modernization*); a studio over a Chinese takeaway (*easy access to local amenities*); and a first-floor flat (*ideal starter home for young professional*) in the apartment block in which he's already renting. All of them are significantly more expensive than the butchered girl's place.

He catches sight of his own reflection in the window, where the scar on his left cheek stands out, livid and inflamed. It's always worse in hot weather; no wonder the estate agent seemed so edgy. The town hall clock chimes the half hour.

He might be getting a bit hung up on the girl. He knows her name, of course, knows all the names of the cases he reviews, but he prefers to distance himself whenever he can. He has a tendency to get too close, as the detective chief inspector often reminds him. *Review, append, move on.* How would she feel about him revisiting a three-year-old crime scene?

He considers, not for the first time, whether the Cold Case Review Unit (or "sea-crew," as it is so inelegantly referred to by his superiors) was ever really intended to get results. He suspects it was more of a PR stunt, a way for the force to show that no stone was ever left unturned. The plan was simply to apply new techniques to old cases. It envisaged new DNA evidence, advanced techniques for lifting fingerprints, centralized databases that threw up previously unlinked crimes and pointed out the similarities between them.

But Tyler has taken his remit a little further than that. New technology is all well and good—at twenty-nine he hardly considers himself a Luddite—but sometimes he finds it's far simpler than that. All it really needs is a fresh pair of eyes. The sifting through of old case files, the re-interviewing of witnesses and retired colleagues. A question not asked that should have been. The DCI indulges him, as long as he gets results. And he does get them, more often than not. Still, she doesn't appreciate him lingering too long on any one case.

A chant starts up in a nearby pub, someone downing a yard of ale. He checks his phone while he waits for the lights to change at a crossing and finds a string of missed calls from Sally-Ann. He listens to three increasingly excitable messages reminding him about the meeting tonight and considers whether he still intends to go.

He looks again at his watch. He hates this time of day. Sometimes, when people find out what he does for a living, they ask him whether he struggles to sleep at night, in light of all the horrible things he must see. But sleep has never been a problem for Tyler.

No, it's the *early* evening that troubles him. The time when people with lives untouched by tragedy are preparing meals for loved ones, and wondering if they have PE tomorrow and whether or not the kit's been washed. The time that Mum gets home from work and the kids come in for tea. That's the time that reaches out to remind him of all the horror in the world. It's the time when the news breaks.

He hovers with one foot on the crossing. Left would take him to Sally-Ann, right would take him home. He turns left.

He decides not to call her back, for as disjointed as her voice-mails are, Sally-Ann is far worse on the phone. She's forever hesitating, as though waiting for her first sentence to reach its destination before embarking on the second. Inevitably they end up speaking at the same time and the conversation descends into a Norman Collier–style faulty-mic routine. Instead, he texts her: *On my way.*

O'Hagan's is a sports bar and Irish theme pub combined; between each of a dozen or so television screens hangs a pithy limerick picked out in Gaelic script: "It's no health if the glass is not emptied"; "The wine is sweet, the paying bitter"; "Go carefully with a full cup." There's a match on, and the place is filled with a mixture of football fans and the early evening work crowd, a clashing checkerboard of groups: red and white, black and gray. The voices of the largely male crowd create a deep bass rumble of background noise, a roiling sea of testosterone. He wonders who chose the venue since it doesn't exactly fit the group's style.

He forces his way to the bar, ignoring the disgruntled looks of people who have been waiting patiently to be served, too scared or too polite to kick up a fuss. He catches the eye of the girl behind the bar and raises a hand. She comes straight to him. He uses the time while he waits for his pint to scan the crowd, and spots Sally-Ann waving enthusiastically from a booth at the back wall. He acknowledges her with a dip of his head.

Once he has his pint, he makes his way across to her just as the collective rise and fall of an almost-goal cheer cuts across the room. She greets him with a bone-crushing hug and a kiss that misses both cheeks.

There aren't many people who make him feel small, but Sally-Ann manages it. She's an inch or two shorter than he is, but the heels she's wearing tonight give her the edge. She's well built, what his parents' generation might generously have called statuesque. The lads at the station are less charitable. They treat her the same way they do the oversized photocopier, like she's an obstacle to be negotiated rather than a human being. Not just the lads, either. Other women, too. There's something in the way people look at her, he's noticed, as though her physique is a condition that might be catching. For some reason none of them can see beyond the excess flesh to the pretty woman underneath. Probably because she hides it so well. She has savagely cropped blond hair that looks as though she might have taken the scissors to it herself, and wears elaborate Gothic outfits that succeed only in emphasizing her size and shape. It's as though she's ashamed of her appearance and yet stubbornly defiant at the same time. He likes that about her. Tyler has no problem with rebellion.

Tonight she's wearing a long-sleeved black velvet top with furry frills at the cuffs and collar, skinny-fit jeans that turn her thighs into dark-blue sausages, and ruby-red heels à la Dorothy from *The Wizard of Oz*. There's a bit more personality to the outfit than the one she wears for work, but essentially it's the same. He feels the dampness still gathered in the armpits of his own thin cotton T-shirt and wonders how she's managing not to pass out in the heat.

"I'm so glad you came," she says, so gushingly sincere that if he didn't know her better he might think she was being sarcastic. But she's always sincere, Sally-Ann. Irritatingly so. It makes it very difficult to be cynical about her. Not for the first time, he wonders how old she is. There's a freshness to her face, an innocence in her eyes, that makes him think she's a fair few years younger than he is. But the heavy, draped outfits and the excess weight she carries make her seem far older. She has that silky, husky voice that men always seem to find attractive in women, despite the fact it's oddly masculine. The lads take the piss out of her when they hear her on the radio, joking about how she could moonlight as a phone-sex chat-line operator. He doesn't think she knows that. He hopes she doesn't anyway.

"I said I'd come."

"Yes," she says, "and I could tell how keen you were."

She isn't wrong, and part of him is still wondering why he's here.

Sally-Ann introduces him to the rest of the group. "Everyone, this is Adam. Adam, this is everyone." She beams at the group gathered around them and straightens herself for what is clearly a rehearsed line. "Welcome to SYPLGBTSN."

The crowd laughs dutifully, and a young guy Tyler vaguely recognizes from the Family Liaison Unit says, "OMG, people, we need a better acronym." The guy catches his eye and winks.

Tyler does his best to smile and nod at the faces round the table. He recognizes some of them from the station. Civilians mostly, like Sally-Ann, but one or two are from Uniform. Conspicuously, there's no one else from the Criminal Investigation Department.

After a while the group fragments into smaller conversations, and Tyler finds himself standing slightly apart, not quite part of any of them. Sally-Ann leans in to him. "I'm glad you came," she says, "but don't feel you have to stay if it's not for you." She's intuitive, Sally-Ann. Whatever else they might say about her, she's that.

He admits to her that none of this was his own idea, that the DCI made it clear she expected him to mix more. Minority groups being good for the public image and all, she feels he needs to make more of an effort when it comes to networking.

Sally-Ann laughs. "She's making you go out to play, is that it?"

"She wants a tame CID-queer she can stick on the town hall steps at Pride and show off to the world." He's not being entirely fair, but there's some truth in it.

"Poor Adam, a poster boy's work is never done, eh?" She reaches across and ruffles his hair. She's not the sort of person who can get away with gestures like that. "We'll have you on a float lip-synching to Gloria Gaynor before you know it."

"No," he says. "You really fucking won't." He changes the subject by offering to buy her a drink.

"Bourbon," he orders at the bar. "On the rocks with a twist."

"My dad used to drink that."

Tyler glances once at the man standing next to him and then turns to the mirror behind the optics to finish his appraisal. He noticed him earlier. He's the sort of guy people notice. Pretty rather than handsome. All defined cheekbones and chiseled jaw, a triangle for a torso that ripples beneath a skinny-fit white shirt. He has a mop of shaggy-dog hair that frames a face with skin so pale he might have just stepped off the set of the latest teenage vampire movie. He's a few years younger than Tyler. Twenty-three, twenty-four, maybe.

Their eyes meet in the mirror. Long enough for them to both know they're not wrong. The man looks in and away, in and away, like a wildebeest checking for predators before dipping its head to the watering hole.

Someone in the crowd jostles the guy, and he steadies himself with a hand on Tyler's elbow. "Sorry," he says, but the hand lingers longer than is strictly necessary. He has a surprisingly deep voice. Rich and full-bodied. For some reason it makes Tyler think of black-berries.

The barmaid returns with the bourbon, and Tyler orders another pint for himself.

"Not much of a match," says the pretty guy, pointing to the TV screen above the bar with a hand that's still clutching a pint glass.

Tyler looks at him rather than the screen. "Do you really want to talk about football?"

The man opens his mouth, pauses, and then laughs. A plump blackberry laugh. "Actually, that's the sum total of my football knowledge expended." He's too confident by far in his ability to charm.

Tyler watches the barmaid singularly failing to pull his pint, engaging instead in a conversation with a colleague. He considers encouraging her along with a choice word or two but resists the temptation.

The pretty guy tries again. "Can I buy you a drink?"

"I have one."

The man laughs again. "You're not making this easy for me, are you?"

The barmaid finally returns and slops a pint glass down in front of him. Tyler pays her. He picks up the drinks and glances over to the work crowd where Sally-Ann stands out a head taller than everyone else. "I'm with friends," he says.

The man shrugs, not obviously disappointed. "Maybe another time."

When Tyler passes Sally-Ann her drink she immediately asks, "Who was that?"

"Nobody."

"A *cute* nobody, though."

"Drink your bourbon," he tells her.

"So you're actually going to pass on a handsome guy that throws himself at you?"

"He wasn't my type."

"Sweetheart," she says, the endearment sounding false from her lips, "he was *everyone's* type. Even mine."

Tyler drains the remains of his first pint, slips the glass back onto the table, and starts on the second. "I can't stay long," he says. "I have work tomorrow."

"Oh, Adam," she says, shaking her head, but leaves it at that.

He stays long enough that he won't feel like he's lying when he tells the DCI he did his bit. He nods politely if anyone talks to him directly, but most of the others don't. He's not the only one being given the cold shoulder, though. He notices the two from Uniform have subtly shifted their seats so as to appear slightly removed from the group. Civilian workers never seem to mix well with the ranks; Sally-Ann is the exception that proves the rule. They don't want him there any more than he wants to be there. He has nothing in common with these people except a label, and he has no intention of categorizing himself in that way.

Sally-Ann is watching the cute guy at the bar again. He wonders if she meant what she said about him being her type. He's always assumed she was interested only in women, but then, he supposes he doesn't really know her very well at all yet.

"Sal," he says.

She's miles away. He reaches out to touch her arm, and she flinches, snatching her arm away. "Sorry," she says, rubbing at the thick velvet of her sleeve. "You made me jump."

"I'm going to get going."

"Okay." She hugs him again and thanks him for coming.

"By the way," he asks as he gets up, "what was the acronym?"

She looks confused.

"SYP, etc."

"Oh," she says, "South Yorkshire Police Lesbian, Gay, Bisexual, and Transsexual Support Network."

"Right."

She laughs and the whole group choruses, *"It's a bit of a mouthful."*

He leaves them giggling at the feeble double entendre and heads off, making sure to take the long way round the bar to the door.

The pretty guy looks up as he approaches.

"How about that drink then?"

The man smiles at him. "What'll you have?"

Tyler shrugs. "I guess that depends what you've got back at your place."

The man hesitates for a few seconds, but the smile remains fixed in place. "I'm pretty sure I'll have something you'll like." He drains his own glass and gets up, leaving Tyler to follow him out of the bar.

Lily takes sharp tugs at her hair with a copper brush, separating the straw ends with the tips of her fingers. Her right hand moves erratically and the brush jerks, not quite following the path she sets out for it. The doctors tell her this is quite normal, that she may never regain the full use of it, and she has resigned herself to that. There are worse fates, after all.

She examines her reflection in the dressing table mirror and remembers a time when her hair consisted of long, thick tresses that brought her more than her fair share of attention. But now, the woman staring back at her is only vaguely familiar, a shadow image she recognizes but can't quite place. She pulls a handful of treacherous silver hair from the wiry bristles and drops it carelessly to the floor.

Behind this stranger in the mirror sits Edna, propped up in bed, reading. She has on her half-rim glasses and the nightgown with the roses she was wearing the day the ambulance brought her home. Her own feeble hands struggle to hold up the weight of the paperback and, not for the first time, Lily is struck by the recognition that one of them will soon be alone. She knows it will be her. It is her lot. For Edna's sake, for all that she owes her, Lily must be the one to hold vigil. She just wishes she could remember why.

Her cheeks heat, giving away her morbid thoughts. Her voice, when she finds it, is cracked, as unrecognizable as her reflection. "Ed-na?"

Edna continues to read.

"Would you stay? Do you think?"

Edna fails to look up.

Lily takes another savage tug with the brush and explains: "Here in the cottage, I mean. I'm not sure I would, not on my own."

"Hmm?" says Edna, her eyes still fixed on the page. "What's this?"

Lily swallows; her throat feels swollen and dry, but she forces herself to go on. "I was just wondering, that's all. I mean—if it *is* me that goes first—would you want to stay here? In the cottage? I can't imagine you'd want to go back . . ." She hesitates. Edna only ever refers to it as *that place,* but it seems important somehow to give it its full name, to try, as they come to this point so near to the end, to be honest with each other. "To the hospice," she says, quickly adding, "Of course, there might be other options we could look at?"

Edna finally looks up, frowns at her, and uses a crippled finger to mark her place in the pages. She stares at Lily for a moment and then sighs, a long blast of irritated air. "Oh, Lillian." (Only Edna calls her Lillian, and her mother, of course.) She shakes her head. "Do hurry up and come to bed," she says, and returns to her book.

Lily resumes her brushing. Another face appears in the mirror, conjured by her thoughts, perhaps. Lily's mother stands behind her and takes the brush from her hands just as she used to so many years before. One hundred strokes before bedtime; far fewer needed now. "Stop your fidgeting!" her mother would say in much the same tone Edna uses now. And "Oh, Lillian." Yes, she used to say that, too. "Oh, Lillian, why are you headed to London when every sensible person is moving away? Don't you know what sort of people they have down there?"

Her mother is one of the reasons she has asked the question. Lily sees her more often now, along with other faces from long ago. Contrary to what she might have expected, the past seems to be drawing ever closer. Events that once seemed vague and distant are becoming clearer; people whose faces she has long forgotten appear before her like hazy photographs coming back into focus. She feels the weight of them pressing down on her, dragging her backward. She wonders if this is a symptom of her illness. Her "little turns," as she and Edna have taken to calling them; so much nicer than "ischemic incidents," which is the name the doctor uses. Her fractured mind is trying to piece itself back together, even if it has to dive decades into the past to find its material. But there are still huge gaps, too. They warned her there might be memory loss, though she's never let on to Edna, nor anyone else, just how far those gaps extend.

Whatever their provenance, she doesn't want to be alone with the ghosts when Edna is gone. And, despite her earlier question, neither of them has any real doubt who will be the one left behind. Mini-strokes or not, it is Edna who is living on borrowed time.

She looks up to find Edna watching her. The book has fallen discarded in her lap, the page left unmarked this time. She's shaking her head again, a small smile playing on her lips. "For heaven's sake, woman, how many times do I have to ask you to drop your hair in the basket? It's a small miracle we don't have rats in this place."

Now it's Lily's turn to sigh, though she isn't as good at it as Edna. She bends and scoops the ball of hair from the carpet, drops it into the bin. "There's no need to snap at me. I'm not a child."

For all the secrets that lie hidden in the corners of this cottage, thoughts are by now painfully transparent, so Lily knows Edna is thinking, *Yes, you are.* They stare at each other in silence until Edna sighs once more and picks up her book. But rather than resuming reading she finds her page and marks it with a tasseled leather bookmark edged in gold leaf that Lily remembers they bought on a trip to Cockermouth where . . . *they eat a cream tea and listen to the rain drumming against the café window. She asks Edna if she can see the bookmark, and Edna extracts it from the small paper bag given her by the woman in the shop. It has a golden silhouette of Wordsworth and a few lines of poetry. She can't make out the poem; the writing is too small and the glinting gold of the letters . . .*

"Lillian? Lillian!"

"Hmm?"

Edna is staring at her from the mirror. She has put down her book on the bedside table and removed her spectacles, which now lie folded in the palm of her hand. "It happened again, didn't it?"

"Oh, Edna, don't fuss."

"But you were miles away! It was as though you weren't here in the room with me at all." Edna's face evokes nothing but its usual authoritative calm, but Lily knows her better than this; Edna is worried. "Will you please go back to the doctor? Have you even taken your warfarin today? When's your next checkup?"

Lily ignores her. She knows Edna's relentless questioning is only born out of love and concern, but she is so sick of doctors and medicines and checkups! She puts down the brush on the dressing table. "I'm finished now. Let's just get to sleep. Things always seem better in the morning." She stops, but Edna is too shrewd not to notice such a slip-up. She meets Edna's eyes. They make her think of hard, shiny conkers and the rapping of cold, raw knuckles.

Edna raises one eyebrow. "What 'things'?"

Lily filibusters, arranging items on the dressing table as though curating a shopwindow display. "Oh, everything. And nothing. You know. Are you finished with the light?"

The ghost of Lily's mother is shaking her head, her lips tight. *Such a disappointment!* But then Edna grunts and clearly decides to let it go. She pats herself down and folds the sheets around her bulky body. She is no doubt tired, which was largely the reason Lily picked this moment to try to tell her. Edna is easier to deal with when she doesn't have much fight in her. So why hasn't she told her? Well, it's too late now.

Lily lets out a breath she didn't know she was holding and watches her mother slide back into the woodchip on the walls. She gets up and pads barefoot between the beds, enjoying the scratch of the nylon carpet between her toes. By the time she reaches for the lamp, Edna is nestled beneath blanket and sheet. As she turns away, Lily sees the small square indentations Edna's hairnet has left on her pillowslip. She decides not to bother with her own and pushes the switch under the shade, the hot metal pinching the loose skin on her thumb.

"You'll regret it in the morning," says a voice, and Lily is no longer sure if it's Edna's, or her mother's, or someone else entirely. She climbs into bed, trying as she did as a child to slip between the sheets without bunching her nightdress. Slowly her eyes adjust to the dark. Beyond the bedside table a lump of crinkled bed linen refuses to look in her direction.

"Edna?" she calls softly.

Silence.

"Edna?"

"What's the matter?"

For the briefest moment Lily is going to tell her everything. Tell her all about the letter that arrived yesterday morning. The letter that is currently tucked under the lining in the drawer of the bureau where she knows Edna never looks. She could blurt it all out in one go. It would be so easy, and then Edna would take control of the matter and she'd sort everything out. Again.

But then a car passes by outside, and the headlights cause a garden shadow to slide across the ceiling above them like a threatening cloud, and all at once Lily cannot speak.

She says nothing more, just listens for Edna's breathing in the dark. If her breath is shallow or broken, she will force herself to stay awake in case Edna needs something. But tonight Edna breathes deeply and is soon fast asleep.

Lily, however, lies awake in the darkness.

day one

Tyler wakes to a set of Venetian blinds that filter the sun into strips that threaten to griddle his eyelids. He gets up and moves to the window to look out at the view. Last night comes back in snatches, a series of sensations: the warm evening air on his face as they left the pub; the eyes of the taxi driver watching them interestedly in his rearview mirror; the chime on the lift doors that closed in slow motion; the scratch of stubble and the faint transferred taste of tobacco and red wine; the cold bite of steel on his exposed back where his T-shirt had ridden up. And then, later, in the bedroom, the twisting of hard, muscular limbs; the tang of fresh sweat; the heat of two bodies pressed together as one.

He turns from the window and watches the man still sleeping. His soft breathing conjures images of fireside cats that dissipate when he notices the prominent Adam's apple pulsing under the translucent skin of the man's throat. It looks as though it's trying to break out and makes Tyler think of the face-hugger from *Alien*.

The man groans and turns onto his side, light feathers of hair falling across that perfectly chiseled face. A delicately proportioned nose, square jaw, thick lips. A calculated length of fine stubble to set it all off. Too perfect. Perfect never works.

The man shifts, reaching up to the pillow with his right arm and causing the duvet to slide off his chest to expose a sculpted washboard stomach and two hard pink nipples. His left arm, bent at the elbow so the wrist disappears under the duvet, is sleeved in an intricate swirl of Celtic tattoos. Like a bush of thorns, or dancing black flames.

He opens his eyes and looks straight at Tyler, the irises bright green in the morning sunlight. He looks almost reptilian.

"Hey," he says, yawning and sitting up.

Tyler moves away from the window and begins to gather his discarded clothing.

The man watches him dress. "I thought we could get breakfast together?" he says. He has that annoying habit of letting his voice go up at the end of every sentence, turning statements into questions.

"I have work."

The man smiles. "Another time." This time it stops just short of a question.

Tyler tries, just for a moment, to summon up their future: trips to IKEA to pick out furniture, lazy Sunday mornings with the paper listening to the kids playing, brunch with the lesbians. It's a *what if* dream that doesn't quite take shape. Someone else's dream. "Look," he says, "this was great but, well . . ." He shrugs and leaves it there.

"I'm Oscar," says the perfect man with his rich blackberry voice. He doesn't seem in the least perturbed by the knock-back.

"And I'm out of here." Tyler leaves the man smiling at him from the bed and lets himself out without another word.

He has been at his desk for no more than a few moments when he realizes something's wrong. It's too quiet. He's used to working alone by now. His desk is tucked at the end of a small cul-de-sac formed by the plasterboard wall of the inner office used exclusively by the Murder Team. It faces the outside wall. There's a partially frosted window to his right that lets in a small amount of natural light, but all that can be seen out of it is the painted brick of the co-op building opposite. He has to turn almost 180 degrees and crane his neck round the corner just to see another human being, let alone talk to one.

And it isn't as though many are queuing up to talk to him anyway. There's another barrier that separates him from his colleagues, something more robust than the flimsy plasterboard of the Murder Room. It isn't always a lack of evidence or suspects that leads to a case being shelved; sometimes it's simple incompetence. More than once he has been responsible for sending one of his colleagues to stand in front of the Independent Police Complaints Commission. It makes him less than popular, but then, he's not here to win friends.

There's usually background noise, though, a hum of conversation that accompanies his working day that's conspicuous in its absence today. He stands up and moves along what he has heard certain droll colleagues refer to as "The Tyler Wing" and back into the office proper. There are one or two industrious types tapping away at keyboards, and in the Murder Room a young detective constable whose name he can't remember—Linda? Brenda?—is wiping down whiteboards with the enthused energy of someone given a minor responsibility. He's considering the best way to approach her—Carla! Yes, he's sure it's Carla—when his mobile rings.

"Adam?"

"Hi," he begins, "how's your head?" but at the same time she says, "It's Sally-Ann here." They both stop. He waits for her to go on, but she doesn't. He starts to say, "Did you stay much longer last—" and she says, "Have you heard what's happened—" They both fall silent again. This time he's determined to wait her out.

"Adam?" she asks after a moment. "Are you still there?"

"Yes," he says quickly.

There's a lengthy pause and then, just at the point at which he decides he'll have to break the silence, she goes on. "I shouldn't be telling you this, but then you'll hear soon enough anyway." She's virtually whispering.

This time he cuts her off. "Sally-Ann? What the fuck's going on?"

Another lengthy pause. He can hear her breathing down the phone. "They've found him," she says. "They're saying they've finally found Gerald Cartwright."

Tyler drives on automatic, his arms and legs controlling the car semi-autonomously while his mind is fixed elsewhere. The place he is looking for is right on the force's boundary, at the edge of the Peak District; one village further on and Gerald Cartwright would have been Derbyshire's problem. The turnoff isn't easy to find; he passes through numerous hamlets, each identical to the last. He avoids using the satnav, having learned from bitter experience that it's just as likely to send him to the wrong side of the valley. Eventually he spots a weathered signpost at the roadside, its cracked face strangled with weeds. He takes the sharp left turn without bothering to slow, and the wheels of the CID Vectra bump alarmingly across scrubland before settling onto the narrow strip of tarmac that winds ahead of him. After a couple of miles, the road dips suddenly and the car jolts its way violently across the ford of a narrow stream. He eases off the accelerator as the first houses begin to appear. A white sign welcomes him to the village of Castledene and asks him to PLEASE DRIVE CAREFULLY.

It isn't difficult to find the church; the road runs right past it, and a sign next to the gate, its pale blue paint peeling into the grass below, declares that ALL SOULS ARE WELCOME. Tyler brakes, stops, and abandons the car halfway up a grass verge. He steps into the quiet peace of a sunny morning in the countryside, birdsong, the wind rustling the autumn leaves. No traffic noise, no sirens, none of the comforting hum of the city. It's unnatural. How the hell does anyone sleep out here?

He checks the address on his phone. He's looking for a vicarage, but the only buildings he can see other than the church itself are a row of four '80s-built semidetached houses that fail to meet the description he has of a dilapidated Victorian mansion. But the third house sports a small brass plaque: THE VICARAGE. There are no signs of activity. No crime scene.

He has a sudden feeling someone is watching him and looks up to see an elderly man standing in the churchyard. The man stares for a moment and then turns away, disappearing behind the churchyard wall. Tyler climbs the grassy bank, and the man comes back into view. He's raking up cut grass from between the head-stones, a half-smoked roll-up hanging from his bottom lip. Behind him a metal cage crackles with burning garden waste.

When the man speaks, he does so without looking up. "You want the Old Vicarage. Follow the road round, and it's the first gate you come to on the left." He gestures over his shoulder with a grubby thumb, and now Tyler sees the strobe of blue emergency lights coming from somewhere behind the church. The man draws deeply on the tab end, filling his lungs before exhaling slowly. Now that he's closer, the man doesn't look as old as he'd first thought. Late fifties, perhaps.

"Thank you, Mr. . . . ?"

"Wentworth. Joe." He makes a show of pulling some weeds from between the stones in the wall. He fails to make eye contact. "Police, is it?"

"DS Tyler." He shows the man his warrant card and tries his best at a disarming smile. He isn't very good at them.

"Found him, then." It's not quite a question. Wentworth throws the last of his grass onto the smoking heap, the burning stub still clasped tightly between puckered lips.

"You knew Mr. Cartwright?"

"Aye," Wentworth growls. "Not many as don't know each other in this place."

Tyler suppresses a smile and wonders if Joe Wentworth has ever heard the word *stereotype*. Perhaps he doesn't hide it well enough, though, because suddenly Wentworth is gathering together tools and dropping them one by one into his wheelbarrow with a reverberating clang.

"I'll be getting on then." He raises the handles on his barrow and starts toward the church. Tyler considers calling him back, questioning him further, but decides to let him go. Maybe he's got something he wants to say, or maybe he's just a nosy old local. Either way, he'll be easy enough to find later.

He leaves the car where it is and walks the few hundred yards round the bend to the gateway of the *Old* Vicarage. A handful of uniformed officers guard the entrance, a human dam built to keep at bay the washed-up detritus of journalists, TV crews, and curious neighbors. He doesn't recognize any of the officers, but this outer cordon is easy enough to breach. He puts his shoulder to the gathered masses without bothering to excuse himself and flashes his warrant card at the uniforms. They acknowledge him with a nod and step apart, lifting the tape that stretches across the driveway for him to duck under.

The gates have fallen loose, but someone has cleared a path by dragging them aside and propping them against the bushes. Tyler feels the cordon snap shut behind him as the mob renews their questioning of the uniformed officers. Ahead of him, along a wide gravel driveway, a large Victorian house sits among the oak trees, its red bricks pitted and enveloped in some sort of vine. At some point in the past there must have been a fire, and the black scorch marks are still visible above each of the broken windows, like excessive eye shadow. There's something familiar about the place, like it might have been used for a period television drama. But then, it would be familiar. Six years ago the place was headline news.

The cluster of vehicles to the right of the driveway identifies the marshaling point. Among them, a workman's van, half its contents spilled out in front of the house. There's a mobile incident room as well, and more uniforms, arranged to form an inner cordon around the house itself. DCI Jordan has certainly pulled out all the stops on this one.

The young uniformed police constable guarding the entrance raises a delicate, shaky hand as he approaches. "Sorry, sir. No one else in. DI's orders."

There's something about the girl's temerity that irritates him. He raises his warrant card. "DS Tyler," he says. He keeps moving, but somehow she manages to insert herself between him and the doorway again.

"Yes, sir. I know who you are. He did say *no one,* sir. I'm sure if you were to report to the incident room . . ."

Her backbone impresses him, but he doesn't have time for de-lays. "I'll take the responsibility."

Still she hesitates. "Is that an order, sir?"

"If you like."

"So you'll be speaking up for me, will you? When the DI kicks me arse?"

He changes tack. "What's your name?"

"Rabbani," she says.

"Constable Rabbani. It's good to meet you. Now fuck off out of my way!"

The girl is out of options. She sighs but steps to the side, allow-ing him to climb the half-dozen steps that lead to the front door of the house. He feels her eyes boring into his back.

He crosses the woodworm-riddled threshold, entering a hallway patterned with red and black tiles. The plaster on the walls hangs loose, the flocked wallpaper holding it together as best it can. In places it bulges with fallen brickwork while in others it's dark and flaky, charred by fire. A wooden staircase leads up to the next floor, its banisters twisted and blackened. To his right, the floor has given way so that getting into the living room now takes a small leap of faith. Beyond the hole, a team of white-clad scene-of-crime officers are combing through the building's past. He steps across to join them.

The house has clearly been empty for years, but someone has been here more recently than that. Village kids poking round, smoking dope perhaps. He sees the remains of a small fire on the floor; around it a few dozen cigarette butts and spent matches. Much of the room is smoke blackened, and parts of it are water damaged. Curiously, some parts are almost pristine: a standard lamp, dusty, its red shade unfaded; the curtains hanging across the patio doors at the far end could be brushed off and made good. It's as though the fire has moved through the room, picking and choosing its targets with care.

Again he has that sensation of being watched, and he searches the room, half-expecting the country bumpkin gardener to appear from behind the sofa. Then he sees the portrait above the mantelpiece, a small framed oil painting of the head and shoulders of a man. The man is wrapped in a dark coat pulled tight to the neck, around which is tucked a loose red scarf. His face is incongruously large. The gray skin hanging in loose folds round his cheeks and jowls makes him look both fat and malnourished at the same time. Here and there are brushstrokes of oranges and reds that might be the distant reflection of light on the horizon. The eyes of the man in the picture are wide and bright and mad. It is these eyes that follow him as he moves through the room. There's a signature in the bottom right-hand corner, hard to make out, and a plaque built into the base of the frame that gives him the painting's title: *The Fire Watcher.*

The frame is much smaller than the rectangle of paler wall that surrounds it, indicating that another picture once hung here, something that must have been moved after the fire. Something wider than it was tall . . . landscape, rather than portrait. He scans the room and finds the likely candidate propped against a nearby armchair, a dull watercolor of the Peak District. He pulls out his mobile and snaps a photo of it.

One of the SOCOs glances up at him.

"Has anyone moved this?" he asks.

The man stares at him blankly.

"You need to dust it for prints. The one on the wall, too."

The SOCO's eyes open wide, and his mouth falls open in mock astonishment. "Sure, mate," he says. "Good thing we've got you experts round. I'd never 'ave thought o' that." He turns back to his work, shaking his head.

"Tyler!"

The man who speaks is standing at the edge of the hole in the doorway, his finger tapping out a drumroll on the mobile in his hand. "What the fuck are you doing to my crime scene?"

Detective Inspector Jim Doggett is a wiry stick figure of a Yorkshireman held together almost entirely with nervous energy. He never stops moving. Pacing, tapping, head nodding; never still, not even for a fraction of a second. Tyler's grandmother would have called it St. Vitus's dance, but it isn't medical as far as he knows. They call Doggett the Yorkshire Terrier, and not for the first time Tyler wonders what *his* nickname is. Then he decides he doesn't want to know.

"The usual, sir. Making friends, contaminating evidence, that sort of thing." He pauses for a moment, aware he's on shaky ground. "I was told you needed everyone you could get."

Doggett barks out a laugh that causes the SOCOs to stop briefly in their work and look up. "Your sort of help I can do without." Still, despite his words he appears to be considering the idea. Then he says, "Since you've made the effort, I've no objection to an extra pair of eyes." He inclines his head, beckoning for Tyler to follow, and disappears back down the hallway.

Tyler leaps back across the hole just in time to see Doggett ducking through a small doorway under the stairs. It opens onto another staircase, this one made of stone. As he follows the DI down, his arm brushes mold from the wall, dislodging a snowfall of musty flakes. At the bottom of the steps the room opens into a cellar that stretches a good way under the house. At some stage it has been used for storing wine, and many of the bottles still survive, the dark-green glass almost blackened with soot. There are props supporting the beams above, relieving the house of its decades-long struggle to hold itself together. Huge, freestanding arc lamps have been set up by the SOCO team, and the cellar bustles with activity as photos are taken and forensic experts go about their painstaking science.

"Right," Doggett says, all business. "House has been empty six year, as I'm sure you're aware. Monday morning, the builders move in." He gestures to the props holding up the ceiling. "Yesterday, they come down here, knock a wall down, and *bang!* Shock of their bloody lives. Elliot reckons he's been there a while. Smart money's on the former owner of the house."

"Gerald Cartwright."

Doggett nods and beckons Tyler to follow him over to the rear wall. The activity is busier here. The pathologist, Elliot, is a reed-like Geordie who reeks of stale tobacco. Tyler keeps his distance and holds his breath.

"Have you had your breakfast this morning, Detective Sergeant?"

He shakes his head.

"Probably for the best, man."

The wall is built of cinder blocks and cuts across the back of the stairs. It's obviously a late addition to the house, not part of the original construction. An irregular hole has been smashed out of it and the corpse lies half exposed in the rubble, caught in the harsh glare of an arc lamp. The three of them are forced to crouch by the descending beams of the ceiling. The body's little more than a skeleton, its remaining skin pulled thinly over its frame. Doggett, on his left, is watching for his reaction, so he determines not to give one. Elliot, to his right, has a yellowy roll-up tucked behind his ear. "From the clothes and general size," he says, pointing, "I'd say it was a man." He gestures to the wasted hands that jut awkwardly above the cinder blocks. "There's enough damage to the fingernails to make me think he was probably alive when he went in."

The stench of Elliot's tobacco breath makes Tyler shudder again. "What about the fire?" he asks.

Elliot looks at the cellar walls. "Could've killed him. He'd have been protected from most of the heat, but the smoke, mind . . ." He leaves the sentence unfinished. "Depends how soon the fire started after he went in, like."

"Could he have been buried there after the fire?" Doggett asks.

Elliot shakes his head, and the roll-up slides loose but somehow doesn't fall. He points at the rubble at their feet. "The bricks are soot covered, same as everything else. He was in there first, all right. This is interesting, though." He moves closer to the body and indicates a dark patch at the back of the skull. "Blunt trauma. Crushed the skull. Not necessarily fatal, but without medical attention . . ." Again he trails off.

"So," says Doggett without feeling, "it's a jolly murder then."

Elliot looks up at him. "Unless he sealed himself in, Jim, and I can't see a trowel in his hand, can you?" Elliot turns back to the body, ignoring Doggett's scowl. "Hopefully we'll know more when we get him out."

Tyler stares at the ragged fingers on the corpse's hands. "Forgetting the fire for a minute, and assuming he was alive when he went in there, how long would it have taken him to die?"

Elliot blows out his cheeks. "Hard to say. If he had been healthy, with plenty of water, food, and oxygen . . . in theory anything up to nine or ten days."

"Jesus!" Doggett scratches absently at his stubbled chin. "Ten days?"

Elliot barks out a laugh, but the noise dies away again quickly, perhaps embarrassed to be there. "I said, *theoretically*."

Doggett rolls his eyes. "When you've finished theorizing, do you think you might be able to give us something a little more accurate?"

"The rule of three," Tyler says. Three minutes without air, three days without water, three weeks without food.

"Very good, Sergeant—in this case the problem for our friend here would have been water. But if we take into account the fact he'd be panicking, expending energy trying to get out, he'd be losing fluids faster than average. Then there's the trauma to the head, blood loss." He pauses and sucks air between his teeth like a dodgy mechanic. "I doubt he'd have lasted longer than a couple of days. Maybe less."

Long enough, though. How long before a man would attempt to burrow his way out through a cinder-block wall using nothing but his fingernails?

Elliot coughs and hacks up some phlegm. Doggett catches his eye, and the man swallows it again. He goes on. "My guess is he was badly injured. Probably concussed. With a bit of luck the poor sod didn't even know what was happening to him." He doesn't sound like he believes it. "Poor old Gerry, eh? Who'd have thought it?"

"All right, Doc, go do your stuff. I'll catch up with you later."

Doggett is already turning away. He shouts over his shoulder, "Tyler," as though calling a dog to heel.

They leave the SOCOs to their work and head back toward the cellar steps. "Right," Doggett says, planting his hands on his hips. "Murder equals Murder Room. Last time I checked, you sit on the *other* side of the wall."

Presumably that's supposed to be a dig but he lets it go. He has his own rule: the first one you get free. "It's an interesting case," he says. "A *cold* case. I'm good at cold cases, DI Doggett. I can't see why you'd turn down anyone's help at this stage."

Doggett grunts. "Depends who's offering the help. All right, we'll see what the DCI has to say, eh?" He starts back up the stairs.

Tyler takes a last look round the cellar. Something Doggett said about the builders when they came in raises a question in the back of his mind.

"Tyler!"

He turns and makes his way back up the cellar steps.

Outside, the sun sears Tyler's eyes and burns away the damp from his skin.

Doggett leads him across the driveway, slowing as they pass the young officer who let Tyler through. "Constable Rabbani," he calls.

"Sir."

"I thought I said no one in without checking with me first?"

Rabbani glances at each of them in turn before lowering her head. "Yes, sir."

"It wasn't her fault. I pulled rank."

"The only rank she needs to worry about is mine." He turns back to Rabbani. "About you wanting to stay on and work this case . . ."

"Yes, sir?"

"Have a guess what the answer is." Doggett moves on without waiting for a response, leaving Rabbani staring at them, unable to hide her scorn.

Tyler shrugs at her and hurries after Doggett. "Don't take it out on her."

Doggett snorts. "Life's a lady dog! She'll learn." He opens the door to the mobile incident room and holds out his hand. "Right, ladies first."

That's number two. He gets that one free as well, but the tally's building.

Amina Rabbani watches the two men disappear into the incident room.

Bastard. But she can't decide which of them she means.

The truth is she's more annoyed with herself than either one of them. She's blown it. She's been ready to take her sergeant's exam for months now, but she keeps putting it off because it's easier to move at this level. She doesn't want to risk getting stuck in uniform until she retires.

She's spent over a year trying to get into CID. But she doesn't know the right people in the right places. She's spent a year collaring people in corridors, trying to make her face fit, even though her face doesn't fit and never will. Months listening to her parents going on about when she's going to get a proper job, something that pays a bit more, maybe something in the medical profession, like Ghulam. Months that she could have been using the extra money from promotion to save for her own place. All this so she can join some white boys' club that doesn't want her anyway.

And when she finally makes it, what does she go and do? She fucks it all up on day one.

Mina sighs. Maybe Danny is right. He keeps telling her, so maybe it's time she listened. "What do you wanna join CID for anyway? It's hard work. And it's not like you get paid no more." But that's Danny all over. There's just no answer to that.

She can't help how she feels, though. She feels—no, she *knows*—that plodding the beat for thirty years isn't for her. And *he* should, too; they've talked about it often enough. In the past he's suggested Response. Or the dog handlers. He'd got fixed on anti-terror for a while. She could go far in the terrorism squad with her background. "They're always looking for Muslims, aren't they? Positive discrimination and all that."

Fuck off, Danny!

She wants to be a detective. She's only *ever* wanted to be a detective. If she can't . . . well then, she might just as well pack it all in and go and work for the dog handlers.

This case fell in her lap like a gift. She remembers what it was like six years ago when Cartwright first disappeared, the media circus surrounding it. It was watching news reports about this and cases like it that made her want to join the force in the first place. And this is the sort of case that makes your name known where it matters. The minute she saw the poor sod buried behind the wall, she knew this was her chance. They stood there in silence, staring down into the rubble, her and Danny. "You know who that is, don't you?" He whispered it, but the sound echoed off the dank walls, returning to them like the muttering of the dead. She didn't answer but she knew, all right. This case was gonna be massive, and all she had to do was impress the right person.

So much for that.

She looks across to the gate where Danny's still guarding the perimeter. He gives her a weak smile. She wonders if he's as tired as she is, if his feet ache as much as hers do. He certainly looks a state. Like he might start chundering again at any moment. When they came up out of the house it was all she could do to drag him to the bushes before he chucked all over the crime scene.

And while Danny emptied his stomach, she'd gone through her SADCHALETS. *Survey* the scene. *Assess* the situation. *Disseminate* details to Control. All straightforward enough. *Casualties*. Just the one. *Hazards*—pretty much the whole house; she was glad she wasn't the one having to sift through the place. *Access* and *Location*. Getting some of the equipment the SOCOs would need down into the cellar might be a bit tricky. She made a note of it. *Emergency* services. Well, it was a bit late for them. *Type* of incident. Murder. Obvs. Though, strictly speaking, that wasn't her call to make. Finally, *Safety*. Of all staff at the scene. She'd looked down at Danny heaving his guts into the bushes and tried not to laugh.

She was the one who made sure the builders were cleared away from the scene, and *she* was the one who made them promise not to talk to the press. And, when they broke that promise, *she* was the one who single-handedly drove off the first journos who turned up. Well, all right, not single-handedly, but it was *her* idea to send Danny on patrol to make sure no one tried to sneak in the back way.

She used the time while they waited for backup to make meticulous notes in her logbook, and by the time DCI Jordan got there she was able to hand everything over in a professional manner. She'd been sure the DCI was impressed with her. She even managed to corner Doggett when he arrived and, although he was his usual misogynistic, racist, shitbag self, she was pretty sure he was impressed with her, too. At that moment she'd known, like you did sometimes, that this was it. This was her chance. This was her way in.

And then the bastard Adam Tyler shows up.

Why her? What the fuck has she ever done to him? She never joins in when the others slag him off back at the station. In fact, if anything she's always felt a bit sorry for him, the way they take the piss out of him because he's gay and because he's good. Too good, from what she's heard. He shows them up, and doesn't give a shit about doing it. They call him Homo-cop: part faggot, part machine.

But maybe they're right, not about the gay stuff but about the other. Maybe he *is* a coldhearted bastard. Never mind the fact he looks like a prettier Jake Gyllenhaal, even with that scar on his face. All the girls fancy him even though they can't have him. To think, she's even *defended* him in the past! Only to take abuse from the lads because they thought she fancied him as well. Well, maybe she did fancy him a little bit, but that's not the point. The point is she won't be fucking defending him ever again, that's for sure. Bollocks to him!

She sees him standing by the window inside the incident room and makes a promise to herself. No matter how fit he is, if he's screwed this up for her and she ends up having to work with the *fucking* dog handlers, she'll find a way to pay the bastard back. If it takes the next thirty years, she'll find a way.

During the course of one sleepless night, Lily grows more and more certain her hiding place in the drawer of the bureau is dangerously exposed and obvious. What if Edna should suddenly need a stamp and, noticing some crease or turned corner in the lining paper, should decide to investigate further? Never mind that Edna hasn't betrayed the slightest inclination to correspond with anyone for a good twenty-five years or more, what if today is the day that changes?

"If ifs and ands were pots and pans, there'd be no need for tinkers!" says her mother's voice from somewhere.

No, the bureau will not do.

But after their morning routine, during which time Lily must focus wholly on aiding Edna in washing and dressing, she helps Edna negotiate the steep staircase and gets her settled in the back room. Only then does it occur to her she has no way to get into the bureau without Edna asking her what she's about.

Added to this, Lily is certain another letter will arrive at any moment. She uses the excuse of making lunch to stay in the kitchen and watch for the post. But then that leaves Edna alone with the bureau. She can't take the risk of leaving her for too long, so she bobs back in frequently to check on her. Only, as soon as she leaves the kitchen she becomes certain she can hear the clang of the letter box and immediately begins to imagine another of those crisp white envelopes lying obscenely on the doormat, waiting to be discovered.

In this way she spends much of the morning diving back and forth between the back room and the kitchen, one eye on the letter box, one on her hiding place. In the end she comes up with the idea of polishing the door brass, enabling her to hover in the doorway between the two rooms. Her nerves by this time are quite shot.

The one consolation is that all of this seems lost on Edna. Though Lily remembers that seldom is anything lost on Edna. Sure enough, it isn't long before she makes a comment about the smell of Brasso and how Lily is in danger of rubbing the damned thing away entirely if she carries on much longer.

Thankfully, that takes them to lunchtime, and it is after lunch when Edna gives Lily the opportunity she needs.

"It's too hot for indoors. We should go into the garden, don't you think?"

"Oh, yes!" Lily cries, and Edna looks at her sharply. "I mean, if you want to, yes, that sounds lovely."

Between them they manage to manhandle the sun lounger out onto the patio. It's a double-seated swing with a canopy, which has faded in the past four decades from chartreuse to a dusty olive. It's Edna's favorite spot, and once Lily has her settled and gently swinging she uses the excuse of a cup of tea to dive back into the house and finally retrieve the letter.

She opens the drawer and there it is. The relief that washes over her is so intense that for a moment she forgets what it represents. But only for a moment. Then she panics again and wants nothing more than to shove the terrible thing back into the dark of the drawer. She can't, though, not without ending up back where she began. But what to do with it? Every place she can think of seems so inadequate. If the bureau drawer—a place Edna hasn't been for years—isn't secure enough, where else is? Time is ticking on and she hasn't even put the kettle on the hob yet. She quickly folds the envelope in half and shoves it into the pocket of her slacks. Then she makes the tea, one eye still firmly fixed on the letter box.

DCI Jordan is seated behind a desk talking into her mobile while simultaneously issuing silent instructions to the rest of the room. She looks tired and ill, but then she always does. Her uniform is creased and her hair has been hurriedly pulled into a ponytail, leaving odd strands of gray waving out from her head like panicked drowning victims. She pauses as whoever is on the other end of the phone takes over the conversation, and sips black coffee from a polystyrene cup. Around her the SOCOs and technicians buzz like drones round the queen.

It's not unusual to see Jordan at a crime scene; she's known for her hands-on approach to command, sitting in on interviews, occasionally visiting suspects in their cells. She's the sort of detective chief inspector the ranks consider a pain in the bloody arse.

But Tyler has his own theory: she regrets taking the promotion. Her office is a constant reminder of her own entrapment, a self-inflicted ball and chain. She'll do anything, even take paperwork to the public library, to avoid shutting herself away in a room she considers her own eight-foot-square, plushly carpeted cell. It occurs to him she probably had to fight for this case herself. Something this high-profile, the chances are good that Superintendent Stevens is already breathing down her neck. That's probably him on the other end of the phone.

If she's surprised to see Tyler with Doggett, she shows no sign of it. She notes his presence and then looks down at a report on her desk. "Yes, sir," she says into the mobile. She clicks her fingers three times in quick succession to attract the attention of a young constable hovering nearby and throws a manila folder at her. The constable fumbles the catch but saves the contents before they reach the floor. "I agree, sir. One hundred per cen—" The last word is cut off as the superintendent again takes control of the conversation. She takes another gulp of coffee, her face betraying nothing of how she feels. "Yes, sir. I'll certainly—" She stops abruptly and presses the call-cancel button, showing none of the frustration she must be feeling at being cut off in mid-sentence.

"Is it him?" she asks without looking up, still tapping away at the screen of her smartphone.

Doggett says, "Seems likely."

Jordan slips her phone into her jacket pocket, picks up the cup of coffee, and stands. She passes the cup to Tyler to hold as she rummages in her pockets for something and says, "DS Tyler, with me."

He follows her out of the cabin, and together they walk behind the mobile incident room, out of sight of any cameras trained on them from the gate. She pulls out a silver cigarette case, flips open the lid, and extracts a smoke. She offers him the case just as she always does, and he declines, just as he always does.

"What do you know about Gerald Cartwright?" she asks, flipping open a metallic lighter that matches the case.

"Same as everyone."

She lights the cigarette and takes a long drag, closing her eyes as though savoring the smoke that fills her lungs. She leaves the cigarette clamped between her lips and breathes out around it. She takes the coffee cup back from him. "Humor me."

He considers for a moment. "Big shot in the nineties, financial whiz kid with his fingers in lots of pies. Disappeared six years ago, prompting some rumors about his possible involvement in organized crime. It was a bit of a scandal."

She barks out a sharp laugh as she exhales, blowing smoke into his face. "As always, Adam, magnificently understated." She takes another fortifying drag. "Cartwright was into everything, and I mean *everything*. Banking was only his bread and butter. He liked to diversify. Property, transport, the stock market. He owned and operated a chain of restaurants, a local brewery, two golf courses, a stud farm, and a newspaper. When he disappeared he'd just begun negotiating to buy a Premier League football team."

"Yes," he says, "it might have helped them stay up."

Jordan glances at him as though he's missed the point. "He was also extremely charming. He went to Eton but was as happy talking to the office cleaner as to the prime minister. He counted a host of the rich and famous among his closest friends, including at least one peer of the realm. He knew everyone, and everyone certainly wanted to know him. I met him myself a couple of times." She pauses and takes the cigarette from her mouth. "Whether or not this body turns out to be Cartwright's, this case is going to receive an unprecedented amount of attention." She takes one last deep puff on the cigarette and then, despite the fact it's only half finished, throws the butt on the ground. She pushes down on it with a scuffed shoe, and he watches the brilliant orange spark flare and fade away.

"Ma'am, with respect, it's not standard practice to allow the original investigating officer to pick up where he left off six years after the case was shelved. Jim Doggett had his chance. This is a cold case review now and as such falls under my remit. I only want to help—"

"No, you don't," she says, cutting him off. "You want to solve the case before breakfast and rub everyone else's nose in how clever you are."

He opens his mouth but can't think of a response to that.

"You overcompensate, Adam. You always have. Always so much to prove. Well, contrary to popular opinion, I do have other officers, several of them fairly competent."

"Again, ma'am, with respect, DI Doggett—"

"DS Tyler, prefacing your remarks with the words 'With respect' does not alone make them respectful."

He swallows what he wants to say and settles for "No, ma'am."

She pauses again, her hand fidgeting as though she regrets throwing away the cigarette so quickly. "What did I say to you the day I gave you this job?"

"That I had my father's eyes?"

She raises an eyebrow and stares at him.

He drops his gaze. "You said I had one last chance." He sees the dog-end at her feet, flattened but still smoking. "You told me not to fuck it up."

She sighs. "I'm not saying you're fucking anything up. Not yet anyway. Look . . ." She pauses, her eyes drifting unconsciously to the scar on his cheek, as they always do when she raises the subject. "What happened with Bridger wasn't *entirely* your fault. But I took a big chance here—you know that, don't you? I put my head above the parapet, and there's any number of bastards lining me up in their sights right now."

"I didn't ask for special treatment, Diane."

"You got it anyway," she snaps. Then she sighs again and reaches out to place a hand on his arm. "You have so much of your father in you, Adam. How am I supposed to treat you like everyone else?"

She lets the hand fall away. "He was always shit at playing nicely with others as well. Is there anyone in the department you haven't managed to piss off yet?"

"There's a girl in the comms room I get along with quite well."

"I need someone on this investigation who knows how to work as part of a team. Forgive me, but that's not you."

"Diane, I . . ." The eyebrow goes up for a second time. *"Ma'am. This is a cold case."* He stops short of telling her it's *his* case. He stops short of telling her how this case is his way back, a chance for redemption, to prove to her she was right to take a chance on him. "I can behave myself."

She says nothing more for a moment, merely stares at him. Then she says, "What about DI Doggett?"

He hesitates, the words he has to speak refusing to drag themselves out. "Perhaps we could work together?"

She continues to stare, eyebrow still raised. He finds himself looking down at the ground, his eyes drawn back to the smoking dog-end.

He hears her say, "Well?" and a voice behind him says, "I've already got a sergeant."

He turns to find Doggett leaning against the mobile unit, his leg dancing to a rhythm only he can hear. How long has he been there?

"You'll need more than one," Jordan tells him.

He shrugs at her, as if to say *It's your call.*

"Fine," she says after a few moments. "But DI Doggett has lead on this. I have no intentions of refereeing a pissing match, gentlemen. Is that understood?"

As they both mutter their assent, Tyler realizes something. Doggett's easy acceptance of him at the crime scene. They expected him to come. They knew he would want to be involved. Was this all some sort of test? To see if he was willing to fight for it?

"One more thing," he says.

The eyebrow goes up for a third time, but it's less effective now that he knows he's been played.

"Constable Rabbani. I understand she's made inquiries about joining CID. I'd like to see what she can do."

Jordan's mouth actually falls open. He'll show her who plays nicely with others.

"Which one's Rabbani?" she asks Doggett.

"Girl who was first on the scene," he says.

Jordan nods. "Oh yes, wouldn't know a common approach path if she tripped over one. All right, DS Tyler, but she's your responsibility." As he turns to leave, she catches hold of his arm. "And Adam. No more fuck-ups!"

On the patio at the side of the house, the sun rebounds off the red-brick wall of the Old Vicarage and smacks Tyler hard in the face. It feels like someone's left the door to a kiln open. The lawn that stretches in front of them to a wooded copse a couple of hundred yards distant looks abandoned, the grass dry and brittle and peppered with thistles and wildflowers. A lone oak tree stands in the middle of the wasteland, cut off from the other trees, like a scout sent out from an advancing army, now dangerously exposed. Hanging from one branch, a plank of wood dangles limply on a piece of rope, the remnant of a childhood swing.

Doggett is staring at the tree as though challenging it to make a break for cover, or perhaps imagining the cool shade offered by its twisted limbs. "Right then, hotshot," he says, scratching at the several days' growth on his chin. "Next move?" He isn't asking because he doesn't know.

"We get Uniform to canvass the neighbors while we wait for Elliot's results. We can't just assume the body is Cartwright's."

"Bloody big coincidence if it isn't."

"There was a gardener," Tyler says, "up the road."

"Good-looking lad, was he?"

He knows by now not to take it personally, but that's number three. The third one has to be answered. "Not really my type, sir, but I could put a word in for you, if you like?" Maybe he imagines it, but he thinks he sees the trace of a smile.

Doggett's leg jiggles up and down. "Six years," he says.

"Sir?"

"This, DS Tyler, is what we on the Murder Team call 'a right bloody ball-ache.'" The leg slows a little, and he shuffles one foot forward, begins kicking at a clump of weeds caught between the flagstones. "Right, I'll leave you to organize things. Get Uniform started on the interviews; Daley's around somewhere, he'll give you a hand."

"Where are you going?"

"I thought I'd better refresh myself of the original investigation. See if we missed anything."

It comes out before he can stop himself. "Gerald Cartwright was missed."

Doggett stops kicking, turns on him, and stabs a finger into his chest. "Right, listen here, son. Jordan wants you included in this. Fine. I think she must be fucking nuts! But who gives a sweet Fanny A. what I want, eh?" He catches sight of something above them and frowns.

Tyler follows his gaze and looks up at the roof. There's a tile hanging alarmingly over the edge of the guttering. It's flapping slightly in a breeze that fails to reach them on the patio. "Is this place even safe?"

"Builders reckon so." Doggett turns back and smiles at him. "But then, why do you think you're the one who's staying, while I go back to the station?"

The mention of the builders reminds Tyler of his thoughts from the cellar. "Why did they start there?"

Doggett turns and squints at him. He shades his eyes against the glare with one hand. "What?"

"The builders. Why start in the cellar?"

Doggett shrugs. "Makes sense, doesn't it? Ensure the foundations are sound before working your way up?"

"Maybe, but why knock a wall down? Why that one? It's a bit of a coincidence, isn't it? They only started work this week, and they went straight to the wall where the body was buried."

Doggett chews on his lip for a moment and then shrugs again. He seems to enjoy shrugging. "Coincidences happen," he says, but he doesn't sound as though he believes it. Doggett looks over to a door on the side of the house. "Why don't you ask the owner? He's waiting for us in there." He moves off toward the door.

"I thought Gerald Cartwright was the owner?" Tyler says, catching him up.

"'Was' being the operative word. His son just inherited the place when he turned twenty-one. Along with a small fortune. It's him what's doing the renovations. Congratulations, Sergeant. I've found you your first suspect."

The door into the house is stuck, and Doggett is forced to take his shoulder to it. The wood groans stubbornly and then the rotting linoleum behind finally gives and the door flies open, pitching Doggett into the room. There's a man waiting patiently on a rickety kitchen chair. Doggett makes the introductions.

"Detective Sergeant Adam Tyler, this is Oscar Cartwright."

The man with the blackberry laugh doesn't even blink. "Detective Sergeant," he says.

Lily is sitting on a stool in the garden trying to catch a breeze. The heat is like a physical force, pinning her down, holding her in place. She thinks of the year Gerald took them all to Spain and how she spent the best part of the fortnight playing the wilting English rose; Edna said she wouldn't travel well and, as always, she was right.

Edna is seated on the sun lounger, gently rocking back and forth while she reads from a copy of *The Inferno*.

The letter folded into the pocket of her slacks burns a hole in Lily's thigh. It feels remarkably heavy for a single sheet of paper in an envelope. She can see its outline and feels sure Edna will notice it at any moment. When she moves, she worries the rustle and crinkle will give her away. Again Lily considers just pulling the thing right out and confessing. It would be so easy to pass on the knowledge, to pass on the problem. She could make out it just arrived, though Edna will see through this, of course, since they have already had a conversation about the lack of post that morning.

It might be easier, Lily thinks, if she could just get away from this place. If she could get away from all the jumbled-up memories, perhaps then she could decide what to do. They need an outing. "Perhaps we might feed the ducks later."

Edna has stopped reading and taken to fanning herself with the pages instead. She is blowing out air through puckered lips. "This'll be global warming," she says, ever the teacher. "Melting ice caps and the like."

Lily has found an answer. "We could stop by the river and make an afternoon of it." If she can get the wretched thing out of the house, she can be done with it. She can drop it into a litter bin as she pushes Edna ahead of her in the chair. Edna will be none the wiser.

"We never used to have summers like this, I know that much."

This is something Lily has begun to notice, how often the two of them hold separate conversations. And then she wonders if they ever really talked about anything. She feels herself blush. That's hardly fair. In the beginning, they were always talking. Talking was

what brought them together in the first place; there was little else
to do on that rooftop. They would sit up late into the night—into
the morning even—sharing each other's hopes and fears for the
future. When did all that change? Lily feels she should know the
answer to that, but she can't quite remember.

"It'll be cooler by the river. And there's some bread in the larder
we could take for the ducks."

"That bread's stale," Edna grunts.

"Yes," says Lily. "Still, I don't suppose they'll mind."

Edna coughs and wheezes, though Lily is far from sure as to the
legitimacy of this sudden attack; it feels remarkably well timed. "I'm
too tired." And that is that. There will be no grand outing today.

The letter pulls at Lily's leg. A blackbird lands in the apple tree
in the center of the lawn. Below it, a number of wasps buzz lazily
around the pots of jam that Lily has placed there to distract them
from the fruit. She watches a wasp crawl up the glass of a jar, its
tiny feet crossing Mr. Robertson's name. She finds herself urging it
on. What use has a wasp anyway, other than to annoy? To buzz and
sting. How they drone, on and on. Not the productive busy droning
of a bee, but a relentless, irritating noise that serves only to warn
you you're about to get stung for no reason. *Waspish,* what an appropriate adjective!

"Damn woman's forgotten the papers again."

"Sorry?"

"Her next door." Edna gestures at their neighbor's fence with a
pen. She's picked up yesterday's crossword. Her book lies discarded,
facedown, brittle pages flaking on the upholstery. She rocks the
sun lounger, legs that still remember school-day swings lifting her
gently from the ground.

"Shush," Lily whispers, one eye still on her insect's fate. And
then she spots another opportunity. "Anyway, I don't mind going."

"It's her turn," says Edna full volume.

The wasp is nearing the pencil-sized hole in the wax paper. It's going in.

"Oh, I can't do this!" Edna throws the newspaper down on top of the book. Lily imagines the spine developing a new crack, one more infinitesimal line among a thousand others. Her eyes begin to water. Edna hauls herself from the chair, and the springs groan their release.

"Where are you going?"

Edna hobbles to the conservatory doors. "If you're going into the village you might as well pick up a few other bits and pieces. I'll make you a list." She disappears into the house.

Lily has her way out. She lets out a deep breath and turns back to the tree. The wasp has gone, and suddenly she needs to know if it has gone in. She lifts herself up from the footstool, feeling the letter crinkle in her pocket. She places a hand over it and trots up the three steps to the raised lawn.

It had been on the doorstep with the rest of the post, though there was no stamp on the envelope, which means it must have been hand-delivered. That thought is the most troubling part for Lily.

Under the apple tree, the sunlight reaches her in mottled patches. It's cool and dangerously inviting; no wonder so many creatures meet their ends here. She kneels down on the bone-dry grass and lifts the jar to peer through the water-damaged label. It's not jam at all but marmalade.

A single sheet of crisp white paper, folded into three. A single line of text. Typed. Not stitched together out of different-sized letters cut from magazines, which is the way they always do it at the pictures. Typed. On a word processor or a computer, she supposes, rather than a typewriter. Nobody uses a typewriter anymore. There was no telling letter A, set half a width higher than all the other letters. The line was straight and uniform and to the point.

I know what you did.

The wasp works to pull itself from its crystalline fate. Lily watches it tire and slow. Its wings falter, and the creature sinks further into suspension. There are other petrified bodies below it.

Perhaps it's all a mistake? Perhaps the letter was delivered to the wrong door? It wasn't addressed to anyone in particular, so it could be for *anyone*. And yet Lily knows, deep down, that the letter was meant for her.

Edna's ghostly voice emerges from the conservatory. "I think we'll have chops tonight."

Lily replaces the marmalade jar, wipes a tear from her cheek, and walks back to the house. To her left there is the hole in the fence that marks the boundary between their property and their neighbor's. An overgrown path stretches away into the trees. Beyond this copse, its roof just visible over the trees, stands the Old Vicarage. Somewhere ahead of her through the undergrowth she hears a noise she hasn't heard in a long time. A familiar sound at one point, a car skidding in loose gravel. She hesitates, glances back at the cottage, but Edna is nowhere to be seen.

Lily starts up the path, threading her way through the gloomy undergrowth. She hasn't been this way since—

"Lillian!"

She hurries back to the garden just as Edna emerges from the house.

"What are you doing all the way over there?"

"Nothing," says Lily. "It's just . . . I think there's someone over at the Old Vicarage."

Edna shuffles her way along the path and peers through the trees. "They must have started work on the place. Well, we knew it was happening." Edna frowns at her. "You are prepared for what's coming?"

Lily has no idea what's coming, but she won't admit it. "Yes, of course. It's just . . . well, perhaps you could talk to Oscar, get him to change his mind?"

"I already have, you know that."

"I do? I mean . . . yes, of course I do. But you could try again, I know you could. Ever since he got back—"

"You forget," says Edna, "he's not a little boy anymore. He's a grown man. Quite capable of making his own decisions."

"But what if—?"

"Enough! I'll deal with it." But then she coughs and bends double, and Lily has to help her slowly back to the sun lounger. All thoughts of anyone going anywhere evaporate as Edna takes a turn for the worse and Lily's time is taken up with helping her back to bed.

All the while, the letter burns against Lily's thigh. She is certain, beyond any reasonable doubt, the message was meant for her.

I know what you did.

If only she could remember what that was.

The kitchen is fetid and damp. Tyler's armpits are hot and sticky, and his head is beginning to feel the same way. The uniformed officer standing watch over Oscar Cartwright has taken the opportunity to step outside for some fresh air, and he can hear Doggett and Elliot talking together somewhere deeper in the house. Or arguing, possibly. He is alone with Oscar. He paces back and forth across the floor, somehow infected with Doggett's perpetual-movement syndrome. It's as though as long as he keeps moving, he won't have to start. Because he has no idea where *to* start. How is this man here?

Tyler stops pacing and leans forward, placing his hands down on a gritty worktop to steady himself. "What the fuck are you doing here?" he asks, more to get his voice working than because he expects an answer that makes any sense.

"Bit of a coincidence?" Oscar says. Even his voice has a slight grin in it.

Tyler presses his hands down hard, feeling the grit that peppers the surface dig small abrasions into the skin of his palms. It's a coincidence. It has to be. What else could it be?

"You can't be here."

"Adam, it's just a coincidence."

It's the first time Oscar has used his name. He's sure he didn't give it last night or this morning, so how does he know? And then he remembers that Doggett introduced them. It's as though his mind is working in slow motion, and he can't catch up.

He's talked his way onto a case and he's already compromised. He has no choice. He'll have to make some excuse to Jordan, tell her to reassign him. "You'll need to give a statement," he says, "but not to me."

"Am I a suspect or something?"

He can't find the words to answer. It's called a conflict of interest. He looks up to see if Oscar's still there, in case he's conjured this up somehow—this one-night stand that refuses to go away. More penance for his sins. But he's still there, the sleeve tattoo like painted chain mail wrapping his left arm. "This is your house," he says, the sentence falling somewhere between a statement and an accusation.

Oscar stands and reaches out a hand, but Tyler steps away from him.

"Is it him?" Oscar asks quietly. "Is it my dad?" His voice breaks a little, and Tyler remembers he's a victim, too. Not just a suspect. Not just last night's shag.

He tries to recall what they talked about last night but doesn't remember them doing much in the way of talking. Did he mention he was with the police? As a rule it's not something he tells people straightaway, not until he knows them better. Not unless they ask. Did Oscar ask?

"Look, about last night . . ." Oscar leans in, wrapping a hand around Tyler's forearm. His voice is deep and low, almost a whisper. "We can forget it if you want. I mean, I won't say anything." He seems younger than he did this morning. But he is younger, or at least younger than Tyler had assumed. Twenty-one! He seems more vulnerable, too, and Tyler has to suppress an irrational guilt. He's done nothing wrong. Yet. Oscar squeezes his arm, rubs his thumb across the bare skin of Tyler's wrist. "I'm not saying it's what *I* want, though." And all at once he is older again, the cocky, sure-of-himself lad Tyler met at the bar.

Which is the real Oscar, which is the act? Tyler pulls his arm away just as Guy Daley walks through the doorway into the kitchen.

"Tyler, me ol' china. What's all this, then? They finally letting you play with the big boys again, eh?"

For a moment he thinks Daley has seen something, but he's just doing his usual faux-Cockney bullshit.

"Jordan let you out the doghouse, then?" Daley asks.

"Detective Sergeant Daley, I need you to take a statement from Mr. Cartwright. You can take him back to the station."

Daley frowns at being treated like a lackey, but then he glances once at Oscar and nods, apparently satisfied the brusque manner is no more than professionalism in front of a suspect. For once Tyler's cold reputation works in his favor.

He leaves Oscar to the tender mercies of Daley's schoolyard charm and makes his way back through the house, turning up the stairs without really thinking about where he's going. He supposes he's looking for Doggett. He has to confess. Even though he's done nothing wrong, that's what it feels like. A confession.

He steps out onto a long landing lined with doors. Directly

ahead are the main stairs leading back down into the hallway. To his left another staircase spirals up and behind, presumably leading to a third floor. He finds himself heading up, as though the higher he travels, the less constricting the air will feel.

He considers what happens next. Once he's told Doggett. After fighting his way onto this case he'll be forced to give it up again. He'll become the latest joke Guy Daley shares with his mates down the pub. It won't be the first time, and he doubts it'll be the last. Jordan's words come back to him. *Always so much to prove.* He thinks about Doggett's comment earlier about the gardener. *Good-looking lad, was he?* And then the later jibe: *Ladies first.* He knows how it will be after this. He'll always be the bloke who was shagging the suspect. If the suspect happened to be a woman, they'd be patting him on the back and it would be pints all round. But it isn't a woman.

So, yes, of course he has something to prove. He always will.

He reaches the top of the stairs and walks along a narrow corridor and through an open doorway that leads into an attic room. The pallid sky is visible through the rotting rafters, and a single mattress lies beneath, filthy and sodden despite the fact it hasn't rained in weeks. There's a large wooden chest of drawers to the right and, next to that, an old-fashioned wardrobe big enough to climb inside. To the left, a dormer window framed by a pair of heavy winter curtains that reaches from floor to ceiling. Other than that the room is empty: bare floorboards, bare walls.

Very bare walls . . .

He hears the floorboards creaking behind him just before Doggett says, "Nice place. Bit of a fixer-upper."

"I thought you were heading back to the station?"

"I'm just leaving now." Doggett stands next to him and follows his eyes to the wall. "What?" he asks.

Above the bed there's a subtly paler patch of plaster, a square of wall that has been protected from the worst of the elements some-how, around it a border of muck and grime. A border about the size of a small picture frame. About the size of the portrait he saw on the wall downstairs. Why would somebody move it?

"It's nothing," he says.

Doggett frowns at him but lets it go. "What happened with the Cartwright lad?"

This is the point of no return. This is his opportunity. The only one he's going to get. He wouldn't be the first person removed from a case because it struck too close to home. There's no shame in it. All he has to do is tell the man the truth. And there is Doggett staring at him, waiting for him to fail.

"Daley's taken him back to the station. I thought it was better to get him out of here." And it's as easy as that. The moment has passed. He doesn't even have to lie.

Doggett grunts. "Fine. But don't leave it too long to talk to him." He turns to go and then stops. "Oh," he says, "I need you to pick me up from court in the morning. I'm giving evidence in the Kendrick case. I should be done by eleven."

"That's a bit of a late start, isn't it?"

"He's been here six years, son. I reckon he'll keep a few more hours." Doggett turns once again and heads toward the door. "Get yourself an early night, Sergeant. Sleep tight." His voice echoes down the stairwell. "Don't let the buggers bite."

Tyler turns back to contemplate the empty wall.

The irritating buzz of a disk jockey reverberates across the plastic dashboard, down the driver's door, and into Tyler's right arm where it hangs out of the window. He has his shirtsleeve rolled to the elbow, the Vectra's metallic paint warming his forearm. Some-where, far behind in the queue, someone vents the day's frustration by leaning on a car horn. The lights ahead change to green. The traffic fails to move.

On the radio the DJ discusses star signs with the guest astrologist. He finds himself listening for his own. *Gemini—a good week for new relationships, with Mercury ascendant; both romance and work hold opportunities for new beginnings.* Christ! His mother would have loved that. She was into all that crap for a while. Horoscopes and crystals, patchouli oil and cosmic shopping. Maybe that's why she left when she did. Maybe she saw a premonition of what was to come.

The traffic lights complete another cycle; red, red and amber, green, amber, red. Still nobody moves. Another horn sounds.

What the hell is he going to do?

He needs to think it through, but he can't focus on anything. The green man on the crossing light has been knocked aslant, making it look like some drunken office worker off to enjoy the lazy evening. He finds the image strangely soporific as flashes of the day visit him like some bad acid trip: Oscar's pale skin covered in those dark swirls of ink; the desiccated flesh of the corpse with its broken fingernails; the gray, mottled face of the portrait in the living room. A portrait that once hung in the attic. Why does that seem so significant?

Again the lights blink their pattern. Why didn't he tell Doggett? That was his moment. The longer this goes on, the worse it gets. It's not unheard-of to come across someone you know while working a case, especially in a city like Sheffield. A place that's more like an overgrown village, where you're never more than three Facebook friends away from every new acquaintance. But there are procedures for this sort of thing. You're supposed to disclose the information, not just bury your head in the sand.

The lights complete another cycle, and Tyler slams his hand

down on the dashboard. "Fuck!" He glances to his right to see the woman in the passenger seat of the car next to him watching. Fuck this! He starts the engine, flicks the left indicator, and inches his way out into the bus lane. He speeds past the line of waiting traffic, ignoring the disapproving glares of the trapped motorists. At the next junction he finds the first empty parking space and abandons the car on a meter. He can collect it first thing, before the wardens come by. It's insured, and it's not as though it's his car anyway. Maybe they'll sack him for misuse of public property, and the rest of his problems will go away. He presses the lock button on the key fob, the lights flash twice in quick succession, and the car chirrups an irritatingly jovial goodbye.

His route home takes him past the Red Deer and he hovers outside for a moment, wondering if this is where he was heading all along. Once inside, he orders a pint of Moonshine and heads out to the beer garden. He finds a spot on a bench near the back wall and uses the conversations of the postgrad students and after-work crowd as white noise to help focus his thoughts.

He's halfway through the second pint when Sally-Ann calls.

"How was your day?"

He begins to put her off, annoyed with himself for answering the bloody thing in the first place, but she starts speaking again right over the top of him. "Was it him, then? Was it Cartwright? Oh my God, Adam, this is going to be fucking huge! You'll be mega-famous. Assuming you're on the case. You are . . . aren't you?"

He starts to tell her they're not sure of anything yet but she's already talking again, filling him in on the gossip back at the station. How everyone's saying the son did it, how Carl heard from that skinny bloke in Reception how he overheard Doggett telling Jordan they'd have the whole thing wrapped up in a couple of days . . . and on and on.

He tunes out her voice and goes back to his thoughts. He could still go to Jordan, make out it was the shock that stopped him saying anything earlier. She'll be pissed with him, but it would probably be all right. She'd reassign him without any fuss, and maybe no one would even need to know why.

"Adam?" Sally-Ann's voice brings him back to the present.

"Sorry?"

"I said, how did it go last night? With that bloke? I saw you slipping out the door with him. You're a dark horse, aren't you? Only, I said to Carl—"

Last night. It can't have been only last night. It feels like weeks ago. He breaks into her chatter. "I don't think that's going to work out."

"Oh," she says. "That's a shame, he was cute." There's an uncharacteristic pause and then she goes on. "Anyway, the reason I was ringing was to tell you about Saturday . . ."

He lets her witter on for a bit with the details, a friend of a friend's birthday, a nightclub, all the gang will be there. He assumes that means he's part of the gang now. He's not sure how he feels about that. In the end he finds himself promising her a dance just to get her off the phone.

After that, the evening disappears through the bottom of a glass, and before long the guy behind the bar is calling last orders. Tyler drains his pint and takes his leave, helping an old fellow negotiate the steps on the way out. The man smiles at him with a mouth missing most of its teeth, and then staggers away into the night. The evening is warm and quiet. A group of lads burst from a nearby pub and cheer at nothing in particular. Tyler crosses the street and leaves the high street, moving into the industrial suburbs. The noise of the city begins to fade, and the orange-tinted darkness settles down into standby mode. At one point, an ambulance siren sounds close by and rips the night into action again, but it, too, fades away into the distance and the city returns to its watchful slumber.

Because his flat is part of a reclaimed industrial estate, there are few people around at this hour. He begins to imagine an echo to his footsteps. He turns and looks behind. He listens for the sound of footfalls, but there's nothing. When he reaches his apartment building, however, he pushes the door firmly shut rather than allowing it to close on its own. He waits until he hears the sound of the lock re-engaging before letting go of the door.

Only as he turns does he notice the figure sitting hunched over next to the lift. Oscar looks up, his head bobbing on his shoulders like a nodding dog. He has the same vague look in his eyes as the old man at the pub.

"What the fuck are you doing here?" Tyler has a sudden flash of déjà vu even as he notes the slight slur in his own voice.

"I had a few drinks . . ." Oscar tries to stand but loses his balance and falls against the partition wall, the flimsy plasterboard buckling a little under the pressure. "One of . . . your neighbors . . ."

Tyler slams his finger onto the button that calls the lift. "You can't be here, for fuck's sake!" How the fuck does he even know where he lives?

"I wanted to see you."

Tyler presses the button again.

"Adam, wait . . . please . . . Jus' two minutes . . . then I'll go."

Tyler swallows. His mouth is dry and stale with beer. He turns to look at Oscar. "What do you want?"

Oscar looks out through the glass doors into the dimly lit parking lot. "Is it him?" he asks again. "Is it my dad?"

"I can't answer that."

The foyer is hot and stuffy, and Tyler feels the sudden urge to be outside again. His head is swimming and it's hard to breathe.

"I don't know what to do," says Oscar. "I can't go home."

"There must be somewhere. Someone."

"It's fine. I'll be fine." He starts toward the door and then stops again, swaying slightly. "I fucked this up," he says, standing with his back to Tyler. "I'm sorry. I didn't mean to cause you any trouble. I mean . . . I didn't . . ." The lift arrives with a gentle chime just as Oscar falls to his knees and vomits noisily onto the carpet.

"Shit." Tyler rubs a hand over his face.

Maybe it's because he knows what it is to lose a father. Or maybe in the light of Jordan's identification of his character flaws, he feels the need to reach out to someone, to prove he's human after all. Maybe it's something else. Some primal urge he doesn't let himself dwell on too long. Whatever the reason, he finds himself saying, "All right, you'd better come up."

day two

The Great Fire of London, 1666

So. They have found him.

You find it strange to know he's no longer there, tucked up safely behind his wall. You remember how it used to be, how he might be lurking round any corner, lying in wait to pop up when your guard was down.

You remember this bus shelter. You stare at the ramshackle structure, barely holding itself together after all these years, and in your head he's still screaming. That red-hot anger rippling through your veins. All you can do is find a way to distract him. Remember the fires. Stay focused on the flame.

The most famous fire in history burned for four long days, eating the city of London. Thirteen thousand houses. Eighty-seven parish churches. Fifty-two guildhalls. Four-fifths of the greatest wooden city in the world reduced to nothing but a smoldering ruin. Despite all this damage, hardly anybody died. Some say as few as six. Of course, that doesn't include the dozens who died of hunger and exposure in the refugee camps afterward. Nor does it account for the ones who took the blame. The foreigners and the papists, who were lynched or beaten to death by mobs. And poor Robert Hubert, sentenced to death and hanged after his confession. Only afterward was it discovered the simpleminded Frenchman didn't even arrive in the city until two days after the conflagration began.

67

That is what they do though, isn't it? You know that full well. How they search for explanations for their suffering and loss. Who wants to believe the world is a capricious, dangerous place? Far better to find a scapegoat, some poor sod who was in the wrong place at the wrong time who can take the blame. Then they can rest, safe in the knowledge the world is a warm, well-ordered place with clearly defined rules.

You know it isn't. You know the world is a bastard place, full of evil men.

If a scapegoat can't be found, they blame God.

But the truth is it was just an accident. A terrible coincidence. Nothing to blame for the loss of half a city but bad luck, poor construction, and an unusually strong wind. London was simply a powder keg, waiting for a spark. You might as well blame the Middle Ages. You might as well blame Time.

But sometimes someone *is* to blame. Arson—*the criminal act of intentionally setting fire to one's own or another's property for improper reason.* You soak the bus shelter in petrol and feel the fumes burning your nose, making you light-headed. You pause for a moment and listen to the thick liquid dripping from the wooden roof and pooling on the concrete floor. You remove the gloves carefully, making sure not to get any of the petrol on your hands.

You shake a little as you light the match, watch it spark, flare, and then sputter and settle. See the way it is already reaching out, eager to consume the sacrifice you've prepared for it. You flick your wrist and the burning match soars through the night air, up, up, in a graceful arc, pausing for a moment, hanging in the night sky like a perfect glittering jewel. And then it's falling again, gaining speed until . . . *whoomph!* It hits the surface of the puddle and bursts into furious life, fire skittering out across the oily pavement to the walls of the wooden shelter.

It climbs, reaching upward for the sky. You watch the graffiti blacken and curl, and see Kelly's love for Sam evaporate on the wind. You wonder if they were the ones who left behind the used condom that melts and fuses itself to the burning bench.

You stand and watch as the bus shelter is utterly consumed. But it doesn't help at all because inside your head, still he is screaming.

POSTED BY **thefirewatcher** AT 6:15 AM

1 COMMENTS

DarrenP said . . .

Loser!!

The media is in a characteristic frenzy. Tyler sits at the breakfast bar that is the sum total of his dining furniture and watches the breakfast program on his laptop while scanning through various alternative news feeds. Theories abound as to how Gerald Cartwright ended up bricked in his own cellar, but no one seems in any doubt that it *is* Gerald Cartwright, even though no formal identification has yet been made.

Above him, the spotlight he replaced last week crackles and fizzes, cutting in and out. Perhaps it's just the wrong wattage or something, but he can't shake the feeling it's laughing at him. Some subtle movement in the corner of his eye alerts him, and he closes the laptop smoothly. Oscar is standing in the doorway, watching. He's wearing nothing but a pair of tight yellow jockey shorts. His washboard stomach flexes, and the bold tattoo on his arm glistens in the flickering light.

"Hey," he says, yawning and stretching somewhat artfully, running one hand down his torso to scratch vaguely at the light downy hair above his waistband.

Tyler stands up and moves to the kettle, deliberately turning his back. "Coffee?"

"Black. Thanks."

He flicks the switch and feels, more than sees, Oscar lope his way across the open-plan living area. There's a small cry as he collapses too quickly onto the cheap sofa and discovers the lump of plywood shoved under the cushions to replace the springs.

"You slept on this?" Oscar asks. "You didn't have to, you know."

"I don't have a spare bed."

Oscar grins at him. "That's not what I meant."

Tyler looks away again and goes back to preparing the coffee.

After a few moments Oscar says, "Man, you have a shitload of books." He's on his hands and knees now, in front of the bookcase, bright yellow buttocks raised into the air like a fisherman's shimmering fly. "Did someone nick your telly?" He seems reinvigorated, the forlorn Oscar of the night before nowhere to be seen.

But by the time Tyler carries two mugs of coffee across the room it is the vulnerable Oscar he finds waiting for him, curled up on the sofa, his legs tucked under himself, arms wrapped protectively round that skinny waist. When he speaks it's quietly, almost reverentially. "I think it's him," he whispers.

Tyler places the mug on the coffee table and withdraws to perch on the windowsill. A safe distance.

"Sometimes I can't really remember him?" Oscar goes on, once again turning a statement into a question. "I can smell him, though. That's weird, right? Stale cigar smoke. And that gross aftershave he always wore?" He picks at a raised mole on his left arm. If they were a couple, Tyler thinks, he would tell him to get that looked at.

"I know the papers made him out to be some sort of deviant, but, well, I'm not saying he was perfect or anything, but he was my dad, you know? Even if he wasn't around much?" He stops picking and starts rubbing at the arm with his thumb, as though the blemish is a smudge of dirt he can wipe off.

"Did he go away a lot?"

Oscar nods. "London, mostly. Europe and the U.S. None of us even knew he was missing at first. The media said he'd done a bunk. There was money missing or something?"

It's a highly sanitized version of events, but he can allow Oscar this; he knows what it is to spend years in denial about a father. But in Gerald Cartwright's case, it wasn't just a bit of missing money. Banking irregularities, mis-sold insurance policies and pensions, speculative and reckless trading. And then, later, they discovered the tax evasion, and there were suggestions of money laundering. After that the rumors began about the wild parties, the weekend-long orgies involving a host of famous names, some more believable than others. Prostitutes came forward, again some more believable than others, to tell stories of being bussed up from London in order to satisfy the needs of particularly important clients.

But it was when links were made between a haulage company Cartwright owned and a factory in Eastern Europe that had ties to the Russian Mafia that the rumor mill really went into overdrive. By the time the papers finally got bored, no one believed Gerald Cartwright was anything short of the devil himself.

Oscar sits hugging himself. "At first, they said he killed himself because he couldn't live with the shame."

The words strike a little too close to home for Tyler, and he shivers.

"Then they started with the conspiracy theories. They said he was on the bottom of the Thames in concrete boots, or the Black Sea. Or that he got taken out by MI5 or the CIA; that his bones were scattered across some private game reserve in South Africa." He stops abruptly.

"What do *you* think?"

Oscar traces the thorny end of one branch of his tattoo with a forefinger. "I think it's all bullshit!" he says. "All right, the company was involved in some dodgy deals, but no more so than any other multinational."

How easily he denies his father's culpability. But maybe he's right. Maybe they *are* all at it. The company certainly survived, the board of directors severing all ties with Gerald Cartwright and changing its name. CWI re-floated on the stock exchange and still continued to involve itself in no more dodgy deals than the average multinational. Or so they would have the world believe.

"I think he's dead, though, if that's what you mean. I think I've always known that."

Tyler doesn't answer him. He knows full well how fathers can let you down. Or does Oscar mean something else? Is this a confession?

"I mean . . . he wouldn't just leave. Not like that. Not after Mum . . ." He looks up, as though noticing Tyler for the first time. He straightens visibly, arching his back and flexing the muscles on his arms.

Despite the fact Oscar is the one in his underwear, it's Tyler who suddenly feels exposed, sitting on the edge of the windowsill, the hard wood digging into his arse through his jogging pants. He crosses his legs, then uncrosses them again. *He wouldn't just leave. Not like that.*

Oscar smiles, and the vulnerability is gone again. Is this a scared little boy play-acting at being a grown-up, or a devious man pretending a false innocence? Tyler can't decide, nor which might be the more dangerous.

The cheeky grin morphs into something more bitter. "I guess you know all this, though? About Cynthia—" He stops abruptly. "My mum, I mean. About her walking out and all that?"

Tyler knows she left years before Gerald's disappearance but not much more than that. He knows the original investigation considered Cynthia Cartwright a possible suspect but never managed to trace her. "How old were you when she left?"

"Ten. She just had enough, I guess. I don't suppose Dad was the easiest bloke to live with."

Absent fathers, mothers who abandoned their sons. The simi-larity in their stories is too striking. "Who took care of you when your father wasn't around?"

"The neighbors. They're sort of like elderly aunts to me. Lily and Edna. They pretty much raised me anyway, even before Dad—" He stops abruptly, leans forward, and picks up his coffee. He takes a long sip, his shining eyes never leaving Tyler's own. "Then they shipped me off to boarding school." He laughs. "I don't blame them; I was a bit of a shit back then." He upends the mug and drinks deeply, the protruding Adam's apple contorting as he swallows.

"Why did you start the work on the house?"

When the mug comes down, the eyes have darkened and the sclerae are yellowed and bloodshot. "Why do I get the feeling I'm being interrogated here?"

Tyler takes a leaf out of Doggett's book and shrugs. The dark eyes pin him to the windowsill.

"I just got back from uni? There was some legal shit; I couldn't do anything with the house until I turned twenty-one." Oscar puts down the empty mug, untucks his feet, and places them very delib-erately on the coffee table. His hands come to rest on his upper thighs. "Now I can sell it," he says.

"Why did the builders start in the cellar? Why that specific wall?"

"Because I told them to. They pointed out that the wall had been . . . added." He seems to be considering the ramifications of this for the first time. Or maybe it's part of the act. "They told me it wasn't supporting anything and asked if I wanted it opened up again. I figured the bigger the place, the better the price, right?"

It makes sense. But it could be designed to. The explanation certainly came very readily. Tyler levers himself up from the win-dowsill and returns to the kitchen, but Oscar follows him.

"Is this an official interrogation," he asks, "or can anyone join in?" He perches one canary-colored buttock on the stool at the breakfast bar while Tyler wrings out a dishcloth and begins wiping down countertops he's already cleaned this morning.

"What made you become a copper?"

"My father was a DCI. I guess I grew up with the police." He turns, looks at Oscar directly. "Did you know who I was when we met?"

"I didn't get much of a go, did I?" Oscar laughs. "Did I know you were a copper, you mean? Maybe? I'm not sure. Did you tell me when we met? I was pretty wasted that night, to be fair."

"I didn't tell you."

Oscar leans forward on the breakfast bar, biceps flexing. "I guess I didn't know, then. It wasn't the thought of the uniform that did it, if that's what you're worried about."

"I don't wear a uniform."

Oscar tuts. "Pity."

Tyler leans across and disconnects the charger on his laptop. He gathers it up, shovels it into his briefcase, and turns to leave. "I have to get ready for work now."

But Oscar catches his arm, his grip surprisingly strong. "When will you know?" he asks, and all at once the scared little boy is back. "When will you know if it's him?"

Tyler looks down and very slowly, very deliberately, prizes his wrist free. "I can't talk to you about this case," he says.

When he gets out of the shower Oscar is gone.

The court case is delayed so Tyler watches from the public gallery as Doggett gives evidence. As prosecuting witness, he takes his place in the box, opting to "affirm" rather than swear on any holy book. The Crown prosecutor leads him through his statements. Then Doggett is cross-examined, his evidence tested, his statements double-checked and verified. He occasionally checks his notebook for exact dates and times. The solicitor for the defense does her best to discomfort him, but Doggett speaks quietly, elegantly, and with an authority no one could doubt. He's a different man to the jiggling DI at the crime scene yesterday.

Meanwhile, the accused stands in the dock, a baby-faced millennial in a sharp suit, trying to appear incapable of the attempted rape he's being tried for. The jury looks confused. Tyler considers how it might feel to stand where Doggett is now, with Oscar in the place of the suited rapist. It wouldn't be allowed of course. It would be deemed a conflict of interest and the defense would call for a mistrial.

When Doggett steps down, Tyler leaves the gallery and heads downstairs to meet him, but it's the DCI who's waiting. Jordan flicks her head curtly and he follows her outside in silence.

"Jim's just finishing up with the Crown Prosecution Service," she says. "Take a seat for a minute."

He sits and waits for her to go on. He should tell her now. He *will* tell her. But still he waits.

"How are you getting on with DI Doggett?" she asks finally.

The question surprises him. "He told me he didn't want me on the case."

She huffs out a small laugh. "Yes, that sounds like Jim." She licks her thumb and rubs at a stain on the arm of her jacket. "He asked for you on this."

"Why?"

She glances at the camera crew setting up outside the entrance to the court. "That's what I'd like to know." Jordan smiles at him, the concern vanishing from her face. "Perhaps he thinks he can butter me up by taking you under his wing."

But Tyler has known this woman a long time and sees the worry hiding behind the professional veneer. "You're not sure it's that."

"DI Doggett is a highly capable officer. But he does have a tendency to do things his own way. I need someone on this case who knows how to follow the book."

"And that's me?"

"Don't sound so surprised. I know you've at least *read* the book, even if you do choose to ignore it when it suits you. And it isn't as though you're averse to challenging authority figures when you think they've got it wrong."

"You want me to spy on Doggett for you?"

She swings her head round and fixes him with a dead-eyed stare. "Do try not to be so melodramatic, Adam. I'm saying I can't afford any cock-ups on this. I need you to make sure the i's are dotted. That's all."

"Diane . . ." He's going to tell her, he is, but then the defense team is emerging from the court in a tsunami of flash photography and shouted questions. Doggett slips around them unseen, and Jordan stands to greet him.

"Ma'am."

"Just checking on progress, Jim."

Doggett's eyes swing between the two of them. "Progress? Yeah, well, that bastard's overrated in my opinion."

Jordan shakes her head. "No cock-ups," she says again, this time to both of them. Then she walks away without another word.

"Right, son, shake a leg." The DI heads straight to the parking lot. On the surface he seems undisturbed to find his sergeant in conversation with his superior. But as they reach the car he makes it clear it's been noted. "I've never known the DCI to take this much interest in a sergeant before."

Tyler opens the driver's door. Their eyes meet across the roof of the car. "Perhaps I'm just lucky."

Doggett waits until they're both in the car before he drops his bombshell. "Nothing to do with her being your godmother, then?"

Tyler ignores him. It's not meant to be a secret, but few people know. He's not going to give Doggett the satisfaction of showing surprise, though. He starts the car without another word but, as he reaches for the gearshift, Doggett's hand leaps out and catches hold of the steering wheel. "I'm not against a bit of friendly nepotism now and again. It's the way of the world, I know that." He pauses for effect. "But if I catch you trying to go round me, I'll crucify you. Is that understood?" He lets go of the wheel without waiting for an answer and turns to look out the window. Tyler slides the car into reverse, and Doggett begins tapping out a tune on the dashboard.

The second letter arrives that morning and takes Lily quite by surprise, even though this is exactly what she's been waiting for. The post arrives as normal, just after eleven, and there is nothing but a statement from the building society and a catalog from some company called Rest Easy that sells beds for the incapacitated and infirm. Lily has no idea where they got her details from, but got them they have. *Mrs.* Lillian Bainbridge. Close enough, she supposes. After that she somehow manages to put the whole thing out of her mind for an hour or so and then, all at once, it is there. Another plain white envelope. Staring at her from the mat. No sound of the letter box flapping, nothing. Just one minute it isn't there, and then it is. It makes the hair stand up all over her body.

Edna is already in the garden but still, Lily can't help but snatch the envelope up and scrunch it to her middle. She creeps back through the kitchen and hurries up the stairs and into the bedroom. Only when she is looking down on Edna from above, certain she can't be seen, does she unfold the paper from her clenched fist and smooth it out.

She opens the envelope carefully, though it isn't sealed, just has the flap tucked in at the back. She pulls out another sheet of paper folded in three and reads the printed words.

If you don't tell, I will.

Below her, through the cracked-open window, she can hear the gentle groaning of the sun lounger as Edna swings.

How would Edna deal with this? Lily tries to apply her mind to the problem in the same way she has seen Edna do so many times over so many years. Two letters. The first—now folded into the mechanism of the grandmother clock by the fireplace—*I know what you did.* A statement, nothing more. Designed to unsettle, yes, but not inherently threatening. Lily shakes her head. No, that's not right. Of course it is threatening! Why else would someone send it? She looks down again at the paper in her hand. The second. *If you don't tell, I will.* A statement, but also a demand. But not a demand for money or any sort of recompense. A demand for . . . what? Justice, she supposes. Perhaps a deserving one, if only she could remember.

Oh, it's all too difficult. Her head is swimming and there are too many gaps. The only thing she's certain of is that this is not something she can ignore. Not now.

Lily's eyes stray to the footstool next to the wardrobe. It has a picture of a Cavalier on horseback with three hunting dogs. She crouches down and brushes the woven fabric with her left hand, the letter still clutched in her right. She can't remember exactly where it came from. Perhaps it belonged to her mother? Yes, that's right, she's sure. Edna re-embroidered it a few years after the funeral. Lily has always found the Cavalier rather dashing. She bangs the fabric with the palm of her hand and watches the dust billow up into the air. She pretends it's the dirt kicked up by the horse's hooves as it thunders across the woven landscape, the spaniels yapping at its heels. She thinks that perhaps she used to do this when she was a child.

It is then she realizes the squeak of the sun lounger has stopped.

She jumps up and looks out of the window. Edna is gone. She feels the hair stand up on her arms, and her heart leaps into her throat. She yanks open the wardrobe door and looks for somewhere to hide the letter. Anywhere. There is a pair of old moccasins near the back, and Lily jams both the scrunched-up letter and envelope into one, inside and up into the toe. Then she closes the wardrobe door and presses her back up against it.

She hurries downstairs to find Edna standing in the front room holding an overcoat.

"What have you been doing up there?"

"Nothing," says Lily.

Edna considers her suspiciously.

"I thought I might change into something cooler." Lily can't help but skate her eyes toward the grandmother clock. Has it been moved? Surely not, or she would be hearing about it by now.

Edna blinks. "But you didn't. You're wearing exactly the same thing you were a half hour ago."

"Yes, I changed my mind."

Edna's eyebrows furrow, but she clearly has something else on her mind since she lets the topic go a little too easily. She thrusts an arm out toward Lily. "Here," she says, pressing into Lily's hand a page from a notepad covered in spidery blue ink. "The list I made yesterday." Edna stares at her. "You said you were going into the village."

"I did?" She can't remember saying any such thing. But it would be the perfect opportunity to get rid of the letters. If only they weren't both so irretrievable. She can't think of any reason to head back upstairs now, let alone for fiddling with the clock.

"Well, are you going or not?"

Lily glances at the list in her hand. "I shall never manage all this."

"For goodness' sake, woman, it's only a couple of chops." Edna begins forcing Lily's arms into the sleeves of a coat she hardly needs in this weather. "Look, just do your best. And take your time. It's a nice afternoon; you ought to make the most of it. Why don't you go down to the river and get some fresh air for a change? You could take that bread for the ducks."

"But that's what I—"

"Oh, Lillian, do stop fussing and get a move on!"

Before she knows it, Lily finds herself ushered out of the house and down the path. She glances back to see Edna watching her from the gate. Edna raises a hand in farewell and Lily follows suit. As she turns down the path toward the road a thought occurs to her. If she didn't know better, she might almost think Edna was trying to get rid of her.

He drives with Doggett studiously ignoring him from the passenger seat, apart from occasional flinches at nonexistent near misses, or the odd mumble about the merits of the advanced driving course. No further mention is made of his relationship to the DCI.

Diane Jordan has been in Tyler's life longer than he can remember. Longer, in fact. *Godmother* is understating it slightly; there were times when she was more of a mother to him and his brother than anyone else. Not that she had much to compete with. Jordan and his father were colleagues first, then partners, then friends, and, finally—if their mother was to be believed—more than friends. But then, their mother accused Richard of having affairs with just about every woman he ever came into contact with, so she was hardly the most reliable source. If he was having any affairs, neither Tyler nor his brother knew about them. Then again, why would they?

He can't remember the exact moment Diane Jordan went from being "Auntie Di" to "That Bloody Woman," but he remembers well those end days, when it was just the three of them because Richard was always at work. Tyler; his brother, Jude; and their crazy mother. She would tell them, sometimes in graphic detail, exactly what she thought Richard and That Bloody Woman were getting up to. He would have been ten at that point, Jude thirteen. Yet it was Tyler who saw the holes in these fantasy stories and Jude, the older brother, who was content to go along with them. Later, after their mother was no longer in the picture, Jude wanted nothing to do with the woman he held responsible for their ills, but Tyler could never find any blame for Auntie Di. Perhaps Jude, being older, thought he didn't need a mum anymore, but Tyler wasn't ready to give any-one else up. Of course, it wasn't long before he had to. First Jude, who ran off to fight in Tony Blair's war in the desert. And then Richard, who lost a battle of his own.

Doggett makes a show of stretching out his limbs, as though waking from a long, relaxing journey, and he yawns extravagantly. Tyler realizes he's been driving on autopilot again. They're already at the Old Vicarage.

The SOCO team is still combing the grounds. The incident room is packed full of plainclothes detectives, with Guy Daley os-tensibly in charge. The detective sergeant acknowledges his supe-rior with a cheeky "All right, boss?" but Doggett ignores him entirely. Shuffling with paperwork in one corner of the room, Constable Rabbani does her best to look inconspicuous but fails miserably. Daley has spent the morning collating the information brought in by Uniform. He takes them through it, but it amounts to very little.

"Anything from Elliot yet?" Doggett asks, dropping into a swivel chair.

"No, boss."

The DI snorts and rolls his eyes. "What about visitors?"

"Sir?"

"Anyone been poking around asking questions?"

Daley clicks at his mouse, perhaps hoping the laptop has the answers he needs, but it's Rabbani who answers, her voice squeaky and faint. "There was some vicar over from the church next door." She does her best to ignore Daley's scowl. "He seemed pretty worried about what were happening."

"I bet he was." Doggett spins to face Tyler. "Always note who's paying the most attention. Chances are they're in it up to their eyeballs." He swings back to Rabbani. "Name?"

"The Reverend Thorogood."

Doggett spins a full circle in his chair. "Thorogood? And he's a vicar? He's bloody made that up!" He jumps out of the chair as though springing into action but instead ends up pacing the tiny room like a disgruntled tiger, elbowing past detectives who can't quite keep out of his way. "All right," he says, changing tack entirely. "Gerald Cartwright left home in his car just after six on the morning of Monday, the twenty-sixth of July, 2010, and drove to Hope station." He stumbles as he reaches the end of the room too quickly, makes a frustrated turn, and pulls out a notebook. "We established this because that's where we found his car. It was assumed he caught the six thirty-two train to Sheffield, as was his custom, at which point he would have changed for the seven twenty-seven service to St. Pancras. He was then supposed to be catching the tube to Heathrow and a flight on to Germany. When he failed to arrive for his meeting in Frankfurt, a call was made to his office in London. They tried him at home and on his mobile repeatedly for five days. No one called the police. Finally a neighbor"—he looks at his notes—"Edna Burnside, rang his secretary at nine fifty-six a.m. on Monday, the second of August. She then rang the police. Our investigation proved he never got on the plane to Germany. We assumed that somewhere between leaving his car at the village station and catching his plane at Heathrow, Gerald Cartwright was either snatched or did a runner." He sits back in the chair and then immediately gets up again. "Some poor sod looked at CCTV at Sheffield, on the trains, and along just about every conceivable tube route he could have taken. And found absolutely bugger all." He looks up from his notebook. "Which isn't very surprising with hindsight, since we can now safely assume he never left home in the first place." He collapses back into the chair.

"We don't know it's him yet," Tyler reminds him.

Doggett narrows his eyes. "Until Elliot tells us otherwise, we'll assume it is. Now, assuming he never made the train, whatever happened to him happened the weekend of the twenty-fourth and twenty-fifth of July. We know he held one of his infamous bunga-bunga parties that weekend but—surprise, surprise—we never did track down anyone who would admit to being there. We know it took place, though, because it was catered for in advance and got cleaned away afterward by the hired help."

"Any suspects?" Daley asks.

Doggett looks at Tyler, encouraging him to take over. "DI Doggett believes Cartwright's son could be involved."

Daley nods. "He *was* a bit of a shifty little bastard."

"He was also the last person we know of who saw his father alive," says Doggett. "The kid stayed over at the neighbors' house that weekend, which was par for the course apparently when Gerry was *entertaining*." He gives the word extra emphasis by creating bunny-ear speech marks with his fingers.

"When did Oscar last see his father?" Tyler asks.

"The Friday night. Or so he says."

"What about the caterers? Or the cleaners?"

"The caterers dropped the food round Friday afternoon, and the cleaner was some old girl from the village who let herself in on Monday morning. She never saw Gerry, assumed he'd left for work earlier that morning, as did everyone else. She admitted the place looked tidier than usual, but the food had been eaten, and we figured Gerry didn't scoff the lot all by himself."

"So the last person who definitely saw Cartwright alive was the kid," Daley confirms. He nods to himself, metaphorically preparing the handcuffs. Job done.

"Apart from whoever was at the party," Tyler adds. "We know there was a party."

Daley looks at him. "Maybe the lad was at the party, too."

"All right, all right." Doggett holds up both his hands to them. "Where do we start?"

"We should bring him in," says Daley.

Tyler doesn't realize he's sighed out loud until he sees everyone looking at him.

"I take it you have another suggestion?" Doggett asks.

"I thought we might at least make an attempt at gathering some evidence before we get the thumbscrews out." The room falls into awkward silence, and Daley scowls. This is exactly what Jordan was talking about. He makes an attempt to move things on. "Edna Burnside?"

Doggett nods slowly. "All right. Edna Burnside and Lily Bainbridge. Neighbors and family friends. Apparently they pretty much raised the little sod, and I've never met a pair of old ladies who didn't like a good gossip."

Daley consults his computer screen once more. No one from Uniform has yet spoken to the elderly neighbors. He starts to get up but Doggett says, "Not you. I've got another job for you." He passes Daley a page from his notebook. Daley reads it and then nods. Doggett turns to Tyler. "You can talk to the old dears."

"What about you?"

"You don't need me to hold your hand, do you, Sergeant?" There's a ripple of laughter through the incident room. "I'm going to chase

Elliot for those results. There's not much we can do until we know for sure it's Cartwright. Besides, I have a feeling you'll get more out of them than I'm likely to." Doggett starts for the door. "The rest of you," he shouts at the room, "go over statements, revisit Cartwright's businesses, legitimate or otherwise. From the day he was born to the day he died. Everything you can find out about the man. Well, go on then. What are you waiting for? Pull your bloody fingers out!"

There's a bustle of activity in the room. Tyler calls out over the hubbub, "I should have someone with me at least."

"Take your new pet," Doggett shouts. He stops, turns, and shouts across the room. "Constable Rabbani?"

"Sir?"

"DS Tyler needs someone to look after him. Do the honors, would you? And Rabbani?"

"Yes, sir?"

"You're in CID now, so you can lose the bloody uniform, understood?"

Rabbani shuts her mouth and swallows. "Yes, sir," she says. "Thank you, sir."

"Don't thank me, Constable. You're working for DS Tyler now. May the good Lord have mercy upon your soul." He clatters his way out through the door to the sound of more laughter.

Rabbani stands there staring at the closing door.

"I need that address," Tyler tells her. "Now."

"I'm on it," Rabbani says, dropping into a chair and starting to tap at a keyboard. "And thanks, Sarge."

Oliver Road is a short cul-de-sac that curves up and behind the Old Vicarage. It takes them a few minutes to find the unpaved path leading between the hedges of number 7 and number 25. It snakes up between the two houses and then turns at a right angle and continues past numbers 9 through 23, a row of smaller cottages set behind the gardens of the houses on the road. The final house, number 23, backs onto the garden of the Old Vicarage itself but is completely hidden from the road. Tyler can see glimpses of the red-brick building through the trees. He rings the bell and taps on the front door while Rabbani explores the path at the side of the house. After a few moments her voice slips around the edge of the cottage: "Sir."

He follows her up the path until it emerges into a small cottage garden with a thin strip of lawn punctuated by a sole apple tree. Someone has been sitting here recently; an open book lies discarded on a rather bizarre canopied swing seat. Rabbani points to the open door that is inviting them to step into the unbearably hot conservatory. The fabric of the chairs inside is faded from long years of exposure to the sun. The air is thick with dust, and Tyler has to fight the urge to sneeze. On one of the shelves there is a framed photograph of a young boy, about seven or eight, standing on a stool at the kitchen sink, his hands and arms sunk first into a pair of bright yellow Marigold gloves and then into the sink itself. There are clouds of washing-up liquid bubbles, out of which he grins a familiar smile. Oscar Cartwright. He is everywhere.

The door into the main house is closed. He taps lightly on the glass and cups his hands to the window. The inside of the house is old and weary, a mass of paisley patterns and dark, heavy fabrics. He bangs on the door again, louder this time, and eventually a dark shape slides toward them.

"Who is it?"

He raises his warrant card to the window.

After some fumbling with chains the door opens and a bent figure steps hesitatingly out into the conservatory. "It's too hot in here," she says without preamble, and, rather than inviting them inside, ushers them back out into the garden.

Tyler introduces both himself and Rabbani. The woman takes each identification card and examines it scrupulously. No bogus gasman would get far at this door. It's obvious the crippled, bent-double figure before them once stood tall and imperious because she has lost none of her presence for all of her age. It's not so difficult to imagine this severe, hard-angled woman as the headmistress she once was. Miss Edna Burnside radiates authority and confidence.

She gestures to the garden chairs and offers them tea. He declines for both of them, concerned the effort might just finish her. She lowers herself awkwardly onto the swing contraption and stares at them alternately. Rabbani shifts uncomfortably under the woman's gaze, as though she's been called to the headmistress's office to defend her behavior.

"Ms. Burnside," he begins.

"*Miss!*" she snaps.

He tries again. "*Miss* Burnside, we'd like to ask you some questions about your neighbor—"

"Yes," she interrupts again, "a grisly business." Her tone is matter-of-fact, as though death is an old but unwelcome friend.

He doesn't really mind the bluntness; in his experience these things tend to go one of two ways: either people fall over themselves in an effort to be helpful or are close-mouthed to the point of obstruction. Either way you don't trust them. You trust no one. Believe nothing. Least of all strangers you meet in bars.

Still. There's something a little too chilling in the woman's tone. If it's bluntness she appreciates, he can do blunt. "You don't seem very concerned you've spent the last six years with a mummified corpse for a neighbor."

"Should I be?" she asks. "There's a graveyard of corpses at the bottom of the garden. One more makes no difference at my age." She stares at him. Next question.

"But you were friends with Gerald Cartwright, weren't you?"

She avoids the question by asking her own. "It *is* Gerald, then?"

He decides on a different approach. "I understand you don't live alone."

She looks at him calmly and blinks. He realizes his mistake; he hasn't asked a question. He phrases his words more carefully. "Is Miss Bainbridge at home?"

"No, Inspector."

He's beginning to tire of this. "Sergeant."

"I'm sorry?"

"It's Detective Sergeant. *Where* is Miss Bainbridge?"

Burnside lowers her head. "I'm sorry, Detective Sergeant, I'm afraid Lily will not be able to answer your questions."

"And why is that?"

"She's . . . she's no longer in a position to help anyone." There's the first crack in her voice.

Tyler opens his mouth and then closes it again. "I'm sorry," he says. "I didn't realize."

She brushes away the apology. "She wouldn't have been able to tell you anything I can't anyway."

Rabbani catches his eye; her leg is bouncing up and down with displaced nervous energy. He gives her the nod.

"How well did you know Mr. Cartwright?" she asks.

"Very well," says Burnside. "We were neighbors. And friends."

"*Good* friends?"

"Well, I met Cynthia first, Gerald's wife. She was younger than Gerald, of course, and got terribly bored, I think. It was Gerald's idea to move to the country, and that was all right for him, he was only here at weekends, but Cynthia found it all very lonely. She volunteered to help out at the church, and that's how we met." It's a well-rehearsed story, but it's a story nonetheless. It's all coming out far too easily. "Then she fell pregnant. A blessing for her. At first, anyway. Then along came Oscar; you'll have met Oscar?" Burnside's tone shifts here; the sternness softens a little, the edges melt. "We were at the birth; Gerald was away, of course. He was such a beautiful baby, our little cherub, with that pale skin and those golden locks. Very sweet natured." The voice shifts again, and they're back into the rehearsed speech. "But Gerald was away a lot, and Cynthia found it very hard to cope. The doctor called it postnatal depression, I think. I'm not sure she ever really wanted a child. She was certainly happy enough to leave it to the two of us most of the time. After that there was some talk in the village of her having a lover, but if she did she never confided in me. Still, it wasn't exactly a surprise when she took herself off."

Rabbani's leg is moving up and down like a pneumatic drill. Edna Burnside shoots her a look over the top of her spectacles, and the leg stops.

"Can you tell us more about Gerald's disappearance?" she asks.

"I *can*," Burnside states.

He tries to imagine Oscar in this house, this horn-rimmed tyrant standing over him. She seems a very unlikely woman to take in and care for an unruly teenager. "*Will* you, please?"

"Gerald didn't cope very well after Cyn went. He took on staff from time to time, but largely it was left to the two of us to care for the boy. Gerald threw himself into his work, and then one day he didn't come home."

Tyler's had enough of the rehearsed speech. "Which day was that?"

"I beg your pardon?"

"Which day was it—*exactly*—that he didn't come home?"

"I don't remember *exactly*." She smooths her hands on her trousers. "A Friday, I imagine. He usually came home on a Friday."

"And the month?"

She thinks for a moment. "It was summer, I think . . ."

He doesn't believe this woman has ever forgotten anything in her life.

Then she turns the questioning around again. "You do keep records, do you not? He *was* reported missing. There was some sort of an investigation, if I recall." The subtext is unmistakable—she holds the police responsible for not finding him. She's sweating profusely in the heat, and for the first time he notices how frail she is. The confident bluster is a smoke screen.

He pushes on regardless. "Who reported him missing?" Burnside looks at Rabbani, but Tyler calls her attention back. "*Ms.* Burnside," he pushes her, "*who* reported Mr. Cartwright missing?"

She snaps her head back around. "*Miss.* I did. I rang his office and his secretary told me he hadn't made his meetings that week, so I rang the police." The sweat is pouring from her forehead now, her breathing labored.

"Can you go on?" he asks.

"My pills," she says. "In there." She gestures to the conservatory.

He gets up and steps back into the house.

"On the shelf," she shouts after him.

He finds a wooden pillbox inlaid with mother-of-pearl next to the photo of Oscar. He takes it to her and she extracts a small yellow tablet and throws it to the back of her throat. They wait patiently while she composes herself, and after a few moments Burnside says, "Do we really have to go through all of this again? I told everything to that horrible little man six years ago. You must know it already."

"How did Oscar handle his father's disappearance?" Rabbani asks.

"Oscar?" Burnside frowns. "He coped. We all did. We had to."

"But losing his mum like that, and then his dad as well?"

"He didn't *lose* Cynthia. *She* didn't disappear, she ran off. She even rang to see if he was all right. I spoke to her myself, tried to talk some sense into the selfish woman."

"He must have been upset, mind." Rabbani's thick Yorkshire accent turns *must* into *moost, upset* into *oopset*. It's oddly endearing, a stark contrast against Burnside's Radio 4 pronunciation.

She looks at Rabbani coolly, however. "Of course he was upset. He had nightmares, some behavioral problems, but we got through them together."

"Until you shipped him off to boarding school," Tyler points out.

The imperious gaze turns back to him. "I'm not sure what you're implying, Inspector—"

He interrupts her again, enjoying it this time. "Sergeant."

She blinks but remains unruffled. "Oscar is a perfectly well-adjusted young man. If you don't wish to take my word for that, I suggest you speak to his fiancée. I believe she's studying law. Following in her father's footsteps. Yes, I'm sure Michael would be very interested in your line of questioning. Perhaps I should call him now?"

Her words hit him in the face, and for a few seconds it is as though time is suspended. The moments tick by while Edna Burnside looks from him to Rabbani and back again. Rabbani is staring at him, too, willing him to speak. He manages to say, "I think we've bothered you enough for one afternoon." His voice sounds distant and tinny.

They get up, and Edna Burnside struggles to raise herself from her swing. He reaches out to help her, but the woman pushes him away. "I can manage."

She sees them out, and as they walk back along the path Tyler looks over his shoulder to see her still watching them from the gate. His head feels light and fuzzy, as though he got up too quickly and has left some part of himself behind in the fusty little cottage. Everything—the birdsong, the sunlight—is dull and flattened.

"Well?" says Rabbani from somewhere a long way off.

"Well what?"

"She were lying her arse off about summat, weren't she?"

Her words make him smile. "Why all the questions about Cartwright's son?" He can't even say the man's name anymore.

"Doggett said he were a suspect."

Soospect. The word clatters around in his head, making no real sense. He feels as drunk as he did last night.

"Don't get fixated on that," he tells her. "There are others."

"Like who?"

But he doesn't yet have an answer to that.

"He'd have been what, fifteen? That's old enough to knock your old man on the head if he gives you a reason."

Tyler looks back along the silent country lane. "Find me a death certificate for Lily Bainbridge," he says. "And check Cynthia Cartwright's medical records."

"Could be tricky," she tells him. "Confidentiality and all that."

"Find a way." He wants to know if that business about postnatal depression has any truth to it. He pauses, and then he has to add what he's been avoiding. "You better find out what you can about this fiancée as well."

Rabbani pulls out her notebook and rifles through the pages. "Sophie Denham," she says, stopping to read. "Her father's Michael Denham, the Cartwrights' family solicitor. Her and Oscar were at school together, childhood sweethearts. She were interviewed during the original investigation."

Tyler looks at her, and she swallows. "Research, Sarge. I thought it might be useful."

"All right," he tells her. "Keen is good, but no one likes a smartarse."

There's something about her expression that leaves him considering his words all the way back to the incident room.

———

When they arrive back at the incident room, Rabbani does her best to stay behind Tyler. If the DI sees she's still wearing a uniform he might change his mind about allowing her on board. She doubts it would make the slightest bit of difference that she's not yet had time to change.

It's Guy Daley who greets them, however. "That was quick." His eyes trudge up and down her body, just as they always do. She can feel the muddy footprints they leave behind.

"Shut up, Daley." Doggett's voice makes her jump. He's standing in the corner, tucked behind the door, mobile pressed to his ear. "How'd you get on?" Before they can answer he raises a finger, listens for a moment, and then shouts into the phone: "You can bloody well find him then!" He slams the mobile down on the desk, looks up at the room in general, and starts a new tack. "Next?"

"The gardener," says DS Tyler.

"What gardener?"

"He was in the churchyard when I arrived yesterday."

"And?"

"And I think he's worth talking to."

Doggett taps a pen against the desk. He's always bloody tapping away at something. He turns to Guy Daley, who's watching from behind a monitor. "Any chance you might do some work today, sunshine?" Then he heads for the door. "You better find this bloke's address, then."

"You're coming on this one, then?" Tyler asks.

"If that's all right with you, boss? You can tell me about the old dears on the way." Doggett checks his watch. "Just let me squeeze one out, first. I'll be in the Portaloo when you've found the address." The door rebounds against the flimsy wall and closes behind him.

Tyler turns to Rabbani. "Joe Wentworth," he says. "Can you find me the address?"

She feels the heat that flushes across her face, and she lowers her head quickly so that nobody sees. She has to stop this. One minute she's ready to twat the man, and the next she's lusting after him like he's the first man with a pretty face she's ever seen. She can barely talk to him. Why did he ask for her on his team? Assuming he did. That seemed to be what Doggett implied, and she's pretty sure Doggett didn't just change his mind about her.

Not that she owes Tyler anything. If anything he owes her. That's probably the only reason he asked for her anyway. Out of a sense of obligation, because he were the one that got her in the shit in the first place. So that's that. They're even now. So why does she feel this constant need to impress him?

It wouldn't be so bad if she thought he were even the slightest little bit interested. But of course he isn't. On the other hand, at least he doesn't check out her arse every time she walks past, un-like Dirty Daley. She's not sure she'd mind all that much if he did. She feels her cheeks redden again and risks a glance up from her monitor at the DS. God, he's pretty. Even now, glaring at Daley while that livid red scar tugs at the corner of his mouth and high-lights his disdain for the man. She makes a mental note that when it blows up between the two of them, and she's no doubt it will, she isn't going to let herself get caught in the middle.

"What?" Daley says when he finally sees Tyler watching him.

"While we're gone, how about talking to that vicar, get a state-ment off him?"

Daley screws his face up like the toddler that he is. "I'm not your fuckin' gofer, Tyler!"

The DS's nostrils flare and for a moment Rabbani thinks he's going to explode, but then he visibly takes a deep breath and swal-lows whatever he was going to say. "It's up to you, mate, obviously.

But you heard the DI just now; maybe you could do worse than try to impress the man."

"He's already given me my job." Daley sneers and waves the notebook page Doggett gave him earlier. "I'm watching the kid. Guess he wants someone who knows what they're doing looking at the real suspects. Why don't you stick to the old dears?"

She's sure Tyler's going to react to that one, but he just smiles slightly and turns back to her. Rabbani quickly jots down the address for Joe Wentworth and passes it across to him.

"Set up that interview with Sophie Denham," he tells her.

She watches him leave. There's an edge to him since they talked to the old woman. Like he's grown even colder somehow. As if that were possible. The door clatters closed behind him and she turns to see Daley watching her.

"You're barking up the wrong tree with that one, love," he says.

This time she decides to stare him out.

As an excuse to pass the Old Vicarage, Lily takes the long way round to the village rather than using the shortcut through the churchyard. It is unbearably hot; the weak breeze that followed her from the garden didn't even make it up the path to the gate. She wants to stop, to put down her basket for a moment on the far side of the road and watch the hubbub of activity. She dares not. Instead she slows to a snail's pace. There are numerous cars and vans parked on the gravel driveway and a cluster of people at the gates, a mixture of faces she recognizes and many others she doesn't. The sense of urgency—of a normality interrupted and a great rush to set things right—is palpable; but for all of that, none of these people seem to be getting anything done. It reminds her of the wasps buzzing both furiously and lazily round the jars under the apple tree.

"Rather unsettling, isn't it?"

The voice comes from behind her and makes her jump. She turns to find the solicitor, Michael Denham, smiling at her with his wolfish grin.

"I do apologize, Miss Bainbridge. I didn't mean to startle you."

"Oh, yes, no . . . that's quite all right."

"Yes, a terrible thing. A body, they're saying. In the cellar, of all places. It does make you think, doesn't it?"

The sun is reflecting off his glasses, and Lily can't tell if the man is looking at her or the house or something else entirely.

"Anyway," he goes on, "I understand from Sophie your Oscar is back?"

"Oh, yes," says Lily, on much firmer ground here. "A few weeks ago now. My goodness, but he's grown!"

Michael smiles at her, this time without showing his teeth. It's a curious smile, and suggests he thinks she's said something amusing. She's not altogether certain she hasn't. Of course he's grown, it's what young boys do, isn't it? She's never been good at these sorts of conversations. And then a thought occurs to her. It could be him. She sways slightly and feels herself falling sideways.

Michael Denham catches her arm to support her, but she pulls away from him sharply.

"I thought you were going to go over."

"Yes," she says. "I'm all right now. It's the heat, I expect."

"Can I give you a lift somewhere? I've got the car just round the corner."

"No! No, really, it's very kind of you . . . but I'm only popping into the village." Then she stops, not wanting to tell him exactly where she's going.

"Are you sure that's wise? In this heat." He waves his briefcase like a fan and smiles again.

"I'm sure I'll be all right. Thank you."

"Very well." He hesitates for a moment, as though he intends to say more. Then he simply says, "You be careful then, won't you?" And without waiting for an answer he walks away from her.

You be careful. She wonders what he meant by that and why it sounded much more like a threat than concern.

I know what you did.

Lily hurries on into the village. She has to queue in the butcher's. She stands behind a fat man she doesn't recognize. There are far too many people in the village lately that she doesn't recognize. And yet, unusually, it isn't the strangers anymore that cause Lily anxiety. It's the people who know her. For only someone who knows her could have sent the letters. As horrifying as that thought is, she has to accept it. Ahead of the fat man is the woman she calls Mrs. Mink. She is wearing her trademark hat and stole, despite the weather. And in front of Mrs. Mink there are two women Lily recognizes too well.

"Went up like a rocket," Carol Braithwaite is saying. She is a good twenty years or so younger than Lily but has a hard, weather-beaten face. Lily always thinks this is odd for a woman who has spent so much of her life indoors.

"Right shame," replies the woman standing with her. She's much younger than Carol and wears a headscarf with a paisley pattern. Lily can't remember her name but thinks she's related to Carol in some way. A niece, or a daughter-in-law or something. Yes, perhaps a daughter-in-law. Carol has a lot of sons if she remembers rightly. Some of them from the same husband.

Neither of the women notice her arrival since her entrance coincided with another customer leaving, meaning the bell on the door rang only once and failed to draw their attention.

"They'll not bother with a new one," Carol says authoritatively. "It'll be stand in the rain and catch your death!"

The younger woman hums agreement while the butcher, George,

slices thin slivers of red meat for her. "It'll be kids smoking, I shouldn't wonder," he tells them.

Carol shakes her head. "Arson, according to our Philip. Went up something fierce, it did."

George shouts over his shoulder to the back of the shop. "Where are you, lad? Barry!"

Young Barry emerges from the back absently wiping a finger on his apron. The butcher's boy has also grown since Lily last saw him, but outward rather than upward. "Yeah?" he asks sullenly.

"Any chance you might put that bleedin' phone down for five minutes and lend me a hand?" George points to Mrs. Mink, who gives the lad her order.

Lily watches him cut the meat. He's wearing no gloves and his fingers are reddened with blood. He has his nose pierced in three places. One of them is adorned with a ring that, given his size, makes him look not unlike the fattened pig he is working on.

"Eight-fifty, luv," says George, and as Carol reaches into her purse he adds, "Any idea what the news is up at the Old Vicarage?"

Lily experiences a wave of nausea as the young lad slaps another cut of meat onto the counter.

"I was just coming to that," says Carol, perhaps put out at having her thunder stolen. When she answers, it's the younger woman she addresses. "This body they've found. Philip's saying it's him . . ."

But Lily struggles to hear the rest. Her ears are full of the sound of Barry's rasping blade as he hacks off a strip of thick, white fat, his knife scraping along the bone.

"You used to work up there, didn't you?" George asks.

Carol is in her element. "Always said he'd come to no good, that one. He was a tyrant, you ask anyone. No place to raise a child. And the times I had to throw good food away just 'cause he decided to change his plans!"

Lily wants to turn and leave, but it feels like her feet have taken root.

"Of course, the police will want to talk to me again, no doubt. Not that I can tell them owt I didn't six year ago, mind. I told them all about how it was up there, all sorts coming and going at all hours. I, for one, weren't the least surprised when they found out he was a wrong 'un."

And now George notices Lily.

"Well, here's someone who can tell us what's what. Ey up, Miss Bainbridge? What's all this about a body then?"

Everyone turns at once. Mrs. Mink pauses in the midst of negotiating her snap coin purse. The fat man wipes his nose. The daughter-in-law stares at her blankly. And Carol flushes a bright crimson.

It isn't George's fault. He has spoken in innocence. Being comparatively new to the village, he knows where Lily lives but not about her personal connection to the Old Vicarage. Her connection to Gerald. But Carol knows. Her cheeks blaze like ripened tomatoes and the daughter-in-law looks down at her feet, making Lily wonder just what Carol has told her.

Time stands still. Lily wants nothing more than to turn and leave, but if she does it gives them permission to go on, to talk about it even more. "I . . . I don't know . . ." she manages, and it's true, she realizes. She doesn't know.

I know what you did.

The bell announces a new arrival, and the spell is broken. George's voice cuts across the shop loudly: "Oi, soft, lad! Watch what you're doing." He moves along to aid Barry in a particularly tricky bit of butchery. Mrs. Mink turns back to check on the progress of her order. Carol and the daughter-in-law pick up where they left off, but in much-hushed tones.

Lily's feet come back to life. She turns to flee but walks straight into the newly arrived customer. She mumbles an apology and tries to get by, but the man puts a hand on her arm.

"Miss Bainbridge, I'm glad I've caught you." Reverend Thorogood squeezes her arm a little. "I wondered if you've decided about the Whitby trip on Saturday. Only there's just a few places left, and I know how much everyone would love to see the two of you."

A breeze reaches Lily through the half-open doorway, cooling her burning cheeks. She takes a step forward . . . *to fetch Edna her pills from the bag she's left by the front door. She hurries through the passageways of the Old Vicarage, but by the time she gets back to the kitchen Edna has been joined by Carol. She hears them sniping at each other before she's even back in the room.*

"There's no biscuits again," Carol is saying. "You want to have a word with that lad."

Edna ignores her. Lily hands over the pills, and Edna takes two of the yellow ones.

"Don't suppose you know if he wants me to cook this weekend?" Carol addresses Lily, just as she always does if given the chance.

And Edna answers, just as she always does. "Mr. Cartwright's entertaining this weekend"—emphasizing the title—"so he'll be using the caterers. Not you."

Carol rolls her eyes and tuts loudly. She heads back to the kitchen and Lily laughs nervously, relieved the encounter hasn't escalated.

"What's the matter with you?" Edna is always snippy after dealing with Carol.

"Nothing."

She'll want tea after taking her tablets, so Lily goes to switch the kettle on . . . and the Reverend Thorogood is shaking her and calling her name.

"Miss Bainbridge? Lily? Can you hear me?"

He has hold of her by both arms now and is talking loudly at her. She wishes he'd lower his voice. Everyone is looking again, she's sure of it. She manages to push past the man and then she is out, back into the full heat of the day but free of all the stares. She hurries round the corner and into the churchyard, imagining she can hear the vicar still calling out to her, over and over. She half-closes her eyes and lets the wind carry her name away between the headstones.

The short drive to Wentworth's house takes them past the churchyard where yesterday Tyler first met the man tending graves. On the way there he fills Doggett in on the conversation with Edna Burnside.

Doggett sits perfectly still for once, but as they arrive at their destination and get out of the car he says, "You were too soft, son. You should have pushed the woman."

"Is that what you did six years ago?" he asks. "How did that work out for you?"

Doggett ignores him.

Joe Wentworth answers the door in the same grubby work clothes he was wearing yesterday. Maybe he's slept in them. Doggett explains who they are, and he lets them into the house.

The cottage is shabby and dated; Wentworth looks perfectly at home. He shows them through to the living room, where the two detectives are forced to stand much closer to each other than either is comfortable with. The concept of minimalism has obviously passed the gardener by; every conceivable space is full. Tyler counts three sofas, two armchairs, and an assortment of mismatching dining furniture. It's just possible to make out the shape of a sideboard running along one wall but barely, as it's hidden beneath the cumulative parts of what must be at least three bicycles. *Every* surface is covered with clothing, books, empty boxes, pots and pans, bits of old machinery. The windowsill groans under the weight of myriad ceramic figurines. And in between every item of furniture, there are Babel towers of paper stretching heavenward. Newspapers and magazines, football programs, brochures, leaflets, receipts. As though Wentworth has never thrown away an item of printed material in his life. Only one chair is empty enough of clutter to be functional, and that's soon filled with the crumpled form of Wentworth himself.

A high-pitched yap announces the arrival of a Yorkshire terrier that careers down the steep staircase from whatever flea market the upstairs passes for, and launches itself straight at their legs. It alternates between them, unsure which poses the bigger threat. When he tires of watching their discomfort, Wentworth whistles through a gap in his teeth and the dog jumps into his lap. He strokes it into submission with an earthy hand. "Paper said you'd found a body." He gestures to the arm of his chair, where a folded broadsheet lies open at the crossword page. "Was it him then? Cartwright?"

Doggett gives him the "We are not at liberty" speech and begins the usual routine questions. But Tyler can already see the answers reflected in the room. Does he live alone? There's little enough room in the house for one man and his dog, let alone anyone else. How long has he been in the village? Long enough to accumulate the collected junk of several lifetimes. Was there ever a Mrs. Wentworth? One or two of the figurines show more taste than Tyler would ascribe to the gardener, and an attempt has been made at some point to match the furnishings with the décor, though the pattern's easy to miss among the chaos. Most tellingly, perhaps, the face of a plain middle-aged woman peers out at them from the occasional photograph, smothered by the mess but not yet completely lost.

"Gone," says Wentworth, following Tyler's gaze. "Took off a few year back."

"I'm sorry to hear that," says Doggett. He doesn't sound sorry in the slightest. "Can I ask why she left?"

"You'll have to ask her, won't you?"

Something about this man disquiets Tyler. What is it? Surely not just the clutter and mess?

"Tell us about Gerald Cartwright," says Doggett.

"What do you want to know?"

"What was he like? Did you get on?"

"Didn't really know him." The dog whimpers as Wentworth catches its fur with a blackened nail.

"But you worked for him? At the Old Vicarage. Let's see." Doggett consults his notebook. "Monthly payments to a Joe Wentworth." He looks up. "That's you?" Doggett looks back down at his notes again, goes on without waiting for an answer. "Going back six years before his disappearance. I assume it *was* for gardening?"

So their presence here is not just a whim based on Tyler's hunch. Doggett was planning to speak to the man all along.

Wentworth grunts what might be an acknowledgment. "Didn't know him, though."

"I assume he consulted you on what he wanted. Daffodils here, *pansies* there. That sort of thing." Doggett glances at Tyler and grins.

Wentworth clears his throat. "We talked about the garden."

"So what was he like?"

Wentworth is silent.

"For example," Doggett explains, "did he know exactly what he wanted, or was he the sort what didn't know if he was Arthur or Martha, if you know what I mean?" Again the DI looks at Tyler.

Wentworth's hand begins to shake, and he reaches for his tobacco tin. The ghost of Mrs. Wentworth looks down on them disapprovingly while her husband fidgets in his chair, disturbing the dog. It whines, gets up, turns full circle, and then settles in his lap once more. He begins rolling a cigarette on its head. "I suppose he knew what he wanted. He were used to getting his own way."

"Is that right? What makes you say that?"

"Just an impression. What with his job and all."

"Was he liked?"

Wentworth shrugs.

"In the village, let's say. Was he popular?"

The gardener finishes his preparation and shoves it between his lips without answering. He reaches out for a box of matches.

"Did *you* like him, Mr. Wentworth?" The emphasis in Doggett's voice is unmistakable.

The matchbox rattles in the gardener's shaky hands but as he strikes the match, the shaking stops. He touches the lit match to the end of the cigarette and takes a deep drag, transformed by the tobacco, fortified. He looks directly at Doggett for the first time, exhales a cloud of blue smoke. "Didn't really know him," he says, and his voice is strong and confident now.

Doggett obviously senses the change, and any attempt at a pleasant façade drops. "When Gerald Cartwright disappeared six years ago, you were never questioned. Why was that?"

"No one came."

"That's not entirely true, though, is it? When we knocked on your door you'd gone away."

"Holiday."

"For six months?"

"Didn't want to be around all the fuss. Bloody reporters."

"Or maybe you were avoiding us? You've been in trouble with the police before, haven't you?"

Wentworth remains calm, blowing his sweet smoke in their faces. He chooses to treat the question as rhetorical. He turns the spent match in his hand, over and over.

Doggett spells it out. "Indecent exposure."

"That were twenty year ago."

"Seems they caught you playing silly buggers in Weston Park. Nice spot for it from what I gather." This time Doggett avoids looking at Tyler.

"Charges were dropped," says Wentworth.

"No, Mr. Wentworth, you accepted a caution. That's why we still have it on record. I take it that was about the same time Mrs. Wentworth left?"

The match flicks from Wentworth's hand, arches gracefully through the smoke, and disappears behind a pile of newspaper. "Don't you lot have nothing better to do than come round here, beggarin' about stuff what happened twenty year ago?"

Tyler looks again at the room. Is this what he finds so disturbing? This man's double life? Born in the wrong time, trapped in a loveless marriage, unable to be himself. As he looks at this friendless, dirty man, hidden away in his time-capsule cottage, the house and its treasure trove of bric-a-brac are transformed. It isn't a house at all. It's a prison. A place where he shuts himself away from a chaotic, frightening world that chooses to judge him. The dog has got it right; he and Doggett are the intruders, walking through the man's memories, trudging across his soul. Suddenly Tyler understands his disquiet; one day this could be him.

"DI Doggett, can I have a word?"

Their eyes lock. Doggett turns away first but does so slowly, not a defeat so much as a tactical withdrawal. "All right, Mr. Wentworth, don't bother getting up. We'll see ourselves out. Just don't go booking any long holidays, will you?"

They begin their exit, stepping over the mess carefully and precisely. The dog hampers them by leaping from its master's lap and yapping, their movement a signal to reengage. As they reach the hallway, Doggett raises his voice over the barking. "You want to be careful with those matches, Joe. Especially with all this paper lying around."

Tyler opens the front door and steps into the fresh air. He takes a deep breath, relieved to be out of the smoky atmosphere. Doggett follows, slamming the front door behind them and dulling the dog's objections.

"You realize," Tyler says, "the fact he sleeps with men does not necessarily make him a pervert. Or a murderer for that matter."

"He was cautioned for indecent exposure; he's hardly a pillar of the community."

"He had consenting sex in the park. You know as well as I do that you could go down there any night and find half a dozen men doing the same thing."

"I'll take your word for that."

Tyler follows Doggett back to the car. "That was all for my benefit then? Is that what that was?"

"No need to be paranoid, Sergeant." Doggett looks back at the cottage. "No, he's hiding something. I can feel it."

Tyler follows Doggett's gaze. The yellow nets at the window are twitching. As angry as he is at the DI's attitude, he finds himself agreeing. There *is* something off about the guy; he can feel it, too. Something grubby and unwholesome that went beyond the disarray of the cottage. Still, he's not about to give Doggett the satisfaction. "Clearly the man has been hiding something his whole life, but what does that have to do with Gerald Cartwright?"

"I'm buggered if I know," says Doggett. "And that isn't an invitation."

"You realize I can report you for shit like that?"

"No doubt." There's a smile playing on Doggett's lips as he opens the car door. "Or you could just punch my lights out." He gets in.

Tyler yanks open the driver's door, gets in, and slams it behind him. He turns the key in the ignition and grinds the car into gear. "I'm trying really hard not to do that anymore. At least, not to superior officers."

The car speeds away from the curb, tires squealing.

"Careful, Detective Sergeant," says Doggett calmly. "We're not on a bloody racetrack."

"Fuck you! *Sir*."

"Not on a first date, son. Not on a first date."

By the time Lily reaches the path that leads up to their cottage, she is panting. She crashes through the gate and then bursts through the unlocked front door. "Edna!" She hurries through the kitchen, down the two shallow steps into the dining room, and she stops. "Oh!" They have company.

He gets up to meet her, and her flight is forgotten as he takes her in his strong arms, crushing her against his chest. She's like a kitten caught by the scruff of the neck; she feels herself go limp.

"Oscar," she says, snuggling her head under his arm. He smells of something flowery. Strange how men wear perfume nowadays. He has his own smell, too, one she could never mistake. A clean, wholesome scent that reminds her of when he was a baby.

"Hi, Aunt Lil."

And just like that all the alarm she was feeling is gone. She forgets how tall he's grown. Handsome, too. The years he's been away at school have transformed him into a man.

"What the devil is the matter with you, Lillian?" Edna asks, and Oscar begins to pull away. She clutches him to her a moment longer. Everything is different now Oscar's here.

"Well?" says Edna, spoiling things as usual.

"It doesn't matter," says Lily, finally allowing Oscar to let go.

"It doesn't matter? You came through the kitchen like you had Old Nick up your nightdress." Oscar laughs, so Lily does, too. "It's a wonder you didn't hurt yourself." Edna's added that last attempt at sentiment in order to turn her stinging rebuke into something more considerate. Edna's always at her best when Oscar is present. She supposes they both are.

"Well, since you're here now, you can sort the tea. The kettle's just boiled."

Oscar offers to do the honors, but Edna pulls him back and catches Lily's eye.

"It's fine," Lily says. "I can manage." She turns back to the kitchen and hears them whispering to each other before she's fully out of the room. She pretends not to notice.

She's calmer now she's home. After so many years here, the world seems distant, unable to touch her. As she busies herself with a tray of cups and saucers and tea plates, she thinks of the women at the butcher's. It was only natural. People like to gossip, don't they? She should know that better than anyone. They must think her mad, running out like that. She's not even sure why she did it.

But then she remembers the letters. Perhaps there *is* a reason to be running and hiding. If only she could remember what it is.

There's a healthy slice of Dundee cake left from the weekend. She tests it with the back of a finger. It's cold and a little dry, but she knows Oscar will devour it in seconds. It always was his favorite.

Back in the dining room, Oscar takes the tray from her. "Shall I be Mother?" he jokes, and they all three laugh.

"Don't be silly," says Lily, and pours each of them their preferred cup. Oscar seats himself on a dining chair, leaving the second armchair for her. He's always thinking of them. Since he was a boy, she's never been sure if it was they who took him in or the other way round.

Edna clears her throat to begin what is clearly a carefully staged conversation; she, after all, is the director of this family drama. "Oscar's just been telling me about the Old Vicarage," she explains.

"There's been some trouble with the builders, isn't that right?" She is prompting her lead actor.

"There was an accident, I think. Nothing too serious . . ." He dries up. Lily knows lying does not come easily to him. Edna will have told him not to bother Aunt Lil with the details. *It'll only scare her.* But really it's Lily she doesn't trust. Edna's worried she'll say something out of turn. She supposes she's right to be. How are you supposed to keep quiet about something if you can't remember it in the first place? Why does it always feel as though everyone else knows more than she does? And why can she not just bring herself to ask?

Edna takes over again. "That's why the police are there. They'll straighten it all out, you'll see." She looks at Lily over the steaming brim of her cup, waggling those eyebrows in a manner that's supposed to convey her own set of instructions. *Keep quiet. I'll handle this.* Edna's instructions are always the same.

Lily wants to ask, *Keep quiet about what? You'll handle what?* But instead she says, "I wondered about the police. It's all over the village. People do gossip about nothing, don't they? Goodness, what a fuss!"

"I'm beginning to think you were right," Oscar says. "About the builders. Perhaps it wasn't such a good idea to get them in after all."

"What's done is done," says Edna, practical as ever, and then changes the subject. "Oscar was just telling me he's thinking of booking a trip."

"Oh, lovely," says Lily. "To Whitby?"

Edna tuts. "Honestly, you and this Whitby trip!"

"What's all this?" Oscar is smiling.

"Some coach trip or other, those daft women from the Women's Institute."

Oscar grins widely. "Sounds like fun."

"Oh, yes!" says Lily. "I just spoke to the vicar and he says they still have places. I've always wanted to go to Whitby."

Edna grunts. "You've been."

"I haven't."

"You have. Bert took us up for the day in the Hillman, after Vi had her op."

"Oh," says Lily. She doesn't remember that at all. "Well, I wasn't counting that."

"He's talking about overseas. Abroad, isn't that right, Oscar?"

Oscar has only been half-listening—poor lost little boy!

"What? Oh, sure. It's just a thought really."

"I found you some cake," says Lily. "Eat up." She pushes the plate toward him.

Edna goes on. "Like when we went to Spain that time. Do you remember, Oscar? You were probably too young, I expect. Of course, I couldn't go now, not in my condition."

"No," says Lily, "not in your condition."

Edna gives her another look. "I suppose you'll take that Sophie girl?" Edna's on shaky ground here. She doesn't really approve of Sophie, but Oscar will not allow any criticism of the girl.

Lily couldn't stand it if there was an argument between them. "Oh yes," she says quickly, "I've just seen her father in the village. How is she? Everything all right between you? You will bring her round soon, won't you? We haven't seen her in an age."

Edna frowns at her. "You seem to have seen a lot of people in the village this afternoon."

"She's fine," says Oscar.

Lily takes a sip of tea. She places the cup back on the tray and, as if the move is a signal, Oscar gets up.

"I should be getting off."

"But you haven't touched your cake."

"You can stay over if you want," Edna offers, and Lily pushes down a little monster inside her; she should have offered first.

"Thanks," says Oscar, "but I should get back to town."

"I could wrap it for you?"

Edna struggles to stand, and Oscar leaps forward to help. Again the nasty little creature lurches inside Lily.

"Try not to worry," Edna tells him. "It'll all be fine, you'll see."

"Thanks, Auntie Edie." He hugs her and Lily is a stranger in her own home, and then it's her turn and as he draws her into him everything is warmer and sharper and more alive.

Together they see him to the gate, Edna more agile than she's been for months. They watch him as he heads down the path. But for a little height, and the missing satchel on his shoulder, they might be seeing him off to school. Before he disappears round the bend he waves to them one last time, and they both wave back.

They stand together at the gate looking down the path.

"They've found him," says Edna.

"Oh," says Lily, clutching at the flaking ironwork. She wants to say, *Found who?* But she doesn't. She's fairly certain she probably ought to know.

Edna makes a sucking noise between her false teeth. "Did you get those chops?"

The sun is setting through the branches of the trees, casting jagged black lines across the front of the house. It looks like the house is burning all over again. Tyler kicks around in the rubble left by the builders until he finds what he needs, a broken half brick. The door to the incident room swings open and Rabbani steps out, squinting into the sun.

"The fiancée?" he asks.

"Tomorrow lunchtime at the university." She hovers, not quite meeting his eye, plainly uncomfortable about something.

"Fine," he says. "I'll pick you up."

She hesitates, then nods. He tucks the brick under his arm and jots down the address she gives him on his mobile.

"Anything else?"

Again she hesitates, then, "I can't find a death certificate for Lily Bainbridge, but I'll keep looking into it. And I spoke to Cynthia Cartwright's doctor. He won't release her records without a court order but, off the record, he pretty much confirmed what Burnside said about her being depressed." She stops, waiting for him to say something.

"Good job," he tells her, returning the mobile to his pocket and extracting the brick again. "Where's Daley?"

She looks down at the brick in his hand and her brow creases. "I'm not sure," she says.

"Don't worry, I'm not going to clock him with it."

She smiles at him weakly, as though she's not sure she believes him.

"Do you know if he spoke to the vicar yet?"

She pushes a lock of stray hair behind her right ear. He's seen her do the same thing at least a dozen times today. "He said he couldn't find him, but . . ." She leaves it there, her cheeks coloring slightly as she realizes he might consider this tale-telling. She doesn't need to say any more, however. He knew Daley wouldn't follow it up, certainly not on his say-so. He'd just been drawing Daley out, trying to find out what secret task Doggett had given him. It had been far easier than he'd thought it would be.

"All right," he tells her.

"Was it important?"

"Probably not."

She still seems uncomfortable, as though there's something she wants to say but can't quite bring herself to.

"What is it?"

The lock of hair has fallen loose again and hangs across her face. "I don't mind staying if . . ." She trails off.

He's not used to working with others, with subordinates. He's forgotten that you're supposed to direct them, tell them every little thing. "Get yourself home," he says, and then remembers, belatedly, to add, "Thanks."

She hovers a moment longer, then sighs heavily, turns, and stalks away from him down the driveway. He wonders what he's done now. She can't still be pissed off with him about that business with Doggett. He got her on the case, what more does she want? He goes back over the day, considering her performance at the cottage, the way she pushed Burnside during the interview. She'd shown him up, in a way; they were questions *he* should have asked, *would* have asked, if he hadn't been so fixated on Oscar. Was that why he chastised her about the research she'd done into the girlfriend? That was a bit unfair. It was good work, intuitive. Perhaps that's why she's so narked. He makes a mental note to try harder with her tomorrow. She has the potential to be a good detective, if she can just learn to keep her temper.

He smiles at the irony of his own thoughts and looks down at the brick in his hand. One side is black with soot. He juggles it for a moment, testing the weight. Then he heads back to the incident room and opens the door. The heat radiates out in a wave, like he's just opened the door to an oven. He bends down and places the brick in front of the door. It holds. As he straightens, he takes one last look at the decaying house with its dancing shadow flames before stepping back into the sauna.

He works for another half hour or so, going over some of the reports from the SOCOs, but eventually the stale air is too much. He drains the last of the water he sent Rabbani out for earlier, grabs the jacket he brought with him but really doesn't need, and steps out onto the driveway.

The sun has dropped below the horizon now, and the house looks bleaker than ever in the twilight. He walks up to the front door and nods to the PC standing guard. He steps back over the threshold into the tiled hallway. He isn't really sure why he's here, but his feet take him through the house until he finds himself back in front of the painting that hangs above the fireplace. He stares at the wrinkled, gray face of the fire watcher, and the painting stares back at him.

"Ugly bloody thing, isn't it?"

He turns to find Doggett crossing the room to join him.

"I thought you'd gone."

The DI tugs at a tie that's already hanging loose at his neck. "I thought I'd head back to the station now, give Jordan an update. You all right getting things locked down for the night?"

Tyler nods his agreement and turns back to the portrait. "Can you make out the signature?"

Doggett squints at the painting for a moment. "Lowry?" he says.

"Yeah, that's what I thought. But he was all landscapes, wasn't he? Matchstick cats and dogs and all that."

"So what's your interest in the bloody thing?"

"I think it's been moved. It was hanging in the attic at the time of the fire—there's a patch on the wall that was protected from the smoke—and sometime since then, somebody's moved it down here. Taken that picture down"—he points to the framed land-scape propped against the armchair—"and replaced it. The ques-tion is, why?"

Out of the corner of his eye he sees Doggett looking at the picture again. "Could have been kids messing about. God knows who's been through here, ransacking the place, in the last six years."

But the place doesn't look ransacked. Badly fire damaged, rain soaked in places, but not ransacked. No one has helped themselves to the furniture or the many pictures, some of which would be worth the taking for the frames alone. Tyler's eyes stray back to the portrait of the fire watcher. Why does it feel so important? If it had been stolen or smashed up by vandals he could understand it, but why would someone move it from the attic to the living room? And rehang it, moving the other painting out of the way in order to do so. Would some squatter or dope-smoking teenager do that? He supposes they might, if they liked the thing enough, but he can't help thinking it means something to someone. Someone who was here *after* the fire, *after* Gerald Cartwright was bricked in the cellar. He looks down at the remains of the small fire on the floor and remembers the cigarette butts the SOCOs have since collected and taken away. "I think someone's been living here," he says. "Someone with a connection to the place. Maybe a connection to Cartwright."

It's a bit of a leap, but to Tyler's surprise Doggett doesn't try to bat his theory away. He runs his finger along the bottom of the gold frame. "Did the SOCOs get anything?"

"Nothing usable, just smudges."

"This hideous bastard means something to someone," Doggett says, echoing his own thoughts. "Someone who's familiar with the place. A childhood memory, perhaps?"

That's why he's so keen to listen. It fits his own theory.

"Why would Oscar be living here?"

Doggett shrugs. "It's his house; why wouldn't he?"

"Because the place is a death trap. Besides, he has his own flat in town." He says it without thinking, but there's no reason he shouldn't know Oscar's address for professional reasons. Even so, he feels the need to give Doggett something to distract his attention. "It's possible," he says. And for the first time he accepts that it *is* possible. Oscar could be playing him, using him.

"Tell me about Bridger," Doggett says out of nowhere.

He has been expecting the question, or something like it, ever since Doggett's comment in the car earlier. But now it's here, the question takes him by surprise and he struggles to find an answer.

Doggett folds his arms. He's watching closely, looking for some reaction. "Come on, son. It isn't every day you get to floor a senior officer and get away with it."

Tyler rubs at the scar with his thumb. "I wouldn't exactly say I got away with it."

He can still see the look on Bridger's face, the smug grin that told him, even before the punch fully landed, he'd been played. Months of windups, scores of digs about who he slept with. Usually subtle enough they might be taken for innocent remarks but sometimes so obvious he might as well have accompanied them with a limp-wristed hand gesture. It was laughable, like some dubious performance by a dodgy '80s nightclub comedian. And it wasn't as though the two of them even worked that closely together, so he had no trouble ignoring the twat. He could have complained. He *should* have. But it was all just so pathetic. And besides, official complaints ran the risk of you losing the sympathy of your colleagues. No one likes a grass, not even the police. Best to keep your head down, ignore them. Sooner or later they get tired and move on. It was his golden rule. And it was manageable.

Until Bridger found his Achilles' heel. His father.

By the time he'd joined the South Yorkshire Criminal Investigation Department, it had been years since Richard's death, and it wasn't as though the name *Tyler* was all that uncommon. But the manner of his father's passing had been memorable, and it was enough for some to make the connection. Gary Bridger was one of them. Jordan told him later that his father and Bridger had been rivals. Richard had pissed him off sometime over some case or other, and since he could no longer take it out on the father, he'd gone for the son.

Tyler was queuing in the canteen that day when it started with the usual general comments thrown out casually to his mates so Tyler would overhear. Lots of stuff about bent coppers and how they were a disgrace to the force. Nothing that couldn't be taken at face value if challenged, so there really wasn't any point. Only the sly smirk on Bridger's face told Tyler they were aimed at him. And then he started on about people only getting on the force because their fathers were coppers, and nepotism and all that.

"They say it runs in the family. Like father, like son." Bridger looked straight at Tyler for the first time, making sure his words struck home. "Sometimes they're so racked with guilt over what they've done, they end up topping themselves. Best thing for 'em, if you ask me."

Afterward, he didn't even remember moving. Only the blood pounding in his ears and the mist clouding his vision as he went for the man's smug face.

"He always was a dog's arse of a copper," Doggett says now. "Too handy for his own good. I daresay I've been tempted to smack him one myself from time to time. But there's one thing you can say about Gary Bridger—he's always had friends in high places. I reckon it must have cost the DCI a fair few favors to pull your fat out of the fire on that one."

"I think it helped that I came off worse."

Ironically it had been Bridger's defense of himself that had ultimately saved Tyler. Perhaps he'd underestimated how strongly Tyler would go for him. Or perhaps, after months of fruitless taunting, the thought that he might elicit a response hadn't occurred to him. Maybe he believed his own rhetoric and saw Tyler as nothing but a limp-wristed sissy-boy. Whatever the reason, he'd panicked and picked up the bottle from the tray without thinking. At least, he was given the benefit of the doubt that it hadn't been planned. There were witnesses, too. Not just Bridger's mates either. The woman behind the counter had testified that some of the lads had already pulled Tyler off and were holding him back when Bridger attacked. She said she saw him smash the bottle deliberately. Tyler himself never even saw it coming through the mist. He didn't feel the glass as it slid into his face, or the blows that came afterward. They were much weaker, to his abdomen and chest, most of them deflected by his clothing. The wounds were superficial, but they testified to the fact Gary Bridger was a violent little bastard. There had been other smaller incidents in the past, it seemed, and Bridger found that his friends in high places couldn't get him out of this one. He escaped the grievous bodily harm charge but was forced into early retirement. Tyler, who was widely seen as the one who'd started the incident, was lucky to escape with just a reprimand. And the transfer to the CCRU, of course. The job nobody wanted. He suspects that was Diane Jordan's work. Without the DCI in his corner, Bridger's friends would have found a way to take him down as well. He still doesn't know exactly what it cost her, but by all accounts she should be a superintendent by now. The fact she isn't . . . well, he guesses that's on him.

He becomes aware his fists are clenched, fingernails stabbing hard into his palms.

Doggett is suspiciously quiet, just watching him.

Tyler sighs heavily and realizes he's made his decision. He can't do this to her again. "I'm going to ask the DCI to reassign me."

Doggett's eyes narrow. His fingers begin a silent drumbeat on his thigh. "How long have you known the lad?"

Tyler isn't even all that surprised. "When did you realize?"

"Come on, son, don't take me for a complete mug. I saw the look on your face the minute I introduced the pair of you. Why do you think I had Daley look into him?"

He nods, relieved it's over. "We met the night before last." But that's not enough. He won't lie about this. "We spent the night together."

"I see." The only gauge to Doggett's reaction is a slight increase to the tempo of his drumming.

"I'll speak to the DCI tonight and remove myself from the case."

The tapping continues. "If you think that's best," says Doggett. "Telling her what you should have told her yesterday." He pushes a finger into Tyler's chest. "*You* pushed your way onto this case; don't you think you owe it to her to see it through?"

"I didn't know Oscar was involved then."

"Of course you bloody didn't, and if I thought any differently, you wouldn't be here now."

"Why am I here then? Why did you even want me on this case?"

Doggett is silent for a moment and seems to be considering his words carefully. "Your father was a good man," he says quietly. "What they said about him being on the take, about why he did what he did. I didn't believe it then, and I still don't believe it now." He sniffs, perhaps uncomfortable with this level of intimacy. "Anyway, seems to me we shouldn't be too hasty here. Did Cartwright know who you were when you met?"

"I don't . . ." Tyler is floored. He didn't even realize Doggett knew his father, but he supposes they would have been about the same age, so it's not all that surprising. It's just . . . it never occurred to him they might have worked together. "No, I can't see how he could have."

"Then I don't reckon there's much of a problem. In fact, this might give us an advantage."

"What?"

"You've reported the conflict of interest to your superior. You took your sweet time about it, but we don't need to tell anyone that. The way I see it, this is *my* call. This . . ." He hesitates. "This business you had with the lad, it's over?"

"We only slept together the one time."

"All right. So maybe we use this relationship you've got with him to sound the lad out a bit, have a few off-the-record chats."

"I'm not sure I'm comfortable with that."

"Fine. If that's what you want, *I'll* talk to Jordan. I'll tell her what a pain in the arse you are and that I can't work with you anymore. No need to muddy the waters by dragging conflicts of interest into it."

"I don't think—"

"Look. Take tomorrow morning to think about it. I've got court again in the morning anyway. Daley can handle things here."

Tyler can't bring himself to answer. The thought Doggett might be on his side is laughable, but he seems to be offering a way out. It's hardly by the book, though. This is exactly the sort of thing Jordan warned him about. But if he stays on the case and they find the answers they're looking for . . . it won't just help him and Doggett but Jordan's career as well. Maybe she'll finally make super, and he can make it up to her.

Doggett loosens his tie even further. "Just think about it. As my old man used to say, 'If in doubt, do nowt.'" Doggett turns to leave and then stops. "Where's your little shadow gone, by the way?"

"My what?"

"Constable Rabbani."

"I sent her home."

Doggett just blinks at him.

"What? It's been a long day, she deserves a bit of an evening."

Doggett shakes his head. "That's very considerate of you, son. Only, did it occur to you to wonder how she was gonna get home without a ride?"

That was why she was so pissed off with him! She needed a lift but was too afraid to ask. How the hell was he supposed to guess that?

He can hear Doggett chuckling to himself all the way out of the house.

day three

Chicago, 1871

You lie among the overgrown, discarded vegetables and watch the shed as it begins to smolder. There's a pumpkin, the size of a small dog, its unharvested carcass beginning to rot, lying inches from your face. The wizened husks of potatoes sit like blackened stones, their surfaces grown over with a furry gray fungus. The long grass that has grown up through every spare inch of ground tickles at your face and hands. Some unseen nighttime creature begins to crawl up your arm. You lie perfectly still and breathe in the faint smoke on the air.

The shed will not catch. You should go back, add more kindling, fan the flames. But you don't want to move. You want to stay lying here, down in the dark undergrowth, looking up at the stars. You're thinking of Ignatius Donnelly.

The Great Chicago Fire, as it became known, began in Patrick O'Leary's shed when a cow kicked over a lantern. Another wooden city, more violent winds to fan the flames, more civic-minded officials too worried about keeping their jobs and too slow to act. The resulting fire killed more than three hundred people. It is remembered as one of the worst disasters in American history and is taught to schoolchildren for years to come.

Twenty years after the fire, however, a local newspaperman named Michael Ahern admitted he made up the cow story to sell newspaper copy. The true cause? The authorities couldn't tell. A spark from a chimney perhaps. Or arson. It's a possibility this time—some itinerant passing vagrant with a desire akin to your own. You like that idea.

There's another theory, though, one you like even more. The Chicago fire, despite its infamy, was actually only one of several fires in the same area at the same time. It wasn't even the largest. A little further north, on the shores of Lake Michigan, a forest fire developed into a firestorm the likes of which has never been seen again. This time two and a half thousand people were killed. In the small town of Peshtigo so many died there weren't enough residents left alive to identify the bodies. Hundreds were buried in mass graves. One and a half million acres of land scoured clean.

But that was only the beginning. On the east coast of the lake, the town of Holland was razed to the ground, along with the lumber community of Manistee a hundred miles further north. Further east still, on the shores of Lake Huron, another fire swept through the town of Port Huron, and a few days later both Urbana, Illinois, just south of Chicago, and Windsor, Ontario, were also ravaged.

What chances? All these separate fires in the same area at the same time. Ignatius L. Donnelly had his own theory about that. He was a U.S. congressman and what might generously be called a bit of an eccentric. You wonder if you will get off that lightly. He had some interesting thoughts concerning the lost city of Atlantis, though, and his theory of catastrophism posited that the ancient civilization was destroyed by a global catastrophic event, a volcano or meteor strike. As evidence for his theory, Donnelly put forward the simultaneous fires of the Chicago area of 1871. He placed the blame for the fires on a single cosmic event, the periodic Comet Biela that broke up as it passed over America, raining fiery death upon the population in the form of methane-rich meteorite fragments.

The thought some future scholar might place the blame for your actions on a cosmic event appeals to you. But, you have to admit, that isn't likely unless you upscale a bit; hard to imagine anyone constructing an elaborate theory about the destruction of an old shed on an allotment.

You look up into the clear night sky and you think perhaps you catch a glimpse of a shooting star. At the same time something in the shed catches, and all of a sudden the structure is fully ablaze. You sit up and feel the displaced creature fall out of your sleeve. The shed is blazing brightly, the heat licking at your face and warming your skin.

The scream returns long before the fire is out, though, even before you hear the sirens tearing ever closer through the quiet dark of the night. He wants more, so much more. He needs feeding, and his appetite is far greater than an old shed, or a run-down bus shelter. These things are too easily overlooked, too easily written off as accidents or pranks.

Tonight, you think, will be different. Tonight, they are going to notice you.

POSTED BY **thefirewatcher** AT 5:46 AM

4 COMMENTS

Gengen97 said . . .

Wow! That is soooooo cool!!!

RDAtack said . . .

Meteorites are cold to the touch when they reach the ground. There are no credible reports of them ever causing fires. The weather conditions at the time—a long period of high temperatures, and widespread drought, combined with the fact that the predominant industry in the area, logging, meant the countryside was littered with sawdust and stacks of dry timber—is a far more likely cause.

Babelicious69 said . . .

Wat u gonna burn next?

Firebug69 said . . .

Love u man! I burned a shed once but it wun't tak. What petrol u using?

The receptionist in the Medico-Legal Center on Watery Street eyes Tyler suspiciously, like he's an out-of-date bottle of milk she's just found in the communal fridge. He tries to reassure her with a smile but feels the scar pull at the corner of his mouth. If anything, this seems to raise her suspicions further.

A door opens and Elliot arrives, his skin jaundiced, gray bags suspended under his eyes; he reminds Tyler of the portrait at the Old Vicarage. "DS Tyler, do me a favor, man," he says, yawning and cracking his neck with one long-fingered hand. "Never, ever, ring me again." He ushers Tyler through to the morgue. "Where's Jim?"

"In court."

"What did they get him for this time? Let me guess, missing alimony payments."

Tyler ignores him. "Thanks for pushing this through."

"Your DCI Jordan is a persuasive woman. I had to call in a favor from a colleague. Forensic dentist." His tone suggests forensic dentists are something of a rarity and that they're lucky he managed to find one. Perhaps they are, but he's thanked the man already, what more does he want?

"I'm sure DI Doggett will appreciate it."

Elliot nods, apparently satisfied. "So, anyway, it's him, all right."

"Gerald Cartwright."

"Aye." Elliot opens the freezer door and wheels out a trolley.

Tyler stares at the corpse. He has, of course, seen pictures and video footage of the live Cartwright, but it's difficult to make a connection between those and the loose collection of bones and skin in front of him.

"I can't really tell you much more." Elliot reaches up to his ear for a cigarette that isn't there. He tugs at his earlobe instead. "We can rule out the fire. There's no evidence of smoke damage to the lungs, what's left of them."

This is not a surprise; they know the fire didn't occur until six months after Cartwright's disappearance. By that time the investigation was already being downgraded; Cartwright would have been long dead.

"The wound on his head wasn't severe enough to kill him outright, but it wouldn't have helped." Elliot absently pats himself down but comes up empty. "If you twisted my arm, I might be tempted to say dehydration."

"How long?"

He hesitates. "Two days max. The wound would have made him groggy, perhaps even hallucinatory." He seems determined to limit Cartwright's suffering. Tyler likes the man a bit more for that. "I can tell you he was definitely alive when he went in, though. There's severe damage to the nails on the left hand; his right arm was broken, so he wouldn't have been able to use it as effectively. And it was dislocated—pulled right out of the socket, I'm guessing when he was dragged behind the wall."

"Cartwright was a big man, wasn't he?"

"Eh?"

"In your opinion, could a fifteen-year-old boy have put him there?"

Elliot exhales a loud blast of air. "Depends on the boy, I suppose. It's not impossible. It would explain why he was dragged and not carried. And there's always the possibility he had help, of course."

Tyler thanks him, and the doctor accompanies him out of the building, having finally extricated a cigarette from some unknown orifice. He lights it before they're fully clear of the building, risking the wrath of the eagle-eyed receptionist. While they were inside, a brisk wind has developed and taken the edge off the heat. Elliot draws the nicotine into his lungs, exhales slowly, and blows the smoke onto the breeze.

"Were you around six years ago?"

Elliot breathes in deeply before answering. "I was 'around,' as you put it. But there wasn't a body six years ago, remember? I wasn't involved in the investigation."

A supermarket delivery lorry reverses past them, its shrill alarm bouncing off the walls of the surrounding buildings. Tyler turns back to find Elliot studying him.

"I must say, Detective Sergeant, you've come a long way from playing with toy cars under the dining table."

He's puzzled for a second and then puts it together. "It seems everyone knew my father."

Elliot laughs. "I'm not surprised you don't remember. Loretta and I came for dinner at your house, oh, let's see, it would have been years ago now. Of course, that was before your mother . . ." He trails off and takes another fortifying drag on the cigarette. "I was sorry about your father's death. It was . . . out of character."

That was one way of putting it.

The lorry stops with a hiss of air from its brakes. The wind gathers the litter from the gutter and dances it round the oversized wheels.

"You knew Gerald Cartwright as well, didn't you? At least, that was the impression I got the other day."

Elliot's eyes narrow. "Aye. We played golf together a few times. Not often, mind; he wasn't exactly in my league. Eight handicap," he says, quite literally blowing smoke. "I'm going for the club championship this year."

"Impressive." Tyler has no idea if it is or not.

Elliot coughs. "Aye. Cartwright was strictly amateur status."

The driver of the lorry jumps down from the cab and looks at a clipboard. He glances up and down the road a couple of times and then back at the information in his hands.

"Look at this joker." Elliot drops his cigarette butt on the ground, where it joins a hundred others. He stamps it out with a foot and shouts at the driver, "Are you picking up or dropping off, man?"

The driver looks up for a moment, winces into the sunlight, and then looks back down at his clipboard as though it alone holds the answers he seeks.

Elliot huffs. "I'd better sort this out. We're expecting a meat delivery of our own any minute." He claps Tyler on the shoulder and starts toward the lorry. But as he walks he turns and raises his voice. "If you want any more info on Gerald Cartwright," he says, "I suggest you ask Jim Doggett. I seem to remember he was in Gerry's league." He smiles and turns back to the driver.

The orange spark of his cigarette butt flares once on the wind and goes out.

Constable Rabbani lives with her parents in one of a short row of newly built terraced houses in Sharrow. Tyler parks on a side street overlooking the back of the houses where the gardens have been paved over and joined into one shared courtyard. A group of young boys are playing cricket between rows of drying washing. When they see Rabbani get in the car they begin shouting at the house.

"Cousins," she explains as she gets in, "telling the whole family some bloke's just picked me up."

"Do you want me to go in and explain?" he asks.

"Fuck, no! Sorry, sir. It's just . . . sometimes they forget I'm with the police."

He smiles. "No need to remind them, eh?"

It takes them no more than ten minutes to reach the university. Finding somewhere to park takes nearer fifteen. Sophie Denham is a law student who's agreed to meet them strictly on her own terms. Her suggestion to Rabbani was that they meet her in the coffee shop at the student union. Tyler doesn't want to meet the girl at all, but he can't just ignore the possible lead. He tells himself his interest is professional. They were at school together—Oscar and this . . . so-called fiancée—which means she's likely to have known Gerald Cartwright as well. And anyway, as uncomfortable as the whole interview is likely to be for him, better he talks to her than Doggett.

They find a table close to the door. Rabbani huddles round her corrugated cup of tea while he watches a handful of students and lecturers meander their way through the building. Term may not have started in earnest yet, but already the institution is beginning to wake from its long summer slumber. He knows Sophie Denham the minute she walks in. She's tall and blond and very beautiful. She's wearing a pair of dark jeans, a plain white T-shirt, and unbranded trainers. Her hair is tied back in a functional ponytail, and she carries a brown satchel-style briefcase that no doubt contains her lecture notes meticulously organized and color coordinated. She already has *lawyer* written all over her. She's one step away from a designer suit, paid for by her corporately negligent clients.

But she also spots him. He sees her glance him up and down as he gets to his feet. She comes straight toward him, clearly not doubting for a moment that she has the right man. First Wentworth in the churchyard, now her; perhaps he has the word *cop* written across his forehead. Perhaps it was there the night he met Oscar.

The way Denham holds herself, she looks as though she's heading into battle in the courtroom. "Detective Sergeant Tyler," she says, not bothering with the question.

He holds out his hand and warrant card. "I'm DS Tyler. This is Constable Rabbani."

Denham takes the warrant card from him and examines it closely. Then she does the same with Rabbani's. The gesture reminds him of Edna Burnside checking for bogus gasmen. "Can I get you a drink?" he offers.

She sits, tucking her satchel very precisely under her chair. "I'll have a green tea, please. And a banana." She stares at him, the banana clearly some sort of challenge.

He goes to fetch her order, using the queuing time as an opportunity to examine her more closely. She sits perfectly still and upright. Rabbani tries her best to make conversation, but Sophie Denham shuts her down each time with the barest of smiles. She seems out of place here, surrounded by partying students whose motivations for attending university differ widely from her own. But she's unembarrassed about it. He struggles to work out how the chaotic Oscar might fit into this tidy, focused life.

When he returns she seems to have softened a little. "Thanks," she says. Perhaps the banana did the trick. By contrast Rabbani looks ready to take the girl down and restrain her. He doesn't know what was said but it's clear Denham got the upper hand.

"I'm sorry," she says, "I don't have very long."

"This shouldn't take long."

She eats the banana in small bite-sized chunks, breaking them off with fingernails neither long nor short, coated in clear nail polish. "To be honest, I don't really know what I can tell you."

"We're speaking to as many people as we can who are involved with the case." He watches her chew; everything about her is so measured and precise. "You were at school with Oscar Cartwright, is that right?"

"Childhood sweethearts," she says. She laughs but it sounds a little forced. "All very romantic. There was a group of us used to hang out together, usually up at the vicarage; there was always something to do there. Oscar used to have this enormous treehouse, and there was always the chance Edna or Lil had been baking. We got to do pretty much what we wanted, no parents to tell us off." She laughs again. "It was a teenager's dream house." Then the laugh fades away. "I only met Gerald a couple of times. He was hardly ever there." She's a little too quick to distance herself from Cartwright.

She takes a sip of tea, and he gets the impression there's something else. Something she wants to tell him. Then a thought occurs to her and her face changes. "Is Oscar a suspect?" she asks, appraising him with the professional cynicism of a hardened defense attorney.

"Just routine," he says. "How is he taking all this?"

She answers slowly, obviously working out the best way to phrase her response. "He's doing well. Considering." She falters, perhaps worried she's made Oscar sound too cool about the situation. "I mean, he's not great, obviously." Now she blushes; she'll have to learn to control that when she goes to court. "I haven't seen that much of him lately, to be honest. Apart from last night."

Last night. The words clatter around his head. She was with him as recently as last night.

"Is that unusual?" Rabbani asks.

Sophie Denham answers without looking at her, still talking to Tyler. "We don't live together or anything. I'm in a student house, and Oscar has his own place in town. He stays over sometimes."

"I see," he says. And he thinks he does. He sees them together, this perfect couple with their perfectly skinny waists and perfectly coiffured hair. He sees Oscar's thick lips pressed against her pale breasts.

She misinterprets his silence. "We're not one of those couples who have to be in each other's pockets all the time."

"But you saw him last night?"

She nods. "We had dinner. He stayed all night."

She sounds as though she's providing Oscar with an alibi, but he can't think of a reason why Oscar would need one for last night.

Rabbani takes over again. "How long have you been seeing each other?"

"I thought I just said, we were at school together." Her voice is so much cooler when talking to Rabbani. He wonders at first if it's a race thing. If it is, he'll find a reason to take her in.

"You've been dating all that time?" Rabbani's voice is cool as well. What was said while he was away? Not a race thing; a woman thing then?

"It's complicated," Denham says. "And personal." She puts down her cup. A little of the pale tea spills onto the table. Tyler passes her a napkin. She mops at the spillage, caught between the invasiveness of Rabbani's questioning and the small kindness of his gesture. Good cop, bad cop. Perhaps they make a good team.

Denham lets out a small sigh. "Oscar's a bit of a free spirit," she says, still talking to him rather than Rabbani. "He comes and goes." She hesitates for the briefest moment. "I know he sees other women. That's fine. I have my studies anyway." She blushes again, recognizing how all this must sound to them. "It works for us," she adds defiantly. He suddenly sees her vulnerability; she's a child playing at an adult relationship. She knows what Oscar gets up to, but she chooses to ignore it. She's convinced herself this is what she wants as well. He corrects the thought: she knows *some* of what Oscar gets up to.

His mobile rings. He glances at the screen as it flashes the identity of the caller at him. He has the number stored in his phone only because he thought to copy it from a witness statement last night. Just in case. He should hit the call-cancel button. That would be the sensible thing to do. Instead he excuses himself, stands, and looks directly into Sophie Denham's bright eyes. He smiles at her and leaves the table, answering the phone as he wanders to the window. "DS Tyler."

"Hi," Oscar says. "It's me."

"I know." He looks out at the grassy bank where the students lie cradling their pints. Another perfect couple is lying together on the grass, hands and mouths all over each other. "You have a girlfriend." He doesn't mean for it to come out like that, like an accusation.

Oscar doesn't answer straightaway. "Soph?" he says finally. "Well, it's not really like that."

Tyler glances back to the table. Sophie Denham is finding it hard to look anything other than imperious, while Rabbani makes no attempt to hide her disdain. If he doesn't get back soon someone's going to say something they'll regret. A man in a tailored gray suit is approaching the table.

Oscar's voice whispers at him from the phone. "I need to see you. I can explain. Can we meet?"

"I don't think that's a good idea."

"Please, Adam. It's important."

He remembers he has something important he needs to tell Oscar as well, the fact they've identified the body as belonging to his father. He still has a job to do. The man in the gray suit is arguing with Rabbani. She's holding her own but because he's standing over her the man has the advantage. His body language is intimidating and aggressive. He wills Rabbani to stand up. "Fine. The Red Deer. Six." Neutral territory. He hangs up before Oscar can say anything else.

Rabbani is up now, and Sophie Denham seems both pleased at her discomfort and mortified at the scene they're creating in the coffee shop. As he arrives back at the table, he catches the tail end of Rabbani's attempt to calm the situation down—". . . only a few questions."

"All future questions can come through me," says the man in the suit.

"I'm DS Tyler." He inserts his warrant card into the conversation by way of an opening salvo. "You are?"

The man squares his chest, but the effect is that of a puffer fish, or an elephant raising its ears and making a mock charge. It's all show. He's significantly shorter than Tyler and is forced to look up at him, squinting through thick-glassed spectacles. "I'm Michael Denham," he says. "I'm Sophie's father and her legal representative."

"It's all right, Dad, they're just asking about Gerald."

"It's *not* all right," he snaps back. "And frankly you should know better." He turns back to Tyler. "If you wish to speak to Sophie, you can do so in my presence. Do I make myself clear?"

Tyler holds eye contact with the man and counts to five, drawing out the tension. When he speaks it's calmly and quietly. "You've made yourself very clear, Mr. Denham. I've no objection to you joining us. In fact, I have some questions I'd like to ask you as well."

"Then you'll need to make an appointment with my secretary." He bustles his daughter up out of her chair. Rabbani steps forward to stop him but Tyler waves her off. She bites back whatever she was about to say. Sophie gives him an embarrassed smile and allows her father to drag her away from them, out of the coffee shop into the corridor.

"Arsehole," Rabbani whispers through gritted teeth.

"Wasn't he, though?"

"Actually, I meant her, sir."

He watches the two Denhams arguing outside. It isn't an equal battle by any means. When they say their goodbyes there's no fatherly kiss, just more remonstrations. Sophie looks defeated. Tyler changes his mind; she's going to make a terrible solicitor.

He wonders how her father knew about this meeting. Sophie obviously didn't tell him. But she might have told someone. A boyfriend, perhaps? The phone call from Oscar certainly made for a timely distraction. He watches her neat, organized body move away down the corridor. She takes out her own mobile, and he's fairly confident he knows who she's calling. But there's another question, and that is how, exactly, Oscar managed to get his number. Tyler's far less certain of the answer to that.

Lily has realized something. It could be any of them.

Her visit to the village yesterday has unsettled her, but equally it has awakened something. The need to know. If she can find the person who wrote them, perhaps she can find out what they mean, and all without involving Edna.

She waits in the kitchen for much of the morning until she hears the clink of the gate and then dives through the back door and is across the yard before Her-Next-Door has even made it all the way through. Lily thanks her, taking the newspaper and ushering her back the way she has come.

"Anyway, I can't stop," she says breathlessly. "She's not good this morning. I'll see you tomorrow, then. Thank you."

Her-Next-Door seems a little put out but nevertheless beats a slow retreat back to her own garden. Lily waits for a moment, then lifts the lid of the dustbin and buries the paper below a layer of potato peelings. She returns to the house.

"Lillian! Lillian!"

"Yes, all right, I'm here."

"Where did you go?"

Lily explains the problem. Her-Next-Door hasn't been able to get to the village this morning, some problem with her hip or some such.

"Her hip? The woman's got more hip than anything else as far as I can make out. You think she could have managed."

Well, it doesn't matter, Lily will go instead. It's really no bother. Is there anything else they need while she's out?

It's clear from the furrowed brow Edna is searching for some further reason to object, but her unwillingness to forgo her cross-word clearly wins out. "Just don't be too long."

Fifteen minutes later Lily is crossing the churchyard and thinking hard. Now that she is out, she realizes she doesn't really have much of a plan. She's fairly certain there won't be another letter today. It's a risk, certainly, but there were several days between the first and second letter, so it seems reasonable to assume at least a couple of days before the next. She has little doubt there *will* be a next letter. Part of her is almost looking forward to it. A chance to find out more, a chance for the perpetrator to give himself away. Or herself; she supposes it is just as likely a woman could be responsible.

But she refuses to sit around and wait for it. In the meantime she can investigate further. She goes back over her conversation with Michael Denham. He seemed to be hinting at something. Or was that just her imagination? And then in the butcher's. Carol gossiping about Gerald and the Old Vicarage. But then, Carol was always a gossip; that hardly counts as displaying unusual behavior. Perhaps, if she talks to enough people, if she shakes things up a bit, she can force this would-be blackmailer's hand. Perhaps they will give themselves away in some other fashion.

She sees him before he sees her and only then realizes he might just be exactly who she has been looking for. He's scratching around in the undergrowth at the base of the churchyard wall, plucking and winnowing, pulling weeds and shaking them loose of dirt before hurling them with casual abandon into his rusty old wheel-barrow. Just like Mrs. Blackbird, who plucks and tugs at the worms in the grass of Lily's garden before chucking them into the air to catch them firmly in her greedy beak.

Joseph Wentworth. Curiously, she feels none of the trepidation she would normally on seeing him. She has been avoiding this man for years, crossing roads and examining unwanted goods in shop-windows, taking the longer route to the post office to avoid passing the rain-spotted windows of his cottage. When they have, on occa-sion, bumped into each other, Lily has always taken great pains to look the other way, pretending a sudden interest in whatever is nearest rather than be forced to acknowledge the man. It has al-ways seemed to her that he did the same. But what if she has been wrong all these years? What if this man has been to her front door, invading their lives with his typed missives demanding truth? For this reason, or maybe just because there seems little left to fear anymore, she finds herself crossing the graveyard. Her feet pass silently across the stony path.

He looks up as she arrives and struggles to hide the surprise in his eyes.

"Hello, Joe," she says, and promptly runs out of anything else to say.

For his part he merely grunts and turns back to his weeding, leaving her high and dry.

"You're working hard," she says, and then, to follow it up, "and in this heat as well!"

Again he grunts and carries on.

Lily struggles to think of something, anything. A question, so he is forced to respond or else appear rude. "Are you going on the Whitby trip?" She stops herself from going on. She knows she has a tendency to prattle—Edna often tells her so—but she leaves him the silence, in the hope he will fill it.

He stops working, sits back on his haunches, and sighs. He stands up slowly, using a grubby palm on his knee to lever himself upright. He isn't as youthful as she remembers him, this "handyman" of Gerald's. His eyes are creased and hooded, his posture a little more stooped than she remembers it. But he is still the same man. A man she had found quite attractive when she first met him. Attractive, and perhaps a little dangerous. Despite his reduced vigor he still towers over her, his recently expanded waistline now blocking her path. He looks at her for a moment, studying her.

"How are you?" he says eventually, and she gets the sense he means it not so much the way another might, as a polite opening to conversation, but rather as a genuine inquiry into her being, her state of mind. Or perhaps . . . even as a threat?

"Very well, thank you. This weather is quite something, isn't it?"

Again he just stares, blinking a little as one might at a deer startled in the forest while out walking, unsure whether to go on, to stop and watch, or simply to back slowly away.

"What do you want?" he asks.

She swallows and feels her face heat. "I wondered . . . if you'd heard anything . . . about the Vic—"

Before the word is fully out of her mouth, his arm snakes out and takes hold of her wrist. "Stop," he tells her. "There's things don't need to be said. I thought that was what we agreed."

His hand is so firm on her wrist she can feel the thin bones under her papery skin rubbing together.

"Please, I . . ."

He lets go just as suddenly as he grabbed her and steps away. "I don't see no call to be raking all this up. What's done is done." And the words sound so much like Edna's that Lily feels ashamed.

"I didn't mean—"

"I thought you, of all people, would have sense enough to leave the past be."

"I should be getting on," she says a little desperately, but he is already turning back to his work.

She hurries away down the path. She wants to run, but her ancient legs will not let her. The strength in his arms . . . she had forgotten. There is a bruise already forming on her flesh that makes her wonder just what he's capable of.

She's almost all the way home before she realizes, in her panic, she has forgotten to go to the paper shop. She opens the gate as quietly as possible. Inside the bin she rummages through the peelings until she finds the newspaper delivered by Her-Next-Door. She lifts it free and brushes it clean. It has a number of faint stains that Edna will no doubt comment on, but Lily thinks she can probably get away with it. She props the paper under one arm where it rests against the heart that is thudding inside her chest. Then she carefully lowers the lid of the dustbin and goes inside.

Tyler slams his hand down hard on the horn and inches his way through the knot of press gathered at the gates. He presses his warrant card to the window, and the uniformed constables wave him through.

When they pull up at the house, Rabbani gets out but Tyler hangs back. He looks again at the blackened bricks and the dying creeper and thinks about what Elliot said. Assuming the body was Cartwright's, they have been working under the premise the fire was unconnected to the case since it happened so long after his disappearance. Just kids messing around in a derelict house. They know now the fire didn't kill Cartwright, so on the face of it nothing's changed. Why, then, does he feel so sure the fire *is* connected in some way? Because of *The Fire Watcher*? A portrait that once meant something to someone. But if so, why set fire to the house in the first place?

His thoughts scatter as the door to the mobile incident room flies open and rebounds hard against the wall. A hulking black man in a tight gray T-shirt emerges, his mouth a thin line. He pushes past Rabbani, who shouts something after him. The man ignores her and stalks back down the driveway. As he passes the car he meets Tyler's eye, and then a thick black arm is brushing past the wing mirror. The man is out of sight for a second and then reappears in the mirror itself, this time visible as a muscled back, which folds its way into the crowd at the gate.

Inside the incident room Guy Daley is leaning backward against a desk, his arms folded and ankles crossed, a self-satisfied smirk on his face that melts away into a scowl as Tyler steps into view.

"Who was that?"

"Doggett said you weren't coming out till this afternoon."

"I changed my mind. Who was that?" he asks again.

"Some tosser from the fire brigade looking to waste our time."

Daley scrambles round the desk and rather unsubtly switches off his computer monitor, but not before Tyler catches sight of the telltale green background of a solitaire game.

"And I imagine you listened carefully to what he wanted and promised you'd pass the details on to your superiors?"

Daley blinks slowly and doesn't reply.

"That's what I thought."

"There's been some fires in the area, a bus stop or summat." Daley sits down and immediately starts spinning in the chair. They're *all* beginning to channel the spirit of Jim Doggett. "He reckons it might be connected to this place."

Tyler stops the chair's movement with an outstretched leg. "And you told him to piss off?"

"We're up to our necks in a murder investigation, Tyler. We've got better things to do than investigate a couple of bonfires."

"Like playing cards?"

Daley plucks a small white oblong from his pocket and launches it across the desk at him. "Here. Knock yourself out, sunshine."

Tyler picks up the business card, glances at it, and slips it into his pocket. Then he crosses his own arms and holds Daley's eye. Finally, Daley sighs, turns the monitor back on, and closes the card game.

Rabbani watches Daley raise his middle finger at Tyler's departing back. When he becomes aware of her watching, he scowls. "Can I help you with something, *love*?"

"I just wondered if you'd spoken to the vicar yet, sir?" She means to offer help, but the way it comes out makes it sound like a criticism.

Daley shakes his head. "Jesus Christ!" He stands up. "I'm going for a smoke. How about you try minding your own fucking business while I'm gone?" The door swings back into place behind him, and Rabbani is left alone in the incident room.

She exhales loudly into the silence. She'd hoped it might be different once she was in plainclothes, that they might forget she's still only a PC, not a detective. But if anything, it's worse. It's as though the confidence and ability she's amassed over the last three years were all somehow locked within the black and white of her constable's uniform.

She spent hours last night trying to work out what to wear, trying on different outfits. In the end, she opted for the pantsuit she uses for interviews. But when she tried it on this morning she realized she looked too smart. She compromised by losing the jacket, only to discover that left her with no pockets. Where would she put her mobile, her notebook, her keys? The only thing she had that was vaguely suitable was a Cath Kidston bag but it's too big, and far more conspicuous than she's comfortable with. She remembers the look the Denham girl gave it. The same look the girls at school used when they looked down at her shoes. She can't understand why Tyler gave Denham such an easy time of it.

DS Adam Tyler. She can't work him out. One minute he's completely oblivious, failing to offer her a lift home even though he knows she doesn't have a car—she'd had to walk all the way to Hope for the train last night, and then wait for over half an hour— the next he's being supportive and encouraging, offering to pick her up, including her on the interview with Denham.

He's not aggressive like Daley, but she wonders if that wouldn't almost be better. She can handle the Daleys of this world. It's more like he just doesn't think of her at all. Doesn't even notice her. Like just then, when they got out of the car and he was too busy staring after that hulk of a fire officer to notice that she was waiting for instructions. How can she make an impression on a man who doesn't even see her?

She places her elbows on the desk and buries her face in her hands. Maybe she should just go for that dog-handler's job after all. At least dogs only bite you; they don't humiliate you first.

She sits up and wipes her face with her hands. She's being ridiculous. She has a head on her shoulders, she needs to use it. She can't expect Tyler to spoon-feed her all the way. She needs to prove to them she belongs here.

And she knows just how to do it. She hesitates, though. If she pulls this off, it will make Daley look bad. Then she shrugs to herself. It isn't as though he can make her life any harder than it already is. She picks up her giant floral bag and slips out of the incident room.

She sees Daley smoking and chatting with a couple of detective constables on the patio, but none of them pay her any attention. Perhaps being invisible to people isn't always such a bad thing. She hurries through the crowd at the gate, keeping her head down and avoiding eye contact with anyone. Normally she'd get some hassle off Riley and Stuart about not being in uniform, but luckily they're too busy dealing with the journalists. She sees a break in the crowd, and she's through and away.

It takes her only a couple of minutes to reach the church. The bricks of the building are blackened with ancient pollution from the city, the pointing crumbling. A cardboard thermometer by the front door proudly announces that the parish restoration fund has reached triple figures. The front door is locked, so she follows the footpath that leads round to the back. At the far end of the church-yard she sees an old fellow bent over tending the graves. The gardener, Wentworth, who Tyler and Doggett spoke to. He looks up at her for a moment and then buries his head back in his work.

She turns toward the church and the small modern extension that leans up against the back wall. Some sort of community center, she guesses. The door is propped wide open, either to let in the pitiful breeze or to let out the interminable heat.

The Reverend Thorogood looks far calmer in his own habitat than when he visited the Old Vicarage the other day. He is seated at a desk, busy with paperwork of some kind. Even though he's sitting down, she can see how tall he is, wisps of gray at his temples but still relatively handsome for his age. He'd towered over her when he was trying to get information about the body, but she hadn't let him intimidate her. Of course, she'd had Danny with her then. And her uniform.

He doesn't even look up until she speaks. "Excuse me," she says, and winces at the way her voice cracks. Not a good start.

The vicar looks up, frowning. "Yes? What is it, my dear?"

"Constable Rabbani," she says.

He looks her up and down, presumably confused by her outfit. She delves into the flowery bag in search of her warrant card, eventually finds it, and fumbles as she pulls it out.

"Oh," he says. "Yes, I see. Well, what can I do for you?"

She steps forward, still holding up her warrant card as though it's a talisman. "You were at the Old Vicarage the other day. I wondered if I could get a statement from you." Too weak. Too uncertain.

The frown deepens. "But I've already spoken to someone. A detective. DS Daley, is it? I gave him my statement an hour ago."

Rabbani drops her arm and slips the warrant card back in her bag.

"Don't you people talk to each other?"

"I'm sorry," she says. Don't apologize!

The reverend looks back down at his papers and leaves her hovering there. Then he looks up again. "Was there something else?"

She hesitates, and she knows it's a mistake even before she begins talking. "Did you know Gerald Cartwright well?" It's too late. He is unimpressed by her, has seen self-doubt in the way she's clutching the hideous bag in front of her. He stands up and moves round the desk. She steps backward instinctively and curses herself for doing so.

"Look, my dear, there's obviously been some sort of cock-up at your end. I suggest you go and read my statement and then"—he looks her up and down again, his eyes lingering on her longer than she's comfortable with; he makes Daley look amateurish in the perv stakes—"if one of your *superiors* needs something clarified I'll be happy to speak to them again." He ushers her backward with a fake smile, kicks away the doorstop, and shuts the door in her face.

Rabbani stands on the stone paving staring at the wooden door in front of her. She feels as though her face is on fire. She's never let anyone treat her like that. Not since she joined the force anyway. Not since she was given the uniform. How can everything she is, everything that she's trained for, be undermined simply because she's no longer in body armor and helmet? Why should it matter that she's replaced her checkerboard tie and hi-vis jacket for a crappy suit with no pockets? It shouldn't matter!

But it does.

"I'm back!"

There's no response. She finds Edna watching the telly; some wildlife program or other, her feet up on the Cavalier footstool. Lily doesn't bother much with the TV, unless it's the snooker. She drops the blemished newspaper onto the arm of the chair, but Edna doesn't acknowledge it.

Lily looks at Edna properly for the first time in days. The disease is taking its toll; her face shrinking in on itself like a deflating balloon. She's never been a small woman—and she's hardly that now—but she is certainly . . . diminished. All skin and hair, her eyebrows too large for her face, great hairy caterpillars that wriggle across the top of her glasses. Her breasts no longer fill the ample room inside her blouse. She has been reduced, consumed from the inside out, and Lily is sure this cancer is somehow all her fault. A punishment from God for her past sins . . . whatever they may be.

She knows what Edna would say. *Don't be silly, Lillian.* *What's done is done.*

Edna has gone on far longer than anyone predicted, but Lily knows *that's* her fault as well. She would have stopped struggling long ago if not for Lily. She's so lucky to have had her all these years. When she thinks back to how things were when . . . *there's a knock at the door.*

"Who the devil can that be?" says Mam. "At this hour?" She looks at Lily. "Well, answer it then." Lily pulls herself up out of the chair, her insides complaining where she's still sore. "And don't let them in," Mam shouts. "I'm hardly dressed for visitors." There's nothing wrong with the

way she's dressed, of course, a floral housecoat, perfectly respectable, even at this late hour.

Lily doesn't recognize the dark shape visible on the other side of the frosted panel but curiously feels no fear at opening the door at almost nine o'clock at night. Funny, really, since fear seems to be all she does feel these days. She wrenches the door open.

She recognizes the woman straightaway, of course. And yet . . . it can't be. It's as though her mind won't accept it. "Ed-na?"

"Well? Are you going to let me in, or not? It's got to be a good ten degrees cooler up here than in London."

"Oh, Edna," she cries, and hugs her fiercely.

"All right, all right, give me a chance to get through the door." But for all of the sting in her words she hugs Lily back just as hard.

The introductions are brief; Mam can't wait to get away, perhaps embarrassed to have been caught less than proper. But even so, something passes between them. It's as though in that brief introductory meeting, Edna still in her coat, cheeks flushed with cold, her mother clutching her housecoat up to her neck, they reach an understanding.

"Well," says Mam, as jolly as Lily has heard her in weeks, "I'll leave you girls to catch up. Oh, Lillian, make sure you put some clean sheets on for Edna. I'll not have her saying we're slovenly in the North. And mind you keep to your side!" She stands and addresses Edna. "I hope you sleep soundly. She's all elbows, this one." And with that she's away to bed, and they can really talk.

"What are you doing here?"

"I came to meet your mother," Edna says. "What do you think I'm doing here?"

"It's just . . . I mean, I hadn't heard anything."

"I wrote. Several times."

"I've been away," she says.

"Yes," says Edna. "I know."

The silence stretches away from them until finally Edna speaks again. "Your Auntie Vi said to say hello. I still see her sometimes, in the shelter under the theater. We were all sorry to hear about your father."

Lily smiles to acknowledge the kindness in the words, but she can see Edna knows mentioning the theater was a mistake.

"Anyway, I'm here to stay. If you'll have me."

"What? For good?" *She can't mean it!*

"As long as you can put up with me, anyway."

"What about London. What about your job?"

Edna sneers. "London's getting a bit hairy, if I'm honest. I could do with a break from it all."

"But what about the office. Mr. Grainger and the girls?"

Edna snorts. "Yes, well. I'm finished with those sorts of people. It was getting a bit much listening to them gossip all day."

Gossip about Edna. Or about her?

"I'll find something anyway. I thought I might try my hand at teaching. And in the meantime I can help out with the housework. And your mother."

Oh, yes! Yes, please, yes!

Something occurs to Lily about Mam's easy acceptance of this un-expected guest. *She knew. They've cooked this up between them. They think she can't manage by herself.* It occurs to her perhaps they're right.

"You'll need to get a job," Lily says.

"Why, Lillian Bainbridge, you sound just like your mother!" Edna laughs and Lily laughs and then Edna takes her hand. "It's going to be all right, Lillian. You've got me now."

Lily looks up at her friend. *She is not a pretty woman, not really. Handsome, maybe. And those bright hazelnut eyes . . .* fixed so in-tently on the screen.

Lily carefully wipes a tear from her cheek. She looks round at the room, the same room in which she had that conversation with

Edna all those years ago. It feels like yesterday. It feels like a life-time ago. Suddenly she hates this place. She needs to get away from it. Even if only for a short while.

Edna is looking at her, her caterpillars folded together into a thick line. "Are you going to go to the doctor's?"

"What?"

"It's happening more and more, isn't it? When are you going?"

"Monday," says Lily without thinking, and changes the subject. "I was thinking about that trip tomorrow."

And she has been thinking about it, even more so since her meeting with Joe Wentworth. She's confident now he's not behind the letters. His reaction was too strong. He had seemed surprised she would even want to talk to him. He obviously knows some-thing, but the thought of going anywhere near that man again has her breaking out in a sweat. So it must be someone else. And not a stranger, either; it must be someone they know. Most of the people they know will be on that coach. Perhaps somebody will say some-thing to give themselves away. If not, then they might return to find another letter. She will need to make an excuse to Edna so that she, Lily, is the first into the house. Then, if there is a letter, she can hide it quickly before Edna notices.

And another thought occurs to her. If there *is* a letter, then it won't have been delivered by anyone who was on the coach. At worst she will have narrowed her list of suspects.

"The Whitby outing? The coach leaves at eight. I know it's a long day, but I thought it might be nice to—"

"I thought we agreed we were better off staying home."

No, thinks Lily, *you agreed*. There's always someone making de-cisions for her. Edna, or her mother. When does she get to decide something for herself? "I thought it might be nice, that's all. A bit of sea air will be good for both of us."

"I don't think so, Lillian, do you? I don't think that would be very sensible, given the circumstances."

"Oh, bugger sensible!" *What circumstances?*

Lily hasn't seen that look on Edna's face very often. Nothing much takes her by surprise. The last time she saw it was probably when it was directed at Oscar after a particularly cheeky bit of naughtiness, and even then it would only have been mock horror; this face is genuinely shocked. But the look fades, replaced with the more usual steely determination.

"Is there something you want to tell me, Lillian?"

Lily looks down at the floor. "No . . . I mean . . . I don't know what you mean."

Edna turns back to the screen. "I thought there might be." She adjusts herself in the chair, wriggling her toes in her moccasins. It's an odd movement given the conversation they are having, almost playful in intent, her feet flopping back and forth like windscreen wipers. In *moccasins*! That she last saw propped up on the Cavalier footstool.

Edna must see the realization in Lily's eyes, because she suddenly lets loose with a devastating smile. She reaches into her cardigan and pulls out the crumpled letter. "How long has this been going on?"

Lily can't speak.

"Well?" A pause for effect, then, "Lillian Josephine Bainbridge, I asked you a question! Clearly this isn't the first, so how many have there been?"

Lily rises and fetches the first letter from its hiding place in the grandmother clock. She passes it to Edna, who reads it slowly, frowning. It takes her an inordinately long time for a message consisting of just five words. But then, Lily supposes she herself must have studied those words in much the same way when she first read them, as though the answers to their author, not to mention their meaning, might be visible on the page somewhere.

I know what you did.

"Why didn't you tell me?" Edna asks.

Lily shrugs.

"Of all the stupid—"

"Edna, please don't call me stupid. I'm not stupid."

Edna stares at her. "No," she says. "No, you are not. I'm sorry. But that is exactly why I would have expected you to tell me about this. This . . ." She waves the crumpled letters in her fist. "This isn't something we can ignore."

"I'm not ignoring it."

"Oh, Lillian, what have you done?"

"What?"

"Please don't tell me you've done something stu—" She changes what she was going to say. "Something inadvisable."

Lily sighs. She's standing in front of Edna with her hands behind her back. She begins to tell her everything, just as though she's reporting to the headmistress. How easily she gives up control. Edna listens silently, nods occasionally. Finally, Lily mentions her meeting with Joe Wentworth.

When she is finished, Edna says, "You are to go nowhere near that man ever again." As though she has any intention of doing so! "If he talks to you, you will tell me. Immediately."

Lily bristles at this but finds herself saying, "I won't. Of course I won't. But I'm sure he isn't responsible for this. It's why I think we should go on this trip. We can talk to people. See if anyone is behaving unusually."

"Lillian, this is not a game!" Edna slams her hand down on the arm of her chair. "This isn't some pulp-fiction detective novel, you do realize that?"

"Of course I do, Edna, I—"

Edna tuts over her. "Such nonsense. Of course we are not going to Whitby, and there's an end to it." She folds the letters in her hand and tucks them back into her cardigan, taking ownership, taking back the reins.

Lily is furious. Edna has no right to cut her out of this. "Well, you can please yourself," she says, "but I think I'm going to go."

"You can think again."

"I have, and I'm going."

Edna doesn't reply, and Lily realizes she is physically exhausted. It must have taken every last ounce of strength she had to get up the stairs and carry the footstool back down. It makes Lily wonder how she knew. She must have, of course. How had Lily given herself away? Perhaps it was earlier when Edna asked what she had been doing upstairs. Is she really so easy to read? Or is there some part of that conversation she can't remember? Lily wants to cry. To be unable to trust your own memory; it is so terribly unfair. But she refuses to ask. She *will* remember!

Lily turns away and moves into the kitchen to start on dinner. In this way the conversation ends, since Edna will not shout between rooms and has no energy left for pursuit. Lily wonders why she's never thought of this before. It's the perfect escape strategy.

This won't be the end of it, of course. Edna will raise the subject again at bedtime, but far from dreading the argument, Lily finds herself ready for it. She has made her decision. This time she will not quietly acquiesce. She has done far too much of that in her life already. She knows Edna only wants to protect her, but it is becoming increasingly obvious to both of them that she won't be able to for very much longer. It's Lily's turn to do the protecting now, and to do that she needs to find out what happened—what she did—to make someone attempt to blackmail her. She is determined to piece it together, whether Edna likes it or not.

———

When Tyler gets to the pub, Oscar is waiting outside. He's sitting in a silver BMW convertible, the top down, the black flames of his tattoo wrapped round the headrest of the passenger seat. "Get in," he says.

Tyler folds his arms across his chest. "Come inside, Oscar. We need to talk."

"We will. It's just . . ." The cocky Oscar is gone again, replaced by the vulnerable one. "Please? I want to show you something."

Tyler hesitates for a moment and then climbs into the car.

They pick their way through the early evening traffic, negotiating tram tracks, bus gates, and the one-way system, until they are out of the city center and winding along the curves of the A57 toward Manchester. The Snake Pass. Sharp bends give way to intermittent stretches of long, straight tarmac. When they reach these spots, Oscar puts his foot down, taking the car to its limit before braking hard again for the next turn. They travel in silence. Tyler wants to ask where they are headed but refuses to give Oscar the satisfaction. The erratic driving feels like a challenge, a deliberate attempt at breaking rules, of disregarding Tyler's authority. So he says nothing, just closes his eyes, slumps in his seat, and forces himself to relax. With the top down on the convertible the wind blasts across his face, but the air is warm and far from unpleasant. Tyler smiles to himself.

How does he end up in these situations? He still hasn't decided what, if anything, to tell Jordan, but he's damned if he'll pose as Doggett's honey trap. Then again, isn't that exactly what he's doing right now? This is hardly a conventional interview with a suspect. He wonders why he hasn't heard anything from the DI yet. Perhaps because he knew what Tyler would do all along. And then he wonders why Doggett didn't mention that he used to play golf with Gerald Cartwright. Doesn't that make *him* guilty of not declaring interests as well? But then, playing golf with someone and sleeping with someone are hardly the same thing.

The car slows for another bend. Tyler opens his eyes and sees a set of traffic lights ahead of them. The lights change to green, but Oscar takes the left turn at the junction. Tyler recognizes the place as Ladybower Reservoir. He remembers one particular Sunday when his father brought them here on a family outing. And he remembers how they'd left early when Richard was called into work. Jude sulked half the way home until Richard shouted at him, while their mother spent the entire journey in silence. Tyler kept his eyes on her all the way. He knew something was wrong even then. How did the others not? Why didn't he say something? Looking back, he supposes it wouldn't have made much difference. She must have already made her decision by then. A couple of weeks later she walked out of their lives for good.

Oscar stops the car in a small unpaved parking lot and switches off the engine. Still he doesn't speak, but gets out of the car and walks to the edge of the reservoir. Tyler takes his time to catch up.

The evening sun glints across the surface of the huge man-made lake that stretches out before them. Beyond it and all around them, the Y-shaped Derwent Valley is lush with green foliage, and the occasional splash of pink heather. They stand together, looking out across the wide expanse of golden water.

"The body we found," Tyler begins.

"I know." Oscar wraps his arms around himself. "I got a call from a reporter at the *Star* earlier."

Damn Elliot for letting that out. "I'm sorry. I didn't want to tell you over the phone."

Oscar shrugs. "It's not exactly unexpected, is it?"

The water laps gently at the shore just a few inches from their feet.

"My father used to bring me here," Oscar says. "With Edna and Lil. They told me the story of how they built the place during the war. Do you know it?"

He does, but he lets Oscar tell it. How they flooded the two villages of Ashopton and Derwent, first demolishing one but leaving the other just as it was.

"When the water level's low," he goes on, "you can still see it. Like a drowned world. The clock tower of the church sticking right up out of the water. At least, you used to be able to."

"I think they blew it up for safety reasons."

The sun is beginning to drop behind the hills.

"I think about this place sometimes," Oscar says. "A village frozen in time." He moves forward, crouches down close to the edge of the water. "I've been waiting six years to find out what happened to him, but nothing's really changed, has it? I thought things might be different now. Knowing for sure that he's never coming back."

"It takes time," says Tyler. But only because it's what you're supposed to say, not because he believes it.

There's a single crystal-clear droplet of water sliding down Oscar's gaunt cheek. It winks in the dying light of the sun.

"You asked why I joined the police," Tyler says. Oscar looks up at him. "When I was sixteen my father committed suicide. I joined the force to get closer to him, a man who consistently let me down, right to the end."

Oscar takes Tyler's hand and squeezes it. A car speeds past them on the main road, its horn blaring as one of the occupants leans out of the window and shouts some obscenity at them that's lost in the slipstream.

"I'm sorry I didn't tell you about Sophie," Oscar says.

"It's not my business."

"I hoped it might be." Oscar looks away again, out over the lake. "I thought maybe afterward, you know, when this is all over . . . ?"

Tyler lets go of Oscar's hand. "We should get back," he says, as the last sliver of sun slips behind the hills and dark shadows turn the water to ink.

Tyler lets the hot water pelt his face, massaging life back into his features. He imagines what it might be like to come home to something other than an empty flat, a quick shower, a microwaved meal. To have someone to confide in, to talk to about his fucked-up childhood. Someone he could go to about his concerns regarding Doggett. Why didn't the man tell him that he knew Cartwright? And the fire at the house that he's sure now, more than ever, is somehow connected to Gerald Cartwright's tattered corpse. And the painting.

Not that he could share any of those things with Oscar even if he were here. Strangely, the image that forms in his head is of the broad frame of the fire officer wrapped in thin gray cotton. Tyler lathers his hands with shower gel and rubs them across his body, working the kinks out of his tired limbs.

As he turns off the shower he hears someone banging loudly on the front door. He grabs a towel and steps out of the bath, drips his way quickly into the corridor.

Another pounding threatens to take the hinges off. He looks through the fisheye lens and sees Doggett's fun-house-hall-of-mirrors nose filling his vision. He can make out the sharp brown hairs in his nostrils. He opens the door.

Doggett looks him up and down, his fingers rapping out his

theme tune on the doorframe. "Get your kecks on, son, the SOCO boys have dug something up."

The water drips from Tyler's body and gathers in cold pools around his feet. "What sort of something?" he asks.

Doggett's fingers stop abruptly.

"Another body sort of something."

day four

San Francisco, 1906

You've always loved that Judy Garland song. It reminds you of your mother, her broken voice warbling in competition with Judy's, not helped by the vodka and Coke in her hand. For years you thought San Francisco was some sort of magical place, like Narnia. When things got bad, near the end, you would lie staring at the wardrobe door, willing the doors to open and whisk you away to that fairy-tale land in your mother's song.

San Franciscans talk about "The Big One," the moment when their house-of-cards city will be swallowed by the San Andreas Fault. They wear their vulnerability like a badge of honor, partying hard, awaiting the inevitable end. You'd like to think of yourself as that sort of person.

Did they think it was the end back then? The morning of April 18, 1906. 5:15 a.m. The earthquake measured 8:25 on the Richter scale. It lasted for just one minute. That doesn't sound long, does it?

Just sixty seconds. But how long does it feel when the earth is moving under your feet? With buildings cascading all around you, and explosions ripping holes in the sidewalk. Ruptured gas mains blowing concrete and dust high into the clear bay sky.

Then come the flames, roaring down Market Street. Fire officers set dynamite charges in order to destroy buildings and create artificial firebreaks. Unfortunately, the fire officers had no training in this, and ended up contrib-

163

uting to the problem more than solving it. As word spread that their in-surance policies didn't cover earthquake damage, desperate homeowners and crafty businessmen began setting fire to their own properties. But the quake had ruptured the water main, and all attempts to bring the fires under control soon began to falter. People trapped in burning buildings begged the police to shoot them rather than be burned alive. The police obliged.

Three thousand people were dead before the end. But then, that wasn't the end, was it? There's never an end for those who survive. They have to go on living with the memories, trying to forget.

Do you remember the first time he took you to that place? The cold draft from the wind whistling up through the slatted floorboards. You thought it would just be the two of you, but he had other plans. He told you that you didn't have to do anything you didn't want to. You remember how his face changed when the others arrived, and you realized you didn't know this man at all and that even if you did you no longer had any choice. You remember the pictures and the trophies lining the walls, boys and girls in green and brown uniforms looking down on you. You remember how they watched and they laughed.

But you survived all that. And more than that. It wasn't the Big One for you.

The Big One is still to come.

POSTED BY **thefirewatcher** AT 9:57 AM

5 COMMENTS

KHainsworth said . . .

Dude, what's the Judy Garland song?

helenM1972 said . . .

It's San Francisco from the 1936 musical of the same name about the 1906 Earthquake. It stars Jeanette MacDonald and Clark Gable and was nominated for 6 academy awards.

RDAtack said . . .

Earthquakes are no longer measured on the Richter scale but by means of the Moment Magnitude Scale: *Mw1* where w represents the mechanical work accomplished. The moment magnitude is a dimensionless number: *Mw = 2/3(log10M0–16:0)*. Although this method wasn't developed until the 1970s.

Dublinsmouse said . . .

Fuck off @RDAtack you boring wanker

PerryA said . . .

Actually, the Richter scale was invented in 1935 so we can only really guess the magnitude of the SF earthquake. Fun fact! I used to work in the Audiffred Building, one of the few buildings in SF to survive the quake *and* the demolition. It was slated for demolition to create a fire-break but the owner gave the firefighters beer so they'd skip it.

DarkHorsey said . . .

(This comment has been removed due to inappropriate content. For a full explanation of terms and conditions please contact the administrator.)

The second body lies curled in a shallow grave of half brick and rubble, returned in death to the fetal position in which it began life. Since the extraction of Gerald Cartwright, the SOCO team has been painstakingly sifting through the debris behind the ruined wall, a routine search for evidence that has unearthed something far from routine. Tyler inches his way backward out of the partially demolished cellar wall and straightens.

Behind him, Doggett shuffles his feet in the rubble. "Definitely a woman?" he asks.

Elliot looks paler than ever, his white scene-of-crime suit shining in the light of the arc lamps. "Aye."

"The body's been here longer," Tyler points out. The skeletal remains are further decayed than Cartwright's, despite their being buried deeper.

"My guess is ten years plus." Elliot turns and places a gloved hand on Tyler's shoulder. "You'll notice the use of the word 'guess,' mind."

Doggett snorts. "All right, Doc, we won't hold you to anything. God forbid you should give us any specifics."

Elliot's face creases with a tight smile. "How's that lovely wife of yours, Jim?"

"Still banging her gym instructor as far as I know. Speaking of wives . . . ?"

"The missing Cynthia Cartwright?" Elliot shrugs.

Tyler considers that possibility. "If it is her, then Edna Burnside lied to us. She said she spoke to Cynthia after she left."

"There was a mistress as well," Doggett says. "A Sandra or Sarah or something or other. We never did track her down. Not to mention any number of prostitutes who visited the place. Some of them might not have been missed."

Elliot gestures to the other SOCOs to carry on, and the three of them move as one away from the body and back toward the cellar steps.

"Did you know her?" Doggett asks Elliot.

"Who?"

"Cynthia Cartwright."

"No." Elliot frowns. "Why do you ask?"

"You knew Gerald."

"I played golf with the man. As did you, I believe." He's calm enough outwardly, but there's an edge to his voice. "Am I a suspect now, Jim?"

"You did go to one of his parties."

"With my wife, Loretta. I can assure you it wasn't anything like the ones written about in the papers. If memory serves, your DCI Jordan was in attendance as well. Perhaps you'd like to ask *her* what went on?"

Doggett holds his gaze for a few seconds while Elliot stares him out, then he shrugs and turns to Tyler. "Let's get out of here."

They leave Elliot in the cellar muttering obscenities under his breath that call Doggett's parentage into question. The DI either misses them or chooses to ignore them. They climb the uneven stone steps back up into the house.

"Why didn't you tell me *you* knew Cartwright?" he asks Doggett as they walk back along the long corridor to the front door.

"You didn't ask."

"Wouldn't you call *that* a conflict of interest?"

"I don't know, would *you*?"

From ahead of them there comes the sound of raised voices. They emerge into the early morning air, the darkness ripped away by the stark illumination of police floodlights. Oscar Cartwright is barely recognizable. He seems almost possessed. There are dark bags under his eyes, and his forehead is furrowed with deep lines. The floppy fringe of hair has been swept back off his face, revealing the early signs of a receding hairline and a glimpse into the future. It has been only a few hours since their conversation at the lake, and yet the man looks ten years older. He doesn't look as though he's slept, which raises the question of where he's been all night.

"It's my *fucking* house!" he shouts at Daley. This is neither the vulnerable, boyish Oscar nor the self-assured, cocky lover. This is a new version. One not seen before. Angry and ugly.

Tyler claps a hand on Daley's shoulder and steps around him. "This is a crime scene, *Mr.* Cartwright." He emphasizes the title, trying to make it clear that however things were between them earlier, it's different now. "You can't go in there."

Oscar deflates a little. "Look, Ad— . . . DS Tyler. I just want to know what's going on."

"Who says anything's going on?" Doggett answers for him.

"The reporters . . . they said . . ." Oscar trails off; the vulnerable boy is back with his big glassy eyes and quivering lip. He turns to Doggett. "You must be here for something. It's the middle of the *fucking* night!"

The DI smiles, but there's nothing pleasant about it. "And what are *you* doing here, Oscar? You were told not to return until we gave you the all clear."

"I was visiting a friend in the village."

"It's a bit early for house calls, isn't it?"

Oscar doesn't answer.

"Since you are here, perhaps we could have a little chat?" Doggett gestures across to his car. "If you'd like to step into my office."

When Tyler moves to go with them, Doggett blocks him with a hand across his chest. "Maybe I should handle this."

He wants to argue but he's suddenly aware Daley is still there, watching, taking it all in. They stand together and watch Doggett and Oscar pile into the battered old Saab. Daley frowns, his bald head wrinkling with the effort. "How come he's not using the incident room?"

Tyler glances at the car and then back at Daley. It seems unlikely he noticed Oscar's slip with his name. On the other hand, the man *is* a detective, even if he's a shit one. "I don't know, mate. Maybe he doesn't want him in there with all those blown-up glossy photos of his mummified father's corpse."

Daley's lip curls and he storms off back to the incident room, no doubt to finish an interrupted game of solitaire.

Tyler relaxes a little and turns back to watch the car. There are two dark silhouettes visible in the pre-dawn light of Doggett's car, one with its head bowed while the other gesticulates wildly. It's while Tyler's watching them, trying to imagine what's being said, that he smells the smoke. The early morning air is thick and still, and at first he thinks he might be imagining it. But gradually the scent grows stronger and he becomes certain.

Despite the early hour, the news about the second body is well and truly out, and he has to inch his way through the flashing white lights of press photographers, his hand placed firmly on the car's horn. He drives through the village slowly, windows rolled down, letting the smell come to him on a new breeze. Woodsmoke. Then he sees it, an intermittent twinkle of blue and orange lights through the trees that guides him to his destination.

It's a big wooden structure, a church hall or something. At least, it was. Black smoke billows high into the night sky, but there's a relaxed nonchalance about the firefighters that tells him the hard fight is over. This is mopping-up work. A uniformed police officer he doesn't recognize detaches himself from the operation and trots over to the car. Tyler raises his warrant card.

"Old scout hut, sir," says the officer. "They've got it under control."

"Arson?"

"Looks like it. Probably just kids, little bastards."

"Can you keep me informed? You know where we are." He's about to pull off again when he thinks of something else. "Who's the fire officer in charge of the investigation?"

"Enfield, sir. Paul Enfield." He looks over his shoulder. "He hasn't arrived yet, but I can probably get his contact details."

"That's all right," Tyler tells him, remembering the small white business card Daley threw at him. "I think I have them already."

He sits there for a moment and considers. He's not keen to head back to the vicarage again, not with Oscar still there. He pulls out his mobile and the card from Guy Daley and dials the number.

Paul Enfield is curt with Tyler on the phone, no doubt because of Guy Daley's poor attitude, but the fire officer is still keen to meet and so, forty minutes later, Tyler is pulling up outside the brand-new headquarters of the South Yorkshire Fire and Rescue service. As he gets out of the car he stifles a yawn. It's not even 8 a.m. and it already feels like he's done a full day's work. Then he remembers, he has.

The building is an orange-bricked sore on the sandstone face of the city. Tyler gives the designers their due—they've at least *tried* to insert some architecture into the project; the front is dissected by a ground-to-roof slash of colored glass. Unfortunately, or quite deliberately for all he knows, the chosen colors—reds, yellows, and oranges—appear to be licking their way up the side of the building like so many PVC flames. Inside, a smell of fried and baked goods hangs in the air, mixed with a chemical odor, like burning plastic. He sits in an enormous tub of a chair in the reception area, all chrome and faux black leather, his back to the flaming window. It throws panels of colored light over his head and across the tiled floor.

"DS Tyler?" A giant of a man looms over him, his broad frame blocking out the fluorescent glare from the ceiling. His black skin is mottled by the colored light from the window, making him look like something from a psychedelic movie from the '70s. He smiles broadly, exposing a row of even white teeth. "Paul Enfield," he says, extending a deep-ridged palm. Tyler takes it, the calluses rough against his fingers. He stands, still holding the man's hand so they end up standing too close to each other. Enfield is half a head taller; Tyler has to crane his neck to meet the man's eyes. He becomes aware of a tight gray T-shirt that cuts into biceps the size of most people's thighs. They let go of each other's hands.

"Would you like a coffee?" Enfield holds out a tree-trunk arm in the direction of what Tyler supposes is the cafeteria. The smell of burning plastic, however, forces him to decline and, whether or not Enfield takes this as a slight, the smile fades. He pulls across another of the gigantic faux-leather tub seats with a casual single-handed movement. On him it looks normal sized.

"Thank you for seeing me," Tyler says, sitting back down. "Firstly, I should apologize for my colleague."

Enfield shrugs but says nothing. He's clearly still smarting from Daley's cold shoulder at the incident room. He pushes a folder across the table. Tyler opens it and flicks through the reports inside. "Three fires in the Castledene area over three consecutive nights: a bus shelter, an allotment shed, and the scout hut you saw this morning."

"Linked?"

Enfield stares at him and raises a thick eyebrow. "Two fires within a mile of each other in the same week? That's not exactly within statistical norms. What do you think the chances are of three?" He speaks quietly and precisely, but there's an edge to his words.

"Arson, then?"

"There were traces of accelerant at each of the scenes. Petrol. We'll probably narrow it down to a specific company, but other than that, it could come from any forecourt in the country."

Tyler thinks about the words of the officer this morning. *Probably just kids*. "Are we talking about a single arsonist or a group?"

Enfield hesitates. "One," he says.

"Why? Why not just a bunch of kids messing around?"

Enfield brushes a square jaw with thumb and finger, looks down at the table while he thinks. He seems to be working out exactly what he wants to say before he opens his mouth. "There's usually other stuff first," he says. "Cigarette butts, candles, that sort of thing. There's no evidence of this kind of experimental fire setting in the area. Castledene's a quiet country village. They don't have kids roaming the street at night setting light to things. If they do, someone notices and the kids' parents get a visit from a concerned neighbor." His brow creases with faint lines. "I suppose, to be honest, this just *feels* different."

"Different how?"

Enfield frowns again, apparently at a loss to know how to articulate what he means.

Tyler lets it go. "What made you come to us?"

Another long pause; he can almost see the cogs grinding. Enfield is clearly not a stupid man, just careful. But what is he frightened of giving away exactly? "The fire at the vicarage," he says. "I think it's related."

"What do you know about it?"

"Only what the records say. I came to Sheffield a few months ago, so it was before my time. I assume you've read the file?"

"The file says it was kids. Squatters. Why do you think it's related?"

Enfield just stares at him, but this time Tyler waits patiently for an answer. After a few moments Enfield says, "Considering what you found out there this week, I think we're moving out of the realms of coincidence, don't you?"

"I agree. But is that all you have? Coincidence? Or is there something more concrete? Something that indicates this is the same arsonist as six years ago."

Enfield frowns again while he thinks.

It's excruciating. Tyler tries to bite his lip, and fails. "Look, if you know something that relates to my case, I need to hear it."

Enfield snorts out a laugh. "Jesus Christ, one minute you're not interested; the next you're accusing me of withholding information." His hands tighten on the arms of the chairs. "If you don't want to hear this, don't waste my time."

A temper. He thinks before he acts because he's a big man with a short fuse. Tyler holds his hands up in mock surrender. "Sorry. I just want to know what you think. You clearly have more experience of these things than I do."

The hands relax and Enfield smiles, the tension gone as quickly as it appeared. He laughs again, but this time he seems genuinely amused. "Nice try at buttering me up."

"I thought I was being subtle."

"As a sledgehammer."

He has a nice smile, nicer than the scowl anyway.

"Same arsonist, or not? Gut feeling."

"Six years is a long time," Enfield says, rubbing his chin again. "Arsonists are creatures of habit. It would be highly unusual for someone to stop setting fires for that length of time and then start up again."

"But not impossible? What might cause it?"

"Pyromania is an impulse-control disorder, a mental illness. The fire starting is either for gratification or to relieve tension. In either case, a major event in the perpetrator's life could stop the cycle. And restart it."

"A death in the family?"

Enfield nods slowly. "It's possible."

"What about the discovery of a body?"

The hand moves round to the back of his head, and there's a crunch as the man cracks his neck. "There's another possibility. He could have been in prison, or he could have moved to the area recently from somewhere else. I can look into that."

"'He'?"

Enfield grins again. "Ninety percent of pyromaniacs are men. Other than that there's nothing to exclude the possibility this is a woman." Then the brow furrows and he grows serious again. "Look. I've seen this before. I can't prove it, I don't have the evidence you're looking for, but this is a pyromaniac. Sooner or later someone is going to get hurt, probably by accident, but still, that's why I came to you. You need to take this seriously."

Tyler meets the man's eyes and nods solemnly. "Will you keep me up to date?"

Enfield extracts another of the small white rectangles and scribbles a number on the back. "My mobile," he says. "You can reach me on that. Anytime." There's something about the pause before the last word that suggests something more.

Tyler takes out his own card and they make the exchange silently, fingers brushing lightly against one another. They stand and shake hands, and once again the handshake lingers a moment too long. Then the fire officer is walking away without another word. As he reaches the lift, though, Enfield turns and glances back, and Tyler is sure he didn't imagine it. Then the giant of a man ducks his head and disappears into the lift.

When he gets back to the Old Vicarage, Doggett is standing in the driveway.

"Where the bloody hell have you been?"

"Auditioning for *The X-Factor*."

Tyler sketches out his visit to the fire station and the possible link between their case and the recent arson attacks.

The DI grunts and stares up at the scorched bricks around the windows. "I'm not convinced."

"I felt sure you wouldn't be."

Behind Doggett, Rabbani emerges from the incident room with a sheet of paper in her hand and tries to catch Tyler's eye.

"What do you think, then?" Doggett asks.

"I think he might be right."

"I felt sure you would do. All right, look into it, but let's get some sleep first. Neither of us are gonna be use nor ornament if we don't get at least a couple of hours."

He wants to ask about Oscar, but with Rabbani hovering within earshot this isn't the time. "I've set up an interview with Michael Denham this afternoon."

"The solicitor? You think he's involved?"

"I got the feeling he might be trying to hide something. He certainly didn't want us talking to his daughter."

"Could just be a protective father."

"I don't know, there was something about the way she tried to distance herself from Gerald, making out they only met a couple of times. I felt she was being a little disingenuous."

"Disingenuous, is it?" Doggett's smirking at him now. "Well, we can't have that now, can we? You'd better speak to her again." Then, without turning round, he shouts to Rabbani, "All right, Miss Marple. Out with it. What have you got for us?"

Rabbani steps forward. "I've been looking into the vicar, sir?" She's clutching the paper in her hand as though her life depends on it. Or at the very least her career. "You said you thought he might be a bit dodgy and—"

"All right, luv, final score, eh?"

She hesitates, mouth open.

"He means give us the highlights," Tyler says before Doggett can start shouting again.

There's the tiniest trace of frustration on Rabbani's face, but she hides it well. "When Gerald Cartwright first put his company together, he had a number of regular business partners, including a bloke named Felbridge. I checked them all out, but Felbridge is the one that stands out. He's got convictions for drug possession and assault. He never did any time, though. I'm guessing his money, or his friend's money, got him off. Then, in the late eighties, Felbridge disappears."

Doggett looks at Tyler and shakes his head in mock frustration. "I hope this is going somewhere, lass, because I'm not getting any younger here."

Rabbani bites her lip. "Felbridge changed his name by deed poll, sir. Shortly before he was ordained. Sebastian Felbridge is the Reverend Sebastian Thorogood, vicar of All Souls Church, Castledene."

Doggett's mouth widens into an evil smile. "I knew that *bastard* name was made up!"

"There's more." Rabbani thrusts the page in her hand at Tyler, and he reads it as she speaks. "Thorogood came to Castledene in 1995 after an allegation were made about him at his previous post. A woman accused him of molesting her. The case was thrown out when the woman withdrew her complaint, but guess who arranged his transfer for him?"

"Mister Gerald *Bollocking* Cartwright, by any chance?" Doggett doesn't wait for a reply. "Right, I'll bet you my last pint of Blonde he paid the woman off as well. Come on, then." Doggett's already heading for the car. "Rabbani," he shouts over his shoulder.

"Sir?"

"Well done, girl. Top of the class!"

Rabbani shakes her head at Tyler behind the DI's retreating back, but she's all smiles.

"Well," Tyler asks, "are you coming with us then, or not?"

Her mouth drops open again. "Yes, sir," she says, beaming at him. There's something about the way she carries herself to the car, her chest puffed out with pride, that makes him smile.

Unusually, Edna is the first one up that morning. By the time Lily has donned her dressing gown and negotiated the stairs she is already standing at the stove.

"I'll do that."

"I can manage."

Lily settles for making the toast. As she takes the loaf from the bread bin she pretends not to hear Edna grunting and wheezing with exhaustion. She slices the dark-crusted bread and avoids watching Edna's hooked hands as they attempt to drop eggs into the saucepan, each one sending up a splash of scalding water that reaches her fingertips. Edna steps away from the hob and stands breathing quietly, rubbing her fingers together while Lily browns the toast under the grill. Eventually, and without a word, she shuffles into the dining room, leaving Lily to take over.

Lily finds herself wondering how much of all this is an act, this sudden frailty that seems almost designed to make her change her mind. It's curious; that thought would never have occurred to her before today.

As they eat she says, "I'll get the papers before I go."

"Can't *she* do it for once?" Edna snaps.

"*She* did it yesterday."

"No, she didn't. *You* did!"

Lily has to think about this. "Well, anyway, I don't mind."

The rest of their breakfast passes in silence.

When she gets back from the paper shop, Lily helps Edna wash, and lays out a blouse for the day. She avoids mentioning the increased police activity next door. She doesn't want to consider what that might be about and besides, she is certain it won't help her cause.

Once Edna's comfortable in front of the telly, Lily begins to get ready. She's buttoning her cardigan when Edna finally breaks the silence. "Please, Lillian. I'm begging you not to go."

Lily moves to the window and looks out at the bird table. "It's only for the day, and then, when I get back, I'll see about getting some of the garden furniture in. They said on the news this morning that the weather's going to break." A tiny female blackbird and a great, fat wood pigeon are battling for supremacy. *Surely* she's allowed one day.

"Lillian, I'm not trying to be mean but . . . you know how things are, you can't just go swanning off—"

"Mrs. Blackie's back. I knew she'd like those mealworms."

"Lillian, will you listen to me, you infuriating woman!"

She can see Edna's reflection struggling to stand. She fights the urge to turn and rush to help. Let her struggle. Edna falls backward, frustrated, and bangs the arm of her chair weakly with her palm. Lily focuses on the blackbird, beak dipping into the tray on the bird table while the wood pigeon flutters and splutters around it in ungainly bursts of flight.

"Ungrateful woman," Edna says, changing tack. "After all I've done for you. You might at least listen when I'm trying to protect you."

Lily tries to block out the voice, but she can't.

"You don't understand, Lillian. It's not your fault. It's mine in all likelihood. Or your mother's. We've sheltered you too long, made you vulnerable. You can't trust other people; you know that."

"Like Gerald, you mean." She whispers it so quietly she's not even sure she says it aloud, though Edna's silence is testimony to the fact she has.

"You're right," Edna says finally. "*I* was wrong that time. But don't you see? That proves my point. Look what happens when we take strangers into our lives. We're better off on our own. Just you and me."

"And Oscar," says Lily.

If they hadn't let Gerald into their lives, they wouldn't have Oscar. And how could they have known about Gerald back then anyway?

But that wasn't how it was really, was it? She thinks hard. She *did* know. She turns from the window . . . *and opens the door to a thickset stranger in a camel-hair coat. She knows immediately who he is. He looks so exactly like an older version of his father that a question she's been asking herself for fifty years resolves itself.*

She lets him in, and he tells her how he's tracked her down. She's scared. Edna will be home from Mrs. High's retirement do soon. What will she say to this stranger in their house? But when Edna gets home she's delighted to meet Gerald. They get on wonderfully, as though they've known each other for years. And then, later, when the church sells off the Old Vicarage, Edna tells her it's a sign. Gerald and Cynthia need a place away from the city, and this would be ideal for them. It's less than six months before he and Cynthia move in for good. Edna and Gerald plan everything together. Lily and Cynthia have no say about anything; it's their only real bond.

One day Cynthia comes to the cottage crying and tells them she's pregnant. Oh, happy news! Edna hugs her and tells her it's just hormones playing her up, but they both notice the bruise on Cyn's cheek and . . .

"Lillian! Lily! My God, Lily, wake up!"

Lily is lying on the floor. What *is* she doing down here?

"That's it, try to get up now." Edna inches forward in her chair, leaning over her.

Lily stands slowly and brushes down her slacks. "I'm fine, just a dizzy spell."

"I thought you banged your head. Oh, Lillian, please ring the doctor!"

"I will, don't fuss." Her arm feels a bit tender; she'll have a bruise there tomorrow.

"This is what I've been trying to tell you. You need help. You never have been able to look after yourself on your own. Look at the trouble you get into."

"Please don't be spiteful."

"How are you going to manage when I'm gone?" She's speaking loudly enough that Her-Next-Door will hear. "Look how it was when your mother died. Who made all the arrangements then, eh? And what about that night? What would you have done without me then, Lillian Bainbridge?" Edna stops, exhausted by her own tirade.

What about that night? Does she mean the night her mother died? Lily doesn't think so. She could just ask but . . . then Edna will know how bad things have got. She needs to be the strong one this time. She needs to work it all out . . . somehow.

Lily turns back to the window in time to see the blackbird lift itself off the table and into the air, its beak full of tasty mealworms. Of the wood pigeon there's no sign. "The coach will be here soon," she says. "Do you want me to fetch you anything before I go?"

"You're not to go! Do you hear me?"

But Lily is already leaving the room. "I think I'll wait for them down by the road. I won't be too late. If there's any problem, I'm sure someone will have a mobile telephone."

Edna calls out to her, "Lillian! Lillian, please! There's no need for this. I can deal with the letters. I already have a good idea who might be—"

"Cheerio then," she shouts as cheerfully as she can manage. She steps forward across the threshold.

"Lillian! Lily, wait!"

Lily closes the door, cutting off the sound of Edna's increasing desperation.

The new vicarage has none of the grandeur of the old one, but it would certainly be cheaper to heat. When they arrive, Thorogood, or Felbridge, has his coat on.

"You're lucky to have caught me, actually. I was just on my way out the door. Coach trip."

Doggett smiles widely. "This won't take long, Reverend."

The three of them are ushered into a perfectly presented living room while Mrs. Thorogood fusses over bringing them tea.

"That's all right, Mrs. T," Doggett tells her. "If we could just have a few moments with your husband."

"Are you sure?" she persists. "It's no bother. I've just put the kettle on and—"

"Enough, Jean!" Thorogood doesn't quite shout, but his wife jumps nevertheless.

"Yes," she says quietly. "Sorry." She withdraws, closing the door behind her.

"I'm sorry about that—"

But Doggett cuts him off. "Right, you can cut the crap now, Felbridge."

"Ah . . ." Thorogood sits down in an armchair and sighs as though a huge weight has come off his shoulders. "I knew it would come out. Just a matter of time. I think I'm actually rather relieved." He looks up at them. "It's not nearly as bad as you think."

Doggett starts twitching his way around the room.

"Why don't you tell us about it then?" Tyler asks.

"It's not a very pretty story, I'm afraid. Fell in with the wrong crowd, the usual sort of thing, you know."

Doggett looks at Tyler and then at Rabbani. "I'm not sure we do, do we?"

Thorogood ignores him and plows on. "Drugs, Detective Inspector. That was the root of it. A few years later, and"—he actually looks up to the ceiling—"thanks to my calling, I cleaned up the act. In case you think I'm some sort of fraud, you'll find my superiors are fully aware of my past transgressions. I have nothing to hide. The name change was just something to distance myself from a terrible time in my life."

"What about Bow Chapel?" Tyler asks him. "Was that a terrible time as well?"

Thorogood keeps his composure. "The allegations made against me were false, as I'm sure you are aware. There were no charges brought against me." He turns back to Doggett. "It's a hazard of the job, I'm afraid. Sometimes vulnerable people lash out at authority figures."

"So your good friend Gerald Cartwright arranged for you to end up here?" Doggett asks.

Thorogood straightens in his chair. "I knew Gerry from Eton. He used to come in and give talks sometimes, and mentor some of the students. We lost touch for a while during the 'Wilderness Years,' as I like to call them. You're right, he did donate a sizable sum to the church restoration fund, but it wasn't a condition, as such. I'm not naïve, though. I imagine Gerry made some sort of request. That was Gerry, after all, always putting others before himself. He knew I was looking to move away from London. In my profession, the mud tends to stick. I imagine it's much the same in your own." He addresses this to Tyler, and the words strike a little too close to home.

Thorogood stands up again. "Now that that's cleared up, was there anything else?"

"We're not finished yet, Mr. Felbridge."

Thorogood makes an effort to control his voice. "I believe we are, Detective Inspector." He glances at his watch. "I have a coach full of pensioners waiting for me, and I don't see why—"

"*Sit down, man!*"

Rabbani jumps, and Thorogood drops back into the chair like he has been punched. In the silence that follows, a phone rings somewhere in the house. The vicar keeps his hands folded in his lap but can't hide the fact they're shaking.

Doggett towers over him. "I want to know what happened to Gerald Cartwright, and I want to know what *you* know about it."

"I don't . . . know anything."

There's a timid knocking on the door, and the mousey wife pokes her head back into the living room. "It's the phone, Sebastian. The driver is getting a little worried about the traffic and . . ." She trails off, picking up on the tension in the room. Then she adds, "I can take a message if—"

"No, that's fine, Jean, thank you. I'll take it."

The woman looks relieved to have got it right for once and makes a hasty retreat.

"I really do have to be somewhere." Thorogood seems fortified by his wife's submissiveness, reassured who wears the trousers in this house. "Unless you plan to arrest me?"

Doggett drags the silence out for a moment. "All right, Sebastian, go tend to your flock. Just don't go leaving the country now, will you?"

The man virtually leaps out of the chair, and they follow him into the hallway, where his wife hovers with the phone in her hand. The vicar takes the receiver from her but waits while his wife shows them out.

Before the front door fully closes Doggett shouts his final farewell loud enough to reach whoever's on the phone. "One last piece of advice, Reverend. Next time you change your name and move away to avoid the scandal of sexual assault allegations, you might want to pick something a bit less obvious."

The door closes firmly in their faces.

"Did you enjoy that?"

Doggett smiles. "It was mildly amusing." He sets off fast, crossing the road back to the Old Vicarage, leaving Tyler and Rabbani to follow.

"We need to keep an eye on that one," he says as they catch up. "Rabbani?"

"Sir."

"Do a bit more digging. I'm not taking his word for it that this past of his is all out in the open and aboveboard. If we can make a few waves for him while we're at it, so much the better."

"Yes, sir." Rabbani clears her throat. "Sir?"

"Yes, Police Constable Rabbani."

Rabbani hesitates. "Sorry, sir, it's just . . ."

"Spit it out."

"Well, I were wondering if we actually learned anything there."

Doggett grins. "What did we learn, DS Tyler?"

"We learned that the good reverend wants us to think Gerald Cartwright was some sort of saint."

"Indeed. And what do we know about Gerald Cartwright, DS Tyler? Above anything else."

"He wasn't a saint."

"Indeed he was not. Which means, Police Constable Rabbani?"

She thinks about this for a moment, chewing her lip. "That he were in it up to his eyeballs, sir?"

"Well done, girl."

When they get back, there are still a number of reporters mingling in the hope of further pickings. Doggett searches the faces until he finds the one he's evidently looking for. "Gina," he calls to a young woman at the edge of the pack. "How'd you like an exclusive?"

Gina's eyes narrow suspiciously. "What sort of exclusive, Jimmy?"

"Dodgy vicar?"

She cocks her head to one side. "Tell me more."

Lily's feet are tired. It feels like they've been walking all day. She stays near the back of the group, where she can keep an eye on everyone, but all she can see is a procession of white heads, snaking its way through the winding streets of Whitby. The harsh screams of the seagulls are beginning to hurt her ears. What do they want with all that incessant crying? The sounds come from all around her, and yet she feels as though they are dogging her, swooping and calling at her back, so she finds herself constantly wheeling and turning. It feels as though she is being followed.

The Reverend Thorogood leads the procession, holding aloft a small gray flag for them all to follow and waving it occasionally back and forth toward the oncoming crowds as though he is Moses parting the Red Sea for the Israelites. Now and again he glances back to look at her. She has thought about the reverend. He seemed awfully determined she should come on this trip, but could he really be responsible for blackmail? A man of the cloth? Unless . . . perhaps the letters are not the work of a man intent on causing harm but instead the work of one determined to force her into doing the right thing. But if so, why not just talk to her? Blackmail, whatever the motive, hardly seems a particularly Christian endeavor.

She thinks, too, about Edna's final words. *I already have a good idea who might be*—what had she been going to say? *Be behind this*? She hadn't wanted to know then and had closed the door before she could hear any more. Oh, it would be so like Edna to step in and work everything out just like that. Well, it just wouldn't do! Lily wanted to be the one to solve the mystery. Now, of course, she can't think about anything else. What has Edna worked out? And how? When Lily has discovered absolutely nothing. She supposes she will have her answer in a few hours' time at any rate. After all, there's nothing she can do to stop Edna from telling her when she gets back.

They lunch on fish and chips in a small restaurant by the bridge. Lily settles for a child's portion and ends up leaving half of it. She has little appetite. She sits opposite Carol and the daughter-in-law, who smile politely but avoid engaging her in conversation. She tries to think of a way to talk to them, but the phrases she rehearses sound just that—rehearsed. Besides which, she's really not sure she wants to talk to either of them. If they do know something, does she really want to get into it all right here, in public?

She sighs heavily and pushes a fat chip through a puddle of vinegar. Perhaps Edna was right, perhaps she shouldn't have come. She's no detective, amateur or otherwise. And it isn't as though the blackmailer is just going to announce himself across the luncheon table. *Any unusual letters lately, Miss Bainbridge? Would you mind passing the ketchup?*

After lunch there's a visit to a fudge shop, but the atmosphere in the shop is stifling. Lily selects a small box of treats with a picture of a sailboat on the front for Edna and escapes back outside as quickly as possible. On the opposite side of the street she sees the vicar and his pretty wife. They are standing close to each other, the reverend with one hand on his wife's arm. She has her eyes downcast but is shaking her head almost violently. When she glances across and spots Lily watching them, she pulls away from her husband, smiles expansively, and folds her arms. The reverend picks up on the gesture and looks across at Lily as well. He, too, smiles, and the two of them cross the road to join her.

"Miss Bainbridge. You are enjoying yourself, I hope?"

"Oh, yes," says Lily. "What a lovely day! Though I admit all the walking is taking its toll."

"There you are, you see?" says Mrs. Thorogood. She turns to Lily. "I was just telling Sebastian the very same thing, but he's determined to see the abbey."

The reverend's mouth curls a little in one corner, but it quickly turns back into a smile. "Well, it's hardly a trip to Whitby without a visit to the abbey, now, is it?"

"Oh," says Lily. "I didn't mean to sound as though I were complaining."

But the couple ignore her and resume a sort of gentle argument, of the kind Lily supposes comes so naturally to married couples. She wonders if this was indeed the conversation she had inadvertently interrupted. There's a stiffness to them both that makes her wonder if it wasn't something else entirely.

"I just think it's a bit much to expect them all to yomp up that great hill, Sebastian. Some of these people are getting on a bit!"

Mrs. Thorogood turns to Lily as though only just remembering she is there. "Oh, goodness, Lily, I meant no offense."

"Nobody's yomping anywhere, Jean. For goodness' sake, you do exaggerate . . ." And so it goes on.

Finally it's decided the vicar will accompany any of the group who wish to pay a pilgrimage to the abbey, while Mrs. Thorogood will remain in the town with those more advanced in years, or less inclined to Christian devotion. They will settle themselves on the benches by the quayside and watch the boats on the river until the rest of the group returns.

As tired as she is, Lily opts for the abbey, taking the opportunity to stay close to the reverend. But the going is far steeper than she anticipated, and she has long since lost sight of him—and lost count of the 199 steps—by the time she gives it up as a bad job and settles herself down on a bench to enjoy the view.

It seems only a matter of moments before he reappears, but given how she is with time these days it might well have been longer.

"Well now, here she is, the lovely lady. We were worried, Miss Bainbridge, thought perhaps you might have come to some harm."

"Oh, no, I'm fine, Reverend. Just taking a breather. It's a long way up."

"That's good," he says, standing over her now and blocking the sun so that, for the first time today, she begins to feel a chill. "Jolly good. We wouldn't want you to stumble. It would be all too easy to lose your footing on this path. It's a long way down."

He smiles down at her, or at least she thinks he does, his face obscured as it is by shadow. He stretches and works some kink out of his back with a hand. He has very large hands, she notices.

"Miss Burnside couldn't join you today, then?"

"Edna? No. It's her health. I think all this walking would have been a bit much."

"I'm sorry to hear that," he says, and she thinks he might even mean it. "You must let us know, Jean and I, if there's anything we can do to help."

"That's very kind of you. Please, don't let me keep you if you want to get on to the abbey."

He frowns and then joins her on the bench. "I've just been up there. I thought I'd better get back before Jean leads a revolt." He laughs. "Let me keep you company for a bit. I must say, these old legs of mine aren't getting any younger either. Then we can walk back together."

Now she *can* see his smile, but she almost wishes she couldn't. There's something about it that makes her think of the Big Bad Wolf in the fairy tale.

"I expect you've had your work cut out for you, organizing all this, haven't you?"

"Oh, I don't mind at all. It's something different." He glances out across the town. "So, Edna's home alone, is she? I'm sure she'll be all right without you for one day."

Lily doesn't answer. So it's *Edna* now, not *Miss Burnside*?

"How long have you had that beautiful old cottage of yours?"

Lily is thrown for a moment by the sudden change in the direction of the conversation. "It belonged to my parents," she says. "I've lived there all my life. Well, most of it anyway."

"That's right, of course; you were in London during the war, weren't you? I'm sure I remember someone telling me that."

Lily marvels at the idea someone might have been talking about her, but at the same time finds the thought more than a little alarming. "Only for a short while. I moved home when . . . after my father died. Then Edna was bombed out and she came to live with us, too."

"That was kind of you, to take her in like that."

She's never thought about it that way before. If anything, it always felt like it was the other way round. "It's just what people did."

"And then you took in another stray."

She frowns, not understanding.

"Oscar? . . . Oh, Oscar isn't a stray. He's a lovely boy. No bother at all." Listen to her, talking about him as though he's still a child.

The reverend smiles again, a lazy, crocodile smile. "Teenagers no bother? Not in my experience."

"It was lovely having a little boy around the house. I think we both thought we'd missed our chance."

"You never had any of your own, then?"

Lily feels the hair stand up on her neck. She says nothing.

"It must have been very hard for you, though, after what happened to his father. To Gerry." He pauses for a moment before he goes on. "I regret . . . I didn't do more to help you both back then."

"Oh, there's really no need. I mean, there wasn't really anything you could have done."

"Still. At least you had Michael to help. I understand he helped arrange Oscar's schooling?"

"Well . . . yes . . ."

"And now here we are again, the village full of police and all those horrible journalists poking around and raking everything up."

Lily can feel Edna screaming inside her head. But if she doesn't talk about it, how will she ever find out anything? "When Gerry . . . disappeared, Edna and I, you see . . . we agreed we wouldn't say anything . . . for Oscar's sake." She can hear Edna shouting, *Be quiet, woman! Stupid, stupid woman!*

"Very wise," says the vicar. "I think that's exactly the right course to steer. Even now. I don't see what good will come of digging up the past all over again." He grimaces slightly at his choice of words and then changes the subject. "And what about Edna, does she still think the same way?"

"Yes. Yes, of course."

He seems to relax a little, and suddenly Lily is sure he's not the blackmailer. He has his secrets, she realizes, but he doesn't seem the least interested in hers.

"Good. Good. Well, you're lucky to have her. You're lucky to have each other." Already he's turning away, his attention wandering back up the path toward the abbey, searching for the others.

I am, she thinks. I am lucky to have her. "We worked for the same company. In London, during the war. I only did mornings, in the typing pool, so I could still dance in the theater later, but Edna was much more important. Personal secretary to the director." Lily thinks about this. "Do you know, the first time we actually met we were on the roof."

This brings back the reverend's attention. "The roof?"

Lily laughs at his reaction. "We were firewatching. That's what they used to call it. During the Blitz. We all took turns on the roof overnight, watching for fires. If we saw anything we ran downstairs to raise the alarm."

"That sounds . . . a little dangerous."

"Not really." She remembers it being quite good fun actually. Edna would bring up the blankets and she would bring the tea. She supposes there must have been others present as well but, it's funny, looking back on it, it's only Edna she remembers.

"And did you ever spot any?"

"What's that?"

"Fires."

"Oh, yes. But they usually knew about them anyway."

They often watched right through the night, but if the raid was fierce or headed their way, they were supposed to . . . *head for the shelter in the underground. Lily tries to pull Edna by the arm, but the woman shakes her off.*

"You go," she says. "I'm stopping here. They're not driving me out."

Lily can hardly leave her on her own, so she stays. The city explodes around them and Lily is petrified, her whole body trembling.

But Edna holds her hand tightly, and soon Lily begins to forget her terror. Edna sticks two fingers high into the air. "That's for you, Mr. Hitler!" she screams into the violent night, and they both laugh loudly.

Once the planes have passed over, they watch in silence as London burns. It's terrible because Lily knows that each one of those fires means a home lost, a family destroyed, and yet she's never felt so alive. All those dancing flames lighting up the sky, it's just so beautiful!

When the all clear sounds they're still holding each other tightly on the cold roof. Lily begins to cry, and Edna leans down so their faces are so, so close and . . .

Lily is falling, the ground rushing to meet her and then . . .

He has her by the arm. "Lily?" The reverend has hold of her, and suddenly she realizes they are not on the bench anymore at all but much further across the path, dangerously close to the edge of the cliff. There's a small fence right behind her and then nothing else but a short plummet down the jagged rock to the streets below. She wants to step away from the edge, but he is standing so close, blocking her path.

"You need to be a bit more careful," he says. "I thought you were going over then."

"Yes," she says quietly, "I will."

"Much more careful. After all, I dread to think what might happen to Edna if anything were to happen to you."

She can feel his fingers digging into her arm, and then they are back off the grassy verge and onto the path proper and the others are returning to meet them and the reverend is all smiles and full of hearty congratulations.

All around her the seagulls dive and screech.

Tyler manages Doggett's prescribed couple of hours but not much more. Soon enough the alarm on his mobile is screeching at him, and he pulls himself out of bed. He decides to walk to the appointment with Denham, crossing the ring road and slipping up behind the cathedral onto Campo Lane, the road where the city's solicitors and estate agents huddle together in a small enclave behind the cathedral, perhaps in the hope of some form of redemption. The offices of Denham, Carter & Carter are in a small cobblestoned courtyard just off the main road. When he arrives, Denham is waiting for him and unlocks the door, letting him into the sparsely furnished reception area, empty on a Saturday afternoon.

"Thank you for seeing me," he says without really meaning it.

Denham eyes him through a pair of designer frames. "Your DCI didn't give me a great deal of choice." He crosses his arms and plants his feet firmly, a man who will not be moved. Tyler has no idea what Jordan said to get Denham here on a Saturday afternoon but whatever it was, he congratulates her. Something else he owes her.

"I only need ten minutes of your time."

"You have my attention, but the clock's ticking."

"A few questions." Tyler paces slowly around the room, examining the Peak District photographs that hang in frames on the walls. He's damned if he's going to hurry, no matter what Denham says about the clock.

"I can't tell you anything that breaches client confidentiality."

"Your client is dead."

Denham pushes his glasses up his nose and swallows.

Tyler steps forward. "I want to know what happened at that party."

Denham readjusts his glasses. "Gerald held lots of parties—do you have a particular one in mind?"

The reaction had been slight, and if Tyler hadn't been watching for it he might have missed it. But he was watching. A small twitch, the slightest tic in the man's left cheek.

"Why don't we start with the one at his house the night he disappeared?"

Denham folds his arms across his chest. "I wasn't there, but I would imagine it was one of Gerry's *poker* nights." The emphasis is unmistakable. "I wasn't invited to those."

"But you knew about them?"

Denham's lips part in a humorless smile. "In my profession it pays sometimes to limit what you know."

Any concern Tyler might have about badgering this upstanding member of the community evaporates. "You mean you turn a blind eye to anything that compromises you or your client."

Denham holds out a hand, open-palmed—just so.

"How morally upstanding of you."

"I don't particularly like your tone, Detective."

"Is that right? Well, I don't particularly like your selective blindness. How far *are* you involved with your clients' affairs, Michael? Maybe I should make it my business to look a bit more closely. I wonder what other skeletons I might dig up."

The choice of words is effective, but Denham is not a man easily intimidated. "You're skating dangerously close to charges of harassment here, Detective Sergeant." He's rattled about something. "Look," he goes on, somehow managing to convey in that one word a sense that they're all on the same side. "Gerry wasn't a saint. Yes, I knew about the parties and the drugs and the whores, but I didn't have anything to do with that. That was for him and his public-school mates. Our relationship was strictly business. Always."

"What confuses me, though, Mr. Denham, is why you would allow your daughter to be involved in it? Knowing what Cartwright got up to, didn't it concern you when Sophie started spending time there?"

The glasses have slipped down again. He pushes them back up. "My daughter makes her own friends. I'm not her keeper."

Tyler doubts that but he can see Denham frowning, putting together his meaning.

"What's this about?" Even as he says it, his face drains of color. "Do you have . . . some kind of evidence that he . . . that Sophie was . . ."

Tyler lets a beat go by before putting the man out of his misery. "No, nothing like that."

Denham breathes out heavily.

"And you can rest assured, Mr. Denham, in my profession we don't turn a blind eye to things like that."

He leaves Denham collapsed in one of the reception chairs, unsure if the meeting has revealed anything substantial. The poker parties are hardly a revelation, but the fact Denham knew about them is interesting. What else did he know about? There's something he isn't saying. Tyler glances back through the window to see the man sitting alone, looking ashen and weary. If nothing else, perhaps he's given him something to think about.

Tyler spends the rest of the afternoon at his desk going over the notes from the original investigation. It isn't that he doesn't trust Doggett. Not exactly. But he can't shake the feeling the man has his own agenda. Why did he request Tyler on this case? He can't bring himself to believe it was simply because Doggett knew his father, because he felt sorry for him in some way because of what happened with Bridger. And why is he so keen to keep him on the case now he knows he's compromised? It doesn't make sense. Tyler likes things to make sense.

He intends to spend the evening on the Internet, doing research into arsonists, but when he gets home Sally-Ann is waiting for him outside the main gate. She's dressed for a night out—another long velvet dress, dark purple this time rather than black, although it still has long sleeves. At her neck she wears a thick choker with a repeated skull motif, and her hair is sculpted with some sort of product so that it sticks up wildly in short yellow peaks that make her look like Lisa Simpson all grown up.

"Now, I know you won't have forgotten," she tells him, "so I'm just going to assume you got held up at work. Am I right?"

"Largely," he says.

"You were supposed to meet me an hour ago."

"I thought that was Saturday?"

"It *is* Saturday!"

"Shit! Sorry. Look, maybe we could rearrange—"

"Nope. You're taking me out, whether you're up for it or not. You owe me at least six drinks for leaving me in that pub on my own for the last forty-five minutes. Besides, I feel like dancing."

"Sal, this really isn't a good time."

"You're not going to win this one, Adam, so save yourself the hassle and go and put your glad rags on."

Tyler sighs heavily. "Fine, one drink."

Despite her words, when they reach the Red Deer it's Sally-Ann who insists on buying the drinks. Tyler finds them a table and tries to think of an opening for the conversation, but he realizes he knows very little about her. When she gets back he takes a sip of ale and starts with the one thing he *can* remember her telling him. "So what made you study art?"

She laughs, a deep, throaty chuckle that reminds him what a great voice she has. "God knows!" she says. Then the laughter dies and she is suddenly serious. "I guess I thought it would piss my mother off. But the joke was on me. I don't think she even noticed."

"You don't talk much about your past. Your family."

Sally-Ann smiles. "You really don't want to hear about *that* particular shitshow."

And there's something so incredibly sad about the smile that he decides to change the subject. "So you studied art but somehow ended up . . . ?"

"Working in a glorified call center? Doesn't everybody?" She laughs. "I realized art was going to be pretty much useless to me, so I went back to college and studied IT. Computers are the future. Art is history. Besides, you went to Oxford, didn't you? What did you read?"

"Mathematics and philosophy."

"Exactly. I imagine that's the ideal combo for joining the police force."

He grants it's a fair point, but he isn't going to get drawn into his own reasons for joining the force. If he's honest, he's not that sure about them himself. He tries to steer the conversation away from him. A thought occurs to him. "What can you tell me about Lowry?"

Sally-Ann frowns. "Lowry?"

"It's work related," he says.

"This is supposed to be a night out. We're not at work."

"Humor me. After this, I promise, no more work."

She sighs but answers him. "Fine. Not a great deal. Laurence Stephen Lowry, mostly famous for his paintings of industrial scenes. Sometimes considered a naïve artist because of his characteristic matchstick figures. How am I doing?"

"Did he paint portraits as well?"

"I'm sure he painted hundreds of them."

Tyler pulls out his mobile and shows her the photo he took of the painting at the crime scene. "Do you know it?"

Sally-Ann squints at the photo; her brow furrows and she shakes her head. "I'm hardly an expert, but yeah, it could be a Lowry, I guess. What's all this about?"

Even if he could tell her he's not sure he knows. "Never mind," he says, slipping his mobile back into his pocket. "Come on then, drink up." He drains the rest of his pint.

Sally-Ann assumes he means to leave. She looks crestfallen.

"I guess I did promise you dancing."

Her face lights up.

———

The club is packed.

Sally-Ann leaves him at the bar and immediately heads off onto the dance floor. He watches her throw herself round the room, totally out of time with the music yet wholly relaxed. She soon catches the eye of a brunette girl wrapped in plastic who gyrates and wiggles ever closer. The girl is squeezed into a PVC dress that's too small for her and that ends just past her hips. She's tall but hunched over, struggling to stand in four-inch heels. It gives her the look of a newborn foal learning the use of its legs.

Tyler drains his pint and orders another. The rest of the SYPLG-BTSN are here and before long he's once again dodging the advances of the Family Liaison guy. The only thing left to do is get pissed.

"Drink?" says Sally-Ann, squeezing his arm.

"I was just wondering how you managed to browbeat me into coming to this place." He has to lean in close and shout over the music. She pulls away from him slightly.

"What happened to Bambi?" he asks.

"Who?"

"Never mind. What are you having?"

"Bourbon," she says, and this time he finishes *her* sentence for a change: "On the rocks with a twist." They both laugh, and he orders the drinks.

Her face is red with exertion; a bead of sweat runs along her jawline and drips from her chin. She tugs absently at the choker round her neck. She notices him looking at her and correctly intuits what he's thinking. She pinches the fleshy fold of her underarm through her sleeve and jiggles it. "Arms like saggy tree trunks," she says. "I don't like getting them out in case someone faints." She reaches out and squeezes his bicep. "We don't all have muscles to show off." She picks up her drink. "Speaking of which, are you aware you have an admirer?" She uses her head to point rather unsubtly along the bar.

He turns to follow her gaze and sees Paul Enfield. The fire officer raises a glass in his direction.

"I'll leave you to it." She upends her glass and drains the contents in one, then disappears back into the crowd on the dance floor.

Enfield moves round the bar to join him. "Can I buy you a drink?" he shouts.

He's about to decline since he still has half a pint in his hands, and then changes his mind. "Fuck it! Why not? Dark rum and Coke. Cheers."

They wait while Enfield catches the eye of the young guy behind the bar and places his order. Then he turns and says, "Small world."

Tyler laughs. "Small scene."

"True." Enfield hands a twenty to the barman. "You know, I got the feeling earlier on you suspected me of something." It's an odd conversation to be having when both of them have to shout to be heard over the music.

Tyler smiles to take the sting out of his words. "I understand that, in the past, a number of arsonists have turned out to be fire officers."

The crowd parts, and he spots Sally-Ann again. She's standing alone at the edge of the dance floor. The brunette foal from earlier has moved on and is all over a pretty blond woman now, their hands moving frantically across each other's backs while they attempt to suck each other's faces off.

"You seem to know a lot about arsonists all of a sudden."

"I've been doing some research." Tyler turns back to see Enfield eyeing him closely, the frown back on his forehead. "*You* suspect *me*."

Enfield cocks his head to one side, perhaps embarrassed to have been found out. "It's the authority pyromaniacs fixate on, not firefighting. Just as many turn out to be coppers."

"It seems we both fit the profile."

"Are you an arsonist?"

"No, are you?"

"No." Enfield grins widely. "Now that's sorted, maybe I can take you for a proper drink." He's interrupted as somebody careers into the back of him, pitching him forward.

The man who sent Enfield flying is a big bear of guy. Beyond him stands Oscar, swaying slightly. The bear starts toward him and Tyler moves quickly, stepping between the two of them. "That's enough."

The bear squares up to him. "What the fuck's it got to do with you, princess?"

Tyler pulls out his wallet and flashes his warrant card in the man's face.

The bear's attitude crumbles. "Look, sorry, luv, all right? I'm not looking for trouble." A hand strays subconsciously to his back pocket. He's carrying. Pills or dope, most likely.

"Walk away then."

The bear nods and melts into the throng of clubbers.

"I could've handled it," Oscar says. His words are slurred.

"Sit down for a minute." Tyler orders a glass of water, and the barman thanks him for interceding. He glances at Paul Enfield, who nods his understanding. Then he has to half-carry Oscar to the sofa in the chill-out corner. The barman brings over the water.

"Doggett thinks the woman they've found is Cynthia." Not *Mum*, or *Mother*. *Cynthia*. Oscar upends the glass and downs the water in one. "I don't know what to do."

"Getting your face smashed in isn't going to help."

Oscar puts down the glass and cradles his head in his hands. "I'll be all right." He looks up at the door. "Sorry I ruined your evening."

Tyler glances back to the bar in time to see Paul Enfield heading out the door. He doubts the man is just going out for a smoke.

Oscar touches his arm, drawing back his attention. "Let me buy you a drink. Just to say thank you, for everything."

"I don't think that's a good idea."

"Please. Just one drink. I don't want to be on my own right now." He smiles, and the innocent little boy is back. The water seems to have sobered him greatly, but his eyes are still red and haunted. His fingers brush lightly across Tyler's wrist.

"One drink," he says. And he knows, even as he says it, that it's never just one drink.

The journey home seems much shorter.

Once they had met up with the others down by the wharf, everyone was a lot less inclined to any further walking. Someone suggested they retire to a local pub until the coach could pick them up. It was shortly after the third sherry that Lily noticed the man in the corner staring at her. A grizzly fisherman with a nicotine-stained beard that collected the foam from his ale with every mouthful. His eyes never left hers, and though she tried to avoid his gaze, there was something about him that kept drawing her back. She was so relieved when someone announced the arrival of the coach, she determined to look him straight in the eye as she passed him on the way out. But when she turned to do so, he was gone.

On the coach, the seat belt cuts across Lily's bust, causing her brassiere to dig into her bony chest. Her feet don't quite touch the floor. The seat next to her is empty, and she keeps glancing up the aisle to make sure the reverend doesn't suddenly decide to sit with her and continue their conversation. She squirms in her seat trying to adjust her undergarments and then lurches forward as the coach brakes and swerves. Someone calls loudly down the bus, "Missed 'em!" There's a smattering of laughter.

The buzz of the sherry in Lily's blood makes her nauseous. She looks out of the window and watches the scrubby gray verge at the side of the motorway as it whizzes past them, her reflection merging with the panning background. It makes her head spin, and she feels like she's melting into ash. She thinks about Edna all alone back at the cottage, and suddenly she wants to be home. Whatever was she thinking? What a fool she's been! Edna was right.

Edna is always right.

Lily closes her eyes and then, before she knows it, they're pulling up at the end of Oliver Road.

"I'll walk you up," Mrs. Thorogood offers.

"Really, there's no need."

Mrs. Thorogood doesn't argue for long. "Well, if you're sure." She gives Lily a tight hug, which Lily finds a little overfamiliar, but then, that is what it's like these days, isn't it? All kissing both cheeks and public displays of affection. The reverend hangs back, thankfully.

"We must do something soon. Coffee or something?"

"Yes, that would be lovely," says Lily, though she's never liked the taste of coffee and the thought of it now makes her feel sick again.

Mrs. Thorogood gets back onto the coach to a stern word from her husband and Lily watches it pull away, listening to the pistons firing as it negotiates the bend past the Old Vicarage. She decides to cut across the churchyard, and as she turns to do so a chill breeze ripples along the hedgerow. The weather has turned. It is as though they left in summer and have returned in autumn. The wind whistles between the headstones, eddying small whirlwinds of leaves. It's late, almost midnight, but she can still see well enough, the dark shadow of the church picked out against the industrial glow of the city in the distance. Lily's eyes dart, as always, toward the grave where her parents are buried. Sometimes she sees her mother here, as she was when they came to visit Dad, moaning and weeping like the women you see on the news after an earthquake. Auntie Vi used to say Mam was very Mediterranean in her grief.

A sudden gust of wind tears open her cardigan, and one of the church bells tolls faintly, as though it's a little embarrassed. The shadows slide and merge along the churchyard walls. Ahead of her and a little to the left there is a darker, thicker patch. Is there someone crouched there? She hears the echo of her footsteps and resists the urge to turn and look behind. She tries to shake off morbid thoughts. Daydreaming. Unproductive, her mother would call it. Self-indulgent, Edna would add.

She negotiates her way past the kissing gate, using the opportunity to look back through the churchyard. She sees no one, but she can't shake the feeling there's someone there. Someone watching. She crosses the road and makes her way up the path to the cottage. As she steps through the gate she suddenly feels blissfully, inexplicably happy. Everything seems distant and fuzzy, as though the events of the day happened to someone else. She is home. She is safe.

She pushes down on the handle of the front door and finds it locked. It's nighttime; of course it's locked. But something is wrong. She can feel it. She reaches into her purse for her keys but can't find them. Her mother has joined her now. *Hurry up, Lillian, what will the neighbors think?* They're hardly likely to be watching at this hour. Why is *she* here? What use is *she* in a crisis? Edna is the one who always knows what to do. It's Edna she needs. It always has been. *Edna!*

Lily drops the purse and runs down the path to the back door, a snail cracking underfoot as she turns into the garden. The back door is unlocked, and this alarms her even more than the locked front door. She steps into the trapped heat of the conservatory, clambering past all the folded-up garden furniture. A wasp batters drowsily at the plastic roof. She steps into the living room.

Here is Edna. Facedown on the carpet. She has fallen forward into the fireplace, and the coals form a reddish halo around her head. The room smells of burned hair and makes Lily think of freshly chopped fingernails. She falls forward onto her knees and lets out the oddest noise—a sort of strangled, keening note. Edna's lumpy body is heavy and stubborn but she pushes on one arm, gets her up, turns her over. The coals shift and spill, the fire flaring back to life until Edna's head comes to rest once more in the embers. The orange glow of the firelight pulses in its charcoal prison. The heat licks at Edna's hair, causing it to blacken and curl, the smoke launching heavenward in a sweet, sickly incense.

Edna.

The right side of her face remains largely untouched, just a brush of soot like she's been up the chimney. But the left . . . The left is a half-mask of black and red ruin, her dentures lying half exposed and melted, her hair—that wispy, half-dead hair that she coveted so—is gone, exposing the scarred pink dome of Edna's skull. The eye is the worst, though. The left eye. Sitting loosely in its socket, a bubbling, hissing mess of milky jelly. There's no chance this eye can see anything anymore, and yet it looks straight into Lily's heart.

She backs away and sits down heavily in the armchair.

You have to ring for help, says an echo somewhere behind her. Edna always knows what to do.

Call Oscar, Edna says.

"Yes," says Lily. She glances out through the conservatory door and registers the furniture is in, all wrapped up and put away neatly. She wonders how Edna could have managed it all on her own.

day five

The Library at Alexandria, circa 48 BC

Plutarch tells us of the siege of Alexandria, how Julius Caesar was forced to set fire to his own ships, the fire ultimately spreading to the docks and on through the city to the great library, with its 400,000 scrolls, parchments, and tablets.

You're no great historian, but you do like reading. What would you have done without the library? You spent more time there than anywhere. It was warm and dry, and generally the librarians left you alone. Provided they didn't notice you. But then you were always good at hiding, weren't you?

Imagine what it must have been like for those bearded scholars, their togas flapping in the wind fanning the flames ever higher. Think of how much human learning was lost and never recovered. Perhaps one of those scrolls eaten by fire might have led to the early discovery of gravity. Or the invention of penicillin. How different human history, but for a single spark?

What knowledge was destroyed in the grubby little offices of a solicitor? Less important perhaps, but you don't want to take the chance. Admit it, though, your heart wasn't really in it. Especially after your visit to the old woman's cottage. The scream didn't even fade this time, just pulsed in syncopated counterpoint with the crackle and roar of the solicitor's case files. You didn't even stay to watch. Outside, the flames dancing behind the windows seemed dull and gray. You knew at once it wouldn't catch. You don't even know for sure the solicitor was involved. Did he know?

The schoolteacher knew. You can still see her, standing in her little cottage, her back arched, her face contorted in pain. She saw you; you know that, don't you? She saw you peering in through the window, and she knew. And you knew that she knew. Then her eyes rolled up into her head and she dropped, falling in slow motion, head crashing down against the stone hearth.

That's exactly how she went. A life extinguished. A snuffing out of all that past. All that knowledge and experience, all those long, long years, gone in an instant.

Consumed by fire.

POSTED BY **thefirewatcher** AT 6:08 AM

12 COMMENTS

Firebug69 said . . .

Ah man! I fucking luv u! Check out this fit blaze from last night #firewatching https://twitter.com/twitter/statuses/725597041213247488

Bazzameat1 said . . .

That's sick @Firebug69 I've only done rubbish bins

Jenna1975 said . . .

Is she dead then? How does the story end? I don't get it

Gigiono@hella said . . .

This blog is boring af #getalife

1 Next

Tyler splashes cold water onto his face and rubs at his temples. He opens the door of the bathroom cabinet in search of help that isn't there. Not so much as an aspirin. In the shower, he turns the water temperature down until it's the colder side of lukewarm. The droplets of water evaporate against his overheated skin. He holds that position, face raised to the showerhead in supplication, cheeks radiating heat like the radioactive rods of a power station.

Oscar is gone. He can't remember when exactly, just that he *was* here and now he's not. He has an image of them dancing in slow time across the laminate flooring to some jazz tune. A favorite of Gerald's, apparently. Why did that idea not seem creepy last night? There's not much he can remember about the evening at all. Just the two of them dancing forlornly in the dark. And the fact that Oscar kept buying them drinks.

When he gets out of the shower his mobile is ringing. He grabs a towel and stumbles, stubbing his smallest toe hard against the shower tray and creating a new pain in his foot, a sharper, tighter version of the one arcing across his forehead. He makes it to the phone just as it rings off. He doesn't recognize the number.

Having found no remedy in the bathroom, he turns to the

kitchen, brewing up a thick black sludge that might just be classifiable as coffee. He waits for the drink to cool and then downs it in one. He makes it back to the bathroom just in time to vomit the concoction down the pan. He crouches there for a moment, the porcelain cool against his forehead, trying to work out how this has happened. But his cotton-clouded mind struggles to focus on anything. The ringing in his ears refuses to subside.

Ringing. The mobile again. He wrenches himself off the floor, wipes his mouth, and hurries back to the phone, the blood pumping sluggishly round his limbs as though he's engaged in heavy exercise. The same number. Why did he not think to ring it back?

"DS Tyler?" It's Paul Enfield. Another part of the evening slots into place.

"Yes, hello."

"There's been another one."

Tyler feels his head beating in time to the rhythm of his thumping heart. "Where?"

This time the fire is in the city itself, not Castledene, but he doesn't need to ask why Enfield thinks it's relevant. As soon as he has the address he knows. He decides to walk, unsure if he's fit to drive. It's only a few minutes, and he's hardly likely to get lost since he was there only yesterday. Perhaps he and Oscar even walked home this way last night. Right past the scene of the crime. Assuming they did walk; he can't remember that either.

It's still dark; the morning air, fresh and cool, helps clear away some of the fog in his head.

When he arrives at the scene, Enfield is waiting for him and holds out a palm for a bone-crushing handshake. An awkwardness between them now. Because there had been the start of something and then Oscar arrived and now they're . . . what exactly? Regardless, something has changed.

The building is still surprisingly intact, the only difference from yesterday a couple of smashed windows and a little charring to the bricks above them. The fire is already out.

"I can't let you go in," Enfield tells him. "The structure's not sound. We'll need to shore up the properties on either side."

Tyler eyes the little brass plaque by the door. *Denham, Carter & Carter.* No doubt now that the fires are somehow related to the Cartwright case. "Was anyone hurt?"

Enfield shakes his head.

He points to the plaque. "Is this why you called me?"

Enfield looks at the name and shakes his head. "No. I called because there are similarities between this and the other fires. Petrol again, though we'll have to do tests to make sure it's the same type. But also, there's the same sense of control." He doesn't sound sure, though. He looks up at the building, still frowning. "There are some differences. The fire didn't take hold; the epicenter was a rubbish bin soaked in petrol, but he didn't soak the whole place like he has before."

"Perhaps he ran out."

"Then there's the location. We're a long way from Castledene." He goes back to his study of the building, and Tyler notices a small vein throbbing on the man's neck as he concentrates. The vein is bisected by a deep scar, a raised white ridge that begins close to his collarbone and widens as it disappears under his T-shirt. "This feels different. I don't think the fire was meant to do much damage. It's more like a message."

"But you *do* think it's the same arsonist?"

Enfield thinks about this. "We've seen a dramatic increase in the number of incidental fires over the past week, right across the country. It isn't that unusual for this time of the year, especially given the weather we've been having. But the spike this week has been greater than the statistical norm. We can't work out why."

"They can't all be the work of one man."

"No, most of them are far less serious. Fires in rubbish bins, bonfires on wasteland, that sort of thing. Kids' stuff. We'll invest some time in going round the schools, and hopefully it will settle down before anyone gets seriously hurt." He frowns again. "This is different. I suppose it's more of a feeling than anything. A signature you learn to recognize." Enfield is more than half-talking to himself. "If this *is* the work of our guy, though, then he's broken his pattern. That would indicate to me this place wasn't just a random choice. That means in all likelihood the others weren't either."

Tyler's eyes move down from Enfield's neck and along his thick, dark-skinned arm. He can't help but compare it to Oscar's pale, wiry frame. What time did Oscar leave? Did he come back this way? "It sounds like you understand him." He doesn't mean it to, but it comes out as an accusation nonetheless.

"So we're back to doubting each other, then?" Enfield's dark eyes sparkle. "I had a similar case to this a few years ago. A serial arsonist." He stretches, works his shoulder with one gigantic hand. "Have you ever seen a serious fire, Adam? Not like the scout hut the other day, I mean a *big* fire."

So it's *Adam* now? Tyler says nothing, assumes the question is rhetorical.

"At first glance it seems random, chaotic, but it isn't. There's a pattern. For example, a flame will always travel toward the oxygen feeding it. It happens all the time. The first thing people do in a fire is open the door to get out, and the fire goes straight for them. Like it's reaching out for them." Again Enfield tugs at his T-shirt. "The experts, like me, will tell you this is predictable. That's how we fight fire. It's governed by the same laws of physics as everything else." Their eyes lock together; Paul Enfield's pupils are glossy black coals. "But it's easy to believe otherwise." He pulls down the collar of his

T-shirt, exposing a mass of white and pink scarring across his shoulder. "Sometimes you get it wrong. Sometimes things don't happen the way they're supposed to and all of a sudden the flames are coming for you out of the darkness, and you know, beyond logic and reason, that this fire is alive. That it wants you." He breathes out heavily. "So yes, you're right, I do understand him. So do you, if you let yourself think about it. It's like Bonfire Night when you're a kid. It's just that this guy is still staring into the flames, hypnotized. I know exactly what that feels like."

"Did you get him?" Tyler wants to say more. He feels an urge to apologize, but he senses it's too late for that.

Enfield nods. "Caught in the act. Sooner or later that's how we always catch them. The compulsion to watch overrides their self-preservation."

"I don't want to wait until then."

"We won't. I have people looking at the crowd." He nods subtly to the small crowd gathering around them in hushed whispers, in spite of the early hour. "Looking for familiar faces. Anyone that might have been present at the last fire. Or the next one." He points at a security camera mounted on the wall of the cathedral. "And you never know, maybe this time we'll get lucky."

Tyler nods. "The locations aren't random. At least, this one isn't." He fills Enfield in on Michael Denham and his relationship with Gerald Cartwright.

Enfield listens in silence and when Tyler's finished, he says, "Where does that leave us?"

"Who did the allotment belong to?"

"It was rented to a Cyril Armitage. I've got someone checking, but so far we can't see any obvious connection."

"And the scout hut?"

"Run by the parish council."

"The bus shelter—that would be council owned, too."

"You think someone's got a grudge against the council?"

Tyler smiles. "They wouldn't be the first."

Enfield laughs, and the tension is broken. "I suppose it's worth looking into."

Michael Denham has arrived. He's arguing with a young fireman and gesturing at the building. Tyler points him out to Enfield, and something about the action must alert Denham to their presence. He sees them, falters slightly, and then straightens. Enfield nods to his colleague, and Denham is waved through the cordon.

"Detective Sergeant Tyler. I would've thought you had more important things to do."

Paul Enfield answers for him. "An arson attack isn't exactly a minor misdemeanor, Mr. Denham."

Denham snorts. "Probably just students. Too much to drink."

Perhaps it's the reference to alcohol, but Tyler is suddenly irritated. "If you don't mind me saying so, Michael, you don't seem very upset for someone whose office has just gone up in smoke."

"The insurance will cover it. The damage seems largely superficial."

"Someone out there seems to have a grudge against you."

"I'm sure there's plenty, Detective, but if you think I'm handing you a list of my clients, satisfied or otherwise, you're very much mistaken. Now, if you'll excuse me I need to make some phone calls." He uses his briefcase to cut a path between them. They watch him for a moment, standing alone in front of his building, talking loudly into his mobile.

"Maybe this isn't connected to the others," Enfield says.

Michael Denham's eyes dart quickly in their direction and then away again.

"No," Tyler says, "there was nothing random about this." He turns back to the fire officer, holds out his hand. "Thanks for including me."

Enfield takes his hand but makes no attempt to shake it. "You okay?" he asks.

Tyler winces at being found out. "I'll be fine. Just a few too many last night, that's all." But he never gets hangovers like this. How much did he drink?

"Be careful," Enfield says. "This arsonist, he thinks he knows what he's doing, but this is getting out of hand. He's obsessive, and I wouldn't be surprised if there's a sexual element to this as well. If you find out something, please, talk to me. I can help." Enfield stares at him for a moment as though to cement his point, then he lets go of Tyler's hand and walks away.

Tyler heads back to his flat, the thin purple light of dawn mushrooming over the city. He doesn't even get halfway before his mobile rings.

Summer has fled. It's cold in the garden, where Lily sits on the wall of a flower bed, the bricks scratching at her legs; she's still wearing the floral-print dress that she wore the day before. It *is* still the day before, the dawn only just beginning to break through the apple tree. A breeze sweeps through the house front to back, blowing away the ash and the smoke and the smell. Cleaning away Edna. On it are carried the various strangers that seem drawn to this disaster: men in white plastic suits that look like spacemen; young girls not much older than Oscar, sporting uniforms that are supposed to make them look respectable; bleary-eyed, unshaven men who fail to hide the fact they've been wakened from pleasant dreams in order to share her tragedy. *Flies to a corpse,* isn't that the expression?

The role of the young Indian girl seems to be to offer comfort and tea. But the comfort consists of meaningless words spoken in whispers, and the tea has grown tepid in Lily's hands. The girl does her best, but what is there to be said on occasions such as these? To her, what is Edna but another old woman gone the way of old things? At least she's quietly spoken, though. Unlike some of the others who shout and tear their way through the cottage. One of the men in white suits, a tall, loud, thin man with a space-age silver suitcase, stubs out his cigarette on the patio and shouts, "In here, is it?" apparently under the impression he's here to shift a piano. Even after he has gone the cigarette butt remains, giving off wisps of pungent smoke. Lily shivers.

Dawn arrives in earnest, and the morning light begins to force the garden shadows into retreat. The birds begin chirping their morning chorus. The world has decided to continue. Her-Next-Door puts her head over the fence to see what all the fuss is about. She's still wearing her nightgown, her hair in curlers. Lily straightens and tries to assume a face for visitors, but the woman withdraws again quickly.

She'll have to get used to that, she realizes, contaminated as she now is. They'll avoid her in the street just like they did after Gerald . . . disappeared. At least then she had Edna, though; this time she's on her own. She wants to close the cottage doors, stop the house from bleeding Edna out.

One of the men from the ambulance comes up to her and says, "We're going to move her now."

Lily gets up. Do they need her permission?

"Is there somewhere else you might like to go?" he asks. It isn't the first time they've tried to make her leave, but where do they think she has to go? Then she realizes: Edna's bulky mass is too great for manhandling through the house. They need to bring her out the back door and take her down the path. She thanks him for his concern, but she'll stay.

As it happens, he needn't have worried; there's nothing of Edna left in this lump of spent flesh wrapped in plastic. Lily remains standing, as is proper, and watches them pass out through the back door, round the corner of the house, and down the path. Edna's final exit.

She is gone.

All at once, everything is quiet. Lily is alone.

"Good God!" A loud voice at the end of the path. Mrs. Thorogood appears, narrowly avoiding being flattened by Edna's departing corpse. She walks briskly along the path to Lily full of sorry-for-your-losses and you-poor-things. She sits and folds her arms around Lily's shoulders, holding her closely. They sit together in silence, and Mrs. Thorogood takes her hand.

Who's this, then? Edna asks. *The vicar's wife? That's a little gauche, even for you, isn't it?* She settles on the wall to Lily's right, sighing as the weight comes off her bad leg; death, it seems, has done little for Edna's health.

So that's how it is? One out, one in, eh?

Lily looks at her and Edna stares back, one milky, jellied eye set within a ruined face.

Tyler looks down at the carpet where Edna Burnside fell. In his hand he clutches a plastic evidence bag. According to Rabbani, Elliot reckons it was a stroke. But considering the cancer that ravaged her body, the actual cause of death could be any number of things. All of which might be considered natural causes. He and his team saw nothing at the site to indicate anything different. Nevertheless. Head thrust into the fireplace, it's hardly a *natural* end. He looks down at the evidence bag. And then there's that.

Tyler moves through the cottage. The inside is much as he expected it to be. It's an old property and has seen none but the most

basic home improvements in the last fifty years. The small kitchen
is tidy, but not very clean. The tiny bathroom smells of mold and
rust. The dining room and living room are mirror images of each
other, except for the table and four chairs in one and the sooty outline of a body in the other. He moves up a steep staircase to the two
bedrooms, one to front, one to back. The front bedroom is pristine,
the small double bed neatly prepared for visitors who never come.
The back bedroom has two beds separated by a small gap. He as-
signs each of them to the two women by the assortment of items on
the bedside tables. A book of poetry, a *Times* crossword, a box of
pills on Edna's; a copy of *Pride and Prejudice,* the spine unbroken,
on Lily's. He could go on; rifling through drawers, checking the
bureau for documents, but he can't bring himself to do it. Besides
which there's the plastic bag he is holding. He doesn't want to put it
down, and he is certain there is nothing here of more importance.
He'll leave the mopping up to Rabbani.

Back downstairs he glances again at the fireplace. Natural causes.

"Bloody hell," says Doggett. He's standing in the conservatory
doorway staring at the floor. "Burnside by name . . ."

"Don't, Jim. Please, just don't."

Doggett swallows his words. "What does Elliot think?"

"Says it's natural causes."

Doggett lets out a huff of air. "Yeah, and no doubt he's busy tee-
ing off as we speak, so forgive me if I don't take his bloody word for
it. That man will say anything to get back to the fairway quicker.
Where's your mate Fireman Sam, then? Shouldn't we get his people on this?"

He tells Doggett about Michael Denham's little office problem.

Doggett listens carefully, then nods. "That changes things then.
All right, I'm convinced. What's it all about?"

"We need to talk to Lily Bainbridge."

Doggett shakes his head. "Let's wait until we get confirmation about the second body in the vicarage." Doggett stops at his choice of words. "Bloody hell, we're living out an Agatha Christie novel here. My point is, if it *is* Cynthia Cartwright we've found, then we know Burnside lied to us."

"We already know she lied. She told us Lily was dead." But when he thinks about it, he realizes she didn't. *She's no longer in a position to help anyone,* she'd said. "Implied it, at least."

"Yes, and aren't you two a prize pair for believing her? Anyway, we're not going to get anything out of her now, are we?"

"Maybe that was the point. What if Burnside was killed to stop her talking to us? We need to speak to Lily Bainbridge *now*."

Doggett frowns, considering this.

"And then there's this." Tyler holds out the evidence bag. Doggett leans forward to examine it while Tyler tells him where the evidence was found.

"Ah, now. Well, that makes all the difference then. Where is she?"

"She was here earlier. She's gone home with Jean Thorogood."

"The vicar's mouse? All right, let's go see the grieving granny. But can we at least get some breakfast first?" He steps into the garden and takes three sharp sniffs at the early morning air. "You know, for some reason I could murder a bacon breadcake."

Tyler stares at him.

"What?" Doggett asks innocently.

Lily wakes slowly, piecing herself together from half-remembered dreams. She knows there is something she has forgotten, and she's running out of time to remember. There's something coming for her out of the darkness. Something heavy and hairy that smells strongly of cologne. She opens her eyes and turns toward

Edna. Instead she sees a wooden door, its white gloss thick with multiple coats that have bled into streaks. She doesn't know this place. She shouldn't be here. She fights her way out from under the bedclothes and is shocked when she throws them off easily. The duvet falls with a dull flump off the end of the bed. And then it reaches for her, the monster from the darkness, arriving like a great slavering beast here to feed on her sanity. She feels it clawing at her stomach, raking its bony digits through her mind, pulling her back with it, down into the shadows. And then she is simply lying in the sun, still fully clothed, in a strange room. And she remembers. She remembers that Edna is gone.

The vicarage. Not the old one that she knows so well. The new vicarage, the home of the Thorogoods. Yes. She remembers, but only vaguely. It's hard to separate dream from reality. Except for Edna. That was real. Edna is gone.

She raises herself up on one elbow. What on earth convinced her to come here of all places? Someone, Mrs. Thorogood presumably, has taken her shoes off for her and placed them neatly by the bedside. It feels like a very intimate act from a comparative stranger. But she is certain it is not the sort of thing the reverend would have done. God help her! She swings her legs round, sits up, slips her stockinged feet back into her shoes, and laces them. She brushes down the floral dress. When was the last time she slept in her clothes? Perhaps that night on the rooftop. After the noise and the fear faded, after the flames died and their violent vigil subsided into quiet contemplation. She'd slept then, her head cradled in Edna's lap.

She *has* slept, she realizes. It seems almost disrespectful how easily sleep claimed her. Not that she feels rested in any real sense, but still, she's sure Edna wouldn't approve. She stands and walks to the window. The day is to be bright and hot. The weather has made no allowance for her loss. On the contrary, the summer has made another assault on them, fighting to the last. The end of the world is surprisingly pleasant.

On a chair next to the bed Mrs. Thorogood has left a towel. Lily picks it up and goes in search of a bathroom. How long has she been here? How long has Edna been gone? Judging by the sun it's late morning, but on what day? Was it only last night that Edna fell? Or perhaps she has slept longer, right through: a day, a night, another day. "A healing sleep," her mother would call it. A year, even. Perhaps this is the next summer or the one after that. Not that it matters. From now on they will all be the same: empty and long. She can't breathe in this place. The corridors seem to go on and on. She quickens her pace, hurrying toward the stairs. When she reaches the top she trips on the rutted carpet, begins to fall, saving herself at the last moment with a wobbly banister. She hurries down the stairs and tries the front door, but it's locked. She dashes along a hallway, finds the kitchen; the door into the garden stands wide open before her. And then she's out, out into the warm morning air where she can finally breathe again.

It's a small garden, only a few feet long, once well-kept but now the grass is a little overgrown, the flower beds thickening with weeds. For some reason the Thorogoods appear to have had other priorities than gardening lately. Lily sits down on a bench by the back door and considers all the things that will need doing. Funeral arrangements, solicitors, notifications. All the things Edna tried to tell her about, but she wouldn't listen. She'll have to see the man at the bank—what's his name? Edna would know—and the house will need cleaning, too, since she can't very well invite people back for tea with that stain on the front carpet.

Then what? Life goes on, isn't that what they say? But what for and for how long? She is so full of questions suddenly, questions only Edna can answer. Why had she so stubbornly refused to ask them when she had the chance? But there is one question she steadfastly refuses to acknowledge. Edna. Lying on the floor with her head smashed into the fireplace. No, she won't think about that.

Lily steadies her breathing. Stick to the practical things; that's what Edna would say. First she has to contact people.

Oscar.

The grief hits her like a physical force. It takes her down and pins her under its weight. She cries out into the choked garden, her body heaving with sobs that threaten to burst her chest. She can hear herself crying, like she's listening to some kitchen-sink drama on the wireless. She wants to stop but the more she tries to, the worse it gets. How will she tell him? He'll blame her, and he'll be right to; after all, all of this is her fault. When Edna needed her most she wasn't there.

The rotting bench groans under her insubstantial weight and shocks her into silence. Oscar. She has to be strong for him. She's the adult now. She is all he has left, and for a moment that treacherous thought thrills her. The shame helps dry her tears.

Mrs. Thorogood arrives back full of apologies. She just popped out for some milk. She wouldn't have normally left her alone but Sebastian had been so intent on getting to the church, it being a Sunday and all. Is Lily feeling any better? Lily thanks her for her kindness, but she must get back.

When she gets home the cottage is still being invaded by strangers. Lily sits back down on the steps leading up to the lawn and stares at the house. Funny how once, not so long ago, she had felt trapped by this place and now it feels as though the cottage is shutting her out, rejecting her. As though this was Edna's place and she has no right to be here.

You're too hard on yourself, says a voice behind her. It's accompanied by the sound of the canopied sun lounger groaning as it swings. But the sun lounger is still inside, folded up where Edna left it.

Lily says, "I thought you'd gone."

Yes, says Edna, *that's always been your trouble, Lily Bainbridge. You think too much.*

"You were right about the trip. I shouldn't have gone."

Edna grunts. *What's done is done.*

The phantom swing continues to creak. For a while they sit together in silence watching the strangers moving in and out of their home.

After a while Edna says, *They'll be coming to ask you questions now. I can't protect you any longer.*

"I know," says Lily. "But I don't think I have the answers."

We knew this was coming.

"Did we?" Lily asks.

The swing stops.

Rabbani is on her way back from the café in the village, Doggett's bastard bacon sandwich tucked under one arm. After a morning of poking round both the old ladies' cottage and the Old Vicarage, Doggett had been complaining that his stomach thought his throat had been cut. She'd spent the morning looking into Thorogood, or Felbridge, or whatever he liked to call himself, and she'd actually found something. Something important. But did he want to hear it? No. Just banged on about her knowing her place, and how she better not forget the brown sauce. She knows this is just his way of testing her, that she won't be fetching the sandwich orders forever, but still, it rankles. She should have gone to Tyler with what she'd found, but there's something about him she finds even more intimidating than Doggett. Well, she won't make the same mistake again. When she gets back she'll go straight to him and . . .

It's then she sees him, the Reverend Thorogood, hurrying along the road ahead of her. He moves quickly, hampered only by the fact he keeps slowing to look over his shoulder. He stops once at the churchyard gates, does the perfect impression of an amateur spy, and then rushes up the path and into the church itself.

Now, what was he acting all furtive-like about? It isn't as though he doesn't have a reason to be there. She checks her watch. Morning service would be over by now, but he must have other chores to be getting on with. Still, there was something about him. . . . She revises her opinion. Not furtive exactly, more . . . scared. She thinks about it for a good thirty seconds or more before she decides to follow him in. If she's going back to Doggett with a cold butty, she'd better have something to show for it.

She opens the iron gate of the churchyard and it squeaks its resistance. She hurries up the path, the greasy sandwich still warm under her arm, and places a hand on the big iron ring of the door. This time it turns with a loud click. She pushes on the heavy wood and it creaks loudly. She steps inside.

Inside, the church is in better repair, although the prayer cushions are faded and frayed and the pews are pitted with age. To her right, against one of the central columns, stands an ornate golden cross on a pedestal, chained to the floor so no one can steal it. She wonders how much that would add to the cardboard thermometer outside. There's no sign of Thorogood.

She wouldn't describe herself as a devout Muslim—she doesn't pray five times a day, she has the occasional drink with the girls—but still, this place is a long way from what she's used to. Stained-glass windows, statues, ornate carvings. The decadence is astounding. Perhaps part of it is the age as well—the oldest mosque she's ever been in was built in the '60s—but there's something about this place that seems almost obscene. Why would you need all this to feel closer to God? There's a crucifix hanging behind the altar, four feet long, the ornately carved wood covered with dust. She's always hated those things. It's just plain gruesome. How can they expect you to pray with that hideous thing looking down on you?

There's no denying there's a serenity about the place, though. She has second thoughts about her reasons for being here. Can she really question a man of God in his place of worship? Even if it isn't her god, and, let's be honest, who's to say that it isn't? But then she remembers how Thorogood treated her a couple of days ago, the lascivious look he gave her. She decides she can. She'll be respectful, of course, but he's up to something and it's her job to find out what.

Where is he? She considers calling out for him, but something stops her. There's a doorway tucked to the left of—whatever that bit round the altar is called. The chancel? The apse? No, an apse has a dome, doesn't it? They did all this at school, but she can't remember it.

She moves quietly toward the door. It probably leads into the vestry. Or maybe *that's* the chancel? The door is ajar, and from behind it comes the sound of voices. Something makes her slow her pace a little, and when she reaches the door she stops to listen for a moment.

Two voices. Raised. She still can't make out the words; they come to her deadened by the thick wood of the door. She can see nothing through the gap but a thin sliver of wall. She leans in, puts her ear to the space between the door and the jamb.

She recognizes the clipped, pious tone of the vicar. The other voice is unfamiliar, though. A rougher, deeper voice.

". . . not a coincidence, is it?" asks the deep-voiced man.

"Why now?" The high-pitched reverend.

A grunt. "You think they don't know you were involved?"

"Who, for Christ's sake? Who's doing this?"

The deep-voiced man says something but Rabbani misses it.

"Christ, Wentworth, you shouldn't have come here! What do you want?"

"Some journalist woman's been asking questions. About you."

"Thank you for the warning, but I'm well aware of her."

There's silence for a few seconds and then the deep-voiced man—Wentworth—speaks again. "I'm going away for a bit."

"Brilliant! And that's not going to look at all suspicious."

"I need some cash. Not a lot. Few hundred, maybe."

Now it's the reverend's turn to go quiet. When he finally speaks, it's quietly, so Rabbani can barely make out the words. "Jesus Christ, you're serious!"

"There's stuff I could tell her."

Rabbani jumps. He's right on the other side of the door. She hurries back down the aisle, missing Wentworth's reply. She hears the door squeak behind her and Thorogood's voice chases her through the church. "Get out of here!"

She's halfway down the aisle when she realizes she isn't going to make it without one of them seeing her. Why does that matter? She has every right to be here. But then some small element of self-preservation reminds her that one of these men could be a murderer. Possibly both. She veers to the right and ducks behind a screen, her heart hammering inside her chest, the grease of the sandwich oozing across her palm. She sees now that the screen is in fact a paneled noticeboard. The blue felt is covered with line drawings and artist impressions—the restoration plans for the church, tacked up for public viewing. If they discover her here she can pretend she is merely curious about the renovation of a local landmark. They won't know that she heard anything. If she can just get her breathing under control.

Their footsteps echo through the church and instinctively she ducks, crouching low behind the screen and ruining her alibi.

"Get out," the vicar shouts again.

"You want to be careful, Sebastian. You've got just as much to lose as me. More, come to think of it."

"And if it comes to it, it's your word against mine. Who do you think they'll believe?"

"What about this fire starter, eh? You think he gives a toss about words?"

There's a narrow gap in the bifold screen, but when she puts her eye to it she's in time only to see the back of someone leaving the church. Wentworth, she supposes, the gardener Tyler and Doggett spoke to. She sees Thorogood's face is red with fury. He stands there panting for a few seconds, recovering his equilibrium. Then he kicks the backmost pew, and the wood lets out a harsh screech as it grates across the flagstones. He sighs, turns, and walks out of the church. The door closes with a loud thunk, and the turning of the key reverberates round the church, echoing through the rafters above.

"Wait!" Her voice booms out across the pews. She runs for the door. She bangs on it and rattles the handle. "Hey!" She's sure he's still out there; she heard him grunt. "Hey," she shouts again, "I'm locked in here." She listens, thinks she might be able to hear him breathing. "This is the police. Open the door." She rattles the handle again and then waits. Nothing but silence.

She looks round the church. There must be another way.

The room where the argument took place is hot and stuffy in comparison with the cool interior of the church. There's a smaller door on the far side that must lead into the community hall she saw when she was here before, but this door is locked as well.

This is ridiculous. How long is he planning to leave her here? Not all night, surely. Fuck that. She reaches into her pocket for her phone. The lads are going to have a field day with this. Her hand finds nothing, and an image forms in her mind of her mobile on the desk in the incident room, Doggett shouting at her about bacon and Muslims. She had grabbed her purse and pretty much run to the village. She looks down and finds she's still holding the greasy sandwich in her left hand. "Oh, for f—" She throws it down on a table, closes her eyes, and takes a deep breath.

She sees an old kitchen chair draped in discarded robes—*cassocks*—the word comes to her in an unsatisfying flash of inspiration. This is bullshit! She pushes the garments onto the floor and sits down. Now what? She can't just sit here until he comes back. She coughs a little and clears her throat. She'll look a complete twat, which is exactly what he wants, of course. There must be a phone . . . or something. She coughs again. It isn't as though she can even climb out the windows; most of them are too high to reach, and the ones that aren't are patterned with stained glass and leaded lights. Even if she could find a way to climb up there and smash the glass, there's no way to get through the lead. Not to mention how much they must be worth; Jordan would crucify her! What is that smell? Something like car fumes or . . . she coughs once more, violently this time, struggles to catch her breath. And now she notices how dark the room has grown while she's been sitting there. A sense of movement draws her eye back to the door that leads into the community hall. Rolling clouds of dark gray smoke begin to billow up and fill the room.

Tyler decides that persuading Doggett to forgo his sandwich in order to question Lily Bainbridge is probably going to turn out to be marginally easier than persuading him not to sack Rabbani when she finally gets back. The wasted journey to the Thorogoods' house does nothing to improve his temper either. By the time they return to find Bainbridge sitting back in the garden of her own cottage, knees up to her chin, arms wrapped protectively round her legs like a schoolgirl waiting for the bus, Doggett is ready to kill someone.

Tyler decides he'd better take the lead. "Miss Bainbridge?"

She looks up. "Oh, are you finished now?"

He glances at Doggett, who shrugs his approval to go on. "Not quite," he tells her. "We just have a few more questions."

"You'd better come in," she says, getting to her feet.

Danny Atkins from Uniform is standing guard in the conservatory and he turns, intent on barring her path, but Bainbridge stops anyway, before she even reaches the doorstep. The smell comes to Tyler over her head. He watches her as she stares beyond the conservatory to the stain on the living room carpet.

"We can get a cleaner for that," he tells her.

"No. I'd rather do it myself. Thank you, though, that's very kind, Mr. . . . ?"

He reintroduces himself and Doggett. "Perhaps we could sit outside?"

She nods absently, and Tyler gestures to Atkins to fetch one of the patio chairs.

"Would you like some tea?" she asks. "I think there may be some cake left as well, if you'd like it?"

"Miss Bainbridge," Doggett tells her. "We are treating your house as a crime scene for now. You won't be able to stay here for a while."

She looks confused. "No, no, that can't be right."

Atkins guides her into the chair and she sits. He returns to his post.

Doggett is making little urging motions with his head, trying to convince Tyler to push her, but Tyler shakes his head. Kid gloves. The woman is clearly in a state of deep shock.

"I'm sorry we have to do this now," he says.

Lily looks up at him for the first time, a frown on her wrinkled brow. "I don't understand. What crime?"

"We need to ask you about Gerald Cartwright," he tells her.

Suddenly she's all smiles. "Oh yes, Gerald. He's a lovely man. No trouble. A wonderful neighbor. We're very lucky." Her eyes flick toward the conservatory for a moment, and the smile fades.

"You got along well, then?"

"Of course."

"And Mrs. Cartwright? Cynthia?"

"Oh." Lily's face hardens. "Yes, silly girl. I'm not sure she ever really wanted a child." She glances at the conservatory again, and a faint color appears in her cheeks.

"You didn't like her, then?"

"Cynthia? Oh yes, she was very nice."

"But silly?"

"A bit flighty," she says. "A will-o'-the-wisp." She laughs lightly. "Yes, always off somewhere. Never happy with what she had. Edna said—" She stops abruptly.

"Yes?"

"Well, it isn't right to speak ill of the dead, is it?" It isn't clear if she means Edna or Cynthia.

Tyler is painfully aware of Doggett fidgeting just out of his sight line.

"Have you seen anything of her in the past ten years?"

"Edna had a call," she says all at once, her words tripping over themselves, "after she left."

"She did? Can you remember where she was ringing from?"

"Canada."

"Canada?"

"I'm not sure. Yes. Canada, I think. Or Ireland. You won't tell Oscar I said that, will you? About Cynthia. I wouldn't want him to think . . ." Again she trails off.

Doggett sighs heavily.

"Have you met Oscar?" Lily asks. "We're very proud of him.

Such a beautiful little boy, and so caring. He wouldn't hurt a fly, not our Oscar." She flinches slightly. Again her eyes flicking toward the conservatory. Tyler wonders if it's Atkins's presence in her home that has her spooked, but it doesn't seem to be him that she's focused on. If anything, she seems to be eyeing the garden furniture piled neatly to one side of the door. He recognizes the strange swing contraption he saw on their last visit.

"Do you remember what happened when Gerald went missing, Lily?"

"Yes," she says. "Or rather, no. I mean, I wasn't there, was I?"

"Where?"

"Hmm?"

"You weren't where?"

"Wherever he was when he went missing?" She smiles, apparently pleased at her logic.

"Lily, I don't think you're being entirely truthful with me. Is there something else? Something you want to tell us?"

She looks at the swing again—yes, he's sure now that it is the swing that has her attention. "The furniture," she says.

"What about it?"

"It's just . . . I don't see how she could have managed it. The sun lounger. Not on her own. I think I would've struggled myself and . . ." Once again she trails off.

Doggett lets out a huff of air, a pressure valve that is perhaps the only thing that saves Lily from being on the receiving end of a significant rant. He places his hands on the arms of her chair and leans in. When he speaks, thankfully, he's lost some of his irritation. "Miss Bainbridge, you need to stop lying to us now." Behind his back he clicks his fingers at Tyler, who extracts the evidence bag that is nestled in his back pocket and passes it forward. The DI snatches it from his hand and holds it in front of Lily's face. She frowns at the charred paper visible through the clear plastic. Her lips move as she reads the words that are still visible. *I know what y—*

"Oh," she says. "I'm sorry, but I don't follow."

"This was in your fireplace. We think it was protected from the fire somewhat by . . ." Doggett stops himself. It is more than obvious what protected it.

"No," she says. "No. I don't think so."

"Yes," Doggett argues with her, but gently by his standards, as though he's coaxing an insect into a trap before throwing it out the window. "You need to talk to us. You need to tell us what's going on here. We can't help you otherwise. We can't help Oscar."

"Oscar," she breathes quietly.

And as though summoned, he is there. "Auntie Edie! Aunt Lil!" His voice echoes down the path from the front of the house.

Tyler moves to head him off. He hears the officer guarding the front door shout, "No, lad, you can't just—" But he breaks off when he sees Tyler blocking the path ahead.

"You? What are you—?"

"It's Edna, Oscar."

Oscar pushes past, his eyes going first to Lily, then Doggett, then to Danny Atkins watching curiously from the house. Oscar pushes his way into the conservatory and straight into Atkins's arms. There's a brief struggle, and then Oscar plainly notices the mark on the carpet because he breaks away from the tussle, his hands flying to his mouth. He staggers back out into the garden and retches, dropping into a crouch and clutching his stomach.

"Get him a glass of water or something," Doggett instructs, and Atkins heads off into the house. Tyler grabs another of the fold-up patio chairs, glancing at the swing—the sun lounger, as Lily had called it. When he gets back outside, Oscar is sitting on the garden wall where they'd found Lily earlier, elbows on his knees, hands over his mouth. He looks paler than ever, and the bags under his eyes are so dark they could be makeup. He wipes the fat tears from his cheeks with the palms of his hands and suddenly he seems to be aware of his surroundings for the first time. "What's going on?" he asks. "Lily?"

But Lily is staring off into space, her jaw slack. Oscar gets up and goes to her. "What have you been doing to her? Lily? Lily, can you hear me?" He rounds on them. "What the *fuck* is wrong with you people? Can't you see she isn't well?"

"We need to ask—"

"What the *fuck* is wrong with you?" He says it again, but this time he's speaking to Tyler alone. "Do you actually have any feelings at all? Do you? Jesus Christ, Adam!" He turns to Doggett. "I want you out of here. All of you!"

"This is a potential crime scene," Doggett tells him.

"What crime? She was an old lady. For fuck's sake, are you saying someone killed her?"

"We don't know what happened yet."

At once Oscar calms. Tyler sees the change in his eyes. "There are rules about police harassment," he says. "From now on both Lily and I will be speaking through our solicitor. You can direct any further questions to Michael Denham's office. Is that understood?"

Doggett eyes him closely. "I think we're all a lot clearer on things," he says.

"Oscar?" Lily is back.

"It's all right, Auntie Lil. Let's get you somewhere a bit more comfortable." Oscar helps her to her feet and guides her down the path. "Then we'll have a chat with Michael. I'm sure he can sort everything out."

By the time Atkins gets back, Lily and Oscar are gone. Doggett grabs the glass from his hand and downs it in one. His eyes lock on

to Tyler's, and he smacks his lips. He looks about ready to kill someone, but he clearly doesn't want to say anything in front of Atkins.
Instead, all he says is, "Where's that bloody girl with my breadcake?"

The wood of the vestry door is beginning to blister. The smoke
is thicker now, as though the fact she's noticed it has given it permission to be there. It stretches out to fill the room. Rabbani coughs
her way back into the church and closes the door. The smoke begins to billow underneath almost immediately.

She moves back down the aisle. On her right-hand side she can
see the fire on the roof of the annex, the flames flickering and
dancing behind the colored glass of the stained-glass windows
even as the images begin to blacken with smoke. Never mind how
much the bloody things are worth; if she could find a way up there,
and a way to get through all the lead on the windows, she would.
She wonders how long the wooden doors will hold. But then, she'll
probably suffocate long before the flames reach her anyway. She
finds some more cassocks folded in a pile next to the font and uses
them to plug the gap under the door.

How does a church burn? It's bloody stupid. Isn't it mostly stone?
In answer, there's a loud crack from overhead and she looks up to
see a mist of wispy gray smoke suspended between the wooden
rafters.

She runs back to the front door. "Help!" Her voice sounds so
pathetic she almost laughs. This can't be happening. Her arms
ache as she pummels on the door. Her throat aches from shouting.

"God!" She screams it.

And saying His name out loud makes her think properly about
Him, perhaps for the first time. She sits down on the rearmost pew.

She needs to calm down, but all she can think about is the fact she's about to be burned alive in a church. She can hear her mother telling everyone, "This is God's punishment!" And it's not even her god. She starts to laugh hysterically, but this soon breaks into another choking cough. The hall is filling with smoke fast now. Through it she sees the first flicker of red light from the area next to the altar. What is it called? Why can't she remember? She's going to die in a place she doesn't have the proper terminology for. Her eyes sting, but she can't work out if she's crying or if it's the smoke.

"No!" She hauls herself back to her feet. There must be something. She won't just curl up and die.

She's considered her own death before, of course. Who hasn't? For a while, in Year 5, she thought she might want to be a foreign correspondent, a war journalist or something. Report from Afghanistan and Iraq or wherever Britain invaded next. It seemed worthy and would at least get her away from home, which was more than half the point. But it was just a dream. She never got the grades, and she doubts university would have suited her anyway. Still, she used to fantasize about what it would be like when the bombs were falling and the bullets flying. She wouldn't hide somewhere waiting for the inevitable. She'd run through the dust and shrapnel, fight tooth and claw to get back, pass on the message about what was happening to innocent women and children who had the gall to get in the way of the blokes and their guns.

She has to get out of here. She has to tell them what she heard. She has to tell them about Wentworth and Thorogood. *They* did this to her. She won't let them get away with it. She'll make a promise to God if that's what it takes. Maybe it isn't her god, or maybe it is, or maybe they're all the same—the Muslim god, and the Christian god, and Buddha, and aliens, and God knows what else. Whatever it takes. She'll give in to her mother and go to Mecca next year, complete the hajj. Just whoever He is, please, God! Not like this!

There must be a way. There must be something.

She tries to pry off the metal covering on the latch, but it's solid and weighty and she might as well try scratching at a wall with her fingernails. She thinks of Gerald Cartwright buried alive and shivers.

Through the fog she makes out a shape—a candlestick on the table next to the font. She pulls up the collar of her top so that it covers her mouth a little and forces her way closer to the flames. The heat is terrifying. Like that time she picked up the pan on the stove and for a second it didn't register and then she was dropping it, spilling boiling water across the kitchen floor where it splashed against Ghulam's leg and turned his soft brown skin a livid pink. She thought she would die that day, when their mother found out. Poor Ghulam, the favorite, scarred for life by his clumsy, useless sister. Maybe that's what this is. Her punishment. Maybe she's already burning but can't feel it yet, just like the pan.

She can barely breathe but she forces herself to go on, one foot in front of the other. Wraps her hand around the candlestick. It feels hot, but it can't be; it's just her imagination. She runs back to the door, and the effort sends her into another fit of coughing. She brings the candlestick down hard on the lock. Clang. The vibrations travel up her aching arms. Again. Clang. Again. Fifty blows. More. She stops and examines her progress. There's a dent in the lock mechanism, but she can't be sure it wasn't there already. The candlestick, on the other hand, is bent completely out of shape.

"Bastard!" She pulls back her arm and launches the candlestick at the window. There's a small tinkle of glass; the candlestick bounces off the leaded lights and drops to the floor with a dull thud.

Rabbani falls to her knees and presses her forehead to the cold flagstones. Above her, the roof timbers break, raining fiery droplets down upon the pews. One of the wooden benches begins to smolder and catch. The air thickens, the heat on her face doubles.

No! Not like this. Up again. Fight!

In front of her, she sees the golden cross chained to its pedestal. Behind that, on the wall with the altar, Christ hangs burning on His crucifix. Something black and molten drips across His face, making Him weep dark tears. Is He mocking her?

She grabs the cross with both hands, pulls it up. It's so incredibly heavy and it won't reach anywhere near the door. But there is some length to the chain. She untangles it as best she can and rams it hard against the smashed window. More of the glass breaks, but when she tries to pull the cross back out it sticks fast, jutting into the cool air. The fresh air is glorious but makes her cough even more. The sun glints off the golden surface of the cross, and she sinks to the floor for what she knows will be the last time. She has nothing left.

"Shit," she says softly, or she tries to. The smoke seems to be all around her. In her. She can't even cough anymore; there's nothing left to inhale or exhale. Let it be over now. She can't fight any longer.

Constable Amina Rabbani falls sideways.

They are on their way back to the incident room. Doggett has changed his mind about them reliving an Agatha Christie novel. "It's the bleedin' *Stepford Wives,*" he says. "That's what it is. Or something out of a Shirley Jackson story."

Tyler has no idea what he's talking about but makes a mental note to google it later.

"You know this Denham character lives here an' all? Got a mansion the other side of the village. No doubt paid for by Gerald Cartwright's millions. They all bloody live here! And they're all in it up to their bloody eyeballs. I tell you, if we don't unearth a flamin' coven sacrificing vestal virgins before we're finished here, I'll— what the . . . ?"

Doggett is the first to see the smoke, but Tyler is the first to start running and soon outpaces the older man. When he reaches the church the flames are already racing across the roof, clouds of black smoke rolling like filthy waves into the sky.

He sees a man looking in at the window. "Police! Come away from there."

The man looks up, startled, and Tyler sees that *kid* would be a more accurate description; he's no more than seventeen or eighteen. "There's someone in there!" he says, pointing at the golden cross sticking out of the window through the leaded lights, smoke curling around it and evaporating into the sky.

The key is still in the lock. Tyler turns it and pushes on the massive wooden door, and a curtain of gray smoke reaches out to engulf him. He covers his mouth with his T-shirt as best he can and plunges into the church, eyes stinging. He can hear the crackle of flames, feel their heat on his face and hands. He inches his way, half blind, toward the window, virtually tripping over her before he even realizes she's there. Rabbani. Her slight figure is facedown on the flagstones, her hair loose across her face. It makes him think of Edna Burnside and Cynthia Cartwright. It makes him think of the girl in the flat. Victims. But not Rabbani. She can't be a victim; he won't let her be. He snatches her up, surprised at how light she is before he realizes the kid is with him, helping to support her weight. They stumble back toward the door, or at least where he thinks the door should be. He's got himself turned around; he has no idea which way is out, which way is closer to the flames. He's starting to panic, then, all at once, they are out, the fresh air burning his throat.

Tyler coughs. The kid coughs. Even Doggett is coughing, either from the smoke that still surrounds them or perhaps just from the exertion of the journey here.

Rabbani doesn't cough.

Doggett leans down and puts his ear to her face, tries to find a pulse. He looks up at Tyler. "I dunno," he says, then, "Wait . . . yeah, she's breathing. I think."

Time passes. The next thing Tyler notices is the sound of the sirens approaching. Doggett has vanished; the kid is lying on his back on the grass, wheezing. Then they are surrounded: firefighters, paramedics, reporters temporarily relocated from round the corner, other curious gawpers. *He's* here somewhere. Watching them, watching his handiwork.

Doggett returns with DS Daley and a handful of uniforms. They begin setting up a cordon to keep back the crowd. Their next job will be to begin combing the area around the church, as closely as they can without disturbing too much evidence.

The paramedics strap a mask across Rabbani's face. Tyler thinks that must be a good sign. They wouldn't be doing that if they were too late. Her lips are dry and cracked, and still she doesn't cough. There are smudges of dirt all over her skin. She looks frightened. Even unconscious she looks terrified.

He asks the kid his name. Barry. He shakes Barry's hand, congratulates him, and thanks him for helping and for raising the alarm. Barry smiles sheepishly, and Tyler wonders what the boy was doing here.

Paul Enfield arrives, surveying the gathered spectators as he walks. Tyler pulls himself up off the ground and tells Barry not to go anywhere; they'll need a statement. He leaves Rabbani to the experts and meets Paul halfway. Interesting, how he thinks of the man as *Paul* now, rather than *Enfield*. A uniformed fireman intercepts Paul ahead of him, and they speak with lowered heads and whispered voices. He's seen that talk before. Many times. He knows what it means. It never occurred to him to go back, to check if there was anyone else.

He sees the confirmation in Paul's face before he speaks. "Round the back."

They walk round the smoking church in silence. Before they can enter, Paul speaks with another uniformed fire officer. The flames are out in the small annex at the back, but the fire is still burning in the church itself. He's reluctant to let them in but finally relents.

Tyler sees the hands first, curled up into blackened claws. He thinks of Gerald Cartwright's damaged fingers, and a cooked dog he once saw outside a restaurant in China, laid out on the pavement so the customers could choose their cut. Its flesh was the same mottled collage of black and red, the only difference the large slash of pink where the chef had carved out a portion of its belly for a diner. Its claws hooked into talons, its lips curled back from its teeth. The guy he was traveling with at the time told him a colorful story about the local culture, how the animals were cooked alive so the adrenaline in their veins enhanced the flavor. He never did find out if that was true, but even if it was he could justify it to himself. A different culture. Not wrong, just different. He can accept that intellectually. He can understand it. He looks down at the charred corpse. This he doesn't understand.

"The door wasn't locked," says Paul. Meaning the victim was dead before the fire started, or at least incapacitated in some way.

"The keys were in the front door."

"It would have been quick," Paul says. But spoils it by adding, "Comparatively."

"Who is it?"

"The local vicar, we think."

Now he sees it. A trace of unspoiled dog collar visible beneath the griddled chin. The Reverend Sebastian Thorogood. Felbridge. Gerald's old school friend.

There's an ominous creak above them and something gives. A crash of falling masonry toward the back of the room. They move as one, diving for the door. Fire officers rush forward to grab them and usher them back into the daylight.

Back at the front of the church Rabbani is no longer visible, surrounded now by men and women in fluorescent jackets.

Paul touches his arm. "You saved her," he says.

"That kid was already here."

"No need to be modest."

"No," Tyler tells him. "I mean, we need to check him out. He was the first one on the scene."

For some reason Paul smiles. "I'll get Forensics to check him for traces of accelerant." He starts to leave and then stops again, looks up at the smoking church. He has an intent look in his eye, almost . . . worshipful. Only, if Tyler had to put money on what it was this man worshipped, it wouldn't be the church so much as the fire that almost consumed it.

"What is it?" Tyler asks.

Enfield snaps out of his reverie. "Oh, nothing. I was just wondering when all this was going to end. With all these extra fires we're pretty stretched. One more serious incident and . . . Well, best not to think too much on that." He smiles and heads off in the direction of his colleagues.

As soon as the fire officer has left, Doggett is there, appearing at Tyler's shoulder as though he's been waiting for his moment. They watch silently as the paramedics continue their work on Rabbani. One of them breaks away from the pack and runs toward the ambulance.

"Do you think she was the target?" Doggett asks.

Tyler shakes his head. It's too ridiculous. What could she have to do with any of this? But then, why was she here in the first place?

Doggett motions for him to follow, and they move toward the church door. Water is still cascading from the ruined roof, and one of the fire officers tries to keep them back. Doggett argues but it's a glance and a nod from Paul Enfield that gets them through.

Doggett points down to the ground.

Tyler kneels to examine the flagstones. There are traces of blood. "Someone hit him with something while he was locking up."

"They dragged him." Doggett points to the flattened grass at the side of the path. "Felbridge was tall, but not particularly bulky; any number of people could have managed it. Any number of people." Doggett taps him on the shoulder and points back out to the road.

Tyler stands up again and scans the crowd.

Doggett nods. "Like I said. It's the bleedin' Village of the Damned. I'll get Daley and a couple of the lads to film them."

But Tyler can already pick out a number of faces from the crowd. There's the solicitor, Michael Denham, his arm wrapped tightly around his daughter's shoulders. They both look shocked, ashen and gray. Not far from them the old gardener, Wentworth, is leaning on a rake and staring at them intently. As soon as Tyler makes eye contact he looks away and shuffles a little further into the crowd. He isn't the only one watching, though. Paul Enfield is talking to the young lad from the church, Barry. But he, too, keeps glancing over at Tyler. And the vicar's wife, Jean Thorogood, who may well be in shock but has yet to shed a single tear. She is being comforted by friends and neighbors but seems to be listening to none of it. Instead she stares at Tyler. There's a man in a butcher's apron, splattered and crusted with dried blood. Gerald Cartwright's old cook, Carol Braithwaite, with several members of her extended family. Half the village must be here, or more. All of them staring at him, waiting for him to do something. Or accusing him of not doing more sooner. The only one who isn't here is Oscar.

"He could have saved her." Tyler looks at the keys still hanging from the lock. "He just left her there to die." He doesn't mean Oscar. It can't have been Oscar. He was at the cottage with them. But as soon as he thinks that, he thinks about how close the cottage is, how quickly a young, fit man could set fire to a church and then hare it across the churchyard to where he knows the police will be, to establish an alibi. And if he knew they were there, then he knew what had happened to Edna as well.

Doggett puts a hand on his shoulder. "*You* saved her," he says, misinterpreting Tyler's silence.

Did he? He's not so sure. The paramedics scatter suddenly, and Rabbani is lifted quickly onto a stretcher and bundled into the back of an ambulance. There's an urgency to the operation that is frightening. In seconds the ambulance is tearing its way through the village, sirens blaring, assorted journalists chasing after it, their cameras flashing.

"Sir!" DS Daley trots up to them. He's holding aloft a backpack and grinning like a cheeky schoolboy. He's enjoying himself immensely. He opens the bag for Doggett. "Found it in some bushes by the main gate. Matches, lighter fluid. Right proper little arsonist's kit."

Some movement makes Tyler look up in time to see the young lad, Barry, speeding toward them across the graveyard. Paul Enfield shouts after him, but Tyler is already moving. Barry realizes his escape is cut off and changes direction. He stumbles slightly and Tyler gains ground. His lungs feel like they're on fire and he resists the urge to cough again, knowing that if he does, he'll stop and he won't be able to get going again. The distance between them closes. Barry is slowing, limping slightly where he's twisted something on the sudden turn. But Tyler is running out of time. His vision is blurring, darkening, and he's sure he's about to pass out. He's not going to stop, though; even if it means his lungs burst, he won't stop. It's now or never. Tyler hurls himself forward, arms outstretched to take Barry around the waist, and then they are falling, barreling over each other in a twisted tangle of limbs. Tyler feels the gravel of the path digging into his hands and face, and something heavy lands on top of his stomach and pushes the last of the air out of his lungs.

Tyler watches the kid sitting opposite him. Barry Nelson is seventeen, but he looks a lot younger with all that snot dripping freely off his nose ring, and the tiny balled-up fists he uses to try to staunch the tears leaking from his eyes. The "appropriate adult" sitting next to him is Helen Cooper ("Call-Me-Hels"). Doggett clearly knows her of old, and the vein in his head has been pulsing dangerously for the hour and a half they have been waiting for the social worker to arrive. She is an ephemeral woman in a floaty dress who spends a great deal of time asking Barry if he is okay, rummaging through her handbag for tissues, and apologizing profusely for keeping them waiting despite the fact she is still the one holding things up. Most AAs see themselves as something only slightly short of a solicitor. They are squarely on the side of the poor little blighters they have been called in to represent, and most have watched too many courtroom dramas and barely resist the urge to shout "Objection!" to every question put to their clients. Conversely, Call-Me-Hels is doing her best to be on everyone's side and no one's, which for some reason Tyler finds even more infuriating. He has to admit he's with Doggett on this one; he dislikes this woman immensely.

Despite her presence in the room, Barry appears completely alone. It seems he is estranged from his parents, who threw him out when he was just fifteen. Since then he has been working for the butcher and living above his shop, but when they rang George

Simmonite and asked him to come to the station, he refused on the grounds "the lad" had nothing to do with him.

Tyler's head is pounding, and every now and again he is forced to cover his mouth while he coughs up black crap from his lungs, though the coughing fits are shorter and repeat less frequently. He had been unconscious in the churchyard for only a moment or two, but the paramedics tried to make him go to the hospital with them.

Once Call-Me-Hels has finished doling out tissues and checking her makeup in a compact, she sits quietly and stares into space, smiling. It's a little unnerving how switched off she looks. Doggett deals with all the usual *persons present* housekeeping, and Barry sits sniveling throughout. Finally, Doggett reaches down to his feet under the table and brings up a plastic evidence bag containing the backpack Guy Daley recovered at the crime scene.

"Is this yours, Barry?" he asks.

Barry looks up and immediately down again.

"Because it has your initials written on the label in felt-tip pen, mate? See, here?" The plastic crackles under Doggett's fingertips. "B.N. Barry Nelson. So . . . I'll ask you again, does this belong to you?"

Barry nods his head without looking up.

Doggett says, "For the benefit of the tape, suspect is nodding." He asks the lad to explain himself, but Barry refuses to look up. His shoulders are shaking, but he's not saying anything.

Tyler has seen this before. It's always the young ones that freeze.

Doggett glances at him for a moment and then goes on, in a softer tone than Tyler has ever heard from him before. "You need to talk to us, lad. All right? I think you realize how serious this is, don't you? Now, you're clearly no stranger to trouble, but by all accounts you'd put all that business behind you. You've got a home, an apprenticeship—that's no small thing these days. I'm surprised you'd jeopardize all that. Mr. Simmonite weren't too thrilled to hear we were taking you in, so you're going to have a lot of explaining to do when we take you home." Here he pauses for a moment before going on. "That's assuming you get to go home. Right now, that's looking far from likely." Doggett reaches down to two more evidence bags at his feet and places them one by one onto the table. A bottle of lighter fluid. A large box of kitchen matches. "All this stuff . . . things aren't looking so good for you."

Barry mumbles something.

"What was that, Barry, lad? You need to speak up for the tape."

"I said, it was just meant to be a laugh."

Doggett nods. "We've all been there, haven't we, DS Tyler?" He winks. "Well, maybe not DS Tyler, he's too much of a Boy Scout." He breaks off to raise his eyebrows at Tyler. Tyler mouths a "Fuck off," and Doggett stifles a grin.

"But I'm still young enough I can remember how it was," he goes on. "Still, you're not a little boy anymore, so you know how serious this is. A man is dead." Doggett's tone hardens. "One of my police officers is in a critical condition in the hospital."

Barry shuffles in his seat but still says nothing.

Call-Me-Hels shuffles in *her* seat. "DI Doggett, I . . ."

"Be quiet!" Doggett snaps, and she does so, closing her mouth and sitting back. "Now," Doggett says, turning back to Barry, "I don't think you meant for anyone to get hurt, did you, Barry? But you need to start talking to us, telling us how this all came about. What the connection is with the body we've found. Because the only other alternative is I book you for murder. Right here, right now."

Barry looks up, wide-eyed. Tyler can't help but feel sorry for the boy. They had fought alongside each other to rescue Rabbani from the church. He doesn't want to believe this teenage lad is responsible for the fires in Castledene, and even less so the death of Gerald Cartwright. And yet . . . he was there at the scene with his homemade fire-starting kit. He lives and works in the village that was Gerald's home. And Tyler has been sure, for a long time now, that the perpetrator of the fires is linked somehow to the body found in the cellar at the Old Vicarage. His head is pounding. Could he have been wrong all this time? Maybe it *is* just a coincidence, all these fires occurring in the same place as their murder investigation. Barry Nelson would have been eleven when Gerald died.

And Oscar was fifteen. Doggett's words when they had gone over all this while waiting for Call-Me-Hels to show up. *Old enough to knock your dad over the head and drag him behind a wall. Especially if you had a friend to help you.*

Could there have been some connection between them? They hadn't gone to the same school. Barry had been at the local comprehensive, a far cry and several miles distant from Oscar's three-grand-a-term prep school. Could they have met somewhere else? Where else did boys of different ages meet other than school? Football practice? Something Doggett said earlier jumps into his head.

Barry snivels into his tissue. Call-Me-Hels stares into space, no longer smiling after her telling-off. Doggett is shaking his head, losing his patience. Tyler catches his eye and Doggett nods his permission.

"Barry," Tyler says, "were you ever in the Cub Scouts?"

The question takes him by surprise, and Barry nods before he can remember not to.

"Did you like it?" Tyler asks. "I did." He's lying. He hated the Cub Scouts. Richard had made him go, following in Jude's footsteps. He'd left as soon as he was allowed to. *Why can't you just learn how to play nicely with others?* "Camping out under the stars, learning all those survival skills. I bet that's where you learned how to light fires, isn't it?"

Barry shakes his head but hesitantly, unsure perhaps if this wasn't where he *had* first learned how to light a fire. Of course, matches and lighter fluid made it a lot easier.

"Was that you as well, then? The scout hut the other day? Why would you want to burn that place?"

Barry shakes his head more forcefully this time. "I di'n't! I mean, that weren't me. I swear, I've only done a couple of bonfires."

At least he's talking.

"Okay, mate, listen. I believe you. I don't think you set the fire at the scout hut or the church. You certainly didn't mean for anyone to get hurt. That's why you helped me save PC Rabbani. I bet you would have helped me save the vicar, too, wouldn't you? If we'd known he was in there. You knew him, didn't you? You knew him by another name, though. *Akela.*"

He had found the word in Rabbani's notebook, circled three times in black ink. But only now, in light of Doggett's comment about Boy Scouts, has the significance clicked.

"He was your old Cub Scout leader, right?"

Barry's eyes are filling up with new tears. He wipes his nose on his sleeve.

"I don't think you wanted to hurt him, or anybody else. But here's the thing, Barry. Somebody did. And it's too much of a coincidence you just happened to be there at the same time. You know something about this, don't you? Do you know who killed your old Akela? If you do, and you don't say anything, that makes you an accessory to murder. Regardless of the punishment for that, I don't think you could live with yourself. So come on, mate, why don't you just tell us who killed him?"

Barry starts to open his mouth, probably to deny everything all over again, but then something gives. Tyler sees it in the way his shoulders drop. The boy leans his head in his hands and lets out a long sigh.

"I don't know who he is," he says. "But if you let me have my phone I can show you."

Tyler looks at Doggett, and they both smile.

"How on earth did you put that together?" Doggett is staring at the computer screen in front of them.

Tyler shrugs. "I didn't, Rabbani did. There was a word circled in her notebook. The last thing she'd written in it. 'Akela.' I didn't make the connection until you mentioned Cub Scouts. Then I remembered. The leaders all take the names of characters from *The Jungle Book*. My old Cub Scout leader was Baloo. He was a right little bastard, about as far from a bear as you could possibly imagine."

"So Rabbani had been looking into Felbridge and discovered he used to lead the Cub Scouts at the hut. That's why she went there? To question him? What the fuck was she thinking? Stupid girl! Why didn't she just tell us?"

"No news yet then?"

Doggett shakes his head.

They stare at the screen together in silence.

"So what the fuck is this?" Doggett asks.

"It's a blog."

"I know it's a fucking blog, I meant . . . I mean . . . well, I don't know what I mean."

Tyler glances over the entries again. "This is him. This is the killer. The fire watcher."

They read the screen in silence for a while and then Doggett says, "This explains Fireman Sam's statistical spike. Looks like Barry isn't the only copycat out there."

"We need to tell Enfield about this. If they can shut it down, it will help stop people copying."

"Hang on, let's not be too hasty," Doggett says. "This might be our only chance to catch the bastard. If we shut the thing down, won't that just tip him the wink that we're on to him? Can't we just . . . trace it?" He asks hesitantly, as though he's unsure whether it might be a stupid question.

"We should be able to trace the IP address. But I don't know how long that would take. In the meantime someone could get hurt."

"Well, let's find out at least."

Tyler thinks about it for a moment. "I know someone who works in IT. Hang on a minute." He pulls out his mobile and finds Sally-Ann's number. While he's waiting for her to answer, he says, "So what have you done with poor old Barry?"

Doggett grins. "I read him the riot act a bit, but to be honest my heart wasn't in it. He'll probably catch far worse when he gets back to the butcher. And we'll pass his details on to your fireman friend, just in case he decides to start lighting bonfires again. I almost feel sorry for the lad."

"Careful, Jim, you're growing soft in your old age."

Before Doggett can respond, Sally-Ann answers without saying hello. "This isn't a good time. Can I call you—?"

He cuts her off: "Actually, this is work related." Has he pissed her off somehow? Probably.

"Oh," she says. "Go on then."

He outlines what they know about the fire watcher and gives her the Web address. She's silent at first and then seems to get excited, as though she can't help getting drawn in, despite how pissed off she might be. "So you think this is your killer then? The Cartwright case?"

"I can't give you any details at this point, but I can tell you you'd be helping us out. A lot."

She giggles with excitement. "Sure. I should be able to trace it. Unless your killer is some kind of computer whiz and has managed to cover his tracks. It shouldn't take too long."

"How long?"

She hesitates, then, "I should have an answer for you by tomorrow."

"Great, thanks, Sal."

"Adam, wait! Don't hang up."

He waits, but she's fallen silent. Eventually he says, "I'm still here. Go on."

"It's just . . . I need to tell you something."

"Okay. Can it wait? I mean, I'm sorry if I upset you the other night or something, but I've got a fair bit on at work at the moment and—"

"I know, I know. I get it, only . . . this might be about work." There's a long silence, which he resolves not to break. Finally her voice comes to him, quiet and tiny. She says, "It's just . . . I think I might have done something really stupid."

"I set you up," says Sally-Ann.

They are standing outside the headquarters of the South Yorkshire Police. The soon-to-be *old* headquarters; the building is less than a month from demolition. With a backward stretch, and standing on tiptoe, it is possible to see the shiny new building a few streets over, twice the size. The move has begun; around them huddle numerous unmarked white vans filled with paperwork no one knows what to do with.

Sally-Ann plays with her earring, picks at her nails, and fails to meet his eye directly. She's still draped in fabric; a thick, long-sleeved turtleneck that must be ridiculously hot. As if that wasn't enough, she's topped it off with an incongruous paisley summer scarf that even Audrey Hepburn couldn't have pulled off. She must mistake his interest in her because she says, "Please don't look at me like that. You're a terrible person to disappoint, do you know that?" She looks round as a group of people exit the building. One of them, a short woman Tyler vaguely recognizes, waves to Sally-Ann, and she smiles and waves back. Then she sighs heavily. "Oscar," she says, "I set you up with Oscar."

A bus pulls up at the light and lets out a sharp hiss of pneumatic brakes.

"I didn't know, Adam. I didn't know about any of this, I swear."

At least now he knows how Oscar got his number. "Tell me," he says.

Sally-Ann swallows. "We were at school together. I hadn't seen him for years, and then we bumped into each other out clubbing one night. We got talking and he seemed different to how he used to be. Not like when we were at school, all full of himself and throwing dirt in your hair in the playground—"

"Sally-Ann."

"Sorry. So he took me for a drink one night, old friends catching up sort of thing, and then he told me he was . . . well, that he was exploring his sexuality. It wasn't long after I'd met you, and I thought, you know who might be good for each other?"

The bus pulls away, covering them in a blanket of dark fumes.

"Why didn't you just ask me?"

"You'd have gone along with that, would you? A blind date? Come off it, Adam. You're a nice guy, mostly. You're intelligent, and you look great, but, well, you're not exactly sociable. So I gave him the hard sell and convinced him it might be better if you met sort of spontaneously."

"The pub. He chatted me up at the bar while you watched."

"I'm sorry, it seemed harmless enough."

"So he knew I was with the police? That I was in CID?"

Sally-Ann looks away, and he has his answer.

"I didn't think it at the time, but looking back I think he might have been angling for me to set him up with someone. Not you specifically but . . . he was really interested in my job. I told him what I did, working in the comms room, and he asked loads of questions about CID."

"He asked you about CID specifically?"

Sally-Ann thinks about it. "Well, no, not exactly, but he kept coming back to the same thing, did I know anyone involved in the juicy stuff, drugs, murder? It was just one of those conversations you have in the pub, you know?"

He thinks he's beginning to.

"But I've been thinking about the night I first met him. It was when I told him I worked for the police that he started to get more interested. I remember because it's weird; most people run a mile when you tell them you work for the cops, but if anything I got the impression he was flirting with me. He asked me out, and when we went on our 'date,' and I made it clear I wasn't interested in him, that's when he suddenly came out."

"Why didn't you tell me this . . . ?" He stops. He's been a fool. "Last night, you set that up, too. That's why you were so adamant I go."

"I didn't know, Adam. I swear I didn't. He said he liked you but that you were . . . difficult. I said I told him that at the start." Sally-Ann looks up at him. "Sorry. Anyway, he said he needed to see you again on neutral territory, like the night you met, that it was better that way."

"And you never thought anything was wrong with that? In light of what we found in his house?"

"No, I mean, I don't know, maybe. It's just . . . he has this way about him. You sort of feel you can trust him. He's always been like that, actually, overly charming. But when I saw you together in the club last night, and I saw him put that pill in your glass—"

"What?"

"I think he slipped you something. I asked him about it and he said you'd asked him for it. It was just an E, something to take the edge off, make you relax."

"You went along with this?"

"Of course not! I tried asking you about it, but you were already wasted. You told me to piss off and stop bothering you. You said some pretty hurtful things actually."

Tyler can't remember any of that. "He spiked me?"

"Oh, God, I'm sorry. I know I shouldn't have left you, but I was upset and—wait, Adam, where are you going? Please! Don't leave it like this . . ."

day six

The Church of the Company of Jesus, Santiago, Chile, 1863

God's house is no refuge.

On December 8, 1863, the townsfolk of Santiago gathered for the Feast of the Immaculate Conception. The church had been decorated for the fiesta: the walls draped in veils of gossamer-thin fabric, the eaves hung with oil lamps that lit every darkened corner, helping to speed the prayers of the congregation on their way. Everyone wanted to attend, but room in the church was limited, forcing many of the townsmen to give up their places to make room for the women and children.

How did it come to pass? A slight breeze, perhaps. A veil blown into a naked flame. And suddenly the scene was changed. The congregation turned to flee. The women, dressed in their yards of linen and giant hooped skirts, were caught and entwined in their own clothing. They began to fall. The side doors to the church had been locked to make more room in the aisles for the congregation. The women and children had only one way out, through each other. The bodies piled up in the doorway, and those trapped behind in the flames pushed all the harder. They clamored and fought with each other, sealing their own fates. The

261

men outside, their would-be rescuers, could only stand and watch in horror as their loved ones burned. Three thousand people were burned alive that day. It could only have been God's mercy when the walls of the church began to collapse in the heat.

In some cases whole families were lost, leaving no one to mourn but friends. Perhaps they were the lucky ones. The cleanup took ten days and, since identification was impossible, the bodies were buried together in a mass grave.

No, God's house is no refuge from fire. But you know that. God's house is no refuge from anything. You didn't mean to kill the policewoman. She just happened to be in the wrong place at the wrong time. It happens.

But the other one, the one who called himself God's servant. The Reverend Sebastian Thorogood got exactly what he deserved.

POSTED BY **thefirewatcher** AT 7:18 AM

18 COMMENTS

BP12realSticko said . . .

You're sick mate! You need some serious help.

JPBrown82 said . . .

Why isn't anyone doing anything about this guy? Is this for real?

Firebug69 said . . .

Shut the fuck up, douchebags! *#firewatching*

   <u>Bazzameat1</u> said . . .

Check this out *<u>#firewatching</u>*

<u>1</u> 2 3 Next

Bright sunlight is shattered by the frosted glass of the window, creating a dance of fireflies across the polystyrene ceiling. Doggett is standing next to him, his leg twitching, and Tyler finds the movement oddly comforting. DCI Jordan is standing on the other side of the desk, her back to them, talking into her mobile. Or listening for the most part; Superintendent Stevens is the one doing all the talking. After a few minutes, she ends the call without saying goodbye. She turns and then sits down at the desk. "Rabbani?" she asks.

Doggett shakes his head. "No change."

"Any idea what she was doing there?"

Doggett employs his trademark shrug.

"She was looking into Thorogood," Tyler tells her.

Jordan sighs loudly and sits down behind the desk. She looks at him, and he knows what's coming before she speaks.

"I'm taking you off the case." She says it quietly, and Tyler nods.

Doggett says, "Ma'am, I don't think—"

"No, you don't, do you?" She slams her hand down on the desk.

Doggett opens his mouth to go on and then evidently changes his mind.

Jordan sighs again and rubs her forehead. "Just wait outside, Jim. I'll deal with you later."

He hesitates, then turns and places his bony palm on Tyler's shoulder. He squeezes it in a peculiarly intimate way and then he's gone, the door closing behind Tyler with a soft click.

Diane Jordan says, "I can't protect you this time, Adam."

"I know."

She shakes her head. "Why didn't you come to me? Why didn't you just tell me you knew him?"

He wishes he could answer that.

"I'm sorry," she says.

"You have nothing to apologize for."

"I'm sorry we no longer have the sort of relationship where you feel you can talk to me."

And he realizes she's right. They don't have that relationship anymore.

He thinks back to how it used to be, how much she did for him in the past. He was a scared sixteen-year-old. A child, forced into becoming an adult before he was ready. He can still see the light that sparkled on her face then even as it does now, only back then it was the reflected light of a glitter ball, and the electric-blue glow of the alcopop in his hands. He doesn't know how she found him, but then it's hard to lose yourself in a community as small as the Sheffield scene. Hard to lose yourself, but easy to be lost.

It had been just six weeks since the death of his father. Six weeks of hedonistic excess. Drinking in bars and clubs, talking to other lost souls. Accepting the kindnesses of strangers, though they weren't always that kind. Six weeks living out of a rucksack, and sleeping on floors and in beds of varying degrees of warmth, simply because he couldn't bear to go home.

He doesn't remember exactly how she convinced him to go with her, but somehow she did. Then she helped him pull himself back together, taught him how to go on. He has no doubt that without her his life would now be very different, assuming he still had one. And this is how he repays her.

"You know what happens next?" Jordan asks.

"You're suspending me," he says.

"I don't have any choice."

"I understand."

She escorts him to the door. She pauses before she opens it and says, "I'll do what I can."

"I know," he tells her. "For what it's worth, I'm sorry."

He isn't sure it's worth much.

Doggett is waiting outside. They fall into step together and walk down the corridor. After a moment or two Doggett says, "Did Cartwright know who you were when you met him?"

Tyler says nothing.

"I'll take that as a yes, then."

"A friend of mine set us up. I didn't know that until last night."

They walk on in silence for a few minutes and then Doggett says, "Elliot ID'd the second body."

Tyler stops. "Cynthia Cartwright?"

Doggett nods. "Oscar's mother. Strangled. The body was so well preserved they even got DNA from under the fingernails. Gerald's. I'm not sure it would hold up in court, but it's good enough for me."

"So Gerald killed his wife and buried her in the cellar. That means Edna Burnside lied to us. She must have known what happened. Helped him cover up Cynthia's disappearance."

"All that business about a bloody phone call. Then Oscar finds out and takes his revenge. Bricks his dad up in the same cellar where his mother's buried. Then the old dears help him cover that up as well."

He wonders if Doggett is really asking his opinion. He gives it anyway. "No."

"Why not?"

"Oscar hired the builders who unearthed the body. Why would he do that if he knew what they'd find?"

Doggett smiles. "That's the clever bit. I've been looking into his finances, and Rockefeller isn't half as loaded as he likes to make out. He only inherits his fortune properly when Daddy dearest is legally declared dead."

"That would happen soon enough without the body. It's been six years. Why go through all this? It's incredibly risky."

"His trust fund's gone, the mortgage on his flat's in arrears. He even owes money on his council tax. The only thing he owns outright is that bloody house, and he can't sell it till his father's declared dead. I'm telling you, he needed that body to be found. Involving you was his get-out-of-jail-free card. The minute we get close, his tame solicitor starts shouting about conflicted interests."

Oscar couldn't have wasted any time after leaving Lily's cottage, because Denham had been on DCI Jordan's doorstep before she'd even arrived this morning. Threatening to file harassment charges: his own, Oscar's, Lily's. Jordan suspected they were empty threats for the most part, but it was enough to derail the investigation and put Tyler well and truly in the firing line. The worst thing was, he'd been on his way to Jordan's office to come clean when she called. Maybe it wouldn't have made any difference, but if she'd just heard it from him, instead of Michael bloody Denham . . . It might have saved their friendship at least, if not his career.

He suspected Doggett and Jordan were at risk, too. If the superintendent had anyone else to take over the investigation, they'd both be joining him in the doghouse. They might still.

"Fuck," he says.

"That pretty much covers it."

Tyler shakes his head. "No, it doesn't make sense. How could he know I'd get the case?" But even as he asks the question he finds the answer. *Sally-Ann*. A few carefully worded questions about who handles cold cases in the department. He wonders which came first the night the two of them met, Oscar's revelation to Sally-Ann about his sexuality or Sally-Ann's mention of her "friend" in CID. Could Oscar really go that far? Sleep with someone? Pretend to be . . . something he isn't just to get away with murder? Perhaps. People have done far worse for less.

He shakes his head again. "What about the fire watcher?"

Doggett heaves his shoulders up. "Who knows how unhinged he is? Or maybe we were wrong; maybe the fires aren't connected."

Tyler shakes his head. "You've read that blog. It's the same village. We're talking about a place where the last crime reported was someone failing to register in the Domesday Book. Come on."

Doggett acknowledges the point with another shrug. "Well, maybe it's not connected in the way we think."

"What about Thorogood? Why would Oscar kill him?"

"Maybe it was an accident? Or maybe the vicar had something on him." But the doubt is creeping into Doggett's voice. Too many maybes. He looks at Tyler closely. "We're bringing him in anyway. Jordan wants to show him and Denham their threats aren't going to shake us."

"You're wrong," he tells Doggett. "Not about the money maybe, but about the fires. It was the discovery of Gerald's body that set the arsonist off. The two things are linked in some way. You need to follow that blog."

Doggett nods. "I'll keep it in mind. Speaking of which, how's your friend getting on with tracing the Internet thingy?"

"I'm not sure," he admits. "We're not really talking at the moment. You'll have to follow it up with her yourself."

Doggett grins at him. "Christ, you really do know how to piss people off, don't you?" He lifts a hand and again touches Tyler's arm. "Stay away from the Cartwright lad, eh?"

"I'm suspended," Tyler says. "I can't damage the case any further."

"It's not the case I'm worried about."

They're trying to protect him, Doggett and Jordan both. They don't want him to end up like Rabbani.

"Just go home and think of this as a few days' holiday. The DCI will straighten it all out once the super calms down."

He wants to believe that. He wants to believe they can somehow go back to the way things were before. But he thinks of Rabbani lying in the hospital struggling to breathe on her own, and Jordan still trying to protect him in spite of everything he's done behind her back. He's let them both down, just as he lets down everyone sooner or later.

Tyler stares at Rabbani through the window. They won't let him go in to see her because it's "family" only. Her chest moves up and down too slowly. Now and again the breath catches in her throat and she coughs through the mask. It's a small sign, but a comforting one. He knows the reason she's here is his fault. He neglected her, spoke up for her on a whim to prove a point to Jordan and then forgot all about her. Like a pet he begged to have and then gave up feeding. He leaves the flowers he brought with the nurse and heads back to the car.

He doesn't realize where he's headed until he's almost at the gates of the cemetery. He hasn't been here for years but it looks exactly as he remembers it, the newest graves laid out in neat little white rows, the older ones more haphazard, overgrown and crumbling. Eventually the dead *are* forgotten.

From the visitors' parking lot, he follows a network of paths that meander through a rose garden, and then he is searching the pale white headstones for the one he has come to visit. When he finds it, the grave is bare; he should have brought flowers, but from what he remembers his father was never really a flowers sort of person. He certainly can't remember him ever bringing any home for their mother.

There's a funeral taking place at the crematorium. He imagines they rarely bury anyone here nowadays; perhaps his father was one of the last. Perhaps Jordan somehow pulled strings to get him in. He doesn't remember that time well. He missed the funeral. He watches the mourners emerge from the building, an older woman dressed in black surrounded by friends and family. The way she leans on the arm of the young man walking next to her makes him think the man is probably her son. Another father being buried then. They are a fair distance away, but he can see the sweat break out on their brows as they step into the blazing heat. The crowd that spills out behind them begins to pay its respects while everyone waits for whatever comes next: a taxi to the house or a local pub, sandwiches and tea, stiff drinks and reminiscence. Soon the enforced quiet that has been laid on them lifts and evolves into gentle chatter as their cars begin to arrive. The son helps the mother into the back of a silver Mercedes and they are gone. Life goes on.

Tyler looks down at his father's gravestone. This is where they all end up; the girls butchered in their apartments, the football crowds and the Friday night drinkers of O'Hagan's. Gerald Cartwright. Oscar Cartwright. Adam Tyler. They all end up here, tidied away in their boxes, vases, and urns. Cramped together, as though still searching for the same human contact.

He thinks back to that day. He's coming home from school and he's happy. Perhaps for the last time. His mother is long gone and Jude is mostly away in the army, but he and Richard are doing okay. He has plans. A-levels next year, and then university to read mathematics or physics. After that, a job doing something important. He doesn't know what exactly, just that it should count. The one thing he is sure of is that he's not going to follow in his father's footsteps and join the police. His tutor, Mr. Barton, tells him it's too early to be making concrete plans, and he should try not to put so much pressure on himself. It's a funny thing for a teacher to say, and he remembers it in the months to come. Wonders if perhaps Mr. Barton had a premonition and knew what was waiting for Tyler at home that day.

He remembers things differently from the way they must have been. For instance, in his memory, he sees his father through the frosted glass in the front door before he actually goes in. A silhouette, a shadow. An unfinished Tarot card—the Hanged Man. He knows this can't be real; otherwise why would he have closed the door behind him and flicked down the latch? Why would he kick off his trainers and drop his school bag just as he always did? Why would he have opened the *fucking* door in the first place? But this is the way he remembers it.

In truth, it must have been only after he'd finished all those everyday, habitual actions that he looked up. Richard—and it is at this exact point he begins thinking of the man as *Richard,* rather than *Dad*—is hanging from the groaning banister, a thin red cord cutting deeply into the folds of flesh at his neck. They try to hide the detail of the rope's origin from him, but he finds out. It's Japanese bondage rope, bought the week before. They find the receipt on his study desk, with the receipt for the paracetamol. Perhaps he had plans to claim them back on expenses.

Richard's eyes are bulging from his face as though, at the end, this event has taken him by surprise. There is crusted vomit still drying on his collar and chest, and a puddle of urine soaking into the deep shag of the hallway carpet. There is the stench of loosened bowels. Does he remember these things? Or are they, like the silhouette, just ghosts of memories? Things he has put together after the fact. Things he has learned from attending similar scenes.

Much later they say his father was on the take. Bent as a nine-bob note and about to be found out. They say he had a broken marriage and an estranged son. They say he was struggling to cope as a single parent in charge of a wayward teenager (it's the first time Tyler realizes he's wayward). They say he was overworked and underpaid and struggling to handle the stress of the job. They say he took enough paracetamol to fell a horse before lowering himself over the banister. They say it wouldn't have made any difference if the lad—that's Tyler—had been home an hour before, or two hours, or had come home sick from school the minute he'd got there; Richard would still be as dead as England's chances of winning the European Championships. But in Tyler's mind is the thought that, as Richard hung there, perhaps regretting his decision and clawing at his throat, perhaps just waiting patiently to be found (and truly it doesn't matter which), at that exact moment, his *wayward* son, the last hope in Richard Tyler's crumbling life, was using silly string to draw a giant cock-and-ball motif on the back of a butcher's stall in the Castle Market.

They don't have all the answers, though. They don't explain why he canceled the hired help that day, but didn't consider his sixteen-year-old son would find him. They don't explain why he would go out and buy a bottle of paracetamol when there were packets of the stuff—used for years by his strung-out wife to self-medicate—in the medicine cupboard already. They don't explain why he didn't leave a note, some explanation for young Adam. A final farewell. An explanation for yet another abandonment.

Tyler shivers. The sun is setting, and the trees round the grave-yard have draped him in shadows. The parallels between his life and Oscar's are astonishing. A missing mother. A dead father. The only difference being that Richard didn't kill his wife and bury her in the cellar. What would Tyler have done if he had? Would he have taken the law into his own hands? Taken revenge on Richard?

Gerald Cartwright was a bad man. A liar, and a thief, and a murderer. No doubt a terrible father as well, far worse than Richard. Did Oscar lash out one day? Perhaps it was an accident. And *of course* Lily and Edna would help him cover things up. They would want to protect their precious little boy, just as Diane Jordan had tried to protect him.

This is Doggett's theory, and the more Tyler goes over it, the more it makes sense. Was the uncovering of Gerald's corpse an accident? Or did Oscar, desperate for cash, arrange it? He digs up his father's body but is unaware of the effect it would have on him. Grief-stricken, racked with guilt, half mad, he begins setting light to things. In a few hours they'll arrest him, if they haven't done so already. The psychologists will do their bit, and they'll argue about what it is that drove him to do it. He once mentioned his father's cigar smoking; perhaps the link is as simple as that.

Tyler's mobile rings. He checks the caller ID. Sally-Ann. He lets the phone ring off and a few seconds later his voicemail calls back with her message.

"Adam? Oh God, I'm so, so, so, so sorry. I really thought I was helping. I heard what happened to you, everyone's talking about it. I mean, not *everyone's* talking about it but . . . oh, you know what I mean. Look, I'm sorry, okay? Literally, like, really sorry. If I'd known what he . . ." She trails off for a few moments, then, "Anyway, I just wanted to update you about the blog. So . . . it's taking longer than I thought to . . . oh . . . I probably shouldn't even be telling you this, what with you being suspended and everything . . . I should probably ring DI Doggett, right? Look, just ring me. Will you? Please? Plea—?" The message cuts off.

He knows he's being a bit unfair. She couldn't have known Oscar's true motivations when they met. But she did watch the man spike his drink and did precious little about it. He should ring her anyway, have it out with her. But he doesn't.

Why can't he bring himself to subscribe to Doggett's theory?

Surely not just because that would mean admitting that he, Tyler, was wrong? Is he too proud to admit he's made mistakes? No, it isn't that. He knows he's made mistakes. Big ones. Mistakes he's unlikely to get away with this time. But it isn't that.

He won't believe it because he can't believe it. Oscar is spoiled, changeable, overly confident in his ability to charm. He's grief-stricken, certainly. At least, he seems it at times; the rest of the time he's too busy channeling the confident charmer. Could that be it? Schizophrenia or something? Perhaps there are other Oscars he has yet to see. A crazy Oscar, racked with guilt. A serial arsonist with daddy issues. But he just doesn't buy it.

Daddy issues.

The mobile is still in his hand. He finds the number he needs still saved on his phone, and Sophie Denham answers in two rings.

"Hello?" She speaks hesitantly, obviously not recognizing his number.

"It's DS Tyler." It's not exactly a lie; he still has his rank on the telephone at least. For a short while anyway.

She's quiet at first and then she says, "I'm not supposed to talk to you."

"I understand. I just need to ask you one question."

"If my father finds out . . ." Her voice is light and whispery.

"He won't."

More silence. He's beginning to wonder if she's hung up on him, but then she says, "Just a minute." He imagines her getting up, closing the door to her bedroom.

He wonders who she is with, and when she gets back to the phone he can't stop himself asking. "Is Oscar there?"

This time she doesn't hesitate. "No, I'm round Dad's. I haven't seen Oscar for days. We're . . . well, we're not together anymore."

"Right," he says, and then realizes that's probably not enough. "Sorry."

"Don't be. It only started up again because of Dad." She laughs. "That probably sounds a bit weird, right? What I mean is, he never really liked Oscar, so I figured it would wind him up a bit if we started hanging out again."

"Did it?"

"More than a little."

"Why doesn't he?"

"What?"

"Why doesn't your father like Oscar?"

"It's nothing personal. I think he just didn't want me to get involved with Gerry's son." She sighs lightly, perhaps wondering if she's made the right decision. "He thinks Oscar's a distraction. And . . . well, I guess he's right." She laughs again, a relieved sort of giggle. "The ironic thing is, in the last few weeks he's probably seen more of Oscar than I have."

"What do you mean?"

"I guess they have business to talk about? Dad's on the CWI board of directors. Every time he comes round they're talking business about something."

He wonders about that. If Oscar is as broke as Doggett claims, how does he afford Denham's services? He's an old family friend, so he might do Oscar the occasional favor, but on the other hand he disapproves of the man's relationship with his daughter, so why would he help? Perhaps the two of them are closer than they appear. Perhaps this isn't the first time Denham has helped Oscar out of a sticky situation.

Sophie clears her throat, and he realizes neither of them have spoken for several seconds. "Is this what you wanted to ask me about?"

"No." He watches the last car depart the funeral. "When you told me about the Old Vicarage, about Gerald, you said there was a group of you used to hang out there."

"Sure. The place was always full of all sorts of people. Staff mostly, but sometimes there would be a model or an actor. Once we hung out with a band Gerald was thinking of promoting. I don't know if they ever made it, but I've still got a pair of drumsticks the drummer gave—"

"Do you remember anyone who was . . . particularly close to Gerald?"

The line goes quiet for a moment. "I don't know." Again she pauses. "What do you mean by *close*?"

The mobile beeps in his ear, the battery dying. "Sophie, I think you know what I mean." She doesn't answer, so he pushes her harder. "When I asked you before about Gerald, I felt there was something you weren't telling me. This is really important. Anything you can tell me might help."

When she speaks, it's quietly. "I didn't like him," she says. "None of us did." She clears her throat again, and when she speaks her voice is a little more confident. "Gerald was hardly ever there, but when he was he used to creep us out. He was always watching us."

"'Us'?"

"Me, I suppose. There was one day we ended up on our own together. I think he said he had a message he wanted me to pass to Dad." She takes a deep breath, and then it's all out in a rush. "He started touching me. Running his hands over my legs. And . . ." She trails off.

"I'm sorry. I know this is hard, but I need to know what happened."

"Nothing happened. I froze. I just couldn't move. I wanted to tell him to stop but I didn't. Then Edna walked in and Gerry laughed it off and I ran home as fast as I could. After that, I made sure I was never alone with him again."

His phone beeps again. "You never told anyone?" Her silence gives him the answer. "Who did you tell?"

He hears another voice somewhere in the background. "It's just a friend from uni," she shouts out. Then she says, "I have to go."

"Wait . . ." But she's already hung up.

Lily can't get in the house again.

After they left the cottage yesterday, Oscar had escorted Lily to Her-Next-Door, who'd been surprisingly gracious in offering Lily a bed for the night. She won't pretend she was anything other than relieved, however, when Her-Next-Door—Judith—had answered the telephone this morning to a Superintendent Stevens. He told her the matter of Edna's death had been settled, and that the pathologist was confident Edna had died of a massive stroke brought on by her condition. The police would be taking no further action. She wasn't sure what *action* they might have taken, but anyway the main thing was she would be allowed back into the cottage.

Now, though, she stands, one foot hanging over the threshold, as though some other, physical, force is keeping her at bay. Everything is so quiet, and she feels a renewed sense the cottage doesn't want her anymore. As though Edna, dissolved into ashes, has blown her way through the house and locked herself into its fabric, claiming the place as her own. She's in the pile of the carpet and the weave of the bedspread; she's collected in the hem of the curtains. No longer will Lily be able to slap the Cavalier's footstool without breathing her in. Edna has become the house. There's no room for Lily anymore.

"Aunt Lil?" Oscar says quietly.

She looks up to where he hovers on the path. Perhaps it's the angle, but he looks even taller than before. Older, too. He seems tired, almost dirty. She didn't notice that when he arrived. It reminds her of how he often looked as a child. Never immaculately turned out, this one. A grubby little urchin, her mother would have said.

He comes to her, and she puts her arms around him and he begins to cry. She rubs his back, and he shrinks in her arms and he's a boy again. She coos at him as though she's consoling him over a grazed knee. There, there. It'll be all right. No harm done.

It occurs to her that she has him all to herself now. There's no one to share him with. She can hold him as long as she wants, and Edna can't interrupt them. Instead, she pushes him away.

He wipes giant drops of water from his cheeks and takes an almighty sniff. "I'm sorry I wasn't here sooner. I had to sort everything out with the police."

"It's all right," she says without really meaning it. "You're here now."

"They won't bother you again. I'll make sure of that. How are you coping?" he asks, though it seems to her she's coping better than he is.

"I'm fine," she says. "We knew it was coming, after all."

"Not like this. Can I do anything? Can I get you anything?"

She shakes her head. What does he think he can get her? A cup of tea? A wireless for company in the evenings? It's almost as though he's desperate to put something right, almost . . . The thought comes to her, and once it does she cannot push it away. If she didn't know better she'd say he was guilty of something. He looks just as he used to when they caught him up to some mischief or other. She hesitates. She supposes there is something that needs doing but . . . she can't ask him that, can she? It wouldn't be fair.

"Can you help me clean?" She nods to the mark on the carpet. "Perhaps we could do it together?"

"Of . . . course," he says.

"I'll get a bucket." And now the barrier is gone. Lily walks into the house and gets to work. When she returns to him with the gloves and the bucket and some soapy detergents, he's sitting on one of the chairs in the garden, biting at a filthy nail. "Oscar," she calls sharply. His hand drops into his lap. "Come along then."

Together they sponge at the marks on the carpet. It's easy now, like cleaning the step for Mother. The water in the bucket turns to a sludgy, muddy puddle. Oscar's face drains of the little color it had. Lily begins to tire and stops for a breather. She watches him from the conservatory, where there's a faded photograph of the man . . . *at the bar next to her says, "Steady, old girl!"*

He's one of the most handsome men she's ever seen. He's with the Royal Air Force, an officer, and his uniform is pressed so neatly. Not like some of the army boys. The man on her other side is American. He's not as pretty as the RAF boy, but he certainly has more charm. She can't decide which of the uniforms she prefers.

She knows she's probably drunk too much. When she laughs, she giggles like a schoolgirl but she can't help it, they're both so funny. Edna is giving her funny looks. Disapproving looks. Lily's thankful for this new friendship. She was so lonely when she first came here, and the girls at the theater hardly fell over themselves to welcome this up-start girl . . . this northerner! . . . to dance among them. With Edna it's different. Different from any friendship she's ever had before. It's just that she can be so boring at times! And put a foot wrong in Edna's eyes, and she's quick enough to tell you where you've gone wrong. Susan at the office says she's sharp as lemons. Lily laughs to herself. She's not wrong about that. But Lily sees something in this prickly, hard-nosed woman that intrigues her. She is just so confident. She is a force of nature. Susan and the others from the office have already gone, leaving Edna to watch while Lily flirts at the bar. Lily giggles again. Poor disapproving Edna sitting all alone. She will go over. In a minute.

The RAF boy wants to buy her another drink. She's had enough really, but she doesn't want to look like she's inexperienced. She glances back to see if Edna is still watching, but she's gone. Just like that. Without so much as a word. Well, the blessed cheek! She turns to look round the pub and stumbles against a table.

"Whatchit," slurs the old fellow whose drink she spills.

She feels sick. She's really not used to drinking. This isn't like her, but then the war has made them all reckless. She needs some fresh air.

It's dark outside. No moon, and the blackout keeps the night pristine. She breathes deeply, but the fresh air only makes her head spin faster. She hears someone say her name and then she's falling. Bang. Suddenly the night is full of bright lights and crackling noise.

She feels something tug at her clothing and knows that she should say something. This is wrong, but she can't move. She wants to lie here and wait for the world to stop turning. There's a great weight on top of her now. She tries to speak but there's something over her mouth, a hard woven fabric. The cuff of a greatcoat. Then comes the sharp pain between her legs, and the dirt and grit beneath her head dig into her scalp. The pain only lasts a few minutes and then the weight is gone again.

She lies there drifting, afloat in the night.

"Lily. Lillian? Lillian!"

Someone slaps her hard in the face. Edna.

Lily says, "I thought you'd gone," and is surprised the words come out all right.

"I went to the lavatory. Oh, Lord, Lillian! We need to get you home."

"No," she shouts. Home is Auntie Vi's. "No, I can't go there!"

"All right, all right," Edna says. "You can come back to mine. We'll get you all cleaned up."

Lily starts to cry. "Oh," she says. "Oh." There really isn't anything else to say. She doesn't even know which one it was. Which uniform would she have preferred?

"Don't think about it," says Edna. "Not now . . ."

After all, you have a guest . . . Edna is back, swinging on the sun lounger, watching Oscar clean up her mess. He must sense them both watching him because he suddenly looks up.

"Aunt Lil?"

"The police were here earlier," she says.

He stands up and comes to join her outside. "No," he says, "that was yesterday. I was here with you, remember?" He's looking at her now, as though he's concerned about something. "Are you all right, Lily?" He strips off his Marigolds and crouches next to her.

"They asked about your father." She no longer feels the need to protect him. "They think it's him they've found, in the cellar."

"Yes," he says. "It is. They confirmed it."

"He was a lovely young man," she says, "that policeman. Very polite."

"They've found another body, too," he says. "A woman."

They've never talked like this before. So honestly. Edna would never have allowed it. But now Edna just watches, smiling her ghastly toothy smile.

"Awful," says Lily.

"Do you know who it is? The other body?"

"What's that?"

He doesn't say anything else for a bit, then, "I think . . . I think I'm going to go away for a while. I can't stay in this place anymore."

"I see," she says.

"I wondered . . ."

"Do come on, Oscar," she snaps, "spit it out." She has never spoken to him like that before. It's as though, with Edna gone, Lily has to fill in for her, become the authoritarian.

He looks shocked but recovers enough to ask, "It's just, I'm a bit short . . . I wondered if . . . ?"

So it's money he's after. She pretends to consider it for a moment. "I don't think so, dear," she says, and looks across at the sun lounger. "I don't think Edna would approve. Perhaps Michael could help out in some way?"

"Yes, of course. I'm sorry, I shouldn't have asked."

"Well," she says. "Never mind. I'm sure you'll get by."

He stares at her sullenly, the way he used to when he wanted his own way on something. But it won't wash this time. Lily glances at Edna where she swings on the phantom sun lounger. She's sure now; there's just no conceivable way Edna could have managed the furniture on her own, and she wouldn't have asked a stranger for help. Edna smiles and nods at her. *I already have a good idea who might be . . .* she'd started to say before Lily cut her off. Then what had she done? Rung that person perhaps? Asked him to come see her?

"Where will you go?" she asks. "Overseas, I imagine?"

"Yeah. I dunno yet; I might travel for a bit. I guess I'll let you know where I end up. Maybe you could visit."

"Oh, I don't travel well, dear. And anyway, there's Edna to think about."

"Lily," he says, "Edna is gone."

"Yes." Her eyes stray to the sun lounger again. "You won't go until after the funeral, though, will you?"

He hesitates. "No, of course not." He gets up. "I should be getting back."

"All right, dear."

He kisses her goodbye. His breath is fetid and stale. She walks him to the front gate. He pauses for a moment, and she thinks he's going to ask her about the whole business again. This time she will tell everything she can. Everything she remembers. No more lies and half-truths and obfuscations. In return she will demand the truth from him as well. Instead he says, "You're sure I can't help with anything?"

"No, dear," she says, "I think you've done more than enough, don't you?"

She watches him walk away from her down the path, no longer the little boy she once loved. He has grown overnight into a tall, grubby stranger.

No, not a stranger exactly. He reminds her of his father, sneaking about and always so full of secrets. And his grandfather . . . the man in the greatcoat from the pub.

Tyler shivers and breaks from his reverie. The sun has dropped while he has been sitting in the graveyard. He stands up and stretches the kinks from his aching limbs. He takes one last look at his father's headstone and heads back to the car.

On the way home he wonders who Sophie Denham told about Gerry Cartwright's wandering hands. He thinks he knows. It explains Denham's reaction when they spoke at his office, and it explains why Denham wouldn't want his daughter involved with Oscar. He must have had some idea what Gerald got up to, even if he wasn't involved himself. What stronger motive than a father protecting his child? And if so, it might go some way to explaining why the fire at Denham's office seemed different, because he set it himself as a blind. Or maybe, as Enfield said, the solicitor's office just felt different because it wasn't in Castledene. And if Denham *is* the fire watcher, none of this explains why he's setting fires in the first place.

Night has fallen by the time he arrives back at his apartment but it's still as warm, the air thick and close. The roads are empty but for the orange glow of the streetlights. Something catches his eye as he gets out of the car, and he looks up at the abandoned office building opposite. There's a crack in one of the windows on the first floor that resembles a large black candle flame, reaching up to the rooftop.

There's a brief flash of light, the headlights of a car as it swings past on the ring road, and with it he sees a shape in the darkness. Someone in the building. There's a jerk of movement, and the shape vanishes.

It could be anyone, of course. No reason to assume it's Oscar, or the fire watcher, assuming those two are not one and the same. He locks the car and crosses the road to the empty building.

The front door of the building is locked, but he knows there's a side entrance down the alley to the left. The small door has been boarded over, but the wooden planks are loose and he pushes them aside easily. The door behind swings open with a loud creak, and the stench of damp and urine is almost overpowering. He considers calling it in, but what is *it* exactly? A shadow glimpsed in the night? No one's going to come rushing out for that, and certainly not on his say-so. The thought reminds him of his mobile and he pulls it out, uses the light on the camera to negotiate his way through the rubble. The corridor he's in leads directly to a set of stairs, no other doors. An emergency exit. He takes the stairs slowly, broken glass from the smashed lighting above crunching beneath his feet. Another door, its emergency bar long broken, stands open and leads into a wide room scattered with abandoned office furniture. There's a bit more light here, street light filtered by the cracked and missing windows.

The room is enormous and stretches the entire length of the building, but his view is obstructed by a number of pillars that support the roof. There are desks and chairs as well, partitioning that once would have separated the cubicles of bored call-center workers. Plenty of hiding places. Dark corners that neither the diffuse orange street light nor his tiny pinprick torch can reach. He moves forward slowly, edging his way nearer to the windows on the front of the building, his eyes searching the darkness for some telltale movement, a shadow that seems out of place. He glances out quickly through one of the broken windows at the street below, but there's no sign of anyone. The battery on his mobile beeps again. He reaches the part of the building that lies directly opposite his own flat. There's the cracked glass pane that looks like a black flame, only from this side the flame is orange and bright. Through it he can see his own living room, the cheap eBay sofa, the IKEA breakfast bar, the bookcases.

Then the window shatters, bursts into a thousand razor-sharp quills.

Tyler reacts instinctively, dropping his mobile and raising his arms to protect his face. He takes a step backward, crouching down, the sound of the shattered glass settling around him. His heart smashes against his rib cage. He looks down at the stone as it comes to a standstill. He hears laughter and looks outside to see a bunch of kids haring away up the road. He exhales loudly. They must have heard him coming and found another way out of the building.

The battery on his phone beeps three times in quick succession and the light goes out. Tyler picks it up off the floor and stares into the darkness until his eyes adjust a little. He heads back the way he came, inching his way slowly back down the stairwell in the darkness.

Just kids messing about in an abandoned building. Nothing to worry about. Nevertheless, when he gets back to the flat he dead-bolts the door and puts the chain on. He glances through the window at the building opposite where the familiar cut-out black flame has now gone. In its place, there's a large, jagged hole.

Rabbani sits up in bed, staring at the off-white walls of the hospital ward.

There are four beds in her section. The woman in the bed op-posite, Sandra, is watching television, but every now and then Rab-bani catches her staring. She guesses it's the ten o'clock news. She can only imagine what she looks like, laid out in the graveyard prematurely. But that makes her think about the vicar. She's get-ting delusions of grandeur; as if the media gives a shit about what happened to her when they've got him to write about.

She's sorry for him. She didn't like the guy, and he was obviously some sort of perv, but still . . . When she thinks about how he must have died, how *she* nearly died . . .

She shivers. She doesn't think she'll ever feel warm again.

The woman in the bed next to her groans intermittently. They've separated them with a curtain, which seems to stay closed pretty much permanently. Rabbani can't say she's sorry about that.

The fourth bed is empty. And somehow that one unsettles her most of all.

She can't remember much of anything after the church. Not the trip here in the ambulance, nor the night spent in intensive care, though occasionally she thinks she remembers puking up phlegm and pus into a bowl.

Her throat is sore and the water they've given her doesn't seem to help, just makes her need the toilet all the time. She doesn't think the coughing sounds as bad now, but every few minutes she has another fit of hacking up slime and Sandra looks across at her disagreeably from behind her TV.

The immediate danger has passed, it seems; she's here for obser-vation only now, arrhythmia of the heart. But what if they find some-thing else? Who knows what other damage has been done? Maybe now that she's here they'll never let her go. Just like her grandfather.

At least her family has gone. How they all managed to get in she has no idea. There were twelve of them at one point, with Sandra looking over in disgust. Well, *fuck* her! At least Rabbani has people who care. Though if her mother really cared, she might not have spent quite so long cursing her, cursing the force, and insisting Ghulam give her a second opinion—as if a neurologist knows anything about lungs! She could have died with embarrassment. Rabbani hits the button on her mobile for what must be the twentieth time and waits for the line to connect. It's not like there's anything else to do. Besides, she won't be able to sleep until she's talked to him. She's not expecting him to answer any more this time than the last twenty times, so she doesn't even have the phone to her ear when she hears his tinny voice barking up from her lap. "Tyler."

She fumbles the phone as she hurries to bring it up to her ear. "It's Mina. I mean, Constable Rabbani. Sir," she adds.

"Rabbani?"

"Why don't you answer your bloody phone? I've been ringing you half the night!" She speaks without thinking, her frustration bubbling over onto the first person she's spoken to in hours. She's about to apologize, but using her voice so much sends her off into another coughing fit.

When she has recovered, he says, "My phone died. I've had it charging. Just switched it on."

"You shouldn't speak on them things when they're plugged in, you know. My cousin knew this guy once whose phone blew up and—" Again she has to cough, but it gives her a chance to think. What is she talking about? Why does he make her so bloody nervous? She takes a sip of water. Sandra is watching her again. Rabbani stares at the woman until she turns back to the TV. "Still there?" she asks.

"Sure," he says.

"Good. I need to tell you something." And she lays it out for him, the overheard conversation between Wentworth and Thorogood.

"He basically accused the vicar of being involved. Which pretty much implies *he* was involved as well, right? Or at the very least, that he knows something."

"Yes, but involved in what? Gerald's death or the fires?"

"Maybe both." She clears her throat again before she can go on. "Anyway, one of them locked me in. Left me there to . . ." She can't let herself think about that now. "They told me you were the one what got me out. Thanks, Sarge." She probably should have started with that.

"I'm just glad you're okay," he says, although he doesn't particularly sound it. "Rabbani, why are you telling me all this? You need to speak to DI Doggett. I'm not on the case anymore."

"I know," she says. "I heard about that, too. Sorry." Maybe she should have started with that as well. "I spoke to him already, but he was right back on to Oscar Cartwright again." Doggett had basically told her to mind her own bloody business and then made it perfectly clear that without Tyler as her sponsor, once she was well enough, she'd be right back in uniform. "I just don't think he takes me seriously, Sarge."

"I'm not sure what you think I can do."

"Talk to him, make him listen. He's got to find Wentworth before he sets fire to summat else." Or someone.

"You're sure Wentworth was the one who torched the church?"

She hesitates. "Well, I never saw him do it. But he was there. And the only other person who was there is dead!" She sighs heavily, trying to control her temper. "Look, I don't know. I just think someone needs to talk to him. Please!" Why is she crying? She wipes her eyes with her free hand. Stupid girl, he's going to think she's a stupid twat! She can feel her hands shaking as she holds the phone. Sandra's watching her again. "Look, just *piss* off, will yer!" Sandra turns back to her telly, her cheeks coloring.

"Sorry?"

"Not you." Rabbani wipes her eyes and sniffs, but she can't stop the tears falling now that they've started.

"Get some rest," he tells her. "I'll look into it."

"Promise me!"

"I promise."

"Thanks, Sarge."

But when she hangs up she feels worse than ever. She hasn't let herself think about it, but she nearly died! She doesn't try to stop the tears now, and she decides she doesn't give a toss what Sandra thinks.

Rabbani buries her head in the scratchy pillow and cries herself to sleep.

It's almost eleven by the time Tyler reaches the village. He considered calling Doggett to lend his own voice to Rabbani's but decided against it. If she hadn't managed to convince him, nothing Tyler might say would make a difference. So he decided to speak to Wentworth himself first, to see what he could find out.

He passes the empty churchyard, the blackened husk of the church hulking over it. When he gets to Wentworth's house, it, too, is in darkness. He rings the bell and waits. Wentworth could be asleep, of course, or down the local pub. But somehow neither of those things fit with what he knows about the man. He could be out setting fire to his next victim.

He rings the bell again. Nothing. No, there is something—the dog barking. But muffled, as though it's a long way off. Tyler presses the doorbell again and knocks hard.

"Mr. Wentworth?"

He should leave. He has no real reason for being here and certainly no authority to be. If Wentworth is the arsonist—the killer—Tyler's interference is only going to jeopardize the case further. He cups his hands to the dirty glass of the bay window, but the nets and the darkness conspire against him. There's something, though. A shape in the dark.

"Mr. Wentworth? It's DS Tyler. We spoke a few days ago. Can I come in?" The figure doesn't move. "I know you're there, Joe. Can you open the door, please?" The shadow disappears from view. Tyler reaches out slowly and tries the handle. The door opens. "Joe?"

He reaches for his mobile before realizing it's still plugged in back at the flat. After speaking to Rabbani he'd tried unplugging it, but for some reason the phone wouldn't hold its charge when disconnected. The battery's been dodgy for a while now, or maybe something came loose when he dropped it. The sound of the yapping dog comes to him louder now, but still muffled. He steps across the threshold. There's something else, too. A faint smell that seems to get weaker the harder he sniffs at it. In the living room he can just make out the shape of Wentworth in his chair.

"Can you put the light on?" he asks. "Joe?" His hand inches its way along the wall to the switch, but when he presses it nothing happens.

"Mr. Wentworth, I need you to answer me, please."

Tyler trips on something, dislodging a pile of newspaper that slides to the floor with a thump. He coughs. The house is stuffy and it's difficult to breathe. And that smell; he can almost taste it. Something that makes him think of car fumes.

When he gets to the armchair Wentworth's eyes are closed. He reaches out and the man groans, his eyelids fluttering slightly. Wentworth tries to speak, but Tyler can't quite make it out. He leans forward.

It's not so much a sound as a sense of movement, and the door to the kitchen sweeps wide. The room is suddenly flooded with bright orange light. Tyler's still turning when something hits him hard on the forehead, twisting him back around. He falls, spread-eagled across the gardener, his head reverberating, white light flashing across his eyes.

Now he smells the smoke. His knee pushes into Wentworth's saggy groin, but the man is silent and doesn't move. Tyler lurches back to his feet and staggers away. He notes a dark smudge on Wentworth's forehead and puts his hand to his own head. It comes away sticky and red. The pain in his head intensifies. He can't see anything. Just dark shapes and that dull flickering light.

"Tyler?" A voice behind him. He turns to see Paul Enfield, his black skin shining in the orange glow. He seems even bigger in the darkened room, a great hulking shadow of a man. "Get out!" he shouts, but Tyler can't move.

He watches Paul leap Wentworth's junk like an Olympian hurdler. He sees the fireman lean in to the armchair, put his head under Wentworth's arm. What's he doing? He straightens again, heaves the old man onto his shoulder in one fluid movement. It's called a fireman's lift, Tyler thinks absently. He tries to speak but all he can do is cough. Why is it so hard to breathe?

"Adam!" The shock of his name hits him like ice-cold water in the face. "The house is on fire. You need to move!" Paul is already hurtling away from him out of the room.

And now he sees the room burning. The ceiling blisters and rains fire down across newspaper and upholstery alike. Now his feet come back to life, but even as they do he hears the dog bark again. He turns without thinking and steps through the kitchen doorway into hell. The walls are alive with flames, as though the room has become one giant oven. He can hear the dog barking behind the door that leads down into the cellar. Clawing and scratching, fighting to get out. Just like Gerald Cartwright. He reaches for the handle without even thinking about it.

"No!"

Time slows, elongating Paul Enfield's scream into one long syllable, and within that split second Tyler knows the mistake he's made even as he makes it. He opens the door. Time stops. An unmistakable pause, like the change in air pressure the moment before a thunderstorm. And then the fire is coming for him, reaching out to take him in a crackling embrace. He drops low, sweeps the dog into his arms, turns to run, all in one fluid movement. Paul is there, grabbing his arm in a tight grip, propelling him forward. Then Paul is behind him, pushing him. The living room is an inferno, fire running in mercurial streams from one pile of kindling to another. Then they're through, Paul hitting him on the back, thumping him again and again. It hurts. He wants to tell the man to stop but there isn't time and he's not sure he can speak anyway. Into the hallway now, the air from the door ahead deliciously cool. Through the door. His feet try to fall out from under him but still Paul pushes him on. Through the gate, past the car. Surely they'll stop soon?

When the explosion comes it picks him up and throws him down hard onto the road. He notes Paul at his side. He glances back at the house and coughs. He can't stop coughing. The windows of the house are like eyes of flame looking down on them. A demon is taking the house and laughing at how powerless they are to stop it. He hears a wailing noise he assumes must be the dog, but then realizes he still has the dog pressed hard against his chest; he can feel its tiny body shaking. No, the noise is a siren, growing louder. Paul is crouched over Wentworth where he lies on the pavement. Tyler had forgotten Wentworth. Paul touches the man's wrist and then bends forward and kisses him. Why is he doing that? Not a kiss, CPR. He's forcing air between Wentworth's tight lips. It looks strange, Paul Enfield's thick lips pressed against Wentworth's cigarette-puckered mouth. Each time Paul blows he has to pull away for a moment and cough. He hacks up a wad of phlegm and spits it onto the pavement. He has no spare breath to give but he gives it nonetheless.

Tyler kneels in the road and watches the house burn.

day seven

The Second Great Fire of London, 1940

Back then they were like family to you. A pair of elderly spinsters, though perhaps the word doesn't apply in their case. Today they would be labeled lesbians.

Sometimes Edna, and especially Lily, would tell you stories about how they met during the war. How they watched for fires from the rooftop. They both liked stories, though Edna was more interested in "the Greats." Edna, the born teacher; even the smallest exchange of pleasantries came with a built-in history lesson. Nero and Rome, Caesar and the Library. Those stories come from her originally, though you've done your own research since. And the greatest of them, the event she never tired of talking about—the Blitz.

Blitzkrieg. From the German word for lightning, classic weapon of the gods. In this case in the form of the German Luftwaffe, raining down fire upon Britain's cities for eight long months. London wasn't the only city affected, of course; even sleepy Sheffield had its turn in the spotlight as the Nazis attempted to cripple British industry. But almost half those killed by German airstrikes were in the capital. And there was one night in particular. The 29th of December, 1940. The night Lily and Edna sat up watching for fires. The 114th night of the Blitz. The night that would come to be known as the Second Great Fire of London.

297

One hundred and twenty-four thousand explosives and incendiary devices were thrown down on the city's head, twenty-nine around St. Paul's alone, one striking a direct hit and lodging in the cathedral's dome. The area destroyed by these bombs was greater than that of the first Great Fire, and the casualty list was higher, too, 160 civilians and 14 firefighters. But Churchill ordered the cathedral saved, and a group of volunteers fought back the firestorm that swept across the capital and halted it at God's door. Every other building in the vicinity of St. Paul's was obliterated.

One of the men who worked tirelessly to save the church was a man named Wentworth, a simple dockworker who happened to find himself in the thick of the action. Later, he would tell his son about the night of his heroic endeavors, just as Edna and Lily told their stories to you. But his son was far from a simple man, nor was he heroic. Not even much of a storyteller, though he did once mention this to you. He was working on the garden at the time, listening in as Edna told her tale.

He was a coward, a bully, just another sad, pathetic creature. The world should not mourn him.

You feel as though you've come full circle. But none of this has helped at all, has it? What have you achieved? Other than to add the screams of Wentworth and Felbridge to the other. To Gerald. Is this really what he wanted? No. You know what he wanted, what he still wants. He wants peace. An end to it. He whispers a name to you. Detective Sergeant Adam Tyler. You should have finished it last night at Wentworth's house. Or before that even, at Tyler's flat. That's two opportunities he's given you. Now it's third time lucky.

Now it's up to you to finish it for him.

POSTED BY **thefirewatcher** AT 6:24 AM

119 COMMENTS

DonkeyHoTay said:-

Yeah, man! You fucking stick it to em *#firewatching*

Nof***inway said . . .

If I want a fuckin histry lesson I gone back to school.

NiceCuppa said . . .

You think this is history but it could happen again. Open your eyes and look what the Toruies are ddoing to the country!!

NiceCuppa said . . .

Tories* and doing* Lol!!!

ActualJeffJones said . . .

Anyone know where I can get an original Klingon bat'leth from Star Trek TNG?

Kaygirlstarchild said:-

Are you single?

Fifitrixibelle said:-

Check out my pictures at http://www.biggirlsbest.com

1 2 3 4 5 Next

The paramedics take away Joe Wentworth in a matter of minutes, but before they depart Paul snatches bandages and antiseptic from them, and cleans and dresses the burns on the back of Tyler's neck. Only then does Tyler realize he was actually on fire. Paul wasn't hitting him, he was beating the flames out with his sleeves. It feels like sunburn, only a lot worse. He can smell his own singed hair.

There are three fire engines, their blue lights battling the orange firelight as the water from their hoses fights the fire. Only two of the trucks are in use; the third stands idly by and after a few minutes departs, ashamed by its redundancy. Finally the police cars begin to arrive. Paul jokes that his lot—meaning Tyler's—are always the last to arrive. Soon the small close is full of people, a mixture of uniforms and neighbors in nightclothes.

Tyler sits on the edge of the pavement. Paul towers over him, places a hand on his shoulder. "Hey," he says, "you all right?"

"You saved my life."

"Some people freeze; it happens. Let me look at that head." Paul puts his hands on either side of Tyler's face and focuses on a point somewhere above his left eye. "You'll live," he says. "The wound's closed. You might have a mild concussion. We'll get you checked out." His hands fall away again. He stretches his fingers, cracks the joints. "Did you see him?"

Tyler wonders how much Paul Enfield weighs. He lifted Joe Wentworth with the smallest grunt. Whoever dragged Thorogood round the church had to be strong.

"No," he says. "He hit me before I saw him." He looks up at the fire officer. "That was just before you arrived." The man has just saved his life, but he asks it anyway. He can't help himself. "What were you doing here?"

Enfield smiles, a sort of disappointed understanding, perhaps. "I was reexamining the crime scenes. You remember the allotment owned by Cyril Armitage? Turns out he was Wentworth's father-in-law. I was on my way here from the scout hut when I saw the flames. You might also be interested to learn that Thorogood was a scout leader."

"Yes, Rabbani found that out, just before . . ."

Enfield raises his eyebrows. "That would have been nice to know earlier."

"There was a lot going on." It's hardly fair, but Tyler doesn't feel like being fair right now. "Isn't it a bit late for house calls?" he asks.

"Yes," Enfield says. "Funny. I was just thinking the same about you."

The fire is under control now, but the engines still pump gallons of water into the small cottage. Enfield goes to speak with the fire-fighters. Tyler watches the flames rage. He understands now what Enfield was trying to tell him. There *is* a beauty here. Something dangerously compelling. He turns and searches the faces lining the street. Is he out there somewhere? Watching.

Another car pulls up and is waved through the police cordon. Doggett's voice drifts across the street. "What the bloody hell are you doing at my crime scene, Tyler?"

"The usual, Jim. Compromising cases, that sort of thing."

"Where's Wentworth?"

"Hospital."

Doggett looks at him closely, notes the cut on his head and the bandaged hand. "Time to piss off then. You can make a statement in the morning."

"It is morning," he says, but Doggett is already walking away.

The dog has given up its barking and is curled round the base of the lamppost, shivering, its head buried under gray paws. Paul Enfield returns and sees him staring at it. "I'll get someone to take it to the rescue place," he says.

"No, I'll take it."

"I think we should get you home. I'll drive, get one of the lads to bring your car later."

They stop at the twenty-four-hour pharmacy to get cream for his burns and some painkillers. The only other customers are meth heads waiting for their prescriptions. Tyler shows the pharmacist his neck. She winces and tells him to go to the hospital. Instead he makes Enfield stop at the twenty-four-hour Tesco so they can buy tins of dog food and a bowl.

When they get back to the flat, Enfield turns off the engine. "I'll help you up."

"I'm fine, really."

"Let me help, Adam. Please."

They have to coax the dog into the lift, where it immediately cocks its leg and pees up the mirrored wall. Great. He seems to spend half his life cleaning this lift. The keeping of pets is directly forbidden in his rental agreement. Once inside, the dog jumps up on the sofa, turns round a couple of times, and goes straight to sleep.

Tyler looks at the fire officer. Then he sighs, loads up his laptop, and shows him the blog. Paul Enfield fixes his eyes intently on the screen. They read the final entry together and Tyler lets out a breath of air.

After a short while Enfield asks, "How long have you known about this?"

"Since the evening before last."

"For fuck's sake, Adam!" It's the first time he's properly seen the man lose his temper.

"We didn't want to scare him off by letting him know he'd been rumbled." It seems wrong to blame Doggett.

"You mean you thought it might be me."

Tyler says nothing.

"And you still do. So why now?"

"I guess because I'm suspended. It's not like I can get into any more trouble. And I'm trusting you. I don't want anyone else to die."

Enfield nods. Tyler can still see the fury in the man's eyes, but he holds his temper in check.

They spend some time discussing the various entries and what they might mean. Whoever this is, it's clear they are damaged, and that the damage was caused in the first instance by Gerald Cartwright.

"Maybe we can trace the IP address," Enfield says.

"We've got someone working on it."

"Yeah, well, forgive me if I don't rely wholly on South Yorkshire's finest. In my experience they're a little loath to share information." He sighs heavily. "I'll get the tech guys on it in the morning."

"It *is* morning," Tyler says again. He reaches out on a whim and touches Enfield's arm. "You were right; he's been talking to us all along. We just weren't listening."

"He hasn't been talking to *us*, Adam. He's been talking to you. You should be concerned about this. He's been to your flat."

They are close now. He can feel Paul Enfield's muscles tense under the fabric of his T-shirt.

Then Enfield is leaning in, pressing his lips to Tyler's mouth. He pulls away again, just as suddenly. "I'm sorry, I shouldn't have done that."

"No, it's . . . Look, I'm tired. Maybe we could talk later."

Enfield smiles. "Sure. I'll get to work on that website."

After Enfield leaves, he reads through the blog entries again. Then he reads them again. It's all here. The reasons, the psychosis. Whatever it is. Unless . . . The thought occurs to him this could just be a game someone's playing. Someone who knows how to manipulate people, how to get what they want.

After his third read he begins to find it hard to focus on the screen. His eyes refuse to stay open despite his best efforts. But when he goes to lie down for a minute or two the words from the blog begin running round his head in broken fragments.

You shouldn't have come back . . . unearthing buried secrets . . . Screaming. Always screaming . . .

On and on as he drifts in and out of consciousness.

So they have found him . . . he wants more . . . remember how they watched and they laughed . . . you survived . . .

Tyler turns over, tries to drive the voice out by humming a tune in his head.

The schoolteacher . . . she knew . . . the one who called himself God's servant . . . got what he deserved . . .

As he drifts off, he dreams he is the arsonist, playing with matches, just like Bonfire Night when he was a kid. Gerry's voice screaming in his head.

He wants peace . . . an end to it . . . it's up to you to finish it for him . . .

A dog barks and he wakes. Tyler sits up sharply, and his T-shirt pulls the skin from his blistered neck, setting it on fire once again.

It's late; he's slept too long. He takes the dog out, letting it run round the grounds of the flats. While he's trying to dig it out from under a bush, Enfield's colleague turns up with his car. Somehow she manages to persuade the dog to come out of hiding. He thanks her and offers to give her a lift home, but she declines.

He showers gingerly, trying to avoid the burns, then spends twenty minutes trying to rub cream into his neck and shoulders. Then he goes back to the blog.

It tells him so much, and yet so little. He prints off the entries and arranges them on the floor. When Doggett arrives the dog launches itself at his ankles. *A* Yorkshire terrier against *the* Yorkshire Terrier. Tyler feels a sudden affection for the creature. Nevertheless, he shuts it in the hallway so they can talk. It immediately begins scratching at the door.

"I wondered what happened to the bloody thing." Doggett is looking down at the printouts on the floor. "How's the neck?"

"Still there."

Doggett takes out a photograph wrapped in plastic and places it very deliberately onto the breakfast bar in front of him. Its corners are singed, and the photo is obscured by crusted black ash. "We found that at Wentworth's, along with a load more."

Tyler picks it up.

"Is it him?" Doggett asks.

It takes Tyler a moment to understand what he's seeing. The angles are all wrong, the camera too close to the subject. Just patches of blond hair. Pale white flesh crisscrossed with marks. Scars, burns, weeping sores. And in the background, hanging in its original place, the portrait from the Old Vicarage. The details are blurred, out of focus, but Tyler is confident it's the same picture.

"We've rescued what's left of Wentworth's PC. The speccy-techies are looking at it as we speak, but I think we know what we're gonna find. More of the same. Is it him?" he asks again.

They both know who he means. Oscar.

"No."

"The hair matches. He's the right age."

"It isn't him."

Doggett takes back the photo and examines it. "Even if it isn't, he grew up in that place." He slips the photo into his jacket pocket. "Wentworth was the gardener, for Christ's sake! Probably babysat the lad. Given what Rabbani's told us about their conversation, and the fire at the scout hut, it's not much of a leap to suppose the very Reverend Akela Thorogood was involved, too. Being abused gives the lad a bloody good motive for murder. I'm not sure I'd even blame the kid."

"How is Wentworth?"

"Dead. On the way to the hospital."

Neither of them voice any sympathy for the man . . . *got what he deserved* . . . But if Tyler had got there sooner . . . Or if Paul hadn't had to come back to get him out of the house . . . *The world should not mourn him.*

Doggett is crouched over the blog pages, reading them. "Well, well. You've been busy."

"It isn't him," Tyler says again, but he doesn't have the energy to argue further, and he knows it wouldn't make any difference to Doggett. His mind is made up.

Doggett leaves with his evidence bag. "Be careful," he says. "If Oscar makes contact with you, ring me. You hear?"

On his way out, Doggett stops and looks at the dog cowering in the hallway. "What are you gonna do with this?"

Tyler shakes his head.

"I'll take it if you like. I don't know why, but I've always had a thing for terriers."

After they've gone Tyler goes back to the floor and the blog entries. He sits cross-legged and reads them through again. He thinks he has most of it now. He visualizes the picture Doggett showed him: the pale, scarred flesh, the steep gabled roof of an attic bedroom, and the corner of an ashen-faced portrait hanging on the wall above the bed. He rereads the last entry. *The night Lily and Edna sat up watching for fires.* The fire watcher. He thinks about what Paul Enfield told him, that desperate compulsion to watch. Where is he? He should be back by now. He googles the words *fire watcher* and *lowry,* and sure enough the first hit is the portrait from the Old Vicarage that once hung in the attic but now sits above the mantelpiece in the living room. *The Fire Watcher.*

He thinks of opening lines. *My dad used to drink that.*

And closing ones. *It's up to you to finish it for him.*

Tyler picks up his keys and his mobile. On his way downstairs he tries Sophie Denham, but she either can't or won't answer. So he calls Rabbani instead and tells her to find out what he needs to know. Then he gets into his car, hoping for the first time he can ever remember that for once he's got it wrong.

There's no one on the gate at the Old Vicarage. The lack of reporters isn't overly concerning; he imagines the bulk of the television vans and photographers are currently camped out at the top of Wentworth's cul-de-sac. But the lack of any officers on the scene is a little more worrying. The police tape that should be stretched wide across the driveway has snapped and is fluttering in the breeze. He leaves his car on the main road and walks toward the house. There are two cars parked outside the front door. Daley's beat-up Mondeo, and a BMW convertible that once drove him to Ladybower Reservoir. Oscar's car.

The mobile incident room is locked. There's no sign of Guy Daley. He takes out his mobile, but the screen is blank. He holds down the power button but nothing happens. It looks like the battery's gone for good this time. He steps across the gravel and shivers; for the first time in weeks the temperature has dropped below sixty degrees. There's a strong wind whistling through the trees, and thick, dark clouds race above the house.

The front door is standing wide open. He waits a moment, listening. There's nothing but the wind rustling the branches above. Even so, he walks past the front door and moves around the side of the house, aware that his shoes are crunching loudly in the gravel. The back door is open too, but he can see through the window that the kitchen is empty.

As he steps into the house there's that same faint, sharp odor that he caught at Wentworth's. This time he recognizes it immediately. It catches in his throat. There's a steady orange glow coming from the hallway. He crosses the kitchen and sees tea lights scattered along the corridor, lining the floor like the emergency lights that mark the exit routes on an airplane. When he reaches the door that leads down to the cellar, he stops and places his hand for a moment on the ravaged wood of the door. It's cool to the touch. He moves on, taking an exaggerated step over the hole in the floor and stepping into the dim living room.

There are more tea lights here. Hundreds of them. On the mantelpiece, the floor, balanced on the brown, moldy arms of the sofas. With the curtains drawn, it's enough to throw dark shadows into every corner of the room. Again he has that feeling of being watched. This time he looks straight toward the portrait on the chimney breast. He moves slowly, stepping carefully across the rotting floorboards, his shoes sinking into the soggy carpet. The eyes of the man in the painting—the fire watcher—follow him all the way across the room, drawing him in. The fire watcher is here in the house with him. And he's sure now he knows who it is.

Rabbani holds her finger against the tiny metallic intercom button and listens to it trill for several seconds. Still nothing. She tries calling him again, but once again her call is immediately directed to voicemail. What is wrong with him? Surely he hasn't switched it off again? On the other hand, she imagines that if she'd been suspended, that would be the first thing she'd do.

But she isn't Tyler. And he specifically asked her to call him, so why isn't he answering? There could be any number of reasons, of course, but she has a nasty feeling something's wrong.

She was given the all clear to leave the hospital that morning but decided to tell her mother they weren't letting her out until the afternoon. That way she could avoid the fuss and finish the job Tyler had given her.

As soon as she left the ward, even as she was negotiating the corridors out of the hospital, she made the call to Sophie Denham. Tyler had told her he was having trouble reaching the girl, so she was surprised when she managed to get through the first time. At first, Denham refused to speak to her, but Rabbani swallowed her pride and begged. She needed to know only one thing. Eventually Denham agreed. Rabbani asked the question Tyler had given her, and Denham gave the answer. Just like that. No equivocation, no reluctance to confide or attempt to find the right words. All of which only convinced Rabbani she was telling the truth. After a couple of hours of listening to the same honeyed voice tell her how sorry she was that her call could not be connected, she'd called in a favor from a girl she knew in HR in order to get hold of Tyler's address.

Now what? She hasn't thought much past this point. She's more convinced than ever that something is wrong and yet . . . how to convey that to anyone who'll give a damn? She can imagine the response she'd get from Doggett.

There's a gentle click, and the gates to the block of flats in front of her swing silently open. A Mercedes swings round the corner and sails past her. She ducks through the gates as they swing closed, but the concierge has his head out of the door before she's made it past the first block. "Excuse me, love? Are you visiting someone?"

"Tyler. Flat 123."

"Popular fellow." The concierge turns and a large black guy steps out of the office behind him. It's the fire officer, Enfield.

"You're looking for DS Tyler?" he asks her.

Rabbani nods.

"Apparently he left about twenty minutes ago."

She introduces herself and then thanks the concierge for his help. The man hovers for a moment and then slips back into his office, clearly put out that he's not to be included in the drama.

"Do you know where he is? He's not answering his phone."

Enfield shakes his head. "I've been trying to reach him myself." He scratches his neck with a massive hand and Rabbani swallows, determined not to stare at his muscles. Well, not too obviously, anyway.

"There was another fire last night," he tells her. "Adam was injured."

"Injured? How?"

Enfield frowns at her. "You're the girl from the church," he says as though suddenly recognizing her.

She lets the *girl* comment go. "What do you mean, 'injured'?"

"Nothing too serious. He probably shouldn't be driving, though."

"Maybe I should speak to the DI," she says.

Suddenly Enfield is in front of her. "I'm not sure that's a good idea." He has his hand on her arm now. She pulls it away sharply.

"Why not?"

"The arsonist. I think he's one of yours."

Her voice, when she finds it, comes out in a rasp. "Police?"

"I managed to trace the blog."

"What blog?"

Enfield looks at her closely. "Maybe we should talk to DCI Jordan. Adam's probably already with her. Why don't you come with me? I can give you a lift."

She wants to tell him to stop calling the sarge *Adam*. It's *Tyler*. Or *Detective Sergeant Tyler*. But not Adam. No one calls him Adam. There's something about this guy that's off, the way he thinks about everything so carefully before he says it.

He gestures toward the gate as though inviting her to go ahead of him.

Rabbani starts to speak, to tell him she'll make her own way to the station, but suddenly her throat is on fire again and she's coughing and rasping and doubling over.

He puts his massive hand on her back. "You look like you need to sit down. Look, my car's just over here."

She wants to struggle, to push his help away, but she realizes that would be ridiculous, so she lets him guide her toward the car. He smiles at her as the coughing fit begins to subside, and then he has the door open for her and she can't think of a valid reason not to get in.

Edna is refusing to pass on; she has joined Lily's mother in the woodchip on the walls. It's worse than when she was alive; at least Lily could escape then.

Lily has been making arrangements. She has had to contact all manner of people by telephone—solicitors, florists, the funeral parlor. It feels almost as though she's organizing a big party, and she supposes that is exactly what this is, in a way. Not that Edna would appreciate the description.

She went early into the village this morning to try to avoid the sympathy of friends and neighbors, but in fact it was all rather novel. The fire at the church has everybody talking. She had whole conversations with people she was previously only on nodding terms with, most of which began with the offering of condolences but then continued on much further than they normally would have done. Had she heard about the church? The poor vicar! The work of an arsonist, the police are saying. Isn't it coming to something? This would never have been allowed to happen in the old days.

She had mostly just listened and nodded, offering very little in the way of her own thoughts, but then it seemed that was mostly what people wanted anyway. It is almost as though Edna's demise has freed Lily in some way, revoked her status as persona non grata and welcomed her back into the village fold. Carol had nodded to her in the paper shop, as close to an offering of deepest sympathies as Lily was ever going to get from that one. And even Her-Next-Door offered to go for the papers and, when Lily declined, stopped to chat for almost twenty minutes about . . . well, almost everything under the sun.

Back in the cold, dry dark of the cottage, Lily has to push down a surge of . . . what? Happiness? She really doesn't want to think about that too much. But she can, if she lets herself, acknowledge that Edna's departure is like the lifting of a dark cloud that has been hanging over her for more years than she can remember. She feels a tremendous guilt about this, but perhaps not so much as she should. Edna's death has been a reality they have both been living with for so long that neither one of them could remember things being any different.

She glances at the clock to find it's past lunchtime. Where has the morning gone? She rouses herself and switches on the kettle, taking down two of the roses cups and saucers from the dresser and placing them on the tray with the milk jug. She makes herself a sandwich, tuna and cucumber, and calls to Edna to see if she wants one. She gets no response.

When she returns to the back room, the local news is on. First there's the accident at the church; a young policewoman was hurt, it seems, as well as the poor vicar. An Indian girl, like the one who was here yesterday offering tea and sympathy. It could even be the same one; it's hard to tell them apart. Then a picture of Cynthia flashes onto the screen. And images of the Old Vicarage, the police tape strewn across the driveway. Lily lets go of the cup in her hand, barely noticing as it breaks into three pieces when it hits the stone hearth.

Don't think you're home and dry yet! cackles Edna, scratching at her milky eye with a blackened fingernail. *Just because I'm dead and gone, that doesn't make everything go away, you know. You can't relax, Lily Bainbridge. You can never relax!*

Lily shushes her. Edna smiles a skeletal crescent and dissolves into dust.

Lily switches off the television set and moves into the front room. But here there is the awful stain on the carpet. It looks better than it did. No one who didn't already know the cause would guess. Of course, everybody *will* know. There's a lingering smell, too, like the remains of spilled food on the floor of the oven that resurfaces every time you light it.

She moves to the patio doors and opens them. The conservatory is hot and smells of plastic—not a significant improvement—so she opens the back door as well and steps out into the garden. The air is fresher than the stuffy cottage, and she breathes out heavily.

There are clouds gathering overhead and she can hear a bird singing. It reminds her of the summer Edna was in the hospital, when Cynthia would bring Oscar over, and the three of them would drink dandelion and burdock on the lawn, spread out on a red check picnic rug.

Poor Cynthia.

Poor Oscar. And then she thinks of him . . . *arms sunk into Marigold gloves, washing the dishes. It's Edna's punishment because he's late back from playing out. Edna always metes out the punishments. She, Lily, is the soft one, the one who'll slip him sweets afterward. You can't buy affection, Edna says. But that isn't it. She needs to spoil him. She's never had anyone to spoil before. And besides, where's the harm? He catches her eye and winks. She giggles, but Edna looks up sharply and Lily straightens her face. It is supposed to be a punishment after all. Poor Oscar . . .* she thinks. But no! Poor Oscar nothing! Why did he send those horrible letters? And if he was here that night, with Edna, why would he not have rung for help? Does he really hate them so? All they ever did, they did to protect him.

What did they do? What did *she* do?

Through the trees Lily makes out the distant outline of the dilapidated Old Vicarage. She shivers in the breeze. It comes to her that for all its beauty she hates this place. And now she's stuck here with that awful smell. Burned toast and warm plastic.

And now what? Will they just fall back into the old routine, she and Edna?

There's a light on at the vicarage. And a noise, too. Something like a drumbeat, a young person's sound. That awful music Oscar used to play, all thump-thump-thump. It sounds like a native call to arms. *Thump-thump, thumpety-thump. Thump-thump, thumpety-thump.* And suddenly she finds herself following the crumbling, leaf-strewn path between the trees, following the noise. *Thump-thump, thumpety-thump.*

The way she came before, all those years ago.

Edna is with her now. Lily can't see her, but she knows she's there. She can hear her soft indoor moccasins, the ones she was wearing when she fell, as they scrape their distinctive lame shuffle along the flagstones behind her. Lily hears the repeated rustle of branches she has already negotiated, even over the noise of the wind in the trees. Above them the storm clouds continue to gather.

What are you looking for, Lillian? Edna whispers. *What is it you hope to find?*

She wishes she had an answer for that. She could ask Edna, of course, but she isn't certain Edna will tell her.

Could Oscar really have sent those letters? If so, what possible reason could he have to do so? She is certain there is something . . . something she can't quite put her finger on. Whatever it is, maybe she can put things right between them. Maybe everything can go back to the way it was. Lily pulls her cardigan close against the chill and moves quickly along the path, emerging from the tree line. *Thump-thump, thumpety-thump.* She knows what the noise is now. It's the sound of her own heart, beating in her chest. She pushes her way through the knee-high scrub, aiming for the door-way that opens into the kitchen. The threshold she last crossed six years ago. Retracing her steps, revisiting the past. And Edna goes with her.

"Hideous, isn't it?"

Oscar is standing in the doorway, framed by it, the flickering tea lights giving him the same hellish background as the fire watcher in the painting. He is holding an open bottle of champagne and two glasses. He crosses the room and Tyler takes an involuntary step back, his heels bumping against the marble hearth.

"Here," Oscar says. He thrusts the bottle and glasses into Tyler's hands, where they clink and chime together, then reaches into his back pocket and pulls out two long, thin white candles and a box of matches. He strikes a match and touches it to the wick. The first candle flares into life. He lights the second candle from the first, then drips some wax onto the mantelpiece and sets the two can-dles upright under the painting. He pauses for a moment and looks up at the portrait. "Lowry," he says. "Laurence Stephen. Nineteen forty-three. It's an original, I think." Then he frowns. "At least, that's what he told me."

"Why are you here, Oscar? Where's DC Daley?"

Oscar grins. "Why? Have you lost him?"

"He isn't at his post."

"How naughty of him."

Oscar pushes him backward into a large armchair and Tyler sits down hard, a cloud of dust and ash rising around him.

"Relax," Oscar says, perching on the arm of the chair. He takes back the bottle and one of the glasses and pours the champagne. "Here, this will loosen you up."

Tyler ignores him. "What are you doing here?"

"Just having a look at the place. One last time. I'm glad you came. I was going to call you but . . ." He swaps the full glass for the empty one and pours a second drink for himself. "I owe you an apology for the other day. I was upset about Edna. It's no excuse but . . ." He takes a long swig of champagne. "I'm sorry. I shouldn't have gone to Denham. I hope you didn't get into too much trouble."

"The police are looking for you."

"I thought *you* were the police?"

"This isn't my case now."

"But you're here?" Oscar leans forward, touches his cool, wet lips to Tyler's cheek. His breath smells of sweet champagne. He feels Oscar's hand moving up his thigh so he stands, stepping toward the portrait and raising his glass.

He stops, the champagne halfway to his lips, thinking about that night in the club. The rim of the glass tickles his lips and tiny bubbles send puffs of air into his nose. He lowers the glass again and puts it down on the mantelpiece.

"I'm sorry," Oscar says again. His words are slurred, and Tyler wonders how much champagne he's drunk. Or maybe he's washed something else down with it. Oscar joins him by the painting. "I know, I've got things I need to work out but . . ." He pushes a fore-finger into the melting wax on the mantelpiece. "I'm ready to do that now." He upends his glass, the prominent Adam's apple puls-ing obscenely as he swallows.

Tyler thinks of the photograph Doggett showed him. The pale white skin exposed by the bright flash. He doesn't want to tell Os-car what he's discovered. Suddenly all he wants is to get out of this place, the fetid air, the damp that seems to creep across his flesh. Instead he asks, "What did you mean, 'One last time'?"

Oscar grins and reaches into his back pocket. He pulls out a white envelope. "Here."

"What is it?"

"Open it."

Tyler takes the envelope and lifts the flap. He pulls out two air-line e-tickets to South Africa. One has Tyler's name on it. He stares at it for a moment and then looks at Oscar. "Do you really think it's that easy? That you can just run away?" Running doesn't solve any-thing. He knows that better than anyone. He thinks of poor Lily Bainbridge, shut away in her crumbling cottage. And Jude, hiding in the army. And he thinks of his father. Of Richard, who ran away from everything in the end. "Things that are buried don't stay bur-ied. Eventually someone digs them up. You don't get to just walk away from this. None of us do."

Oscar allows himself to fall backward into the armchair. He sighs heavily and closes his eyes. "I know," he says. "I just wish . . . I wish . . ." His words trail off.

Tyler bends over and taps his hand against Oscar's cheek. "Os-car?" He stirs a little but doesn't open his eyes. "Oscar!"

And then Tyler's head explodes. He staggers, and falls in slow motion to the damp carpet. He lands hard, on his knees, tries to speak but the words coming out of his mouth seem strange, etched in bright colors. They pour from his mouth and spill out over his

T-shirt. His arms feel heavy, like slabs of concrete. And he feels something warm trickling down his neck.

Tyler falls forward onto his face and hands. He tries to push himself back up, but his body is just too heavy. It's getting darker, the light from the candles and tea lights fading around him. He manages to roll onto his back and sees the ashen face of the fire watcher looking down on him and then, whatever it was that hit him, hits him again. And after that there is nothing.

Lily climbs slowly and steadily. She's careful on the stairs, where one or two have rotted right through, but at least the fire hasn't touched them too badly.

The fire. She never understood the fire. Edna?

Not me, dear.

Joe Wentworth, then?

No, I don't think so. Someone else.

Someone else?

You forget how it was. There were always people coming and going in this house. All sorts. Gerald's women and his business partners. Oscar's friends.

Lily nears the top and places her hand on a banister that falls away and clatters to the floor below. She steadies herself by clutching the top step. It feels just as it did back then. Yes, she remembers! She knew something was wrong. Why didn't she go back? She should have gone back.

You knew what you would find.

She didn't know. She couldn't have known.

But you did, didn't you? We both did.

"The girl. Sophie."

Denham's daughter. He told us what Gerald did.

"But you said she was lying!"

That's right, Lillian. Blame me if it makes it easier.

"We should have told someone."

Are you going to stand here all night? It's all the same to me, of course. I'm not the one who'll catch my death.

Lily goes on. Along the first-floor corridor to the next set of stairs. The house smells. It's the same smell she tried to soak out of the carpet by the hearth. The smell of fire and death.

"I don't want to go up there. I won't!"

Silly woman!

"No, Edna, please! Don't make me!"

Stupid woman! I never made you do anything.

There's a noise from above, the scrape of a chair, footsteps.

Someone is already up there.

Someone else.

She takes refuge in one of the bedrooms, closing the door behind her so very quietly. She turns. Oscar's old room. Even now, ruined as it is, it's far tidier than it ever was when he had it. It had been this very room where it began. Only, on that occasion, she'd been outside listening in. Listening as Edna . . . *argues with Michael.*

"You can't be serious! You expect me to take the word of that girl? Gerald's a good man; you can't possibly believe this nonsense."

Lily can't see them but she knows Michael's frowning, unsure if he's gone too far. He always falters when it comes to Edna. But then, who doesn't?

"I don't know what to think. But I know Sophie wouldn't lie to me. She wouldn't make this up."

"Then the girl's mistaken," says Edna, and her voice is so confident Lily almost believes it herself.

There's a long pause. When Michael speaks, it's quietly and calmly. "I hope you are right, Miss Burnside, for the boy's sake if nothing else." Lily slaps a hand over her mouth to stifle her gasp.

"What are you talking about?"

"Are you really that naïve, or are you in on it?"

"How dare you!"

Lily hears the slap.

When he speaks again it's quietly, and Lily has to strain to hear through the wooden door. "I've seen the money behind it and God help me I haven't said anything. Shipping girls up from London. Boys, too. Did you know that? Do you really think Oscar is safe? Who the hell is safe from Gerald Cartwright? What happened to Cynthia, eh? You know, don't you? He let some of it slip once, when he was so drunk he could barely stand. I just thank Christ he was too drunk to remember afterward that he'd said anything. Otherwise, I'd probably be joining her . . . wherever she is. I know you were involved. Does Lily know about it as well?"

"Leave Lily out of this." Edna's voice is frighteningly harsh. "Don't you even think of going to the police! Do you think they'll take your word over his? He's a powerful man. You know full well who his friends are. If you're lucky, they'll make out you're mad. Lock you up somewhere. Is that what you want?"

Michael's voice is different now. He backpedals. "I don't want any trouble, and I certainly don't want to go up against Gerald Cartwright. What you do is up to you. I just thought you should know what he's capable of."

There's a stunned silence, as though they both realize they've said too much. When Michael comes out of the room his cheek is bright red. He stares at her and they both understand. He steps forward and Lily flinches.

"He's a bad man," he says simply. Then he heads down the stairs.

Lily goes into the room to find Edna sitting on the bed, one hand clutched to her chest.

"Edna?" She rushes over to the bed.

"I'm all right."

Lily crouches in front of her and takes her hands. "It's not true, is it? Please! Say it isn't true!"

Edna shakes her head. "Of course it isn't true. She's a young girl, her head full of mischief and her body full of chemicals. She smokes drugs, you know. I've seen her in the barn with some of the others. At least Oscar wouldn't get involved in that nonsense." Edna's hands are shaking.

"What about Oscar?"

"Never mind."

"But Edna, what if . . . ?"

"Lillian," Edna snaps. Her hand cups Lily's wrist like one loop of a policeman's handcuffs. "You put this nonsense out of your head at once. Do you understand me? Do you understand?"

"Yes, Edna, yes. Please, stop. You're hurting me."

She stares at Edna until she lets go and . . .

When she sits down on the bed next to her, Edna's face is cadaverous. She grins her toothy smile through ruined lips. It's hard to believe those insubstantial claws once held the power to hurt Lily. She rubs at the memory in her wrists.

You couldn't leave it, could you? Edna says. *You let that girl's poison pour itself into your mind.*

"But it wasn't poison, was it?" Lily demands. She can feel the blood rushing though her veins, flushing her cheeks. "She was right!"

Edna's grin falters slightly. *Go on, then,* says Edna. *We might as well see it through.* She falls backward onto the bed and her wasted body sinks into the mattress and disappears.

Lily gets up, walks to the door, and opens it. She steps out onto the landing and listens. The house is quiet.

She moves to the bottom of the attic stairs and begins to climb.

———

Tyler feels the ground cold and wet against his cheek. Hard stone. He opens his eyes, but everything stays dark. His head is pounding and he can feel that the wound from last night has re-opened and is pumping blood from his head at an alarming rate.

His hands and legs are tied with what feels like garden string. He wonders idly if it came from Wentworth's allotment shed. He forces himself upright, twisting his body and trying to ignore the throbbing in his head and the way the bonds cut into his skin. Upright he feels better; the pounding in his head wanes a little. His eyes begin to focus.

He is in the cellar. The cellar where they found Gerald Cartwright and his broken fingers. There's a battery-operated light designed to look like an old-fashioned gas lamp that gives the area a dull orange glow. He sees a row of dust-covered bottles lying still in the wine rack. The smell from earlier is now painfully acute. The same smell as at Wentworth's house. Petrol. There are twenty or thirty cans of the stuff dotted across the stone floor. Ahead of him, in the darkness at the foot of the far wall, there are piles of wood, broken pieces of furniture, pallets, anything that might burn.

He hears a sound, like the scraping of metal on stone, and only now realizes he's not alone. There's someone moving, purposefully, out of sight but somewhere to his left. He has to try to get his strength back. Quickly. He tries flexing his wrists, working at the string binding his arms. It gives a little but only after it slices further into his flesh.

The scraping noise stops abruptly and he freezes. He doesn't think he made a noise, but something has given him away. And then the sounds of movement draw closer.

"You're awake," she says, her voice deep and rasping but still beautiful. A dark shadow falls across his face.

Sally-Ann is wearing a child's nightgown, pink cartoon rabbits dancing through the grass in a repeated pattern. The nightgown is old and faded and made for someone carrying a lot less flesh than Sally-Ann. The fabric pulls tightly across her stomach and waist, revealing her bare arms, legs, neck. It's more skin than he's ever seen her reveal before. Once upon a time, before Gerald Cartwright got his hooks into her, Sally-Ann must have had a similar build to Oscar. They're about the same height, though Sally-Ann walks hunched over, turned in on herself as though trying not to be noticed. They certainly have the same pale skin, the same hair. Though Sally-Ann's blond head is cropped savagely, designed to repel rather than attract. The one striking difference, of course, is the burn marks. Sally-Ann's entire body is pockmarked with small red patches. Scars so deep that some are visible even through the thin stretched fabric of the nightgown. At some time in the not-so-distant past she was used as something like a human ashtray. The marks are the stubbings out of a thousand cigarette butts.

She is the child in Doggett's photo.

Tyler flexes his jaw and tries to speak. His voice when it comes is cracked and husky. "Where's Oscar?" he manages.

She moves closer, crouches in front of him. He sees the soft pink flesh of her stomach rolling over her underpants beneath the thin material of the nightgown.

"You're back," she says quietly. "I'm sorry about that, Adam. I didn't want you to suffer."

"You drugged him?" he asks. Oscar had to have had more than just champagne to pass out that quickly. He realizes something else. "You were the one that spiked me in the club the other night, not Oscar."

"Oscar," she says absently. She reaches out to touch his face with a hand rough with brick dust. He tries to pull away but only manages to swivel his head a fraction.

"Why?"

"Because I wanted to see you out of control for once. Adam *fucking* Tyler, always so confident, so sure of himself. I wanted to see the real you."

"I meant, why are you doing all this?"

Sally-Ann wipes the sweat from her forehead. "You're the detective, you tell me."

When Doggett showed him the photo he, too, assumed it was a boy. At first. There was nothing in it to say otherwise, but then Sally-Ann was still a young teenager at the time. She'd yet to develop those obvious characteristics that make a difference. But what he knew then, beyond doubt, was that it couldn't be Oscar. For the first time, he was 100 percent confident Oscar wasn't the arsonist. He'd seen Oscar naked, after all. He'd seen the man's unblemished body. The scars on the body in the photo could never have healed so completely.

"You've been living here, haven't you?" he asks. "You were the one who brought the picture down to the living room, so you could see it every day." The painting of the fire watcher that once hung in the attic. The one thing she had to stare at while Gerald and his cohorts raped and abused her.

Sally-Ann studies him, a neutral expression on her face. "You knew it was me."

"Not soon enough." He hadn't been sure. He'd hoped he was wrong.

"How?" she asks.

He almost shakes his head but catches himself in time, before it sends the blood pounding again. "I didn't start putting it together until we found the blog. The fire watcher."

"Yes, the blog. I have to admit you were a lot slower catching on to that than I would have expected. Still, you fair put me about when you rang me to ask me about it. Talk about having to think quickly on your feet."

"You offered to trace the IP address and then you stalled."

"I knew I was running out of time. But you can't have suspected me at that point, surely? Or you wouldn't have given me the blog to trace. Unless it was all some double bluff? Was it a bluff, Adam? Oh, please tell me you really are that clever!"

He wishes he could. "It was Sophie Denham. She told me how everyone used to come here after school and how Gerald once tried it on with her. It wasn't a big leap to assume she wasn't the only one. You told me yourself you were at school with Oscar."

"Ah yes, I wondered if I'd gone too far there. I bet it sounded odd, a run-down, ugly, fat, common girl who went to such a prestigious school. But I wasn't always like this, you know?"

It hadn't sounded odd to him at all. Is that really how she thinks of herself? He guesses this probably isn't the best time to argue with her, though. Keep her talking.

"And then there was the bourbon," he says. "A bit unusual these days." Bourbon on the rocks with a twist. *My dad used to drink that.* Oscar said it the night they met. She must have idolized the man to adopt his drinking patterns. "Why did you come back here, Sally-Ann?"

"This is my home. This is where I grew up." She looks in the direction of the wall where they found Gerald Cartwright. "It helps when I'm closer to him."

"I'm sorry," he says. Sally-Ann picks at the scars on her arms. "I'm sorry for what they did to you."

He doesn't see the blow coming. Her hand takes him hard across the cheek, blurring his vision. Blood rushes through his ears.

"I don't want your sympathy!" She spits in his face.

"Were they all involved?" he asks. "Cartwright and Wentworth and Thorogood?" He wonders if naming them might make her lash out again, but she doesn't.

She straightens up and moves away, leans against a broken pallet and breathes heavily, trying to regain control of her emotions. And then he realizes she's listening for something. She's looking for permission to tell him from the voice in her head. She smiles. "It was just me and Gerry at first. I was thirteen. I looked a bit different then. Skinny and pretty. One of the gang. When I met Oscar a few weeks ago, he didn't even recognize me. But I suppose I've changed a lot since then.

"I was flattered, of course. Who wouldn't be? Gerry was the man. And he loved me. I didn't mind that he didn't want anyone else to know; just having the secret was enough. It felt like everyone knew anyway, all the boys at school, the girls, everyone. I was pretty popular, and it was all thanks to Gerry. Like, while I was with him, he gave me confidence. And I knew we'd be together one day. Properly together."

"But Gerry had other ideas?"

The smile fades. "The others," she says. "He told me it was just a bit of fun, a bit of playing around, all boys together."

"Poker night."

"He brought people up for the weekend. Business acquaintances, a judge he owed a favor to. Before long he was bringing them up from London by the busload. Men and women he found on the street or in clubs and brothels. The money was good, but it had to be, because some of Gerry's friends had unusual tastes."

"And Gerry's thing was fire."

She nods. "Cigarettes, mostly. I didn't mind. It wasn't too bad at first and . . . well, I suppose I got used to it."

"You were a child, Sally-Ann. You weren't old enough to make that kind of decision. Where were your parents? Didn't anyone notice anything?"

She laughs. "I used to skip PE, and then I just started skipping school. My mother found a scar on my arm once but figured I was doing it myself. She called me a stupid girl and then got so drunk she forgot about it. It's not hard to hide things from people who aren't really looking. When I went missing she thought I'd run off. And when I came back, eventually, I found out she'd told the school I'd been sick. She covered for me, never even reported it. Made out she'd done me a massive favor."

"When you went missing?"

She sniffs. "It was one of Gerry's parties. Everyone was pretty coked up, including me. If not I might have realized and got out sooner, but by the time I came round enough to know what was going on I was already tied to the bed in the attic." Sally-Ann's hand reaches for her back. "The attic was always Gerry's favorite place. He installed soundproofing, told everyone he was creating a music studio. But it was more like a movie studio. He liked to film me; it was all pretty exciting.

"But that night he had something special in mind. A few days before that he'd got a bit carried away and hurt me. It was my fault really, but I was young and stupid, and I threatened him and told him we were over. He smoothed everything over but he didn't forget."

She straightens up and turns round, lifts the nightdress and pulls it up and over her head, exposing her back to him. The entire surface is crisscrossed with scars and burns. At the base of her spine the word *whore* is etched in spidery white scar tissue. She lowers the top and turns back, and Tyler realizes in his shock he's missed his chance. He might not get another. She must be strong; she dragged Thorogood round the church. Given his current state, if she sees him coming he might not have the strength to take her.

"Sometimes Gerry liked to watch while the other two took turns. For Thorogood, it was always just about the sex, and Wentworth's heart was never really in it; I think he preferred the boys,

to be honest. Gerry said it was because Wentworth's father used to
fiddle with him when he was a boy. He was sad and lonely, and
Gerry let him be one of the gang. He'd have done anything Gerry
told him to. He used to cry sometimes when he was fucking me.
Poor old Joe. Trust me, all I did was put him out of his misery." She
crouches again, pushing her face forward into his. "I was scared
shitless when you turned up at his place. I'm sorry I hit you, by the
way. I just panicked."

Abruptly she gets up and is walking away. She moves out of sight
and goes back to her work on the far side of the cellar. There's a
scraping noise.

Tyler takes the opportunity to stretch his legs. They respond but
are tied more firmly than his arms. He twists and turns his arms,
feels the string cutting into his wrists. She reappears and he stops
struggling.

"They know I'm here," he tells her. "They know it's you."

"You're a bad liar, Adam, do you know that? No, the only person
who knows I'm here is DC Daley, and he's not going to be telling
anyone."

"What have you done, Sally-Ann? What did you do to Guy?"

"You don't need to worry about him. I'm nearly finished now,
anyway."

"Finished with what?"

"You'll see." She disappears again and the scraping noise takes
up once again.

He has to get her attention back. "What about Edna Burnside?"
he shouts.

The scraping stops. Sally-Ann wanders back into view. This
time she's holding a small metal trowel, the type used for bricklay-
ing. "Poor Edna."

"Why did you kill her?"

She frowns. "I didn't."

"But you were there when she died; it was in the blog. You could have helped her."

"I wasn't the only one. I was only there at all because I was following him."

"Oscar?"

"I watched them through the window. He'd been trying to find out what happened to his mother. He told me he'd overheard Lily and Edna talking, years ago, when he was still a teenager, and he knew they'd been involved in some way. He knew his mother hadn't just run away like they'd always told him. The anonymous blackmail letters were my idea. I thought it might shake things up a bit. Funny, really, he was never even interested in what had happened to his father. Now, that I could have helped him with. If he'd asked.

"I couldn't really hear what they were saying, but Edna obviously called his bluff because I watched her rip the letters up and throw them into the fire. Then suddenly she was collapsing and tipping forward. And then she was facedown in the flames. He just stood there and watched her. Didn't move, didn't react. Jesus Christ, but he must have hated that woman! He was right there and he did nothing. Just turned around and walked away."

"Why didn't *you* do something?"

"I did exactly what she did. Sweet F.A. She knew what was going on in that house. They all did, though they were very good at closing their eyes to it."

"What about Lily, then? How come she wasn't on your list?"

She shakes her head. "There isn't any list." Then her face crumples in pain. She clutches at her head. "Shut up, shut up!"

"Sally-Ann?"

When she looks up, her face is composed again. "I couldn't hurt Lily." She pushes the trowel forward until it's inches from his eyeball. He notes the keen edge of the blade, sees how the cigarette burns stop at her neck and wrists. Easily covered by a long-sleeved turtleneck, or a choker. He can smell Sally-Ann's sweet, stale breath.

"Lily," she says, wistfully. "Lovely Lily is the one who saved me."

As Lily moves up the stairs . . . *she's waiting for Oscar to get home. He's late. He's supposed to be coming to stay over like he always does when Gerald has his friends round. Where is he? He should be here by now.*

She prepares the tea anyway and takes Edna up a bowl of soup, but she's sleeping. Lily watches the television for company without taking it in.

He must be out with his friends—that young Sophie and her lies. He's growing up fast. Fifteen; more than capable of looking after himself. And it's only eight o'clock. But that means Gerald's friends will be arriving soon, and Oscar mustn't be hanging around. It's their job to keep him away. Why has that never seemed odd to her before? Why only now after what Michael has told them?

It's not like they didn't know what Gerald was capable of. She's always known. Since the day he arrived with his father's features etched across his face, she knew he had it in him to be the same man. Before that, she knew. When she gave birth she knew what he was— a cancer born of the fire and pain of war. She had no qualms about giving him up. Not that she had any choice in the matter. And then he'd found her, tracked her down through the adoption agency. Why?

Did they do the right thing, helping him that day when he came to them about Cynthia? But what was the alternative—to watch Gerald carted off to prison? See Oscar put into the care of strangers? They certainly wouldn't have let him be raised by two elderly spinsters. Not at that age.

Yes, they know full well what Gerald is capable of. But those things Michael said . . . She shudders.

*It's almost nine o'clock, almost dark. He's never been this late.
Something must have happened. She needs to talk it through with
Edna, but it's so soon since she came out of the hospital and she needs
her sleep.*

What would Edna do?

*She would tell her to calm down for a start. She would go up
there. Never mind Gerald's rules.*

*She sets off along the path, intending just to take a look at the house.
Perhaps Oscar is playing in the garden and has forgotten the time. She
crosses the lawn, but there's no sign of him. She tries the back door just
to make sure. It opens. She hesitates on the doorstep, but in her gut she
knows something is wrong and she knows she has to go on. The house is
too quiet. She remembers the sound of men drinking together and this
isn't it.*

*She moves almost on tiptoe, opens the door to every room, every
cupboard. Like hide-and-seek. Coming, ready or not! Her search
takes her onward and upward until she reaches the stairs to the attic.*

*There's no noise but she's suddenly sure they are in there. She
moves slowly . . .* the floorboards creaking under her shoes. Her
slacks catch on a rusty nail on the banister. At the top she pauses
before . . . *she opens the door.*

*She sees the camera first. It stands out, smack-bang in the middle
of the room on its three metal legs. Then the men. There are three of
them, their trousers round their ankles, their hands busy upon themselves, their eyes focused on the bed. She looks to the bed. She doesn't
want to, but she must. There she sees him. Even now she doesn't want
to believe. It can't be him, not her little Oscar! His sweet little blond
head being pushed into the pillow to muffle his cries. And now she
sees Gerald, her son, the wicked, wicked child of fire and death, forcing himself on his own boy—her beloved grandson.*

*She must cry out, for they all turn at once to look at her. She takes
a step backward. That look on Gerald's face. It is the face of the devil,*

gray and mottled with sweaty exertion. The face of a cornered crea-
ture, snarling its fury. The face of his father, the man who raped her.

And because she's a coward, because this is what she always does,
she turns and runs. Back downstairs, back through the house, voices
shouting after her. She hears the front door slam as she's crossing the
grass and realizes the other men are following her lead.

She doesn't stop until she's home, up the stairs and into the bed-
room. Edna doesn't even ask. She gets up and looks into Lily's eyes.
She knows. This is what they've been avoiding since Michael came to
them. One more secret. One too many. Edna dresses quickly while
Lily sits and silently screams inside her own head. Though she's ex-
hausted, and the chemotherapy has rotted her hair and taken her
strength, Edna knows what must be done. That's what she does; she
takes care of Lily's messes. As Lily trembles while the bombs fall, Edna
keeps silent vigil for the fires.

Lily watches her go, but she can't let her face this alone. She can't
fall apart again. Like on the rooftop. Like in the alley behind the pub.
Like the day Gerald came to them crying over Cynthia.

Edna is the one who fixes things . . . while Lily crumbles.

"Aunt Lil?"

The attic room is much as it was the last time she was here. No
camera, though. No men. Just an incredible number of candles.
And lying on the same bed . . . "Oscar!"

She rushes to him. He seems so tired he can barely keep his
eyes open.

"Oh, Oscar!"

"She's . . ." he whispers at her. He seems confused. "Why is she
here?" he asks. "She brought me up here but . . . Auntie . . . you
need to get help." Even through her terror her heart tears to hear
him call her that. She wants to shout at him, "I'm your grandmother!" She wants him to call her *Nana,* or *Gran* or . . . But he
doesn't know. They all agreed. No, Gerald and Edna agreed. Why

confuse the boy? Why burden him with the truth of his father's ignominious conception? Just the first secret among many. Perhaps if she'd been stronger from the start and told the truth, none of this would have happened.

She tries to move him, but he's too heavy. Who has done this? Who has brought him here? No matter what he's done, he's still her grandson. She has to protect him.

Lillian. Edna is there, standing by the gable window in the roof. *Go now,* she says. *Do what the boy says. Get help before it's too late.*

"Aunt Lil," says Oscar, "please . . . you have to help . . ."

"Oh, Oscar!" Lily sobs, pulling him into her arms. He's just too heavy for her. His body sags back onto the mattress.

Lillian. Go. Now!

Once again, Lily runs.

"I used to come down here sometimes," says Sally-Ann.

Tyler can't see her, but he can hear the scraping of the trowel.

"Sometimes if everyone was out, or Gerry was busy with work. There's a coal chute for deliveries behind you. It was never locked. I'd come down here and sit in the dark, striking matches. Watch them burn down to my fingertips to see how long I could hold them."

He knows now what she's doing. She's rebuilding the wall torn down by the builders. Gerald Cartwright's final resting place. And Cynthia's. He has to keep her talking, keep stalling.

"You don't have to do this." He flexes his wrists again, and this time he feels something give. He twists the string but his hands are still held.

"I'm afraid I do." Sally-Ann reappears, the trowel in her hand. "Someone has to take Gerry's place, you see? At first, I thought it would have to be Oscar. I got him to come here by telling him you wanted to see him. I knew he'd come; he's actually pretty keen on you. All I had to do was drug the champagne and leave it out for him. He thought you'd arranged all this, the tea lights, everything. And then you actually turned up. I would have been angry with you if it wasn't so funny. But then I thought, perhaps it's better this way. Now you get to take Gerry's place instead, and we get to keep Oscar."

"Who's 'we,' Sally-Ann? You mean Gerald, don't you? You still hear him?"

She nods slowly. "He went away for a while, but he never stays gone. That's why I came back the first time. A few months after . . ." She trails off, and then picks up again. "I had to know if he was still here. I came in through the coal chute and listened at the wall. I could still hear him scratching at the bricks."

"He was long dead by then, Sally-Ann."

She grins again. It's a sick sight, no humor in it. "I know that, Adam. I'm not crazy." She rolls her eyes at him. "I could still hear him, though."

"So you set fire to the house?"

"It was my first really big fire. I didn't do a very good job of it, I'm afraid. I wanted the place to burn to the ground, but the flames just didn't want to catch. This time will be different."

"Tell me about Oscar. How did you meet again? Or have you just stayed in touch all these years?"

"No, I told you the truth about that. We met a few weeks ago by chance. Until then I thought it was all over. I was in therapy, and I could keep Gerry quiet most of the time. But then Oscar got back from uni, all grown up and looking just like his father and making noises about renovating the house."

"And that's when Gerry woke up? It was Oscar's idea to bring in the builders, wasn't it?"

"I couldn't tell him he was making a mistake, could I? Not without letting on how I knew, that Gerry had told me he didn't want
to be found. He was happy down here, you see? And then they dug
him up and the screaming started all over again."

"Why me? Why did you involve me?"

She looks down on him. "Poor Adam." She sticks out her lower
lip. "When I realized Gerry was going to be coming up I started
worrying what else might get found. DNA and stuff. I thought it
might be useful to know someone on the case, so I started talking
to you. You're not easy to befriend, though, do you know that? Very
self-absorbed."

He says nothing to that.

"Then Oscar confided in me about his sexuality, and I knew I
could get the two of you together. It's easy setting people up, isn't
it? Especially pretty boys like you two, so used to the world falling
at your feet."

"Why?"

She shrugs. "It made Gerry laugh." She looks back at the wall.
"I think he's ready now."

"Wait, I still don't know what happened. Sally-Ann, please! You
have to tell me."

She scratches her head and narrows her eyes. "You're stalling,
Detective Sergeant Tyler." Her other hand traces the outline of a
burn on her elbow. She leans back against the pallet again. "All
right," she says, hugging her arms. "They forgot about me in their
haste to get away. I'm not even sure Lily knew it *was* me. She just
kept screaming Oscar's name over and over again. The others ran
for it, and Gerry just threw his clothes back on and rushed downstairs to talk the old women out of phoning the police. So I snuck
down here. The old bolt-hole. I knew Gerry was going to kill me
this time, and I knew I had to get away. I thought I'd wait for things

to die down and then get out through the coal chute. I could hear them fighting upstairs. Him and the schoolteacher. I'd never heard him so angry. And I realized something else. He was afraid of her.

"Then that door opened." Sally-Ann points to the top of the stairs. "And down they came."

Lily runs . . . *after Edna through the hallway. She hears her confronting Gerald. Her voice is like acid; it eats at Gerald and he dissolves under her attack. But then he changes. The devil resurfaces. He spits venomous words back at her, accuses her of terrible things.*

"You knew what was going on! Don't pretend you didn't."

"You wicked creature!"

Lily watches as he threatens, and then pleads. He switches between scared little boy and monstrous beast, and through all of it Edna stands steadfast. The unbendable headmistress. She says, "I wish to God I'd convinced her to snuff out your miserable little life before it began." And then she falters, the cancer and the drugs ganging up on her at the worst possible moment. Her tired, aging body lets her down.

He sees her weaken and takes it as a sign. He grabs her by the arm, and Edna cries out. He pulls her after him, down the cellar steps. Lily can only follow. She can do nothing. She can't even speak. She watches as he places his hands round Edna's throat and starts to squeeze. Lily looks into Edna's eyes over his shoulder. They plead with her. Lily. Lily, my love. Lily, please!

She cannot say how it got there but she has a bottle in her hands. The light is fading from Edna's eyes. She watches them darken, the fire going out.

Lily has to choose.

The bottle goes up . . . and comes down.

He drops like a dead weight; facedown, his arms outstretched. Edna collapses next to him, gasping in the damp air.

Time passes.

Edna is no longer there. There's just Lily and her son, his head haloed by a growing pool of blood.

And then Edna is back with the gardener, Joe Wentworth. He's saying, "Jesus Christ, Jesus Christ!" over and over again. Edna tells him to be quiet. Her voice is croaky. She rubs at her throat. She tells him to help them or she will tell the police what he's been getting up to.

He knocks down the bit of wall where they buried poor Cynthia. Lily watches him haul Gerald's body through the hole. Then he rebuilds it. By the time he leaves, he is white-faced and shaking. Edna talks to him in a low, calm voice. After this day neither of them will speak to him again.

Finally, Edna comes for her, tries to take the bottle that's still in her hand. It hasn't even broken. Her hand is paralyzed; Edna has to prize her fingers open one by one. On the bottle's thick green base there are splashes of red and brown, flecks of gray. She lets go suddenly and the bottle falls. It bounces on the concrete floor. Still it doesn't break.

Edna takes her home and puts her to bed.

Much, much later, Edna tells her the rest. She makes Joe Wentworth drive the car to the station. She empties the bottle down the sink and takes it to the recycling point at the supermarket. Lily wonders if it even smashes then, when it drops into the green-glass bottle bank. Edna searches the house for evidence of what Gerald was up to. Some of it, like his shady business deals, she leaves for the police to find, but other bits—the tapes and DVDs, the photos—she takes and burns on a bonfire in the garden.

Oscar comes home the next morning. He apologizes, tells them he stayed at Sophie's. They go along with the story. Lily thinks they should get him some help, but Edna tells her if he doesn't want to talk about it then it's probably best left. They both fuss over him. Edna tells him his father has left early for his business meeting in Frankfurt and that he's to stay with them until he returns.

Lily and Edna spend much of the week talking. Getting their stories straight. Edna tells Lily what she's to say and what she is not to say to the authorities. Lily wants to tell them the truth, but Edna says it's far too late for that. Besides, they must think about Oscar and what's best for him.

The following Monday, Edna rings Gerald's office. The secretary tells her that he missed his meetings. Edna feigns some concern, but not too much. She calls the police. She handles them so well. Her answers are perfect, her timing impeccable. Lily never has to lie, not even once.

They turn their attention to Oscar. He wants to know where his father is. They tell him they don't know. He's a weak link, weaker in fact than Lily. If he should tell someone the truth about what Gerald was doing . . . But strangely, he doesn't. In fact, he stops communicating entirely. He grows cold and sullen. It breaks Lily's heart to see him change. First his mother, now his father. He thinks he has no family left. She wants to tell him differently, but she can't. It's too difficult. There are too many questions to answer.

Months later they wake to sirens in the night. They see the flames through the trees. The Old Vicarage burns. The police say it's arson. Probably kids taking advantage of the empty house. The officer investigating Gerald's disappearance is a suspicious ferret of a man who scares Lily until she can no longer talk at all. Thankfully, and just as Edna said, things begin to die down. As the truth about Gerald and his unscrupulous business dealings comes to light, the police begin to look further afield than sleepy Castledene.

But Oscar is growing more unruly, asking more and more questions. He's no longer their little boy. He's lost his way. Against Lily's wishes, Edna arranges with Michael Denham for him to be sent away to boarding school. He resists at first, but eventually seems to realize there's nothing left for him here. They see him off at the station.

And then Edna's cancer returns to punish them. Why is it Edna that must suffer all the pain? What about her? Why should it be that Edna is dying while . . .

Lily goes on.

"I saw the whole thing. I was crouched down, naked behind that wine rack, ready to bolt the moment anyone saw me. But no-body did. I must have been there for hours. I was weak with hunger and frozen stiff. Even after they'd gone I stayed another hour or two. That's when I heard it. The scratching. Like rats trapped in a box, scrabbling to get out. It was coming from behind the wall. I crept forward and listened. I could hear him on the other side, go-ing at the wall with his fingernails. I must have made a noise or something, because he knew I was there. He called out for help, then he called out for his mum." She marks the points off on her fingers. "Then he said he was sorry. Then he screamed." Sally-Ann licks her lips. "I ran. Naked and dirty and bleeding, I ran all the way home and shut myself in the bathroom. I thought about going to the hospital, but in the end I just dealt with it myself."

"That's the scream you hear?" he asks.

Sally-Ann wipes the tears from her face and looks up, as though seeing him for the first time. "I think we'd better get on," she says. She starts toward him.

He's not ready. He needs a few more minutes to gather his strength and give himself a fighting chance. "Wait, Sally-Ann!"

But this time she won't be distracted.

"Sally-Ann, you don't have to do this."

She crouches over him again. "I'm sorry, Adam, but we're run-ning out of time now. Oscar will be waking in the attic soon and wondering where I am. I have to get back to him."

"Sally-Ann, wait! What are you going to do?"

"Time's up," she says, and leans in to haul him up by the arms.

Now or never. Tyler untangles his wrists and drives his fists hard into her stomach. She wheezes as the breath goes out of her body, but at the same time she lashes out at his head with both arms. He manages to block one of the blows, but the other takes him hard on the side of the head. It wasn't enough; his body wasn't ready. He tumbles sideways, his legs still tied at the ankles. Then she's on him in a fury, pushing him toward the wine rack. They hit hard. He feels something sharp stab its way into his back. There's a pain in his side and another in his arm, and then his head is full of bright white light.

"Do you know her?" Paul Enfield asks from the rear passenger seat.

Doggett glances in the rearview mirror briefly and returns his eyes to the road. Something for which Rabbani, sitting in the front passenger seat, is enormously grateful. The man's not exactly the best driver in the world and is currently doing seventy along a winding country lane that's supposed to be a thirty zone.

"Who?" Doggett asks.

"Sally-Ann Digby. Is she involved with the case somehow?"

Doggett shakes his head. "She's a civilian, works in IT. She's the bloody one we put in charge of tracing the Internet address. When I chased it up with her yesterday, she fobbed me off with some excuse about the servers being busy, and I fucking believed her!"

They fall back into silence. Rabbani has her mobile pressed to her ear, but Guy Daley's phone just rings and rings until it cuts to voicemail again. The car speeds on.

Enfield says, "Does Adam know her?"

Doggett doesn't answer straightaway. Then he says, "Yes, *Adam* knows her."

"And now Adam's missing."

"Trust me," Doggett says. "Jordan'll have half of South Yorkshire Police out looking for him by now."

They drive on in silence. Rabbani clutches at the armrest on the door as the country lanes continue to unwind ahead of them. After a few more miles, the fire officer says, "Are we sure it's this Digby woman?"

Doggett looks to Rabbani to answer, and she realizes that in his eyes she's the computer expert.

The IP address Enfield gave her led to the comms room, where it was easy enough to trace which terminal the blog entries were uploaded from. "Then," she says, "it was just a case of checking who had access to that terminal at the right times. They were mostly posted early in the morning when there were only a few people in the building. Less chance of getting caught, I guess." When she saw the name on the list of employees Rabbani shivered. "*Ask Sophie Denham,*" Tyler had said to her earlier, "*if a girl called Sally-Ann Digby ever visited the Old Vicarage.*" She didn't know who Sally-Ann Digby was when she spoke to Denham, but she knew whatever theory Tyler had, he must be on to something. She just never got the chance to tell him. She hopes that lack of information hasn't cost him.

Again the car is silent for a time, the only sound the straining of the engine and the screech of tires desperately trying to stay on the tarmac.

"Why did she do it?" She's talking to herself more than anything, but Doggett answers her anyway.

"How the fuck should I know?" he says. "'Cause she's a bloody loon!"

"Do you think . . . ?" Enfield trails off.

Doggett glances in the mirror again. "I think we need to find them. Fast."

When they reach the Old Vicarage, Rabbani knows they've made the right choice. The police tape across the drive has been broken. Tyler's car is parked by the side of the road.

"Find Daley," Doggett tells her. He turns to Enfield. "You stay here. This is still a crime scene, and I've got at least one officer missing."

Rabbani notices a movement in the long grass. "Lily!" she shouts, recognizing the woman.

"Oi!" Doggett's voice follows her up the driveway, but she ignores him.

Lily emerges from the grass and stumbles onto the gravel. Her clothes are smudged with dirt, and she has a tear in the thigh of her trousers. "Edna?" she says. "I couldn't stop it." She holds up two red palms. "I couldn't stop the blood."

Doggett arrives behind her. "Jesus Christ!"

Rabbani takes hold of the woman's dangerously thin arms and Lily starts to cry. She can't see any wounds on the woman. "It's not hers," she says. "I don't think it's hers. Lily, whose blood is this?"

"He said it wasn't his fault," she says. "Gerry told us all about it, but it wasn't his fault. Cynthia goaded him into it."

"Where's DC Daley?" Doggett grabs Lily's arm, causing her to cry out.

"That's not helping," Rabbani snaps, and Doggett raises an eyebrow at her.

"Here!" Enfield is ahead of them. He's followed the path of flattened grass back in the direction Lily came from. He crouches down and Doggett runs ahead, leaving Rabbani to shepherd Lily back the way she came.

"It's Daley," Doggett shouts.

"Head trauma," says Enfield. "He's lost a lot of blood but there's a pulse."

"Daley! Guy, mate, can you hear me?"

Doggett pulls out his mobile and dials while Enfield tears off his T-shirt, exposing a tight black chest that Rabbani just manages to appreciate before she sees the scar that covers his neck and left shoulder. He balls the shirt in his hand and presses it hard against Daley's head. Guy Daley groans.

"Oh! Hello, dear." Lily is back. "Please! You have to get him out!"

There's a loud crack and one of the windows of the house shatters, smoke spiraling skyward from the hole.

Lily shouts, "Oscar!"

Enfield takes off in the direction of the house.

"Wait," Doggett shouts. "Shit! Shit! SHIT!" He turns to Rabbani. "Keep pressure on that wound and wait for the ambulance. You'd better call the fire brigade as well." He hares after Enfield.

"Oscar," Lily shouts after them. "No, you mustn't hurt him! Leave him alone!"

Rabbani presses the woman against her shoulder. "It's all right, Lily, love. They'll get him out."

But the woman's eyes have glazed over.

Tyler opens his eyes on a landscape of color. There's a hole in his skull and something sharp and pointed is being jabbed, over and over again, into his brain. He reaches up instinctively and immediately regrets it, as a white-hot lance of pain stabs through him. The burning sensation ripples and courses through his head, making him retch.

He forces himself to be still and wait for the pain to subside. Slowly, carefully, he opens his eyes again. This time he sees only darkness. His fingertips are wet and warm, and when he lifts them to his nose he smells the coppery odor of his own blood. It's a deep wound. But he knows head wounds always bleed badly. It isn't necessarily something to worry about.

He checks the rest of his body, but everything seems to be in working order. His legs are bent beneath him and as he stretches, tries to work them out from underneath his own body, and sit up, he feels them burst into life with pins and needles.

He waits for his eyes to adjust to the dark, but they refuse. He reaches out again, forward this time, and when he feels the brick wall in front of him, rough and dusty under his fingertips, he understands where he is. He cannot see them, but he can feel the other walls pressing in on him from all sides. He can't breathe. He draws in gulps of stale air and beats his fists against the cinder blocks, only stopping when he feels the skin on his wrist tear open.

He falls silent and tries to calm down, but his head is full of dangerous thoughts even as it pulses and spills his lifeblood down his face and neck. How long has he been here? How long does he have left?

He searches his way along the wall with his fingers, looking for a gap, a hole, anything. He forces himself to get up, though there isn't room enough to stand completely, and the pain in his head is excruciating. Using his fingers as eyes, he works his way systematically across the rough brickwork, turning in circles. On and on. The blood flooding across his face burns its way into his eyes, and by the time he lowers himself gently back to the floor, he's panting with exertion, his breath coming faster and faster, as though it's in a race with his beating heart.

How long has he been here? How long does he have left?

The rule of three. Three minutes without air, three days without water, three weeks without food.

He'd be losing fluids faster than average, Elliot had said. *Then there's the trauma to the head, blood loss. I doubt he'd have lasted longer than a couple of days. Maybe less.*

He knows, abruptly and certainly, what he must do.

He starts with the flat of his finger. A downward motion, stroking at the mortar between the bricks. He reasons that the mortar, by definition, must be softer than the brick, and assuming he hasn't been here too long, it may even still be wet. And yes, he can feel something moist beneath his index finger. He stops, uncertain whether the moisture is the wet mortar or his own blood. Perhaps the skin on his finger, already torn, is adding to his loss of fluids. But he goes on. It really doesn't matter. He has no choice.

After a minute or two he reasons that he is running out of time. He might pass out again at any moment. He switches to his nails, the image of Gerald Cartwright's tattered hand clear in his mind. The cement *is* still setting; he can pick out whole chunks of the mortar this way. Then a shard of hardened cement stabs up and under the nail of his index finger, cutting deep into the flesh. He cries out and pulls at the shard with gritty, bloodied fingers. Then he switches to the next nail and carries on. It doesn't matter. He has to do this. Whatever the cost.

Or does he? As he gets deeper into the mortar he finds it's much wetter. Perhaps he hasn't been there all that long. Perhaps there is another way. He lines up his shoulder with the wall and pushes at it gently, leaning in with the weight of his body and pressing himself against the unforgiving bricks. The wall refuses to budge.

He leans backward, trying to gather all of his weight onto his back foot. It takes everything he has to not think about the pain he knows is coming. He will not flinch. He may not get another chance.

He throws himself forward.

After that there is only a world of darkness and confusion. He's not sure if he loses consciousness but when he opens his eyes, light has returned. And with it the smoke. His attack on the wall has worked, and several of the bricks have fallen away to create a jagged hole in the wall, perhaps the size of a ship's porthole. Through it he can see the flames, and the heat reaches him in full force, burning his face and drying the sweat on his brow. He starts to cough, but he is committed now. It's all or nothing. Out there with the fire he has a chance. A slim one, but a chance. In here he has none. He braces himself for the pain and throws himself hard against the wall for a second time.

He tumbles out with the bricks and falls to the floor in a heap of rubble, his head screaming at him. A voice reaches him through the haze of his own agony. "Adam." A voice that cuts across the crackling of the flames. Paul Enfield.

The smoke is so thick and every mouthful of air burns his throat and leaves him gasping for the next, but somehow he gets to his feet. He hears someone coughing. How is Doggett here? Never mind. Follow the voices. The men calling his name.

He finds the bottom of the cellar steps and begins to climb. The voices above are fading as they search for him somewhere deeper in the house, but the cooler air ahead of him drives him on. He won't stop now. And then he is out, into the corridor where Doggett and Enfield are coming around the corner. They stop, all three of them, and stare at one another.

"Bloody hell, Tyler," Doggett croaks. "You look a right state."

"Oscar?" he manages. "Sally-Ann?"

Paul shakes his head. "No sign of them down here . . . no, Adam. Wait!"

But he's already halfway up the stairs. On the first floor every room is alight, the fire eating through the fuel Sally-Ann has left for it; this time she's taking no chances. The second flight of stairs is untouched and Tyler bounds up them, ignoring the light-headed feeling that he knows can't be a good sign. Then along the upstairs corridor to the little attic room. The door is open, but there is a small mound of burning material blocking the way. He can see two shadow figures inside, struggling with each other. Beyond them the room burns brightly, every item of furniture ablaze, liquid flame skating up the walls and licking at the damaged ceiling. The old-fashioned wardrobe smolders, smoke curling across its curlicue decor. The curtains at the window are towering pillars of flame. In the midst of the conflagration stand Sally-Ann and Oscar, locked in each other's arms, grappling like wrestlers. Sally-Ann has the edge, her bulky height pitted against Oscar's skinny, drugged body, pushing his head down into the burning mattress.

Behind him, Paul shouts something up the stairs but Tyler ignores him and kicks at the bonfire in the doorway, pushing the burning fragments to one side. Sally-Ann looks up at him, and while she's distracted, Oscar punches her hard in the face. She staggers back, just one, two steps, and then Oscar is using the momentum to push her away from him, across the room.

"No!" Tyler shouts, but it's too late.

Sally-Ann is swallowed up by the burning curtains. He tries to reach her, stumbling across the room with no real idea what he can do. He thinks he sees her smile and for a split second she seems . . . what? Relieved, perhaps. Then she is gone, transformed into a column of fire. It happens so quickly; her clothes must be saturated with petrol. She glides almost elegantly across the room, squealing— a flickering corpse candle.

Tyler looks for something—anything—to douse the flames, but there is nothing that is not already alight. Oscar stands transfixed, watching. The candle stumbles toward the gable window and Tyler sees what is going to happen just moments before it does. Then the rotten wood and broken glass are disintegrating like paper under her weight and Sally-Ann is gone.

Oscar turns to look at him. "I didn't mean . . ."

Paul arrives, smacking at the flames with what's left of his T-shirt. He smothers the remains of the blaze in the doorway. "Go!" he shouts.

Oscar takes the lead, Tyler following closely behind with Paul Enfield bringing up the rear. Part of the ceiling collapses and the corridor bursts into a ball of fire.

"This way." Oscar takes them to the other end of the corridor, where another set of stairs leads them down, and Tyler remembers coming this way on that first day that now seems like a lifetime ago. It was less than a week.

The fire is waiting for them at the bottom, the kitchen already an inferno; there's no way to reach the back door. He can see Doggett peering in through the glass from outside, gesturing for them to go back. But there is no back. Oscar leads them through the dining room and back into the living room, but the patio doors are locked. It's Paul Enfield who puts his naked bulky shoulder to the glass-paneled frame.

At the far end of the room the flames are jumping from one item of furniture to the next, dancing inexorably closer. Tyler hears the doors crack and give, and then he feels that same change in air pressure, just like at Wentworth's house. Enfield and Oscar stumble out into the night and the rush of oxygen inward fans the flames higher. The firestorm reaches out to engulf him.

As Tyler throws himself backward through the patio doors, the last thing he sees through the oncoming fire is the picture above the mantelpiece. The gray face of the fire watcher, as it melts and runs.

embers

Lily stands in the garden watching the Old Vicarage burn. A woman touches her arm. The Indian girl. The policewoman. The house is almost gone now. She can still feel the heat of the flames, yet she shivers. The girl puts an arm around her shoulders, but Lily can't feel the warmth; the chill is deep inside her, running through the marrow of her bones. She turns to the girl. Something familiar about her. An Indian woman with a pretty face and a button nose . . . *that wrinkles when he screws it up and bawls. Lily asks if she can hold him, just once. The midwife looks round. They're not really supposed to. Lily begs and the woman relents. He's a mottled dark-red color, a perfect little ball of anger. She can feel his strength already. She's not sorry to be giving him up. She wants to put all this behind her and go back to the theater. But that won't happen now. It'll be back to Sheffield and she'll never see any of them again, the girls from the theater or the office. And not Edna. She regrets that most of all. They'll never let her go back* . . . to the cottage where Edna is waiting for her.

"Here you go, Lily." The girl helps her into a chair that's appeared from somewhere. "That's better. You rest a moment, love, all right?" The garden fills with more faces. Faces of the young.

Policemen and ambulance people. Where's Oscar? She saw him come out, she's sure she did. Why hasn't he come to see . . . . *her father laid out; Mam dressed head to toe in black. Lily came straight from the station; didn't have time to change. She can feel them all looking. Is that the one? You remember—went off to flash her legs about on the stage. Can't even be bothered to dress decently! Hasn't she put weight on?*

Hardly anyone speaks to her. She can live with the whispers, but can she live without London? And the dancing. And Edna . . . clutches her hand. "Are you all right, luv?" Not Edna. A man in a yellow and green uniform. The policewoman is looking at her. It makes her uncomfortable. She isn't sure . . . *whether they are safe up here.* "Safe?" says Edna. *"There's a war on. No one's safe!" It's cold on the rooftop, bitterly so. She clutches Edna's hand and they listen to the whine of the Messerschmitts overhead and then the whistle of the falling bombs. Lily closes her eyes. She knows this is the end. There's nothing left. "Edna?" But Edna can't hear her over the crack of explosions and the wail of the sirens. Then Edna looks down into her eyes. They don't need to speak. They have each other. They can read each other's thoughts. Lily reaches up . . .*

But Time is coming unspun. The monster from the darkness is almost upon her. She remembers now, but it is all too much and too fast . . . *Her father stares at her, the disapproval writ large on . . . his screwed-up face as he bawls . . . and shouts and screams . . . she can feel the strength in his hands . . . covered in blood . . . choking the life from Cynthia . . . no, Edna! Poor Edna . . . safe on the rooftop but . . . there's a war on, no one's safe . . . she smashes the bottle down on his head . . . thump, thumpety-thump . . . and Edna smiles her lipless smile . . . wrapped in Edna's arms while the bombs fall around them and everything burns . . .*

Lily remembers.

———

Tyler sits in the doorway of the incident room watching the Old Vicarage collapse in on itself. Every now and then his eyes travel across the gravel driveway to the covered remains of Sally-Ann Digby.

His head still grumbles but the wound has been patched up, and with the painkillers he reluctantly agreed to take beginning to kick in, he can just about bear it. Doggett's fingers drum against the roof of his car. It starts to rain.

"Perhaps you could stop that now," he says, and Doggett's hand does indeed stop. For once. His fingers hang suspended in midair for a moment. Then he places both hands on the back of his head and exhales loudly. His leg starts to jiggle, the squeaking leather of his shoe taking up the rhythm.

"You should be in the hospital."

"Guy Daley got my ride."

"He's going to be all right," Doggett says, but it isn't clear who he's trying to convince. The leg stops. "It looks like they're done with him, then." He nods to the back of the remaining ambulance where Oscar is being treated by the paramedics. "What about you and him?"

"No." It comes out more sharply than he intends.

"I guess I was wrong about him."

"No," Tyler says again. "Edna Burnside wouldn't have asked just anyone to help her bring in the furniture. He was there all right. Sally-Ann told me he was trying to find out what Edna knew about his mother's death. Hence the blackmail letters."

"Burnside died from a stroke."

"He could have rung for help, got her out of the fire."

"I'm not so sure that would have been doing her a favor."

Oscar looks across at them and smiles like a little boy.

"Maybe he hated the woman," says Doggett. "Or maybe he thought she was better off out of it. Anyway, I doubt we'll prove anything."

"And Lily?"

"Nah," says Doggett. "The CPS won't touch that. Maybe she did kill Cartwright, or maybe Sally-Ann killed him and made the whole thing up. Even if we wring a confession out of the woman, she's half cuckoo. There's no way it would stick." Doggett must realize Tyler's staring at him, because he turns. "What?"

Tyler grins. "I just realized, you ran into a burning building for me."

"Oh, fuck off!"

"Just for me." Tyler lets the smile fade now, so Doggett will know he means what he's about to say. "Thanks, boss."

Doggett shakes his head, but he's smiling now, too. He gets up. "You coming then?"

"Where?"

"We still have to interview the shifty little bastard."

"I'm suspended, remember?"

"Jordan'll be here in a minute. She'll probably crucify both of us anyway. Might as well give her something to shout about."

Tyler shakes his head. As Doggett turns to walk away he asks, "Why?"

Doggett turns back, suppressing an irritated huff. "Why what?"

"Why did you really want me on this case? Why did you keep me on it even after you found out about me and Oscar?"

Doggett shuffles his feet and looks away. It's the first time Tyler's seen the man look uncomfortable about anything. "We don't need to go into all that now. Take a few weeks off and let Jordan sort everything out. When you get back we'll talk."

Tyler's eyes drift once again to Sally-Ann's body. "I'm not coming back," he says.

Doggett follows his gaze. "That wasn't your fault, you know. You couldn't have saved her. You're a good cop, DS Tyler, but even you can't save everyone."

He wants to believe that, but he knows somehow he let her down. All she needed was one friend. One friend who could have seen how much she was suffering. If only he'd worked it out sooner . . .

"I'm not coming back," he says again.

Doggett puts a hand on his shoulder. "I wanted you on this because I knew your dad. I knew him very well, and I knew his son would turn out to be just as good a cop as he was. You'll be back, all right. Your dad never let anyone down, and you're not about to either. It's in your genes."

Tyler shakes his head. "Actually, I think my father let me down in quite a big way."

Doggett snorts but doesn't argue. Then he says, "Take a few weeks, then come find me. There are things we need to talk about."

"What things?" When he gets no reply, Tyler looks up to see Doggett walking away across the driveway.

"What things?" he shouts after him, but the DI simply waves a hand behind him.

The rain grows heavier and pelts down on the final remains of the Old Vicarage, dampening the last of the flames.

Tyler sits on the incident-room step and watches.

Acknowledgments

First, a big thank-you to the staff and students of Sheffield Hallam University's graduate writing program. Many people helped get this project under way, but particular thanks to Daniel Blythe, for encouragement when I was at a low ebb; to Mike Harris, for teaching me how stories should work; and to Lesley Glaister, for encouraging me to find a story in the first place (and teaching me the expression "lying fallow"). A big thank-you, too, to the Dark Horseys—Kate Hainsworth, Len Horsey, and Helen Meller. Long may they ride!

Thanks to various coffee shops, pubs, and libraries, and to John Hunter for accompanying me to them. Special thanks to the Red Deer for giving both Adam and me a place to relax after work, and for putting up with me celebrating and drowning my sorrows (I'm not sure which is worse). Extra-special thanks to the booksellers and patrons of Waterstones Sheffield Orchard Square, Meadowhall, Derby, Doncaster, and Chesterfield. You've had to spend fifteen years listening to me talk about my book more than anybody else's.

Thank you to the wonderful writers I've met on this journey for all you have taught me, but especially to the Hallam Writers for their critiques of early drafts. Also a big thank-you to Bernardine

Evaristo, Jacob Ross, and my fellow attendees of an Arvon course entitled "Making Your Writing Sing." I'm not sure if I achieved that goal but you made me believe that one day I might. And to all the students I've taught over the past few years: my big secret is . . . you've all taught me stuff too!

The more recent drafts of this work would just not have happened without the unparalleled support, constant reassurance, gentle nagging, and endless supplying of wine that came from my good friends Susan Elliot Wright and Marion Dillon.

A big thank-you to Anna Jarowicki and to Kevin Robinson for ideas and thoughts surrounding police investigation. Check out Kev's indispensable resource: www.crimewritingsolutions.wordpress.com. All the bits I got right came from them; all the mistakes are mine alone.

I've had three editors work on this book: Anne Perry, Sara Minnich, and Jo Dickinson. I am beyond lucky fate conspired to arrange this for me; I couldn't have asked for more helpful insight. And thank you, too, to the fabulous teams at Simon & Schuster in the UK, and G. P. Putnam's Sons in the US.

The biggest thanks of all must go to my agent, the practically perfect Sarah Hornsley. It's no exaggeration to say this book would not be in your hands right now without her unfailing hard work and erudite advice. Thank you for changing my life.

Finally, thank you to all my friends and family for their unending support but especially to Ed, for telling me to stop talking about it and do it; and to Auntie Norah and Auntie Mart for the inspiration.

To anyone who is a writer out there—keep going, don't give up. Sometimes dreams really do come true.